THE BOXKART REBEL

First published in 2017 by TheNeverPress
Second edition published 2024

A CIP record of this book is available from the British Library.

ISBN 9780956742292

Cover design by Adam Sibley: www.adamsibley.co.uk
Additional artwork by Leighton Johns: www.leightonjohns.co.uk

@TheNeverPress

www.theneverpress.com

For the old man and all those Sundays back then,
with a fry-up and a Grand Prix

We have a saying here:
'In this city, nothing is certain but
Old Tick Tock and taxes.'

But there is an accompaniment to the phrase.
A silent coda that everybody knows. We keep it
inside, we say it only to ourselves and by doing so
we affirm our position in this city and this life...

In this city, nothing is certain but
Old Tick Tock and taxes...

But the Boxkart Rebel drives...

TWO
GIANTS

Chapter 1
Red Rocket

Chris Redding's dad was a silent mountain, taller than the thirteen-year-old boy thought he could ever become and broader than any parent he knew. Terry Redding was quiet, stern, his face tense all the time. To Chris, this meant that his dad was tough – certainly tougher than any of the other boys' dads. This was the kind of man who could happily eat a fried breakfast at any time of the day. If Terry had ever gone to Sports Day, he was a sure-fire bet to win the Dads' Race. But Chris' old man would never go to Sports Day. That was a job for Chris' mum. Janine Redding went every year and cheered her youngest boy on, beaming with pride and collecting every participation medal he 'won'. She kept those prizes in a battered old shoebox inside the bureau by the front door, along with the necklace made of pasta shells and the bracelet made of milk bottle tops that Chris gifted her when he was seven. She kept everything the young boy made.

Chris rested his elbows on the kitchen countertop and made sure his oil-stained hands didn't touch anything. He was a little short for his age, tubby too, and while he knew a growth spurt was around the corner, his patience was wearing thin. Chris looked at the sink as his dad turned on the taps – huge, grease-stained fingers smearing the fittings.

Terry looked out of the kitchen window at the unkempt garden, his eyes focused on something that Chris couldn't quite perceive – some faraway problem dealt out only in adulthood. Terry didn't take his eyes off the garden, but simply lilted his head to the side as he addressed his son: "Get the gunk." Chris ducked down under the sink and rooted around for the tub. Terry had never finished refurbishing the kitchen and only half the units had doors. Luckily for Chris and his filthy hands, it meant that he could get under the sink without mucking up the doors and getting shouted at. He found the gunk – a dirty tub of some green gelatinous substance that was brilliant for cleaning "men's hands", as it said on the label. It was hidden at the back. After a stretch, Chris grabbed the tub and held it up to his dad. Terry took it without saying 'Thank you'.

Chris stood up and held his hands over the sink, looking up at his dad, studying the lines on his face and the stern, squinted piggy eyes that were unlike his own. Chris was fair, his father dark. He was bright and happy, his father stern and grouchy nearly all the time. Terry scooped out a big dollop of green, wet jelly and dumped it into Chris's dirty hands.

"Scrub them properly," he said before taking a dollop for himself.

At the back of the kitchen Janine leaned against the larder doorframe and observed the young boy and his father, both scrubbing their dirty hands in the same way.

She smiled and turned to retrieve some tins of beans for dinner. Janine worked as an administrative assistant in a council building three miles away, and she walked there and back daily. The family car was in the driveway, up on bricks and waiting for Terry to fix her up. She had been like that for two months. Terry's big red Talbot van was the only working vehicle the family had, and the back of that van was filled with Terry's tools. A handyman always on the move, a family struggling to make ends meet. They did what they could. There was a recession on, and times were hard, but all the same, it was a happy home. Rarely any cross words between adults thrown about. At least, none that Chris could hear. To him it was life as usual: bricked-up car in the driveway, scaffolding poles dumped in the back garden and an upstairs toilet that only flushed when you threw a bucket of water down it. He looked at his hands as the green goo slurped between his fingers, gradually darkening in colour as it mixed with the grease and dirt accrued from a hard day's work in the lock-up beside the house.

Terry washed his own hands clean and turned the spout 90 degrees so that Chris could hold his hands under the tap. Chris watched the water wash the dirt away. He looked up at his dad who was drying his hands on a tea-towel.

"Not on that, Tel," shouted his mother, from inside the larder. She had not witnessed the indiscretion, but she knew what was going on. Terry ignored her and handed the towel to Chris who took it and dried his own hands.

"Make your dad a cup of tea," said Terry, patting Chris a little too heavily on the top of the head. Chris sighed and flicked the kettle on.

"That's my boy," he said, turning and walking across the kitchen and out of the back door to return to the lock-up.

"One for your brother too," came his voice as he disappeared from view.

Chris was good at making tea. So good in fact, that his dad near refused to drink tea made by anyone else. Chris was delicate and concentrated when pouring the boiling water, keeping time in his mind while the bags steeped. His mother kissed his crown as she walked past him to throw the filthy tea towel into the washing machine.

"Juice?" she said, opening the tall fridge next to the washing machine.

"Yes please," said Chris, replacing the kettle and spooning the tea bags out on to a little porcelain tray.

"Pass me a glass, then."

Chris handed his mother a mug. His mother poured the juice and Chris carefully took hold of the three mugs. He didn't like the taste of tea too much, but he felt that real men who worked in lock-ups drank out of mugs, not glasses. Chris walked slowly to the back door, eyes fixed on the two teas and juice, careful not to spill a drop.

Chris stepped out of the house, a corner terrace in a hard-up part of the city. Alongside ran a wide driveway that flanked their long garden on the right and housed a row of lock-ups on the left. Theirs was the very last. Chris walked slowly and surely along, his hands steady and his concentration complete until he reached the open lock-up. Inside, Terry stood next to his oldest son Danny and they both pensively scratched their chins in exactly the same way. At sixteen, Danny Redding was already a man. Tall like his father, lean like a young man, focused and steeled like a race car driver. Which is exactly what Danny Redding was – not just any race car driver though, he was the fastest SuperKart racer in the city. That, at least, was what Chris told everyone he met. In fact, when meeting new people, Chris rarely introduced himself as Chris Redding, but as 'ChrisReddingmybrotheristhefastest-SuperKart-racerinthecity'. And Danny was fast in the car, incredibly so. He had nearly every trophy and cup going to prove it: all gleaming and grand, displayed with great pride on top of the bureau by the front door.

To Chris, Danny was everything – a hero, a brother and a gentleman. An ideal to strive for. But it was in his car that Danny became so beguiling. Chris asked his mother once how it came to be that Danny raced so well. His mother paraphrased a line from her favourite film. She said: "God gave us two sons, the eldest to look after the youngest and the youngest to dream big enough for both… but God also made the eldest boy fast." Terry then added: "…and because the car is lightning."

Chris loved being allowed into the lock-up. He was permitted to hang around and hammer nails into off-cuts, while his dad worked on Danny's kart. Oftentimes Chris would look up from his hammer and nail and see the SuperKart, half-built, no cowling, no finesse, just engine and bite. He would see Danny and his father standing over it, hands on chins, talking in some strange quiet code. They would step around the car and, as one, bend down and inspect some nut or bolt. Then they would stand back and nod solemnly. Sometimes they would drink their tea in unison and gasp in exactly the same manner. They stalked around the kart, currently jacked up, nose tilting down and engine exposed. Chris saw the kart as a dormant dragon just waiting for Danny to ride it.

"Teas up, lads," said Chris as he stepped into the lock-up-cum-makeshift workshop. Danny smiled and reached over, taking the two cups and handing one over to his dad.

"She nearly ready to race, Danny?" said Chris, leaning down and inspecting the suspension on the front left wheel and pretending to know what he was looking at.

"Nearly there, bro," replied Danny. "She took a pounding last Saturday and needs a little bit more TLC."

"She'll be right," said their dad flatly.

"Doesn't matter, anyhow," said Chris standing tall. "She could have a bust engine and no steering wheel and you'd still win, Danny. Right, Dad?"

Terry smiled and blew across the rim of his mug, peering into the engine.

Danny lifted his arm around Chris and pulled his younger brother in to his side.

"You going to be a racer one day?" he said.

"Sure, and I'm gonna be even faster than you."

"Oh really?"

"Yeah, I reckon. I am the youngest!"

"So?"

"Well, Mum and Dad had you fine. You're great. Not bad for a first go. But with me they had time to practise the formula. Nobody bakes the perfect cake first time out."

Danny looked at their father with a bemused 'can you believe this guy?' expression. Terry ignored them both, and bent down to the exhausts, his knees cracking.

"That's my bro," said Danny, squeezing Chris' shoulder. "You're gonna be something special one day. You're smarter than me already."

"Better looking too."

"Let's not go overboard,"

"True," said Chris, shrugging out of Danny's arm, "Julie said so. She said that she wished she was a little younger, or I a little older."

Danny burst out laughing. "She's coming over later. I'll have to ask her after dinner."

Chris turned beetroot-red almost instantly. "I wouldn't, she'd get embarrassed and…"

Danny smirked at his brother who mumbled something into his mug of juice.

Terry was about to get back to work when the dinner bell rang. Chris was halfway out of the lock-up before the second ding had sounded. Terry creaked to his full height and he and Danny carefully pulled a tarpaulin over the kart.

"She's going to be great," said Terry.

"She's looking sharp already. Just hope I can keep her under control."

"Son, you're the best damned racer in the city. There is nothing my boy can't do."

Danny smiled, keeping his eyes on the car. It was the only time his father ever cursed and so Danny believed every word. He would fly that car over the line. His old man had said so.

———

The family ate in silence, in front of the television, dinner on trays. Chris had his usual sausages, chips and beans, his father a fry up, his brother a chicken salad and his mother's plate made up of whatever food the others hadn't piled on to their plates. She always ate a mish-mash of whatever was going.

"Chris was a big help today," said Janine, smiling at her youngest as he scooped some beans into his mouth.

"He did 200 photocopies and stapled them too, all in 20 minutes. Didn't you?"

Chris nodded without paying any attention.

"A good little helper around the office."

"Good man," said Danny, pushing his salad around the plate.

"It's okay, Mum asked me to," said Chris. "Besides, it is good to learn new things. Might come in handy."

"What, photocopying?" replied Danny.

"Well, I've never been in an office before. Might be some good ideas for some stories in there."

"Working on a new story for your comics?" asked Danny.

Chris shrugged, "Maybe... I have a few ideas, but you know... you can never have too many,"

Danny nodded to imply he understood, though, truth be told, it was a confusing notion for him. He wasn't particularly imaginative; he didn't listen to music or watch films with any great enthusiasm. He just raced.

"You'll have to tell me about some of the stories," he said.

"Sssh," interrupted Terry as he tried to concentrate on the TV.

"Thank you for coming to work today," whispered Janine, "I know it's your school holidays. Promise to make it up to you. Dinosaur museum on Sunday?"

Chris shrugged and nodded. He was about to cut into one of his sausages when a loud, frantic advert blasted out of the TV. His eyes lit up.

"Look! That's it, Dad! The MegaSystem – it's a really cool games console, Dad, probably the best around. Loads of great games for it already. Look at the graphics."

Danny looked at his mother. They both looked down at their plates.

"Fighting games, puzzle games... driving games."

"Waste of money," said his father, flatly.

"Oh, I know," feigned Chris, "I don't want one, I was just saying. It's cool, isn't it? Just showing you."

Terry turned the channel and Chris slumped down a little in his seat.

"It's a cool system," whispered Danny, "really the bee's knees."

Chris shrugged.

"I don't want one, I was just saying."

"It's very lovely," said his mother, quietly.

"Can I please leave the sofa?" said Chris, sadly.

"Sure," replied his mother.

Chris stood up and took his tray to the kitchen.

"Terry," snapped the mother with a sharp, whispered tone, "don't hurt his feelings. It's his birthday in a few weeks."

Terry ignored his wife and returned his concentration to the programme. Danny muttered under his breath and stood up to leave the room.

"Thanks for dinner, Mum, it was lovely."

He walked calmly out of the room. The parents sat in silence and watched the TV.

Chris kicked his deflated football up and down the garden. The sun was setting, August was coming to a close and the school holidays would soon be over. With every kick, he muttered under his breath, cursing at his father. Danny leaned against the pebble-dashed wall to the kitchen extension and watched his sullen brother skulk up and down the long, overgrown garden.

"You alright, bro?"

"Yeah, fine" said Chris, haughtily.

Danny rolled his eyes and hopped over the garden fence, disappearing from view inside the lock-up just as Chris turned to talk to him. Various bangs and crashes began to emanate from the dark doorway of the workshop. Chris stopped kicking the football and walked across the yellow grass to the peer over the fence. Suddenly, Danny emerged, holding a large electric fan, its chord attached to a long extension lead.

"What you doing?"

"Wanna go racing, bro?" said Danny with a conspiratorial smile.

"What do you mean?"

"Go get the Red Rocket," replied Danny, nodding at the back of the garden.

Chris screwed up his face and looked over to the far corner of the garden. There, half buried in the tall grass where the dog used to play before it got hit by next door's van, lay Red Rocket – Chris's old plastic pedal car. The vehicle lay upon its side, rust claiming most of the axles and the pedals, the sun bleaching the red fairings – left to die in the corner of their garden.

"Trust me," said Danny.

Chris huffed and walked across the garden, heaving the car on to its wheels and dragging it through the tangle of grass. The wheels creaked and flakes of rust coated his fingers. He pulled the small car across the garden to the fence where Danny effortlessly heaved it over and dumped her down on the concrete driveway.

"Hop over," said Danny.

Chris hauled himself awkwardly over the fence, his height and weight working against him in such a way that the battered old fence almost collapsed. He landed on the driveway, almost on his back.

"Now what?" he said, getting to his feet and dusting himself down.

"Get in."

"I can't fit in that. I'm too old."

"Just get in and stop moaning. Badass race drivers don't moan; badass race drivers do what?"

"Burn rubber," said Chris meekly.

"Do what?"

"They burn rubber!" said Chris, this time with more enthusiasm.

Danny held up his hand and smiled. Chris jumped up and slapped it.

"Now get in, fire the beast up and take your position on the grid."

Chris smiled and squeezed into the pedal car, his knees coming up awkwardly beside the crooked steering wheel. Danny retrieved his racing helmet from the lock-up while Chris gripped the wheel and imagined it to be a real SuperKart.

"Watch your ears," said Danny, shoving the helmet down over his brother's head.

The helmet felt heavy on Chris, and his head lolled to the side pendulously as he looked up at his brother.

"Eyes on the road," said Danny, stepping around to the front of the car and pulling the nose around so that it was properly in front of the fan.

"So, where you wanna race? The Oakley Raceway? I have the lap record there – wanna take it?"

"No way, too slow a track!" said Chris, flexing his fingers over the wheel.

"Too slow? Okay, how about the Brant Ring?"

"Too easy!"

"So, where do you wanna race?"

"I wanna race Palmerston Road!"

"That's not a circuit, that's just a street," said Danny.

"Yeah, but it's the steepest in the city. Almost vertical. No track is like that. I wanna do that. What nobody else would dare race down, but I dare."

Danny smiled. "Good man," he said, pulling the flex chord from the fan around so that the footswitch lay by the back of the car.

"You ready?" he asked.

Chris took a deep breath.

"You better believe it," he answered, gripping the wheel even tighter.

Danny bent down and grabbed hold of the rear axle.

"Gentlemen, start your engines!"

Chris simulated the roar of his engine.

"Three," said Danny.

"Two," replied Chris.

"One!" shouted Danny, and he suddenly yanked the rear of the car two feet off the ground, pitching it forward on to its nose. Chris screamed in shock and gripped the wheel, pushing back into his seat and remaining inside the car.

"And they're off!" shouted Danny, "an amazing start from Chris Redding as he leaves most of the pack for dust on the grid. He takes the first sharp left at Peak Corner!"

Danny tilted the car on to its front left wheel. Chris laughed manically as he turned the steering wheel.

"And Redding takes it supremely, finding the perfect line for the straight."

Danny slammed the car back on to its front two wheels.

"Redding floors it through the straight."

Danny began to jiggle the car, feeling no pain in his muscles as he revelled in his brother's giddy laughter.

Chris, in the cockpit, didn't see the paving slab on the ground, nor the faded red bonnet in front of him. He saw a great imaginary track. He heard the roar of engines, the cheers of the crowd and the stench of the motor oil. He was there and he really felt it.

"Oh, no!" shouted Danny, "Redding is approaching the Searle Chicane too fast. Is Redding heading for a deading?"

"No way!" shouted Chris as he spun the wheel right, then left and then right again. Danny, in perfect synchronicity titled the car each way, swinging the back end out each time to add some dynamic emphasis to the turn. Chris's mad laughter intensified.

"A demon driver! How does he do it?"

"Talent! Pure talent!" shouted Chris.

"But what's this, the finishing straight? The famous downhill home stretch? The Palmerston Blitz? Has Redding got the nerve? Has he?"

Danny's arms began to burn with the strain, but he held the car up.

"Has he got it?"

Chris thumped his foot down into the pedal of the car with such force that he nearly yanked the car out of Danny's grip. Danny smiled, knowing that Chris had just 'floored it'.

"This kid is the bravest racer the city has ever seen. Here it comes! The Palmerston Blitz!"

Danny clenched his jaw and began to lift the car a little higher. Chris pressed into his seat, nearly falling out of Red Rocket.

"Here it comes! Three, two… one!"

Danny heaved the car up on to its nose and began juddering it severely.

"Come on!" shouted Chris with gritted ferocity. Danny stamped on the footswitch and the fan turned on, blasting air into Chris's face. Danny shook the car violently.

The wind flew into Chris's eyes, the road ahead blurring, the grandstands becoming streaks of colour. The only thing in focus now for him was the oncoming grid and the chequered flag. The wind whipped through his helmet, the noise taking him. Chris peacefully closed his eyes and lifted his hands from the wheel, raising them high above his head as he passed the finish line. He didn't even see the chequered flag. He didn't need to.

Danny's arms gave out and he dropped the car back down.

"And he's won! Chris Redding has won the Palmerston 500 in his inaugural race!"

Elated, Chris leapt out of his race car and cleanly over the fence. He ran around the garden, giddy and mad, his arms high above his head, fingers fluttering in the late summer breeze. Danny, unable to fight the 'occasion' jumped up on to the car, balancing perfectly with one foot on the bonnet, the other on the seat rest. He cupped his hands over his mouth and simulated the noise of the adoring crowd.

"There he goes!" he shouted, "there goes the racer! The Red Rocket Racer! The Race Car Rebel! That's my brother! That's my brother!"

Chris' run slowed down and he turned to Danny. He removed his helmet and looked up at his brother, standing on the little car and shouting out to the neighbourhood.

Chris held the helmet up high and waved to the sun.

"That's my brother," said Danny as he jumped from the car and cleared the fence with the grace of a cat. Chris ran over and hugged him.

"Told you I would be a better racer," he said.

"Yeah, you did good, kiddo," said Danny, ruffling his hair. "Now go help mum with the dishes."

Chapter 2
The Coolest

aylight was over and Danny had taken himself to his room – the sacred upstairs domain with the 'no-entry' sign on the door and strange, confusing smells within. Every time Chris walked past it, on his way across the landing to the bathroom or to go downstairs, he would instinctively crane his neck and try and grab a few words or sounds from within. Of course, he was allowed in whenever he wanted, as long as he knocked first, but that wasn't enough. That wasn't illicit, for what secrets can be learned by observing giants in their natural habitat when they are aware of your presence? He would creep past and listen, sometimes he would sit on the landing, resting against the wall between his bedroom door and his brother's and read. When questioned by his parents, he would just shrug and say that the light was better on the landing.

But after dinner, though he wanted to be upstairs, Chris was consigned to the kitchen as always to help his mum with the dishes while his dad went about his own business.

"Hand me the towel, piggy," she said as she scrubbed the plates. Chris winced at the pet name that he felt he had outgrown practically at birth. He thrust the towel out begrudgingly.

"Thanks, piggy," she replied, oblivious to his clear protest.

On the breakfast bar, Terry cleaned engine parts with an old toothbrush, scrubbing away, then stopping to hold them up to the light and narrowing his already tiny eyes to see into various cavities and tubes.

"What time is the race, tomorrow?" asked Janine.

"Qualifiers at 12pm, Danny will be on pole by 2pm. Race starts at 3pm."

"Plenty of time, then," replied Janine, looking down at Chris and smiling.

He knew what was coming next but asked all the same.

"Plenty of time for what?"

"You're helping me in town," she said, eyes wide and smile broad as if the very suggestion was akin to asking if he wanted to go on a bold jungle adventure. Chris' shoulders sank.

"Don't worry, we'll get to the track in time, but we need to get some bits for school."

"What bits?" interjected Terry, not through interest but a fiscal concern.

Janine dried her hands and walked around to a side-table behind the breakfast bar and leafed through a stack of papers dumped upon it. She pulled one out and handed it to her husband. Terry took it in his greasy hands, smearing oil over the paper.

"Don't smudge it, Tel, I need that."

"I'm not," he replied, taking his glasses and pushing them up his nose. He cleared his throat like a judge about to pass sentence. Terry read the list, his eyebrow rising incrementally after each line. Chris leaned against the counter and looked at his parents, bored to tears with the drama but unable to leave. He folded his arms and thought of the day when they wouldn't be around any more and he would be free. He drifted into imagination, placing himself into a future of fast cars, crime fighting, freedom and glory.

His father huffed and handed back the paper.

"Obviously, Chris can have mainly hand-me-downs," said Janine, nervous to head-off any protestations from her husband at the pass.

"Obviously," he replied, returning back to his engine block and toothbrush.

"Great," muttered Chris under his breath.

"But there are a few bits on here that he will need."

"Fine, just don't go nuts or we won't have enough for the MegaSystem," he said, his eyes darting up from his machine to meet Chris's, whose flashed with excitement. His mouth opened slightly. His mother nudged his father who broke out into a loud laugh.

"Your face!" he said, pointing to his son. "As if we'd spunk money on that! Ha!"

"Stop it, Tel. Leave him be."

Terry laughed to himself and returned to his work.

Chris' world collapsed. The second before was the greatest he had known. He was the owner of the hottest game console on the planet and a second later he'd been mugged of it. He clenched his jaw and felt the sting of tears rising. Only his father and perhaps a selection of teachers at school had the magic ability to reduce him to sudden, irrational and childish tears with just a word or a glance. He never understood and didn't even know if he would ever shake the affliction, even in his fantasy future. His lip was about to wobble when, with perfect timing, the doorbell rang.

"Get the door," said his father, returning to his work. Chris rushed to the door, thankful to be out of the scene.

Janine leaned into her husband's ear.

"You are so mean to him. Why do you make him sad?"

"Because it's funny to me," said Terry with a genuine smile. "Besides, it's not that mean and he can't stay soft all his life."

"Well, I don't like it," replied Janine, walking back to the dishes and stacking them back in the cupboards.

"Anyway, did you get it?" she said over her shoulder.

"Yeah," said Tel, "I picked it up on the way home yesterday. It's under the seat in the van."

"Will he find it?"

"If he can think to get the keys to the van, sneak outside, and look under the seat on the off-chance that there might be Mega-whatsisname under the seat, then the kid deserves it!"

"He's a wily one," said his mother.

"Yes he is, but his old man is wilier"

"He's a wanker," giggled Janine.

"Guttermouth."

———

Chris knew who was at the door before he even opened it. He could see their unmistakable outline through the misshapen glass panelling on the unvarnished wooden door. He flattened down his hair and reached for the bolt lock, halting there for a second.

"Be cool," he whispered, before taking a breath and opening it.

"Hi, Julie," he said, trying to add some bass to his voice.

"Hey, Tiger."

Julie Finch, Danny's girlfriend, stood on the doorstep. She was short and thin, with tightly cropped black hair and five studs in each ear. She wore what she always wore: a men's biker jacket, denim skirt, black leggings and DM boots. Chris wasn't sure of her exact age; he thought sixteen, but she could even have been as old as eighteen or nineteen. Not twenty – that would be ridiculous.

"Can I come in, kiddo?"

Chris snapped out of his daze and offered the way. Julie stepped across the threshold and ruffled his hair.

"He in his room?"

"Yep."

"Has he cleaned it?"

Chris raised his eyebrow. Julie laughed and looked up the stairs.

"Hi Julie!" bellowed Chris's mum from the kitchen.

"Hey Janine!"

Julie motioned to ascend the staircase when Chris halted her by clearing his throat. She turned to him.

"Forgetting something?"

She furrowed her brow.

For some reason that he couldn't fathom, he tilted his head and tapped his finger against his cheek.

"Little sugar?"

Chris had gone through the looking glass and was acting without any thought or control. Julie furrowed her brow even further.

"You been watching Danny's videos again?"

"Don't leave me hanging baby?" replied Chris with an affected baritone to his voice. He had no idea what he was doing and had gone too far to revert to type. He held position. Julie's furrowed brow turned into a laugh and she bent down to him.

"Chrissy-woo," she said, clasping her soft hands around his face and turning it her. "You're the coolest," she said and planted a huge, loud kiss on his lips. She pulled back and Chris stumbled and bumped into the radiator.

"I'm gonna tell your brother," she said.

Chris's eyes grew wide with fear.

"I'm gonna tell everyone!"

"Bu.."

"People need to know that you have it going on, baby" she said with a wink. She clicked her fingers and pointed at him. "Laters, taters. Keep breakin' hearts."

Julie turned from Chris and skipped up the steps.

Chris smiled, popped the collar on his polo shirt and walked back into the kitchen.

———

Terry didn't notice his son's strange strut as he entered the kitchen.

"Put the kettle on, make your dad a cup of tea," he said, keeping his eyes on the engine block. Janine walked past her son and, without looking either, flattened his collar back down and disappeared into the cupboard to rearrange tins. Chris's shoulders slumped a little as he flicked the switch on the kettle and took a mug from the tree.

"Nobody makes tea like my boy," said Terry.

"Dad?"

"Yeah?"

"When can I start racing?"

"Whenever you like," he replied, still focused on brushing the machine tooled parts.

"Really?"

"Sure, we can get you into a boxkart circuits whenever you like. Could try and get you into the Boxkart Derby. That's coming up soon. Good day that, all the ridiculous machines people have built. Great fun. How about that?"

"How about no?!" snapped Chris.

"Excuse me?" said his father, putting the toothbrush down.

"I want to race SuperKarts like Danny."

"You think you can handle a 250cc engine strapped to your back, sitting one inch off the floor and hitting 60 miles an hour in under 3 seconds?"

"Piece of piss."

He instantly regretted displaying his new-found confidence. He heard the stacking of cans cease and saw his father's eye rise above the rim of his readers.

"I appreciate your enthusiasm, Christopher, but use that language again in front of your mother and I'll take my belt off."

"Sorry, Dad," said Chris, turning back to the kettle and pouring water into the mug.

Terry sighed and sat up from his stoop. Chris walked the mug to him.

"Sit down," he said, offering a stool to his son. Chris climbed up.

His mother returned from the larder and pretended to make herself busy around the counter and sink.

"You want to be a race car driver?"

"More than anything. I'm gonna be fast. The fastest in the city."

"Why?"

"Because that's the job. Be the fastest."

"No, I mean why do you want to be a race car driver?"

"Because Danny is one and you used to race. It's in the family."

"Your Uncle Tone isn't a racer. Never was and he is in the family."

"But he's Uncle Tone. He's strange. He's different."

"Well, yes… that's true. But what do you like doing? What are you good at?"

Chris looked at the engine parts. Two conflicting thoughts hit him. What was he good at? And how was that that his own father didn't even know? He shrugged.

"Drawing. Stories." He offered.

A glimpse of confusion fluttered across Terry's face. How was he supposed to field that? He dodged it.

"Everybody starts in boxkarts. Start there and if you like it, if you stick to it… well."

Chris looked up at his dad. His dad half-smiled, picked up the tea and blew across the rim of the mug.

"We'll see."

That was all Chris needed. "We'll see" was a general, vague term, but in Dad-speak "we'll see" pretty much meant "and so it shall be."

"Yeah," said Chris hopping off the stool. "We'll see and then you'll all see."

He walked backwards around the breakfast bar. His mother and father looked at him. Chris popped his collar, winked, clicked and pointed his fingers.

"You'll see. You'll see what this kid can do. Laters."

Chris spun on his heels and strutted out of the kitchen.

Terry looked at his wife. He smiled and shrugged.

"He's certainly confident," sighed Janine.

"He's an idiot," said Terry, unable to contain his rare smile.

"Reminds me of your brother," she replied.

"That's what I mean" said Terry.

"Speaking of that fool. Will he be at the race tomorrow?"

"Coming down for the qualifiers."

"The soak will be on the floor by 2pm."

"Five gets you ten he will be drunk by 1pm," said Terry.

"Done," replied Janine, reaching across the breakfast bar to shake on it, but Terry grabbed her hand, pulled her across the bar and kissed her. Janine lifted her leg in the way she had seen starlets do in those Fifties movies she so loved.

Chapter 3
Julie Is in the Bedroom

Julie sat cross-legged on Danny's bed and rested her head against the wall. She looked around the small room, regarding the posters of cars, racing drivers and maps of circuits. No popstars, no movies, just cars and drivers. On the floor next to her, Danny leaned against the bed. Julie ran her hand through his blond hair, her fingers softly circling through the locks.

Danny closed his eyes and assumed a driving position on the floor, his bare feet on the imaginary pedals, his hands motioning to grip the wheel.

Julie smiled and rolled her eyes as her fingers softly caressed his hair. Danny began to whisper in his strange code – numbers and names in rapid succession as his feet tapped the pedals, and his left hand operated the gearstick. He leaned into the imaginary curves, his eyelids fluttering as he recalled every aspect of the circuit. His mind's eye focused, his spirit in the cockpit driving faster than anyone in the city dared to. He was really there.

When they first started dating and Julie stepped into his small room, she was giddy with excitement. His parents seemed cool and allowed him to have girls in his bedroom – and with the door closed too. She remembered standing in the room and seeing the posters for the first time, seeing his wardrobe that had no door and offered tantalising glimpses into his life: an old jacket hanging, a few shirts and, wonderfully, his racing overalls. British racing green, yellow chevrons, sponsor badges from the local butcher's, his dad's pub and a few icons and brands that she did not recognise. She felt like she had stepped backstage at a concert, or into the trailer of a movie star. She was in Danny Redding's bedroom and the door was closed. She thought she knew what would happen next. A suggestion to sit on the bed and listen to music, a discussion on the depths of the lyrics – an insight into his soul that was soon sure to be her private universe. Then would come the touch, the undress and the fall into adult experience. It was on a plate and she could hardly breathe. None of that happened at first. Instead, Danny spoke quickly and confusingly about the pictures on the wall and about his SuperKart. Julie sat on the bed, coat still on and boots still laced as he poured some strange language over her. Picking up childish model cars and explaining parts of them that held little interest to her, but meant the world to him. And then, just as soon as he had started, he declared that he had to get ready for the next race and promptly slumped down on the floor, assumed a driving position and began, Julie thought, to meditate. She asked him what he was doing and he said, in a flat monotone voice and eyes still closed: "Rehearsing the circuit. Need to know it inside out."

Julie furrowed her brow and asked why. Danny said "James Hunt did it. I do it."

Julie said "Oh," and that was it. She didn't know who James Hunt was, but she was smart enough to bite her tongue and wait till she got home to ask her dad. It had taken three or four more visits to that room over the next few weeks before Julie felt both comfortable in the environment and also frustrated at the chastity of their Friday nights. Her friends at school constantly asked about Danny, his body and his ways. He was the hottest ticket in school and Julie was the luckiest girl on the block. Of course, they talked cruelly about her behind her back and generally agreed that she had lucked out and that Danny would soon grow tired of her. But to her face, it was a relentless inquisition of gossip. Julie lied, feigned and dodged until she could feel it all compounding upon her. She couldn't keep it up and knew that soon it would unravel unless she did something about it. And, of course, she actually wanted to know. She knew she was lucky to snag Danny Redding, but she had seen into his room and realised the truth and so she felt the little insight she had gained levelled the playing field. And so, on the third week she didn't let him practise his race. She took control of the Friday night to the point that she managed to get both of them on the bed, facing each other with some music on and the door closed. It was all that was needed. Afterwards, Danny panicked that he hadn't practiced the circuit. Julie laughed and he relaxed. That weekend he won and set three consecutive lap records.

Julie ran her fingers through his hair and smiled as she drifted back to the first time. Now, things had cooled somewhat – they made time for each other of course, but in the build-up to a race weekend she knew that he had to practise and learn his turns; so she sat and looked at the posters and ran her fingers through his hair, a constant soothing reminder that she was there – a touch and a gesture that managed to carry itself on to the grid on race-day and remain with Danny until the chequered flag.

Danny crossed the line and opened his eyes, reaching up and touching Julie's hand to let her know that he was back in the room.

"Done?"

Danny stood up and stretched.

"Done."

"You here?"

"I'm here," he said with a smile as he walked over to his stereo, which rested on the desk at which Danny spent the absolute bare minimum of time on homework. Danny was about to press 'play' on a tape when a coded knock sounded at the door.

"Yo, bro!" answered Danny, putting his finger to his lips and winking at Julie.

"Can I come in?" replied Chris through the door.

"What's the secret code?"

Silence.

"No code, no entry."

A mumble.

"Louder."

"Chris Redding is a bummer," came the response.

Danny snorted a laugh and Julie giggled.

"Enter!" he boomed.

Chris opened the door and stepped halfway over the threshold. He caught Julie's eye and she coyly waved at him. Chris changed from flesh-coloured to beetroot instantly.

"What can I do you for, bro?" said Danny, leaning against his desk and crossing his arms.

"You about to do homework?"

Danny and Julie looked at each other and smiled conspiratorially.

"Yeah bro, why?"

"Can I borrow the TV and video?"

"Yeah, sure."

"Some tapes too?"

"You want to watch videos and listen to music at the same time?"

"Yeah."

"Fair enough, unplug it."

"Cheers, bro!" said Chris, crossing the room, around the bed and to the video and TV combination.

"What you going to watch?" asked Julie.

"You can choose," said Chris, absently, as he burrowed under the desk to begin unplugging the machine and wrapping up wires.

Julie rolled off the bed and bent down to the stack of videos, piled up by the door.

"Cartoon?"

"No," said Chris reappearing from the footwell of the desk and bracing the TV.

"You need a hand there, bro?" said Danny, watching Chris prepare himself for the heavy television set.

"No, I got it."

"Here we go," said Julie, taking a few videos from the pile.

Chris heaved the TV from the desk and took the weight.

"You got it?" said Julie.

"I got it," huffed Chris, face red and chin resting on the top of the set.

Danny stepped over to the door and opened it for his brother.

"Want me to hook it up?"

"I can do it!" said Chris as he huffed and heaved the TV out of the room and across the landing.

Julie waved the videos at Danny.

"Back in a sec," she said, nodding to the bed. Danny smiled and turned back to the stereo and switched the music back on.

———

"So, this is you?" said Julie as she stepped into Chris' box room – a single bed under a window, a small clothes rail next to it and a desk on the wall opposite the bed.

Chris dumped the TV down on to the desk and ferreted down into the footwell with the cables.

Julie looked at the walls – plastered with drawings of cars, and racing drivers. But these cars were not SuperKarts (she at least knew one of those when she saw one, after months of hearing about it from Danny). The cars drawn on the walls were sleek, expensive looking and armed with guns and cannons. Each one in front of a generic cityscape.

"You do these, Tiger?" she said.

Chris peeked out from under the desk.

"Yeah."

"They're really good – you're a good drawer. You like art at school?"

"Guess so."

"These guns – what are they for?"

Chris stood up from under the table and turned the TV on. Static filled the screen.

"Fighting crime," he said, silently adding "obviously" to his statement.

Julie smiled and nodded her head in understanding.

"What kind of crimes?"

"Whatever the Midnight Boy is needed for," said Chris.

"The Midnight Boy, is that like Batman?"

"Kinda," replied Chris. "He's a loner with his car. He fights crime. Handbag snatchers, bullies… that sort of thing."

"Oh," replied Julie, a tiny note of disappointment in her voice that sounded like an alarm to Chris. He stopped tuning the TV and turned to her.

"What's wrong with that?"

"Nothing, nothing… it's cool. I was just expecting some bigger crimes. I mean handbags snatchers are horrible and bullies are wankers, but what about something more, I dunno…adult? Like a kidnapping?"

"Kidnapping?"

"Yeah, maybe a ransom…only the Midnight Boy can solve the case. Maybe something else, a rescue of some kind. Something romantic. Heroic. Heroic and romantic. Something for the girls. That would be ace." Julie stopped when she realised she was rambling. She turned to see Chris looking at her with a look of confusion that bordered on disgust. She cleared her throat and returned to the pictures. Chris returned to tuning in the TV.

"So, you going to put these together into a comic?"

"Nah," said Chris.

"You should, they are really cool. People will love to read the adventures."

"I'm going to live them."

Julie looked at Chris and saw a hint of the man-to-be in profile, rim-lit by the flickering TV.

"You're going to actually become the Midnight Boy when you grow up?"

"I am grown up," replied Chris, distracted with tuning the TV to pay proper attention to the fact that a beautiful sixteen-year-old girl was in his room. His friends at school probably wouldn't have believed him anyway.

"When you're more grown up, I mean."

"When I'm old?"

"Yeah, when you're old."

Chris found a channel. "I ain't never getting old," he said, finally turning to Julie and throwing out a corner smile that disarmed her immediately. For a second, she believed him utterly and he suddenly looked her age, maybe even older. Behind his eyes, a flash of maturity, resolve and conviction. Julie handed her selection of videos to Chris. "Then, Tiger," she said, "you're gonna love these."

Chris took the videos and Julie blew him a kiss.

"Don't go changing," she whispered demurely and left the room.

Chris looked down at the two videos and furrowed his brow. "Rumblefish and Rebel Without a Cause," he said to himself, turning the videos over and looking at the blurb.

"Black and white?" he said incredulously at Rumblefish and dumped it on his bed.

"1955?" he sputtered with even more incredulity at Rebel Without a Cause. He laughed to himself and tossed the video on to the other before stepping over to his desk and grabbing his sketchbook and pens.

He sat down on the floor, resting his back against the bed and briefly looked at the pictures of the Midnight Boy and his crime-fighting supercar. Chris slowly closed his eyes and stepped out of his bedroom and into his own world.

Chapter 4
Night-time in the City
of Holstenwall

Night had fallen over Holstenwall City. The lights from the skyscrapers over at Roppongi Heights twinkled against the black, overcast sky. No real stars over the city. Just the stars of the rich and well-to-do living in Roppongi. To the west, the lights fell away as the blackness descended over a great area of the city, as if a dark artist had blotted out a whole section of his canvas. The abandoned docks had closed down years before. No ships came to the city. No export. No jobs. Other than Roppongi and its skyscrapers and casinos, the rest of the city was on the very edge. Tenements and projects pressed together and pushed down under a great network of elevated train tracks and freeways. The only other source of light was to the south: Friar's Island, a great amusement park on the banks of the dried-out river that bisected the city. The attractions were old, but still functioned – great dippers and rollercoasters, boardwalks, penny arcades, casinos and a giant Ferris wheel. It was the perhaps the only place in the city where a kid could get some legal thrills, if they had coins. Music all night, the sights and sounds of the funfair, a 24/7 din that floated through the night sky, over the city and up to the top of the Stivyakino TV Tower – the tallest structure in the city. Built long ago and long since shut down. The 700ft metal tower with its blinking red beacon stood like a sad giant above everything. A God of no use. It was there, under that great red beacon that he stood. Clad in his black leathers with silver piping. Jet-black chinless helmet and a black scarf over his face, covering all his features save for his fierce, ice-cool eyes. He stood tall, on the very edge of the tower, standing above the world at the end of an I-beam jutting out from the tower. The six-inch-wide beam was all that supported him. He stood motionless as he surveyed all. Holstenwall City. His city. Waiting for her cry, her pained wail of sadness to bring him to her rescue. He watched and waited, knowing the signal would come soon enough.

———

The mayoral elections were gaining momentum. Banners had been erected in the most impoverished regions of the city – great posters of smiling faces, beaming down upon the citizens emblazoned with heart-melting slogans like 'Change! and 'We can, we must, and so we shall!' Great future leaders with gleaming white teeth. Over in Roppongi, the rich got more than just posters – they got fundraising balls, they got what was called 'face time'; they had their babies kissed and their egos massaged. All for office. Mayor Dooley fretted about his position. He had seen a successful term, so his advisers told him. City Hall's pockets were strained, but crime was the real issue. Crime is always the issue and all the candidates looking to take his job were hitting the topic hard. They talked and talked. Roundtables and focus groups. Hands shook and hands were wrung. But the one thing they could all secretly agree on was that the Midnight Boy needed to be caught. Vigilantism was not to be tolerated – especially when that vigilante was bringing down gangs left, right and centre, while the cops floundered like lost children in a supermarket. Whoever this anonymous threat to the crime stats was, he must be brought to justice. The mayor, like most in City Hall, knew that some of the cops in various districts knew him, even sought out his help. It did no good to round up these cops and martyr them. The city needed cops on the street. The mayor was in a fix, he wanted his job, he wanted to stay behind his mahogany desk and drink whiskey at 9am. He wanted the fat cheques and the perks. He really wanted the Midnight Boy's head on a plate, preferably before the electoral race moved into its final stages.

Dooley sat in his private office at home, sipping away, feet on desk, braces off shoulders as he pondered the downfall of his misunderstood enemy. He looked to his side and smiled when his eyes fell on a picture on his desk – a happy image of a father with a young girl's arms draped around his neck. The girl was perhaps eleven or twelve. All sweet, all smiles. She held on to his neck in the same way he wore his jumper in the warm autumn evenings at the country club. Their perfect smiles framed their perfect hair. He raised a glass to his daughter and took a long sip, closing his eyes as he drifted back to the matter at hand – how to bring down that damned Midnight Boy. Behind him, outside the widow by his desk, a bed sheet rope fell down. He did not see it. The rope pulled taut as a figure descended. The shadow peered into the window – a young woman of sixteen, blonde hair, perfect smile. She looked at her father, pondering at his desk as always, and she smiled. She continued on her path down the outside of the house, ready to make her getaway into the night. She hit the ground quietly, grabbed the bed sheet and pulled it aside from the window, so that it was out of view from the office. She tied it off against some ivy ready to untie and climb back up to her room when her adventure had finished for the night. She peered into a ground floor window. The inside of the house was dark, still, silent. The mayor's daughter took a cigarette and sparked up. The reflected flame revealed her face, pretty and fair but deliberately altered by over-application of mascara that she had smeared and smudged so her eyes resembled a panda's. She had smeared her lipstick also. Juliet Dooley nodded in approval at her appearance. She popped the collar on her denim jacket that she had customised with rhinestone studs and she hitched up her skirt even further. She checked that her DM's were suitably undone and loose around her ankles before blowing herself a kiss and scampering away across the lawn and into the night, heading towards Friar's Island and towards adventures with boys.

Juliet had hooked up with her three friends Melanie, Steph and Chas the moment she had crossed over the parking lot and under the great, illuminated archway that led the way into the island. The girls had been waiting around by Silvio's Hotdog Stand, eating a portion of fries between them and smoking. Juliet sauntered over to the girls and was immediately handed a cigarette. They called her Letz and never once mentioned her father, or the summer houses and country clubs. All their parents lived like that and though Letz's father was the mayor, their own parents weren't that far behind. They were old, so who gave a damn what they did anyway? They loitered by Silvio's for an hour, changing their positions and poses every ten minutes in a strange unspoken choreography. They pouted at the boys they deemed beneath them, and they giggled and coyly looked through their eyelashes at the real contenders – the guys on motorbikes, the ones with flick-knives hidden about them and just aching to be discovered.

The girls never once saw the motorcycle rider over by the arcade, checking them out. He leaned against his bike and rolled a cigarette, picking apart the girl with his keen eyes. He had seen her before somewhere. He knew she was faking it, that she didn't fit the attitude she was trying to convey, but that wasn't it. There was something else. That face, he knew it.

It wasn't until 9.30pm that the girls' veneer was chipped slightly. Letz was leaning against the hotdog stand, one leg cocked, head back and blowing a plume of smoke into the air. She flicked her cigarette to the side and was about to take another from Mel's stash when she received a violent shove.

"What up, shorty!" came a sharp voice.

Letz fell to her side but regained her balance to see a troupe of girls standing before her. Their leader was tall, older and truly cooler than Letz and her friends.

"What you rich bitches about?" she snapped.

Letz, in an instant, became Juliet. Melanie, Stephanie and Charlotte sheepishly huddled together.

"Nothing," said Juliet.

The rival gang had not applied their make-up or put on clothes in any way to make a fashion statement. They just wore whatever clothes they had. They were the real thing. They were fierce.

"You owe me fries."

"What?"

The leader of the gang shoved her fries under Juliet's face. She looked down to see her cigarette butt resting on top of the pile of greasy chips. She gulped.

"I'm sorry, I'm sorry…"

"You bet your ass you're sorry," spat one of the girls at the back of the group. Juliet and her 'gang' huddled a little closer.

"So?"

"Oh God, yes... of course." Juliet grabbed her purse and pulled out a five-dollar bill instantly. The other girls gasped. Juliet held it out to the leader. The other girl curled her lip and sneered.

"Girl, I already ordered my fries," she said, turning to reveal a path to Silvio's ordering point. Juliet looked at the group of bullies and stepped up to the hatch.

The man by the motorcycle had been watching the whole show. He smiled when the gang of bullies stepped up to the other girls. He had seen them before, everyone had. Harmless girls... harmless, unless you were some rich kids from way across town. He stood up from his bike and began to move subtly towards the stand, stopping to nose around the arcades, all the while with one eye on the situation.

Silvio, in his sixties bent down. He probably understood what was going on, but parlance seemed to have changed so much for him that the girls could have been saying anything. The language he heard every day from the kids around had desensitised him to any and all forms of adolescent hostility. He looked at the young girl and did not register her fear. He looked down at her with tired, old eyes, an inch of ash hanging from the end of a limp cigarette in the corner of his mouth. He raised an eyebrow to say: "Yes?"

"May I have some fries, please?"

The girls behind Juliet instantly creased in giggles at Juliet's manners. Even Silvio managed to half-raise his second eyebrow. He waited for a few seconds. No riposte, no offensive follow-up from the girl. They were actual, genuine manners. He turned to the fryer and began scooping out some fries into a styrene tray.

The lead bully winked at her friends.

"Girl, them fries ain't even a dollar. Get us some sodas."

Juliet swallowed and asked for enough soda to go around.

"How much is that?" she meekly asked Silvio, praying that her ordeal would soon be over.

"A dollar," he said.

The bully overheard.

"And some franks and knishes then," she hollered out, to laughs and cheers from the others.

Juliet's friends had slowly begun backing away from the hotdog van, ready to make a dash for it when the moment came. To hell with Letz.

Silvio laid all the food out on the counter of his stand.

"$4.95" he said.

Juliet gave him the cash and turned around to the bullies.

"Bitch, I ain't gonna serve myself."

"Rich princess been served on enough in her life," added one of the gang.

Juliet turned back to the food and began to hand it out to the group. They snatched their food and began stuffing their faces happily. The lead bully watched the frightened girl hand out the food and for a few seconds felt actual, genuine remorse for her actions. The humiliation in her victim's eyes was evident and great shame rose in her. Finally, Juliet handed food to the bully who stowed her shame away and took it.

"Can I go now?" snapped Juliet.

The bully raised her eyebrow. Juliet shrank back.

"Who are you anyway, rich girl? What you doing in Friar's?"

"Free city."

"To you maybe."

The biker was now leaning against the side of the stand, out of view but overhearing them. Who was this rich girl? He knew the face; he was sure he did. He had to know. If it was whom he dared to suspect, then it could be the greatest thing ever to happen to him.

"You wanna hit me?" asked the bully, leaning a little closer into Juliet's face.

"Yeah, she does!" shouted one of her gang.

"No, not at all," said Juliet, raising up her hands.

"Bet you do, shorty. Pretty little rich princess out here, trying to be bad. You bad?"

Juliet shook her head, the bullies laughed.

"You gotta hit me," said the bully. "You gotta. Shorty, you can't let bitches like me push you around. You got one in you?"

The bully shoved Juliet a little. Instantly, her gang erupted in jeers, knowing that violence was here. Juliet's friends bailed in an instant. They turned and fled, not once looking back and leaving Juliet to take a beating.

The biker darted around from the stand and got in front of the bullies. They backed off when they saw his size. Over six feet and broad.

"I think you had your fun, girls. You got your franks, so how about you leave the girly be?"

He looked into the eyes of the bully and imparted a suave kindness. He winked at her. Her aggressive guard dropped a little and she blushed. Instantly, she composed herself. She looked at her gang, who were awaiting orders. She clicked her fingers.

"Let's split, girls."

The bully stood over Juliet and held out her hand.

"Come on," she said.

Juliet took the bully's hand and was pulled to her feet.

"You should have hit me; I know you wanted to."

"You would have killed me."

The bully smiled and left with her gang, eating their franks as they went.

Juliet turned to her saviour and smiled, wiping a tear and smudging her panda-eyes even more.

"Thank you," she said.

"You're welcome," replied the kind stranger, his gaze held on Juliet.

"You okay, mister?"

"Forgive me, yes… it's just your face. You look really familiar to me."

"Yeah, I get that," replied Juliet. "My dad is kind of a big thing."

The penny dropped.

"Holy hell!" he exclaimed, clapping his hands, "you're the mayor's daughter!"

Juliet blushed a little.

"Ma'am, it's a real pleasure," he said, holding out his black-gloved hand. Juliet shook it.

"Say, how old are you?"

"Eighteen."

"How old, really?"

"Sixteen," she said sheepishly. "You going to say that I should be at home, that I am too young to be in this part of town?"

He smiled. "Just seeing if you were old enough for a beer, as long as you don't tell your dad and get me busted!"

He winked at her. Juliet blushed back and they walked into the Island for a proper drink.

———•———

Juliet opted for a cola, and received instead a large shake. Her rescuer sat opposite and introduced himself simply as "Joe". They sat in plastic deck-chairs on the porch of a wooden cantina that served beer all night. Rows of motorcycles lined up alongside the porch, and the neon 'open' sign flicked green and red in the murky window. Juliet held the glass in two hands, nervous to be so far from home in an environment she had not anticipated finding herself in. Everyone around was older. Not a teenager in sight. Real men, real women. Not the old sort of adult her father and his friends were, but the dangerous sort who occupied the years in between her age and her father's.

She looked around cautiously.

"So, your friends bailed on you?" said Joe, flipping the top off his beer and coolly resting his feet on the porch rail.

"Guess"

"Not the done thing."

"Didn't want to get in trouble."

"Still, not the done thing. Anyway, tell me about your father. Old man got the election coming up, no doubt?" he said.

Juliet shrugged. "I guess."

Joe smiled at Juliet. "Finish your shake, I'll drive you home," he said, taking a large swig of beer. Juliet smiled politely back and dabbed her straw into her shake.

———

The mayor had fallen asleep at his desk, his feet up and the whiskey finished. His contented snoring was suddenly disturbed by the loud ringing of the large telephone beside him. The rings were so violent that the handset seemed to rattle, like in the cartoons. Dooley almost fell back off his chair. He grabbed the receiver.

"Hello," he barked.

"Hello, Mayor Dooley," came a soft, male voice.

"Who is this?"

"Never you mind. Just know this. I have your daughter. She is alive, she is safe. But she will be in grave danger unless you do exactly what I say."

The mayor's eyes widened.

"Who is this?"

"For an elected official, you ain't so smart. Did you hear me? I have your daughter and if you want to see her alive again, you're gonna do what I say, understand?"

"How do I know you have her, you son of a bitch?"

Silence for a few seconds, then the sounds of shuffling and the unmistakable sound of tape being ripped quickly off something.

"Daddy?" whimpered Juliet.

"Julie, baby? Oh my God, are you okay, are you hurt, where are you?"

"I don't know Daddy; I'm not hurt but I'm scared. I want to come home."

"Be brave baby, I'm gonna come get you!"

"I'm in a van… it's moving…. we're driv–"

The voice cut off.

"Julie, baby?"

"There, you hear?" the man's voice returned.

"You sick son of a… you are dead if you hurt her. Understand?"

"No, *you understand*. You have one hour to gather one million bucks. In an hour's time I am going to call back with instructions for the drop-off. Clear?"

"But I can't get one mill–"

"One hour and every minute after that you're late, precious Juliet starts to lose fingers, then toes, then eyes, then… well, you get the picture."

The phone went dead.

The mayor, soaked in a flop sweat, stood up, his hands shaking. He grabbed the whiskey and took a large swig directly from the bottle.

He paced around the room, desperately trying to think of a plan. Suddenly, it hit him. He grabbed the phone and dialled.

"Commissioner Thomas," came a tired voice at the other end.

"Geoff, it's Malcolm."

"You okay, Mr Mayor?"

"Listen, we don't have much time. Juliet has been kidnapped. We have one hour to find her."

"Jesus, what can I do – the full weight of the force is behind you Mr Mayor."

"I need the boy."

"I'm sorry?"

"I need this one off the books, I want my daughter back and I can't have the press knowing about it. Can't jeopardise the race. I know you know how to contact him. Get me the Midnight Boy!"

———

The Midnight Boy stood as he always did, atop Stivyakino TV Tower surveying the city, calm, quiet and waiting. Suddenly, from the centre of the city, a beam of light from a rooftop spotlight signalled to him, the circle of light wavering over the dark clouds overhead. The Midnight Boy silently acknowledged the signal, before turning and walking across the narrow I-beam, hopping over the rail and on to the platform at the top of the tower. He walked to the centre of the metal landing and grabbed hold of a large fireman's pole that ran the full 700 feet to the ground. He wrapped his legs around it and descended at great speed.

Twenty feet from the ground, and approaching fast, the Midnight Boy pushed himself from the pole, flipped over in the air and landed hard and well on a dark metal shipping container in the corner of the ground floor of the TV tower. He walked over to a roof hatch and threw it open, climbed into the dark container and slammed the lid shut.

There was a low rumble, followed by a loud roar. The front of the shipping container raised and a pair of lightning-blue headlights beamed out from the gloom. The growl of an engine seemed to make the ground rumble as it reverberated around the tower – a screech of tyres, the headlights snaking from side to side. At the peak of the engine's roar, the Midnight Boy belted out of the tower. The car, a low, customised SuperKart peeled away from the tower and burned into the night. He gripped the small wheel as he drove faster than anyone else could stand. His SuperKart was low, just two inches off the ground and the cockpit exposed. The beast was jet-black with electric-blue piping and matching lights under the chassis that created a streak of blue lightning as it darted through the night. People in the city who had seen it – or knew people who had – called the SuperKart the 'The Blue Flash' or simply 'The Streak'. The Midnight Boy called it 'The Midnight Special'. He had no identity – no past, no future – just the now, just the mission. The car was weaponised and the car was fast. When he drove it through the city, he became one with the moment. He and the car, the car and he.

———

Joe drove his stolen white van through the dark city streets. In the back, tied and gaged, a weeping Juliet rolled and tumbled from side to side with every turn. Joe cackled with evil laughter as he drove, knowing that with each passing minute he got closer to his million bucks. He knew no police could find him; nobody could stop him. Juliet prayed for someone to come and save her, she prayed she would live and she swore she would never sneak out again. Whatever vows needed to be made so that a hero would come and take her from this nightmare, she made them.

———

Commissioner Thomas met with the Midnight Boy in their secret place – beneath an overpass in the centre of the dried-out canal that bisected the city. The Commissioner smiled when the unmistakable roar of the Midnight Special echoed through the canal, bouncing off the wide, slanted concrete walls. He peered into the darkness and just as soon as he saw the pinpricks of the headlights in the distance, they were already upon him. The SuperKart screeched to halt mere inches from the policeman. He stepped around to the car, bending down to the driver. He knew the Midnight Boy did not waste time getting out of the Special and shaking hands. No time for pleasantries. Instead, the mysterious driver looked ahead into the dark distance, his black leather gloves gripping the wheel. The Commissioner filled the driver in on the mission. The Midnight Boy looked ahead, the Special's engine angry that they were idling in a fixed spot.

"Can you help us, Midnight Boy?" pleaded the Commissioner.

The Midnight Boy gripped the wheel, the creak of his leather gloves answering the Commissioner's question. The Commissioner stepped back from the vehicle and was about to wish the hero good luck, when the car pulled away and the rear lights were pin-pricks before his words came out.

The Commissioner smiled and walked to his parked police car. He turned the engine on and drove away, his headlights reflecting some graffiti a street rat had tagged on the wall of the underpass. It read: '…and the Midnight Boy drives.'

———

Joe laughed maniacally as he weaved the truck through the city, his eyes wild, his character suddenly changing inexplicably from the sweet kind stranger of an hour or so before to that of a psychopath in charge of a vehicle.

"Don't you worry, princess," he hollered over his shoulder to the whimpering Juliet in the back of the van. "Soon this will all be over. I will get my million bucks and then, you know what? I am gonna come back for you! That's right – when the money runs out, we're gonna do this all over again. You think this ordeal will be over? You think it's a one-time deal? Haha! Old Joe Bones is gonna take your daddy to the cleaners over and over again. Baby, you're the prettiest damn ATM I have ever seen, yeeehaaaw!"

Joe slammed his fist on horn in the centre of the wheel three times. He was about to floor the van into the tunnel under the canal and into District Denmark Heights when he looked ahead. He jammed on the brakes. In the back, Juliet tumbled forward and hit her head on the back of the driver's bench.

"What the…" whispered Joe.

Juliet got on her knees and looked through the windshield.

The tunnel was pitch. The overhead lights shut off. A black hole.

Joe fumbled for the gearshift to throw the van into reverse. He stopped when two pin-pricks of electric blue ignited at the other end of the tunnel. And then a revving rumble filled the air.

"No… it can't be" murmured Joe Bones in disbelief.

Juliet's eyes widened.

"It is… it's him," she whispered. "It's the Midnight Boy."

"Shut your mouth," scoffed Joe, palming Juliet into her back while he threw the van into reverse and began backing it up.

The revving rumble turned into a roar and the headlights ahead began to grow faster than Joe could believe.

The Midnight Boy gripped the wheel hard as he shot towards the van ahead. He knew his target. He was the fastest racer in the city, and also the greatest detective. It had not taken him long to track down the villain. He hit the centre buckle of his seat belt and the straps retreated into their housing. The Midnight Boy pressed the gas hard and stood up on his haunches as his headlights illuminated the cabin of the van. He saw the wide-eyed driver, frozen in fear.

The Midnight Boy pointed the Special dead centre at the van and just as he was about to drive under, he leapt from the cockpit, flying headfirst into the van's windshield.

In the back of the van, Juliet looked up as blue light filled her vision. Then, like slow motion in the movies, the Midnight Boy smashed through the windshield. Juliet fell on to her back and watched as the hero sailed over the driver's bench, grabbing her kidnapper by the neck. The force of the Midnight Boy's entry pulled Joe clear out of his seat and the pair sailed over Juliet's head. The Midnight Boy, with his free arm, struck out with his fist with perfect timing and punched the rear doors of the van open. Juliet pressed herself to the floor of the van as the two men cleared her and tumbled down on to the asphalt at the back of the vehicle. The Midnight Boy rolled expertly and got on to his feet in one fluid motion while Joe tumbled like a doll. The Midnight Special had driven itself cleanly under the van and was idling by the Midnight Boy who looked down at a battered and dazed kidnapper. Joe murmured. The Midnight Boy reached down, grabbed him by the lapels and dragged the villain out of the road and sat him down against a lamppost, cuffing his hands around the back of the post securely. Slowly the Midnight Boy walked back to the van and held out his hand to the frightened young woman.

"Thank you, thank you so much mister!" she spluttered, the shock of her rescue still rattling her.

The Midnight Boy took a flick knife from his pocket and cut her bindings. She immediately threw her arms around him, embracing her rescuer tightly. The Midnight Boy held her, his calm breathing soothing her, and his gloved hand ran through her hair. She was safe. Safe from the ordeal and she knew that in his arms she would be safe forever.

———•———

The Midnight Boy did not take Juliet directly home. He had saved thousands in his days, but something about Juliet calmed him. Something about her smell, her hair, the tightness of her embrace. She sat on his lap, his arm around her, her legs across the cockpit and dangling over the edge. They drove fast, but not so fast that she felt anything other than elation. They drove through the city, the lights dancing over the glossy sheen of the Midnight Special. She looked into his eyes, but they never looked at her. They stayed on the road, on the city – steel pearls looking to the future. Juliet pressed herself into him as the wind blew her hair elegantly. Perfection never lasts; all too soon she found herself in the driveway of her house. The Midnight Boy parked up and Juliet climbed out of the cockpit and stood beside the car. The Midnight Boy did not step out to join her.

"Will you come in? My father will want to thank you."

He remained motionless.

"Will I ever see you again?"

The Midnight Boy gripped the wheel, and the sound of his creaking leather driving gloves did all the talking. Juliet sniffed back a tear and bent down to him, her face inches from his. She could see the black scarf around his face rise and fall with his deep, calm breath, his eyes refusing to meet hers.

"You have a family? You have someone?" she whispered.

No movement.

She tentatively reached out to touch his mask, perhaps remove it and see his true face. Quick as a cobra, he grabbed her hand and held it close to his face. His touch was not heavy, his grip tender.

"I'm sorry, I was just…"

The leather creaked as he turned to her. Slowly he tipped his head forward and through his scarf he kissed her fingers and let her hand go.

Juliet stood back and held her fingers up to her lips.

"Go," she whispered. "Someone else out there needs you more right now. There is always someone in danger. But it's okay, because we have you. And I know now that we always will."

The Midnight Boy nodded and flexed his gloves against the wheel. The engine began to rumble. Juliet kissed her fingers and held them over the car before turning and walking up the drive.

She had walked twenty paces when the roar of the engine made her turn back. The car weaved in the road, wheels turning, rubber burning and smoke pluming. And then, as fast as he had come into her life, he was gone – the red taillights out of sight before she could say: "I love you."

Instead, Juliet looked to the city spread out before her, the clouds parting to reveal the celestial bed above. She smiled to herself.

"And the Midnight Boy drives," she whispered, before turning away and walking back into her house.

Chapter 5

...and the Midnight Boy drives

Chris opened his eyes, and left his city and the Midnight Boy behind. It had been a hell of an adventure and though he had made it up as he went along and the end felt rushed compared to the drawn-out beginning, he knew deep down that he really had something. Chris reached behind his head and grabbed one of the VHS tapes he had previously tossed on to the duvet. Without looking to see which of the two he had selected, Chris shoved the tape into the player.

The screen buzzed into life and the film started. Chris only half-watched the movie as his concentration was on the pad of paper resting on his lap and the pencil in his hand. He recalled all the detail and atmosphere of Holstenwall City, of the Midnight Boy and the fabled Midnight Special. Chris never questioned how it would ever come to pass; he just knew with a deep conviction that he would one day become that silent hero. He would become the Midnight Boy. Chris smiled broadly and drew on.

———

Julie and Danny lay on top of the covers, listening to one of the CDs that she had brought over, her leg draped over Danny's waist, her head resting on his chest. This time, it was his hand running through her hair. The music fell into Julie and she really felt it – she felt that nobody understood what the singer was trying to impart in his angst-ridden lyrics better than she did. It was almost as if he were singing to her and her alone. Julie's inner voice made real and presented back to her. Danny, on the other hand simply listened to the music and occasionally noted a pleasant melody here and there. He was not a man of much imagination; he was a racing driver and his analysis was on the task at hand. Danny ran his fingers though Julie's hair and plotted the race the next day, planning and adapting to every turn and eventuality that might present itself on the track. He felt ready.

———

Janine and Terry watched the television, neither paying much attention to the programme. Terry pondered over his cigarette, turning the ashtray that was precariously balanced on the arm of his favourite chair, the light of the TV blurring as he thought about the next day's race. His boy was sure to win and take a great step towards the regional championships. But then what? Move up a league, into the national's maybe? What if he was spotted by a pro team? They would take the boy from him and nurture and mould a true racing driver and then where would Terry be? On the scrapheap or worse, in the grandstand with the other fathers watching their sons race, drinking stale beer from the stalls and without the smell of engine oil in their nostrils and the bustle of the pit lanes in their ears. But if they went their own way, and set up their own pro team – how would he fund that? He knew that what was best for the boy's future was to provide all he could until the moment a real team came along and took Danny away from him. 'Such is life,' he thought sadly as he stubbed out a cigarette and immediately lit another.

Janine sat beside him with a notepad on her lap. She spent the best part of the night jotting down all the incomings and outgoings of the family, hoping that somehow the laws of mathematics would cosmically shift for her and the final tally would be miraculous. It was a futile task but nevertheless, she did the finances nightly.

———

Chris couldn't believe his eyes. It was nearly incomprehensible. He finished his drawing – his best yet, he thought – and he looked up at the TV screen to catch the last few seconds of Rumblefish. There, on screen as if it were a projection of his destiny, some graffiti was scrawled on a wall in a city that he seemed to recognise. He saw 'The Motorcycle Boy Reigns' flash by and his eyes widened. Chris fumbled for the remote control and paused the film, the screen rolling and flickering as it struggled to hold the image steady. He moved closer to the screen, his eyes inches from it and he silently mouthed the words he saw. Chris slowly looked back down to his drawing and saw that he had scrawled over the night sky, above the city, the Midnight Boy's catchphrase – the legend of the city: "…and the Midnight Boy drives". Chris sat back, hitting the bedframe and resting his head on the edge of the mattress. Chris repeated the two phrases and knew he had not copied the film, but had actually arrived at the same legend independently. It could mean only one thing: the film was his. His new favourite. His number one. He grabbed the video case and looked at the liner notes on the back cover, taking in the names of the director and the actors – none of whom he had heard of a few moments earlier, but were now Kings and Knights in his world. Chris put the box down and went to rewind the tape when his mother opened the door without knocking (a habit she knew could not last as the boy was approaching the dangerous years). She stuck her head round the door.

"Bedtime, piggy," she beamed. Chris winced a little at his pet name, turned the TV off and unhappily got to his feet. His mother held the door open for him and he ducked under her arm to go brush his teeth.

Janine waited for Chris to leave before stepping into his room and sitting on the bed. She looked down at the drawing and picked it up, smiling at the landscape. She looked around the room at all the other drawings of the black car and the cityscape and she had a sudden, daring flash of realisation that maybe, just maybe, her youngest child was an artist. She knew that Danny didn't really display much in the way of creative flair and that was fine, that kid could drive and that thrilled her immensely, but her youngest to be an artist? A sensitive boy becoming a sensitive man who would create wonders for the world. "Fine boys, fine boys," she said aloud.

"Who," said Chris, walking back into the tiny room and pulling some pyjamas from a rickety chest of drawers, customised with stickers and doodles, many of which made little sense to him as they had been stuck or drawn on by his brother years before. He added to the stickers, but never tried to peel them off, or stick over them.

Chris turned and stood in the room, holding his pyjamas and looking at his mother. She looked at him and they paused until she realised what he meant by his stance.

"Right, sorry of course," she said, realising that the boy wanted privacy and didn't want to get into his pyjamas with her present. He was growing up, after all.

Janine stood up and laid the picture down on the bed.

"I love the drawing," she said, "better than the rest."

"Thanks," said Chris a little flatly.

"What are they of? Some sort of supercar?"

Chris scoffed a little, knowing that she would never be able to grasp the concept of the Midnight Boy, or what he stood for, of the things he did, let alone that Chris himself would one day assume the role and become the saviour of the city.

"Yeah, a supercar," he said unable to hide the sarcastic disdain that marinated his tone.

His mother smiled at him.

"Cool," she said, uncoolly and she bent down to him, tilting her head and tapping her cheek.

"Night night," she said.

Chris rolled his eyes and pecked her cheek. Janine smiled bravely despite knowing intrinsically that her sweet boy was stepping farther away from her hour by hour. She ruffled his hair and left the room, walking across the dark landing and thinking: 'Make it through the teenage years and come out the other side as a good man. Don't become a terror.'

———•———

Terry turned on the light in the lock-up beside the house and looked at the SuperKart, hoisted up on its stanchions. Everyone else in the house was in bed, his wife no doubt sitting up with that annoyingly huge calculator on her lap, punching in figures from her notepad and causing the printer to chug and clunk loudly as the roll of paper confirmed what her notes had already told her – that the laws of maths remained and that they were in the red.

He walked over to the workbench and turned on the kettle, dumping a tea bag into a mug before stepping over to the kart and running his hands over the sleek cowling. He bent down to the engine and inspected various valves and pipes, smiling to himself as he concluded that everything was in its right place. The kettle boiled and he prepared his tea, blowing the vapour from the rim.

'You're gonna fly tomorrow, my boy, you're gonna take our kart and fly'

"All the way to the top," he added, aloud. "All the way to the top, my boy."

Terry took a sip of tea and grimaced. He shook his head and tipped the mug on to the floor. He smiled and left the lock-up, turning the light off as he did. He walked down the driveway to the house and threw a cursory look up to Chris's bedroom window. The light was off, which told him it was far too late now to get a real cup of tea. This pleased him somewhat and he knew that he was foolish even to attempt making his own tea. If it wasn't made by his youngest boy, it wasn't worth drinking.

———

Chris lay in bed and stared up at the ceiling. The moonlight illuminated the plastic galaxy that was stuck above his bed. Planets, stars, rocket ships – a private universe. The house was silent, it was deep into the night and he had not been able to sleep. He needed to be sure that nobody would be disturbed. At 2am he reached over to the TV and turned it back on, instantly twisting the volume switch down to near minimum. Chris curled up in his bed, pulling the duvet over himself so that he was provided just enough space to view the television and nothing else. He reached out, rewound the video and began to watch the Rumblefish again. This time, he gave it his full attention and in those private ninety minutes in his room, bathed in the blue light from the television, he learned more about himself and the world than he knew he ever would at school. It was clear that somehow, someday, the Motorcycle Boy and the Midnight Boy would team up. Two brothers. Two giants.

Chapter 6
Morning of...

Chris had little sleep that night, but he was the first in the house to rise. It was a perfect morning – puffy clouds that Julie referred to as 'Bueller Clouds', for a reason unknown to Chris, scudded by peacefully. He had slept with the curtains open as he liked, and his room was bright and airy. It had been a hell of a night and he lay on his bed, looking up at the ceiling with a contented smile on his face, hand clasped over his belly, legs crossed. He had watched both videos back-to-back and felt as though he really had lived an adventure as the Midnight Boy. He felt strong, changed; fast. Everything ahead for him now seemed clear and achievable. His life mapped out. His destiny shown to him. The feeling of serene acceptance at the glorious inevitability of his life breezed through him. What made the feeling and the morning sweeter, was that he knew that nobody in the house, or in the city knew. It was his secret, his idea – his.

Chris got out of bed and walked across the landing to the bathroom to wash and clean his teeth. He could hear some rustling from within Danny's room as he passed by – Julie no doubt getting ready to leave for her early shift at the café in town. He walked past his parents' bedroom and heard the pleasant sound of his mother and father snoring gently in their signature ways.

The bathroom was small with the bulk of the space taken up by the chipped enamel bath, and a huge airing cupboard that kept the room lovely and warm in the winter and near unbearable in the summer. The carpet used to have a black and red paisley pattern, but that had been worn down over years having been trodden on by heavy work boots, and dirty shoes despite the protestations of his mother. Chris washed in the small basin, brushing his teeth quickly and trying to style his hair before his face was totally obscured in the cabinet mirror by the condensation from the taps. He managed the task and dumped his toothbrush back into the pot. He turned the taps off and looked at the blurred shape in front of him – a recognisable outline, but a featureless mass. Chris contrived to imagine an ancient version of himself staring back – grown up and fierce, perhaps as old as thirty. He stared for a minute before the condensation began to wane and his young, chubby face was gradually revealed. Chris dried his face and left the bathroom.

He stopped dead in his tracks on the landing as Danny's bedroom door opened and a sleepy Julie stepped out, dressed in a small, black slip. She groggily waved and yawned a good morning to Chris as she walked past and into the bathroom, completely unaware of just how short her slip was, and just what sort of thing that could do to an impressionable young boy. She closed the door behind her, and Chris rushed into his bedroom, a strange fire in the pit of his belly.

Julie yawned and turned the taps on, dipping her toothbrush under the tap. She looked in the mirror and expected to see her smeared make-up panda-ing her eyes from where she had forgotten to remove it the night before. Instead, she saw her face obscured in the mist and the formation of letters appearing. She scrunched up her face and read "…the Midnight Boy woz ere" scrawled diagonally across the mirror. Julie shrugged, wiped the condensation away and began to brush her teeth.

Danny and his father pushed the SuperKart slowly out of the lock-up and turned it forward so that it faced the up-ramp of their trailer. It was still early morning, but the summer warmth was already on the back of their necks. The car gleamed.

"She looks a beaut," said Terry.

Danny nodded and both men regarded the car, arms folded and heads tilted in the same manner. Danny looked up to the sky.

"Perfect weather for it," he added.

"You got the course down?"

Danny tapped his forehead.

"I'm still not sure about Graves," said his father.

"Drop to third, take it wide. Trust me," replied Danny, "I have it."

"It's an expensive gamble," said Terry. "We only got one of these," and he kicked the rear tyre.

Danny shrugged, "That's racing pops."

"Come on then, let's get her up there."

Danny and his father bent down over the kart and pushed it slowly up the ramp and on to the flatbed trailer. Terry folded up the tail gate while Danny secured the car.

"Good to go?" he asked.

"Good to go," confirmed Terry as he walked from the trailer to the attached van. Danny walked to the vehicle and threw a look up at his brother's bedroom window to see Chris looking down at them.

Danny smiled and waved at his brother who did not wave back in his eager way, but simply nodded his acknowledgement that he knew his brother was ready to race. A confident nod that said: 'You got this, bro.' Danny smiled and shook his head at the burgeoning maturity of his younger brother before hopping up into the cab of the van.

Terry fired her up and they drove slowly out of the lock-ups, turning right and parallel to the front garden. Danny's mother stood there, holding a Tupperware box of tinfoil-wrapped sandwiches. She handed them to Danny through the passenger window.

"You ready, Danny boy?" she asked, smiling and squinting as the sun flared into her eyes.

"Yes, Mum. Will you be there?"

"After town, I'll bring Chris along. We'll be there for the qualifiers. What about Julie? Am I collecting her from the café?"

"No, she's finishing early and coming down in a few hours. Uncle Tone will look after her while me and dad are in the pits."

"Uncle Tone? Heaven help her."

"Leave him alone, Mum, he's fine."

Janine raised her eyebrow, and leaned to the side so that she could talk past Danny and address her husband.

"Please try and make sure he's not ten sheets to the wind by the time we get there, will you, Tel?"

"There's no telling him, you know that."

"For me?"

"Alright mum," interjected Danny, "for you."

Janine leaned towards the passenger window and turned her face, tapping her cheek. Danny smiled and leaned out of the window, kissing her cheek with a loud smacker.

"See you in a few hours, boys." she said.

"Bye, Mum."

Terry didn't say anything, but put the van in gear and pulled away, off out of the close and to the circuit, gleaming SuperKart in tow.

———

Chris sat on his brother's bed in his vest and pants, arms folded and petulant. He and his mother had wasted the morning trying on some of Danny's old school clothes and had amassed two piles – those that fitted and those that were for charity. Janine folded the last shirt and looked at the two heaps.

"Looks like we'll have to spend a bit longer in the supermarket if we're to get you what we need."

"Ah what?!" exclaimed Chris, feeling each passing minute as if it were a week.

"Don't worry, we'll have time to get to the circuit. Might miss qualifying, but we'll get to the race."

"No, we won't, idiot. Might as well stay here."

Chris folded his arms and sunk his chin into his neck, instantly regretting calling his mother an idiot.

"Well, that's that, then," she said sternly. "No race for you this afternoon. Straight home after the store. When your dad gets home from the race, I will tell him what you called me and then he can decide what to do with you, how about that?"

Chris went to protest but saw the look in his mother's eyes.

"I'm sorry," he spat with an exasperated tone, implying that his apology was obvious and that she was an idiot for not understanding his remorse. She raised an eyebrow.

"Put these clothes away and get dressed. We're leaving in five minutes," she commanded flatly, before leaving Chris in his brother's room.

As soon as the door slammed, Chris swore at it silently. He turned and looked at the two piles, his anger boiling up. He picked up both piles and threw them against the door, mixing them up.

"Don't care," he said to himself when he saw the huge bundle on the floor. He scooped all the clothes and threw them into the bottom of Danny's cupboard. He turned to leave before stopping to look at the old racing overalls hanging up at the back of the wardrobe. He reached into the cupboard and ran his fingers along the sleeve of a plain black suit, one of his brother's first – jet black, no sponsors, nothing extraneous that might weigh it down. He carefully took the suit from its holding and held it up fully.

He was about to take it from its hanger and put it on when he heard his mother yelling up from downstairs. He couldn't make out her exact words but he knew what she was saying, nevertheless.

"I'm coming!" he bellowed back. "For Christ's sake", he added quietly for his own benefit. He put the racing suit back and smiled to himself, a beautiful idea forming. He quickly left the room and dashed to his own to get some clothes on.

———

They hadn't spoken for an hour. At the bus stop, Janine sat reading her detective novel – a series of books charting the adventures of some guy called Giallo that she loved and that caused much strange derision from Uncle Tone whenever he caught her reading them. She didn't care though; she loved the books so she would read them if she wanted. Besides, Chris knew that his mother thought cool Uncle Tone was anything but. On a few occasions when she had drunk too many glasses of wine at home, Chris had overheard a few choice words his mother had exclaimed to his father regarding Uncle Tone: "drunkard" which was a bit rich, considering; "layabout" which wasn't so bad as she called everyone without a job a layabout; "failure" which was a bit mean; once she heard her call him an "effing loser", which was utterly shocking to Chris. His mother had thought she heard Danny say the F-word once and she belted him so hard that he nearly cried and so to hear even an approximation of that word coming from her mouth was unbelievable. Anyway, she sat at the bus stop and read her Giallo book. Chris sat away from her, deliberately at the other end of the stop, staring at the row of houses on the opposite side of the road. Normally, he thought nothing of those houses given that they were of the same design as his own but whenever he was annoyed, the monotonous design filled him with anger. They presented some sort of prison – an endless, banal prison of dull houses with near-identical cars on the driveway and identical lives inside. He wanted out of the suburbs, he wanted to go his own way. 'They'll be dead one day,' he dared to think of his parents. He half smiled as he reassured himself with that dark realisation. Chris looked up and rested his head against the glass-paned bus-stop, his eyes rising above the rooftops of semi-detached houses and towards the horizon. Though it was late morning, and the sky was utterly clear, he could still make out the never-ending red beacon atop the Stivyakino TV tower at the opposite end of the city. 'When they're gone, that's where I'll go,' he thought. 'All the way to the other side of town where nobody can find me. To the top of the tower and there I will stay. There I will be truly born.'

Chris closed his eyes and smiled as the warm breeze caressed his face. He was drifting into the future, to the top of the tower and to where he now dared to position Julie in her nightdress. A squeal of breaks brought him back to reality. The bus had arrived. His mother folded the book away and paid for them both. Chris skulked on to the bus. Chris sat in a window seat and angled himself from his mother so that she could not see his face and he could just sit and look at the mundane houses as they rolled past. After five minutes, Janine gave in and ruffled his hair, all the while keeping her eyes on her book. Chris knew that she had forgiven him for the insult, but he didn't care. He thought only of the tower in his imagination, on top of which Julie reclined and where the Midnight Special was parked below: awaiting the call to action.

Chapter 7
Supermarket Specials

Chris abandoned his mother in the supermarket mere seconds after they had purchased the clothes needed for the new school year. He badly wanted to get the hell out of there and get to the racetrack to watch his brother cross the line way ahead of the pack. But he knew his mother. She took ages shopping. He knew he could get the items on her list so much faster. He wouldn't 'um' and 'ah' about different brands, he wouldn't succumb to impulse and buy some new product, only to listen to reason ten minutes later and go back to the correct aisle to replace the item. None of that would happen. "Get in, bang, done," as his brother always said when talking about anything that required quick thinking (outside racing, of course – *that* required meticulous preparation and execution). And so, Janine whiled away the late morning as if nothing else mattered and Chris knew there was only one thing that would save him from the slow hands of the clock: the toy aisle.

And there he stood, between the two narrow aisles of toys. A year or two ago, he could have sworn the toy section of the supermarket was at least three times bigger than it was at this point. Not now. Everything was getting smaller. Just two aisles of toys and not even any good ones – most of them were for girls and the boys' toys were for young kids, way too juvenile for Chris to bother with. Great hulks of plastic, painted in lurid colours. His section had been reduced to just a small little portion at the very edge of the aisle, as if slowly being pushed out farther and farther until eventually they would all disappear. A few cap-guns, a few expensive action figures based on films that he had not yet seen. But they had cars. He knelt and looked at the selection on display. The cars were finely detailed replicas – working steering, opening doors. "They are not toys," his dad would say. "They are for looking at."

Terry was half right. Chris had lately found that just looking at them held more joy than tearing them around on his carpet – but then the only car of that 'shop quality' Chris knew of was the green E-Type that sat on his dad's desk and was, most definitely, only to be looked at. Chris thought himself tough and fearless but even didn't dare 'drive' that car.

Chris adjusted his position, moving from his knees and sitting cross-legged on the floor so he could see the boxed cars behind the display models, hoping there might be a few variations hidden at the back. You never know, there might just be a sweet car that had been pushed to the back by some careless shelf-stacker and remained unsold. He pulled the front row of boxes on to the floor as if they were all his own and the supermarket his bedroom. Chris began ferreting around, reaching deep into the shelving and sweeping the rear boxes forward – his desire to find new models suddenly becoming a matter of urgency. Chris did not hear the sound of the man clearing his throat behind him. It took three loud rasps for Chris to snap out of his mania. He turned around to see two blue trunks nearly at his back. He looked up and saw the trunks become a torso, then a man, a man in uniform – and decidedly unhappy. The security guard said not one word, but Chris knew what was what. He looked around to see the boxes of model cars scattered around him. He turned red and hurriedly began replacing the boxes neatly back to how they should have been.

"There's a good lad," said the security guard, before walking away, whistling to nobody as if he were a gaoler. Chris silently swore at the guard when sure that he was out of sight and not about to suddenly turn back. He picked up the last boxed car and went to replace it when he halted. He had not seen the model before. It was a rare one for sure. Rare in its perfection: it was a jet-black Pontiac, sleek and surreal – unlike any other car Chris was ever likely to see in real life. Perhaps on television, but not a chance on the streets. Not only was it jet-black, but it came with electric blue lights and rims. The Midnight Special, in his hands and just a mere £50 from his possession. Alright, so it wasn't a SuperKart and didn't have the customisation that the Midnight Boy would have brought to it, but you couldn't have everything. £50. That was an extraordinary amount for a toy car, that's what his dad would say – even though they weren't toys. But it was Chris' birthday soon…perhaps he could strike a deal? Perhaps not have the birthday dinner he assumed he would have, perhaps not have two or three of the assumed ten other toys? Sacrifice the lame toys that he wouldn't have played with anyway in order to accommodate the replica Midnight Special into the birthday budget – £50 was an extraordinary amount but he was sure it could be done. He would state his case well and, as Uncle Tone said: "There's nothing that can't be done."

Chris smiled and stood up, unable to take his eyes from the toy car. He turned to seek out his mother, who was no doubt moving through the frozen aisles comparing the price of frozen peas. He left the toy aisle, turning left and rushing straight into someone. Chris dropped the car and spluttered an apology. He looked up to see not an adult, but two girls his own age. Worse, in his school, in his year and his class. Stacy Beckett and Jenn Bowler. They were his age, but somehow not. As Dom proudly boasted a few weeks back in the rugby changing rooms: "Stacy has great tits and Jenn is well easy to finger." Same age, same species, but may as well be from another planet. They were with the cool kids – not cool boys and girls, but cool kids and there was a monumental difference. Chris stood, dumbstruck, unable to think of anything to say – let alone a quip.

"You go to our school, right?" said Stacy, forgoing pleasantries and without addressing the fact that Chris had run into them. He shrugged meekly and blushed.

Stacy and Jenn looked at each other and curled their lips as if they had just smelled something odious. Who was this idiot?

Jenn looked to the floor and saw the model car.

"You still play with toy cars?" she gasped, her mocking laughter kicking the ladder of his maturity from underneath him in one swoop. Chris looked to the floor.

"You like toys, how old are you?" added Stacy.

"So gay," concluded Jenn.

The two girls laughed and brushed past Chris. He turned to them hoping to summon some sort of courage and wit with which to slice them in twain.

"Yeah, well..." was the best he could muster.

Stacy and Jenn turned back and laughed at him. They both swore at him with identical gestures, as if it was part of some sort of obscene dance number. They cackled again and peeled off down the make-up aisle to try and make themselves appear like sixth-formers.

Chris's shoulders dropped and he looked down at the Midnight Special on the floor. He kicked the toy box under the nearest aisle with one, sharp kick. He looked up at the huge clock that hung in the very centre of the supermarket, designed to remind adults that they were running out of time to take advantage of the various retail opportunities, and simultaneously to remind children that they were in that bright prison for the long haul.

Not even eleven. Qualifying was due to start in one hour – his dad and his brother were probably tuning the car, probably doing all sorts of manly activities in the pit lane. His father was probably drinking some poorly made tea, Uncle Tone was probably talking to some barmaid in the beer tent and Julie was in the paddock sunning herself.

"And I'm stuck damn well here," said Chris, loudly answering his internal monologue. He huffed and stuck his hands in his jacket pockets. He looked back up at the giant clock. It appeared to be somehow earlier than it had been just a few moments prior.

Chris left the aisle and shuffled through the children's clothes section, trying to circumvent the make-up aisles and somehow get across to his mother and hope to find her ready to get the hell out of there. He turned from the clothes and stopped in his tracks. Had he never been to this section of the store before? Was it nearly Christmas? Ahead of him he saw a cleared section of retail space – no aisles, no shelves – just a line of pristine pedal cars. Lined up, underneath a chequered banner that read: "Rebel Racing New Line, 1994". The plastic and metal machines gleamed under the soft supermarket light. Simple, lean machines: bare chassis, exposed steering columns and minimal cowling. Just a plastic sheath like his shin-pads clipped to the steering arm with a racing number spray painted on. Plastic wheels, even a working handbrake.

Chris smiled incredulously at the sight before him. He looked around briefly, half expecting it to be a trap like in 'Return of the Jedi' – a thousand Sith Security Guards ready to pounce if he so much as touched one. He saw only the security guard from earlier, sat in a little kiosk and appearing to be on the verge of sleep. Chris cautiously stepped to the line of karts. He instantly knew which one he really wanted to look at and, brilliantly, it was at the very end so he could slowly and dramatically walk down the line, running his fingers across the edges of the seats and steering wheels, assessing each in turn. Finally, he came to the kart at the end of the line – of course, it was black. Better still, it had no number and no other markings – no go-faster stripes, no chequers or chevrons. What it did have that the others did not, however, was a large whale-tail spoiler like a 911. Man, it was a beauty!

Chris looked down at the price tag and knew it wasn't even worth entertaining the idea of haggling with his parents for it. Not twenty Christmases and birthdays combined would get that beast in the lock-up next to his brother's SuperKart.

Chris bent down and ran his hands over the wheels – real rubber tyres. He looked to the pedals and regarded the well-oiled chain that powered the beast. It was a perfect machine. Chris then looked up at the kiosk and saw the security guard reading a newspaper. Without moving his gaze from the guard, Chris pushed the kart backwards, expecting the chain that tethered them all together to pull tight, perhaps even an alarm to siren. Nothing happened. The kart rolled out of line and came to a stop, half turned from the area and facing away from the kiosk and to the supermarket ahead.

Chris stifled a laugh. Of course, it would be thus. Of course, he would never be able to afford the car – didn't need to, it was his by destiny. Calmly, he walked around the line of other karts and circled his, all the while keeping an eye on the kiosk. Of course, the kart had no engine, but to Chris it still grumbled and growled like the Midnight Special, eager to get away from its starting position. A final look at the kiosk and Chris eased himself into the seat. It was his. He rested his feet on the pedals and flexed his hands on the wheels, the imaginary sound of creaking leather filling his ears. He cricked his neck as he had seen heroes do in the movies.

"Oi, YOU!" bellowed a stern voice from over his shoulder. Chris gasped and looked around to see the security guard leaving his kiosk and stomping his way over. Chris pushed to heave himself out of the car, but stopped halfway. He looked down at his feet, still on the pedals, one hand on the wheel. He looked over to the guard.

"Don't even try it, son!" shouted the guard as he saw the rebellious glint in the young boy's eyes.

Chris winked at the man and sat back into the seat: adjusted himself, gripped the wheel and took a breath.

"Eff it," he said with a smile. Chris hit the pedals.

And the Redding boy began to drive.

Chapter 8
Midnight Boy, Aisle Seven

Chris knew that his mum perhaps had never been so embarrassed in all her life. She first went red, then burgundy and was seemingly just seconds from emitting steam from her ears by the time she yanked him by the arm out of the security office and frogmarched him to the bus stop, struggling with her bags of shopping. Quite frankly, Chris couldn't give a damn. What a ride, what a rebel.

Chris sat on the bus, his mother purposefully sitting on the bench across from him, not wanting to be near the wretched child. He leaned against the window and softly closed his eyes so that orbs of orange light formed under his eyelids. Strange and beguiling shapes pushed and pulled, moving past his vision like the tail lights and headlights on the highways of destiny as he overtook them at sub-sonic speeds in his future crime-fighting car. Chris felt he had taken a giant step towards that future. He had proved himself to be fearless and strong. Easily the fastest racer in the entire supermarket. He knew that he would not be seeing his brother race after that escapade and probably wouldn't get any dinner and might even have his ears boxed for real by his father. The threat was always there, but never carried out – the threat being enough of a deterrent. But maybe this merited a whack or two? Who cared?

Chris closed his eyes a little tighter, dispelling the orbs of light and he travelled back to his moment of glory, just half an hour before but already cemented in legend. Everybody had seen him, and he knew everybody would speak of it until their dying days... but only one had actually achieved it. Only one of them had lived.

———

Chris pushed his feet down on the pedals and the car lurched into life, off to a great start – perfect timing as the security guard dived for the great rear spoiler on the back of his Special. But the standing start had pulled the kart out of reach by mere inches. The guard lurched, almost toppling over as the inertia barrelled him forward. The Midnight Boy instantly thought of five separate, but equally cool and biting quips to hurl back at the guard as he pulled away, but he said nothing, knowing the terse, serious nature of the Midnight Boy was cooler and more mysterious than some wisecracking kid. He began to accelerate, the kart feeling light and slipping across the highly polished floor. He soon brought her under control, imagining the weave to be the growl of the great engine positioned right behind his seat. He pulled away from the guard and approached a glass counter directly ahead. He saw two spotty lads in white overalls and stupid hair nets behind him, as they stared in disbelief, seconds away from diving for cover in fear when the Midnight Boy took an extreme right, nearly losing the back end of the kart as it swung out and almost clipped the underside of the counter. He had no mirrors – he didn't need them – but he knew the lads were dumbstruck, in awe and rooted to the spot. He didn't look back, he pedalled harder. The guard regained his balance and ran on, turning the corner on one foot and hopping from one side to the other as they do in those juvenile cartoons the Midnight Boy used to watch all those Saturday mornings way back when.

"Stop! Stop that boy!" he yelled as he ran forward, holding his hat to his head and blowing a whistle that just now appeared in Chris's recollection. The Midnight Boy gripped the wheel tightly, his new leather gloves creaking with intent against the plastic wheel. Ahead, the long aisle that ran the length of the store seemed to stretch out in front of him, pulling away; the aisle to the left and all its products flashing by like shop windows and streetlights. He pedalled even faster. The guard had found his pace and was gaining. "I have you now!" he said in a villainous voice that seemed to appear inside the Midnight Boy's glossy black racing helmet before the guard had even uttered it. Chris smiled wryly and leaned to the side, turning the wheel hard, rolling his left wrist over right and leaning into the bend. The Special pulled up on two wheels and he took the impossible bend like a magician, never losing speed. The guard skidded on his heels, kicking his legs up like a Can-Can dancer. The Special landed back on all four wheels and the Boy pedalled on. In the make-up aisle ahead, he saw Stacy and Jenn leaning by the lipstick section, sharing a small mirror at head height and trying on varying shades of the same colour. The Midnight Boy reached to the side and shifted gears, the engine behind him blaring out a warning. The guard got to his feet and scrambled down the make-up aisle after the racer. The girls trying on lipstick heard the growl of the engine, and swooned as the Midnight Boy belted past them, coolly saluting them as the wind from the engine blew their skirts up to reveal their underwear. The girls gasped, put one hand on their lips and tried to suppress their unruly skirts with the other as the Boy drove away. They craned their necks to watch him, their hearts beating fast.

"Who was that boy?"

"Midnight… Boy!" gasped the guard as he rushed past the girls. They looked at each other and giggled coyly, silently vowing to dedicate their lives to tracking him down. One would become a rambunctious investigative reporter at the local newspaper, the other would stalk the night in her own car committing and solving crime in equal measure – anything to draw the Midnight Boy out.

Chris drove through the supermarket, weaving through the aisles and stunning shoppers until it was time to leave. He passed under the chain-rope that sectioned off an out-of-use till and drove along the length of the store, the windows to the city zipping by on his left-hand side. It was now night-time and he knew that somewhere, out in the city, a villain was victimising a citizen. As soon as he conceived it, his signal appeared in the night sky. The Midnight Boy put his foot down and burned through the store, taking a fast left out of the exit and launching from a speed bump clear over the car park and the tall hedge that bordered it, coming down hard and well on the freeway. The guard, out of breath and beaten, came to a halt by the exit of the supermarket, his hat on the back of his head, his shirt undone and untucked, his tie loose as sweat poured down his brow.

"I'll get you one day, Midnight Boy, I will bring you down" he vowed, shaking his fist at the light in the sky and instantly devising a costume, a lair and even a backstory to help create the type of person required to hunt down and kill the Midnight Boy.

———

She had never been so embarrassed in public before. There was a time, 10 years ago at a dinner party with her new boss and colleagues, when Terry and his idiot brother got hammered and proceeded to berate the hosts' cooking and as well as their taste in décor. Tone had started it, as he usually did – saying something deliberately contentious when he deemed the conversation to be straying into the boring, conventional and inane. But Terry had gone along with it. Too many brown ales, and too much wine, which always made him act like a fool. On the Monday, Janine practically had to beg to keep her job. Terry could not have been more apologetic. Tone didn't even remember and had the cheek to refute the claims that he deemed ludicrous, and play down the ones that might possibly have happed. But that wasn't the general public. Having her name called out in the supermarket over the Tannoy, at the checkout and having to leave her shopping and be escorted by security the whole length of the store to the back offices – everybody looking at her, and everybody seeing the abandoned trolley of goods. Of course, they had all created their own ideas of what had happened – juicy stories of thievery and deception, or tragic tales of declined credit cards. Janine walked with her head down. She knew something had happened, but she did not consider it to be anything that could possibly be to do with an accident. Security would not have come to frog-march her to the office if a tragedy had occurred. No, she would be taken aside and calmly spoken to and all the other shoppers would look at her with sympathetic eyes and, not knowing what had occurred, would have feared the worst and given Janine all their pity. That would have been something. But no, she walked to the booth and as she approached, she knew what had happened. Outside the booth stood a black pedal kart. Its front wheel was bent and hanging off, vicious scratching up the front cowling. Utterly unfit for sale. The stern security guard didn't say a word until he opened the door to his little booth to reveal Chris sitting inside.

"Hi, Mum," he said. She almost blew her top. The cheek of it. Not even a trace of tears. Not even a blurted-out vomit of explanation and this and that and the unfairness or if all as was Chris's way.

"Hi, Mum," in a flat, faraway tone as if she had phoned at an inconvenient time. The same tone she deployed when she used to get calls from her own mother, God rest her soul.

Janine went red.

"Took it for a joyride," said the guard.

Janine went maroon.

"Belted down the milk aisle, lost control and hit the counter. Smashed up the car pretty good, broke at least five pints. Surprised you didn't hear the smash."

She could feel steam beginning to rise inside her.

The security guard reached for a carbon pad on his desk and ripped off the top sheet, exposing the green sheet underneath. He folded it up and handed it to Janine.

"Expensive bit of kit, that car. Management don't expect you to have the cover for it on your person at this very moment. That would be unreasonable. So, here you go – you have the standard 28 days to settle up. Think of it like our returns policy."

Janine gritted her teeth and took the invoice and folded it into her purse.

"Come on then, young man," he said, gesturing for Chris to leave the booth. He calmly got to his feet. She grabbed Chris by the arm and yanked him out of the booth. They marched back to the till to collect their bags.

"One thing you should know ma'am," called back the guard. She stopped and turned to him. "He weren't half going some!"

It did nothing to placate her, or to cancel the invoice already burning a hole right through her handbag and about to ignite their desk calculator and financial notebook. Chris smiled wryly. He knew.

And so, she sat on the bus and cycled through all the possible punishments she could dish out. Of course, Tel would have the lion's share of corrective administration but, by Jove, she wouldn't mind a crack at the whip. She gripped the metal rail on the seat ahead of her and gripped it tightly, until her knuckles turned white. She looked over to her young boy. He was sat with his eyes closed, his hands on an imaginary wheel and his feet on an imaginary accelerator and brake. His hands turned the wheel and hit the gear pedals behind, while he silently named every turn and every gear change in an automated fashion. She couldn't help it, there was nothing she could do. He was her son, he was Danny's brother and the boy clearly just wanted to race. Janine smiled and quietly changed seats to sit next to him and absently ran her hands through his hair as she read her detective novel.

Chapter 9
Top of the Hill

Chris knew that for some profound and unsaid reason, his mother had forgiven him. She moved her seat and started to rummage around in his hair while she read her book. It was her way, and he wasn't stupid enough to ask her what he had done to earn forgiveness and perhaps remind her of the "evil crime" for which he was punished. He thought it prudent to just sit there in silence. And, of course, if she had forgiven him for his rebellious act in the supermarket, perhaps her kindly mother's love had deemed him worthy enough to even go to the races. He would soon find out. If they stayed on the bus all the way to the bottom of Palmerston Road then he was sure to go to the races. If they were to stop at the parade of shops at the top of the steepest hill in the city and alight, then he was to be taken home. The bus rounded on to the approach to the parade. Two stops until the grand decision. They stopped at the penultimate stop, at the start of the sad parade of shops with the grotty looking flats above them. Chris looked out at the depressing sight – three betting shops in a row, a café, a grimy fish-and-chip shop laughingly advertised as an 'emporium', a newsagent with metal grates over the windows and an off-licence that was as secure as a vault. At the very end of the parade, and at the top of the hill stood The College Arms. Dark windows, a rickety bench outside, chalk menus nailed to the walls offering "good food, billiards and real ale". Chris was only thirteen and even he thought that they should get done by the board of trading standards. Chris briefly wondered what it would be like inside – what would it smell like, what was the etiquette when ordering a drink, what state were the toilets in?

The only pubs he had ever been in were in the leafy outskirts of the suburb. He was allowed in those nice pubs until 6pm and, on the rare occasions his dad felt flush and took the family out for a Sunday carvery, Chris had spent most of the time in the large garden, swinging around on the climbing frame. The Bell & Bottle, as the only pub he had been in was called, seemed like a nice enough place. But the College Arms was a different matter altogether, that much was clear. Chris even asked Uncle Tone about the pub on the top of Palmerston Road once. Uncle Tone, who was laughing at something else until he heard the name of the pub, suddenly fell stern and silent. He leaned down to Chris and rested his thin, delicate hand on his shoulder and looked deep into his eyes with an expression Chris had seen on soldiers in those war films that he had to endure watching with his father when there was nothing else on. A faraway look that seemed to say: "I've seen too much."

Uncle Tone fixed Chris with that same look and said, quietly and firmly: "Son, I have been around a little longer than you, seen things you wouldn't believe… and done things I hope you never do. Have I learned anything? Doubtful… but if I have learned one thing, one piece of wisdom to impart upon you before I shuffle off this mortal coil it is this: Son, never drink in a pub with a flat roof."

It was a cryptic message that Chris didn't fully understand, but the sincerity in Uncle Tone's voice and the look in his eyes told him that he was right. After all, Uncle Tone should know about these things as Uncle Tone drank in the College Arms – but then Uncle Tone drank everywhere.

The bus waited at the stop for what seemed like an age. A few people got off, a few got on and still they stayed there, engine humming, bus rattling to the resonance. Chris looked at the College Arms and smiled a little, thinking of his idiot uncle. He then looked across to the café and his smile changed, dropping slightly, his eyes narrowing as he tried to spy though the dusty bus window and through the windows of the café. Julie worked in there. Perhaps he could spot her, bussing tables in a tiny skirt that you couldn't even see behind her little apron. Finally, the bus lurched into life and pulled away towards the next stop – passed the Arms and on the very brow of Palmerston Road, the steepest road in the city.

The fact that taking this descent signified to Chris that he would be going to the races was not the only reason he loved that part of the bus journey above all others. The bus would seem to tilt on the edge of the precipice for a few seconds, like a weighing scale before finally tipping and driving down the impossible slope. It reminded Chris of the big dipper at the adventure park he went to a few years back. The agonising moments of ascent, the fear mixed with anticipation, the one last breath and then whoosh!

On some glorious days, Chris was allowed to sit on the top deck of the bus and at the very front seat. What a view. From up there, you could see to your left the flat roof of the College Arms below you and the mangy, angry Alsatian that belonged to the owner circling the roof, its rusty chain pulled tight and threatening to break at any second. But ahead – ahead of that point you could see the whole city laid out, and beyond. It seemed to Chris at that height he was even level with the red beacon atop the great TV Tower above the filled-in reservoir where the dangerous teenagers drank and fooled around. And then the bus would tip forward, the horizon would rush up and Chris would see nothing but the tarmac stretching out, down, down, down that long, straight road and to the heavy crossroads at the very bottom. Palmerston Road bisected an A-road that was said to run the width of the city. Four lanes of heavy traffic, two lanes in each direction rocketing past in a blur.

As the bus trundled down the hill to the crossroads, Chris would always imagine some great emergency, like in the action movies. Perhaps the brakes would fail, or maybe the driver would have a heart attack – "Can anyone drive a bus?" would come a frightened plea from a fellow passenger. Chris would leap at the chance and grab the wheel, steering the huge bus filled with screaming passengers through the crosstown traffic and to a halt at the other side. Or, if the driver was sick but the brakes were still fine, he would grab the wheel and swing it around, hitting the brakes hard and skidding the bus to a halt, side-on to the traffic and perhaps perilously up on two wheels for a few agonising seconds and then back down on to all four, just inches before being broadsided by the traffic. "You did it, you saved us!" they would shout. Chris would wipe the sweat from his brow and step out of the driver's cubicle and calm everyone down with a reassurance that they should still travel by bus as it's still the safest mode of transport in the city. Then they would applaud.

Unfortunately, on this occasion, Chris was not sitting on the front seat and on the top level, but a middling seat above the rear wheel arch and looking across at some pasty-faced old drinker slumped against the wall of the Arms, clamping his pint under his armpit as he swayed and tried to roll a smoke. Poor man. Chris waited patiently as the doors opened. He made no motion to up and leave, to anticipate his mother's exodus from the vehicle. He did not want to prompt her, remind her or even give her any ideas. He waited it out, motionless and staring at the swaying man. Counting in his mind, his heart beating faster and faster. Surely, if they hadn't made a move now, then they weren't getting off the bus…but then maybe his mother was toying with him? Maybe she just wanted to finish the end of the page? Out of the corner of his eye, he saw her index finger reach up to the bottom of the right-hand page and gently brush up the lines until it came to the top of the page and curled around it slightly. Chris gripped the metal rail of the seat in front. She was about to fold the top corner of the page to mark her progress and then close the book. This was it. Her finger paused for a few seconds. The ding from the driver's bell signified that the doors were closing. His mother turned the page and continued reading. The doors closed and the bus lurched forward, tipping down and descending Palmerston Road.

Chris didn't want to beam with happiness or even say anything to his mother. He gritted his teeth and clenched his jaw, like he did to stop himself crying during a sad film and incur his brother's mockery. But this time he was so elated to be going to the races. He was back in her good books and the sun was warmer than it had been all summer.

—·—

Chris carried more than he normally would and, indeed, perhaps more than he could actually handle for the period of time required. They had taken the bus all the way to the nearest stop to the circuit, which was still a good twenty-minute walk away, even when unburdened with cumbersome and unruly bags of shopping. When the bus came to a halt at their stop, Chris and his mother hauled all the bags from the large parcel shelf at the front of the bus. To get them off the bus quicker, Chris had taken seven of them. Janine had expected, as the bus pulled away, for

Chris to hand back two or three and redress the balance. He did not. The bus pulled off and as it did so, Janine noted a smiling old lady in the seat behind looking at the young boy with all the shopping backs, eager to help his beloved mother. "What a lovely, kind and helpful boy," she imagined the old woman thinking as she was driven away. Janine looked down at her son, who didn't look back up or hand her any bags, but instead began to march with purpose off towards the circuit. 'Yeah, he's alright,' she concluded in her mind, also deciding not to tell Terry of his stunt in the supermarket or, if she did, she would embellish it a little – perhaps fudge some of details and of course her level of anger and embarrassment. Perhaps she could paint the lad in a good light. She threaded a few of the bag handles up her wrists and picked everything up and began to follow her Sherpa son.

Sweat was pouring off Chris when he finally rounded the last corner on their journey. His arms ached and the plastic bags cut into his wrists and his fingers. But they had made it – from the tragedy of the morning when he had back-chatted his mum and been denied a race day, though the Battle of the Supermarket where he had assumed his alter ego after Stacy and Jenn had been mean to him, the epic bus journey and the silent prison his mother had thrown him into, and then the forced-march under a desert sun to his destiny. They had made it. He had made it. He put the bags down for a second and looked up. Though he had been here countless times before, the power of the place had never diminished. The racetrack was laid out before him – the grass car park to the left, the pavilion and grandstands to the right and the Drive Team entrance that led to the pit lanes. The looped tyre bridge that led into the centre paddock – the stalls and stands selling food, drink, clothes and model kits. Everything that was great about life and everything he loved was handily laid out for him. Motor racing: other than crime-fighting, is there anything as cool? Chris looked upon it all like a king over his kingdom. His mother trudged past him.

"Come on, piggy, we need to get the bags in the back of the van. Crickey, I'm glad we didn't get any frozen." She walked towards the Drive Team entrance. The grand illusion was broken slightly by the command of his mother. Chris sighed and bent down, setting the bags back into the grooves in his fingers and wrists, the burn returning instantly. He huffed and heaved the bags up and walked on after his mother. 'Just a few more minutes,' he thought. 'Get the bags in the back of the van. Get to the pit lane, see Danny, see Dad. Walk down past the other teams and smile with pity at them all. If they know that Danny is racing and they still want to race, then they are idiots. If they don't know he is there, then they are about to get a lesson in what true racing is. First things first: get to the van before the bags cut your hands off.'

CHAPTER 10
ALONG THE LINE

Chris had been waiting by the van for twenty minutes, resting against the back doors in a variety of poses. He considered each one and adopted them in a staggered fashion so that he appeared cool and casual and not to be fidgeting. He decided on his favourite pose and the one that struck the balance between casual and cool the best: resting his back against the door, head tilted back while resting against the panelling, one foot crocked up and resting on the bumper. He wished he had a cigarette hanging from his mouth and perhaps operating a yo-yo with consummate skill. He didn't smoke, of course, and he was rubbish with a yo-yo and so he stuffed his hands in his pockets and waited. Eyes closed, sun warming his face and hoping that his mother would return with the keys before he got restless in his current pose.

Mere moments before he changed position, Chris happened to open his eyes and see no girls looking over, but his mother approaching, swinging a set of keys around her fingers.

"Finally," he said as she arrived at the van. The first words he had spoken since the security guard's booth.

"Sorry, lovely," she replied, "I couldn't find your dad and when I did, he had his head stuck under the car. Anyway." She gestured to the door that Chris was resting on. He stepped aside to reveal the previously concealed lock. She opened the doors, creaking them aside. The van was on its last legs. Lord knows how they would fix it if it got sick, let alone buy a new one. Chris was only slightly embarrassed by the huge thing. Normally it didn't bother him, but every once in a while, someone from school caught a glimpse of it – even worse if he happened to be inside. Most of the people at his school had a couple of cars – a saloon and what they casually referred to as a 'little run-around'.

Chris bent down and heaved all the bags around his feet into the back of the van. A few of the carriers were splitting. They had only just made the journey. He put the last in and stepped back as his mother closed and locked the doors.

"Right then," she said turning and kneeling down to him – a gesture that only meant he was in for it. Or in for a 'grown-up chat' as she always sold it as. "In for it" is what she meant. This was confirmed by the way she clamped her hands around his shoulders – not on top of them, but at the side as she was about to lift him up and put him on a shelf.

"Listen. You were pretty bad earlier. Very much so and it's going to be very expensive to fix."

Chris looked down at the floor; he had totally forgotten about the green slip the guard had given her. He swallowed and turned his toe into the ground knowing what was coming next.

"Probably means we're going to have forgo a few birthday presents and your meal."

He nodded. He understood and although it was upsetting news, he deemed it to be fair.

"You can still have your party with your friends…but probably not at the Burger Barn. We can have it at home like we did for your seventh birthday, remember?"

Chris shrugged. "Sure, it's fair… fewer people will come because it's a lame idea for a party. It's what the divvy kids do… but I deserve that."

Janine smiled, she could see the crocodile tears in her son's eyes forming but she held true – she was determined not to be such a soft touch on this occasion.

"Do you a deal," she said, folding faster than Danny in the driving seat. Chris looked up and sniffed up a fake tear-induced running nose.

"You promise to never do something so stupid again, I won't tell your father what happened and we'll see about the Burger Barn. Maybe we can trim down the invites to your closest mates. How about that?"

Chris smiled. She was good to him.

"Thanks Mum, it was a stupid thing I did."

"Yes, it was," she confirmed, releasing his shoulders and standing up to signify that the 'grown-up chat' was over.

"Should have seen me though, I was so fast. Proper racer."

"Proper racers don't crash into milk aisles," she retorted as they walked off to the pit lane.

Chris couldn't help but smile to himself. She was correct, and unusually precise in her delivery. 'You'll see,' he thought. 'The Midnight Boy is gonna drive again.'

———•———

Janine and her son didn't need to show any credentials when they reached the entrance to the Drive Team section of the circuit. Danny Redding was somewhat of a legend in those parts – he had lap records in every division he had ever raced on that track and though he wasn't yet champion of the SuperKarts, it was a sure-fire bet. What made it more astounding was that Danny remained independent and unsponsored. The other teams and their directors couldn't understand how some poorish kid and his old man could build and race a car the way they did. In clubhouses around the city, to which Terry remained uninvited, people talked and rubbished the old man and his ways, but they idolised the kid. Danny was independent, and unsponsored – the unsponsored nature being the aspect that piqued their interest the most. It was an open secret among the wealthier teams that if Danny Redding won the SuperKart championship that year and was ready to graduate into the formula divisions then he was sure to be poached. There would be a bidding frenzy as everyone shouted and waved to get his attention. Until that championship was secured, however, they were happy to let his old man get the boy across the line. Let him front the extortionate price it cost to race in the city. He would be broke at the end of the season and grateful for any scraps new sponsors would throw at him. Nobody in the racing world could wait for the season to end and to see what would happen next. Three races to go. Just six weeks.

A few suited men smiled and waved at Janine as she walked along the paddock line beside the huge row of open garages divided into bays. A couple even saluted and smiled at Chris, noting his wide eyes and excitement at seeing all the cars in their bays and the pit crews bussing about. A few thought: 'I wonder if the kid has it,' or 'Get the kid to lose a few pounds and put him in a boxkart… see how he goes.' A possible racing dynasty was potentially going for a song right in front of their eyes, so you can bet your bottom dollar that Janine got the smiles and waves as she walked along.

Chris passed Team Enzo, McTalbot, Rolfe Racing, Team Caligari… all the teams there for this critical race of the season. He hadn't paid much attention to the lower kart divisions as they walked along – they were small fry, too amateur, too goddamned slow to really be worth his time. SuperKarts were where the action was. The karts gleamed, each one brand new for every race, each team with stacks of tyres. Chris could not believe the money involved. His family had one car, two sets of tyres and some customised tools that his old man had knocked up and yet they blasted the competition. He saw the drivers, each one different in their behaviour. They looked like robots in their suits emblazoned with logos. Each of them with their helmets on. Some lounged at the side of the garage bay, keeping their gloves clean of grease and grime and letting the mechanics get on with it; others were right in the thick of it, meddling around with wheels, engines and small, portable computers connected to the karts.

Chris saw the driver of Rolfe Racing, his second favourite if he dared to consider any after his brother. Chris liked Rolfe Racing's driver because he too was called Christopher. This guy was Danny's main rival, which Chris thought was somewhat fitting. Christopher Rolfe's car was dark green, bisected by a stylish yellow stripe. But what Chris loved about this guy was the way he was in the pit. He didn't lounge around, and he didn't get stuck in. He just sat in the car, always. They could jack the thing up, pull it apart, turn it upside down even and he would still be sitting in there as if he were part of it. The guy probably even slept in the car.

"Look, Mum, Rolfe Racing. That guy is so cool."

"Cooler than your brother?" she asked as they left the bay, Chris craning his neck to look back at the team.

"No way, stupid question," said Chris as they came to the last bay in the row.

He let go of his mother's hand as soon as he saw their kart, his father and Danny. The kart was up on its stanchions, tilted forward slightly and looking mean.

"Hi, love," said Janine jovially, as she stepped over the low chain-link partition.

Terry and his son stood, arms folded and looking down at the car, the same stern expression on their faces, their heads rocking back and forth in near-metronomic synchronisation as they regarded individual aspects of the vehicle. The regulated, slow movements of their heads reminded Chris of a pair of desk toys or a dashboard companion. He stepped over the rail as his mother walked over to her husband and kissed him on the cheek, snapping him out of his contemplation.

"Oh, hi love," he said.

Danny too snapped back to reality and looked over at his brother.

"Bro!" he beamed rushing over and grabbing Chris around the waist, tipping him on to his side and heaving him up into the air under one arm with surprising strength. Truly, he seemed to get stronger by the day. Chris began to giggle and thrash around as his brother ruffled his hair.

"You okay, Bro? You got any pocket money for me?"

Chris's laughter attracted the attention of a passing team pushing their car along. They looked into the pit bay and sneered at the strange scene. Some uncouth poor family seemingly having playtime in the lane. The watching driver, who didn't recognise the Reddings tutted and called them bloody poor amateurs as he pushed his car towards the grid to begin his qualifying.

"Alright, alright, put him down," said Terry, the noise of the laughter causing him to wince a little. "Less of the racket."

"Sorry, Dad" said Chris as he was put on to his feet. He gave his big brother a little shove. His father looked over at him, fixing the young boy with a severe look.

"Want to help?" he asked.

Chris sighed and nodded, thinking that he was about to be consigned to 'screw and nail sorting' again. His old man smiled.

"Make your dad a cup of tea. There's a good boy," he said.

Chris fake sighed and walked over to the workbench where his dad's trusty teasmaid had been set up for him.

"So, how we looking?" asked Janine as Danny walked over and gave her a kiss on the cheek.

"No sweat," replied Terry.

"Well, it's really dry out there and Rolfe has posted a hell of a time," said Danny.

"Balls to that joker," scoffed Terry. "You'll smoke 'em."

"Yeah," added Chris, appearing by his dad's side and holding up a cup of tea. Terry took the cup and held his empty hand out to his wife, wiggling his fingers in expectancy. Janine fished in her pocket and pulled out a chocolate bar, placing it in Terry's greasy hand. He thanked neither, as he bit the top of the wrapper off like a lion biting a chunk out of a gazelle's neck. He dunked the bar directly into the mug and stirred the tea.

Janine looked around the pit bay.

"Where's Uncle Tone? No empty cans about."

Danny smirked and picked up a pair of binoculars from the bench and handed them to his mother.

"In the paddock," he said.

His mother took the binoculars and walked to the opening of the bay, looking through them and out past the track and to the central reservations.

"There's the idiot," she said.

"Can I see?" asked Chris.

Janine handed the binoculars to Chris who looked through and saw his uncle immediately. Chris started laughing again.

In the centre of the paddock he saw Uncle Tone: a shade under forty, thin, with a week of stubble, jeans that were more hole than material, an obscure band T-shirt in a similar state to his jeans. Stupidly huge and out of fashion cardigan, unruly explosion of unkempt hair that fell to his shoulders and a pair of ridiculous sunglasses that Chris had once seen on a female Italian movie star from the Sixties. Uncle Tone was sitting on the grass, drinking from a can of lager, a few empties by his side and a blue plastic bag that clearly held more between his legs. Chris knew the type of bag – a heavy-duty plastic bag that could carry twelve cans of beer from the off-licence, no danger. Uncle Tone was yapping away, as usual, sitting in the paddock, drinking his beers and with his arm around a very sober and very bored looking Julie.

Chapter 11
Uncle Tone

Chris and his mother left the pit lane as soon as they spotted Uncle Tone in the paddock, havering to Julie. His mum shook her head and tutted, Chris laughed to himself. To the adults around, Tone was a fool, a nuisance and utterly tiresome but to Chris he was simply a guy who liked his good times.

Being part of the race team meant that they did not have to pay the £10 fee to cross over the tyre bridge and enter the 'exclusive' realm of the inner paddock. From the verdant, slightly undulating field one could have a near 360° view of the track and of the great grandstands by the start line. 'Proper racing,' thought Chris every time they reached the apex of the bridge and he could see the track beneath him. The dark asphalt and the perfect white lines, repainted freshly before each race weekend. Of course, they had missed some of the earlier races that day and even some of the qualifiers for the more important classes – he could already see the racing line burnt into the track, little bits of rubber singed and melted from tyres, the tiny imperfections and skids left by careless and amateur drivers. He loved that texture of the road below: somewhere in that black streak lay the perfect racing line, that direct route around the track to the chequered flag, to lap records, to championships and to glory. Somewhere in the middle of that black texture lay perfection.

Chris smiled to himself as he acknowledged what he thought to be a mature and poetic view of the simple tarmac below as he stepped across the bridge and on to the paddock. He knew that even if his father and brother could understand what he meant, they would never be able to express the idea quite as elegantly. His English teacher, Miss Gardner, would probably swoon. Maybe when term started in a few weeks and he would be told to write a story about his holidays, he would do something a little left-field, a little romantic, a little 'out there' and write about that perfect line within the black streak. He would be a man when term started and Miss Gardner would definitely fall for him, but he would brush her aside coolly and gracefully in favour of a sixth-former.

"You alright?" asked his mother, pulling Chris out of his train of thought.

"Yeah, why?"

"Deep in thought, penny for them?"

Chris tapped his temple. "You ain't got the bus fare, mate," he said cockily, parroting a phrase he had heard from a late-night television programme he had stayed up to watch illicitly on Danny's old TV.

"Cheek," smiled his mother, marvelling at the myriad personalities her young son seemed to display in recent months as he hurtled towards adolescence. 'Just come out the other side as a good one, my boy, just be a good one,' she thought.

"Oi, oi!" came a loud, happy boom from across the way. Janine shut her eyes as soon as she heard it, Chris smiled. They both craned their necks around to see, on top of a small hill, Uncle Tone standing tall and performing a strange little jig, two cans of beer above his head and spilling some wantonly as he danced. Julie cringed and brushed the spillage from her shoulder.

"You lucky people!" he shouted again, jigging around in a circle.

Janine didn't call over but nodded and smiled. Chris waved and together they weaved through the annoyed looking picnicking spectators. Chris noted their looks as he and his mother passed them. He saw their wicker baskets and bottles of sparkling wine, their strange food that came in small portions – raw pink fish on little squares of bread, tubs of rice. All the things he hated, all the things that his family never ate. He took on board their scorn and, for right and wrong, labelled it 'us and them' and threw back his own look of disdain. 'Eff 'em,' he thought as he looked towards Uncle Tone and his beaming smile, his little blue plastic bag of beer cans. The only one smiling among all the other poshos. Uncle Tone and his good times.

Chris let go of his mother's hand and ran the last few steps over to Uncle Tone who knelt down and extended his arms, nearly punching Chris in the face with both beer cans. Chris, who usually leapt into Tone's arms stopped short and held out his hand to shake. Uncle Tone furrowed his brow and looked up at Janine who smiled and shrugged. Tone broke out into another loud laugh and took Chris's hand, shaking it firmly.

"Good afternoon, Kit," he said, formally.

"Alright Uncle Tone, how are you?"

"Me, I am happy as a pig in the proverbial. Got me family, got this frolicking filly next to me, got me beers in a summer pasture and it's cracking the flags. You?"

"I'm alright," said Chris, releasing his grip and sitting down next to Julie, looking out at the racetrack.

"Man of few words. God knows the world needs more of them," said Uncle Tone standing up and holding out his hand for Janine to shake. She looked sternly at him before relenting and breaking into a smile.

"Hi, Tone," she said.

"How's my favourite sister-in-law?"

"Only sister-in-law," she added.

Uncle Tone threw his arms around her and squeezed her tightly. Janine couldn't help it, she laughed.

"Put me down, you idiot."

Uncle Tone gave her another squeeze and plonked her down on her feet.

"So, what have we missed?" she said, flattening her jeans as if it were a summer dress and sitting down on the grass. Uncle Tone turned to address his seated audience.

"Woke up with a bastard behind the peepers, got trounced by the Star in the pool league last night. Got unlucky with a barmaid, got really lucky with a juke box…. some mug had left a few creds in it, and I got me what I liked. Last orders, got a carry-out, which was brilliant as the offie had shut, walked past some old dear trying to get into her house. Offered to help and broke into her house for her. Had to stack two wheelie bins on top of each other and squeeze in the first-floor bog window which was, on reflection, well dodge because it was raining last night. Let her in, she gave me some rum which sent me bandy after the lager. Got home about three. Woke up on the kitchen table. All my breakfast ingredients already staged and awaiting cooking in the morning. Bacon in the pan, saussies on the grill, tomato kinda cut, beans in the can. How good is that? Drunk me looks after hungover me. So cooked that up, yum-yum in my tum and then came down here for about eleven just as the offie was opening and got some cans. Met Tel and Danny Boy… and, of course, the lovely Julie here, and escorted said fine filly over into the pasture where we have since enjoyed the qualifiers, the sun and some racy banter that never once drifted from the racing line. Ain't we darling?"

"Something like that," said Julie half-heartedly, looking off to the starting line and watching a team push their kart out for a time trial.

"See," said Tone, smiling broadly as he plonked himself down and dug around in the bag for a can of beer.

"And the qualifiers?" asked Chris.

"Wouldn't worry about it, mate," replied Tone, "these bunch of cunts couldn't drive rain if they were a rain cloud," he cracked a can and sat up from the bag, turning to the three sitting in a line beside him. He expected laughter and happy faces. Julie looked disgusted, Chris shocked and Janine furious.

"Mrs Redding, I'm really sorry for the language. That's not… that's really not cool," said Tone, immediately understanding that what polite people called 'dropping the C-bomb' was a step too far.

"Julie, it's a disgusting word, I apologise. Honestly."

"It's alright, I've heard it before," she said with a half-smile.

"Still, doesn't mean you should hear it again and we've had a lovely morning and for me to ruin it all by being me – Christ, I can say some awful things when I have had a few and I'm excited. Will you forgive me?"

Julie furrowed her brow and looked at Tone, not knowing if his profuse apology was meant sarcastically or just a product of the embarrassed drunk. She was a graceful woman and gave the idiot the benefit of the doubt.

"It's fine, honest," she said.

"And Kit," said Uncle Tone, darting his attention from Julie to Chris who was hugging his knees, aware and mature enough to know when a real adult faux pas had been committed and what that could mean. It wasn't what would happen to him if he swore – nobody was going to send Uncle Tone to his room without dinner or ground him. Worse, they would just simply not like him and then gradually push him aside.

"Kit, mate," said Uncle Tone, "it's adult language and you are an adult... but only idiot adults use words like that. Real smart adults are knights. Understand?"

Uncle Tone extended his hand across Janine to Chris. Chris smiled and shook his uncle's hand once more.

Uncle Tone then offered it to Janine.

"Friends?"

Janine sighed and shook it, this time the smile on her lips only vaguely appearing.

"Friends," she said.

Uncle Tone turned from the line and looked out with them towards the grandstand and the starting line. He sipped his beer quietly and discreetly as he hugged his knees like Chris, the happy atmosphere having been flicked away like the crumbs on a picnic rug.

———

Danny cricked his neck and interwove his fingers, turning his palms outwards and cracking his knuckles as his dad jacked the car down on to the ground. Danny was dressed in his racing suit, save for helmet and gloves. He watched as his father ran a chamois leather rag over the car, furiously buffing the wings once more. Appearance meant a lot to them both – it wasn't vanity, it wasn't a plea for the audience in the stands to gasp in wonder at the beauty of the car. It was out of respect for the situation, for the work they had put into their car, their team and for the sport itself. Danny, at school, read once of a captain in the Second World War who was dubbed 'Mad Jack' as he was known for going into battle armed with a bow and arrow and a sword. According to lore, he believed that a soldier was not dressed for war unless he had a sword at his side. When he heard that little fact, Danny felt a warm kinship with Mad Jack. His father too. The car had to be perfect, clean and bright, else it was not fit for driving and not ready for the track. Funnily enough, that ethos was not extended to Terry's van.

Terry wheeled the car around so that it was facing the pit lane and slip-road that led on to the starting grid. Danny's qualifying session was about to start. They stood in the alcove of the pit garage and Terry turned to his son, making sure that his fire suit was correctly tied and that his overalls were zipped up. Danny put on his gloves and flexed his fingers. Terry reached to the counter and took the helmet from the side, placing it over his son's head. They stood face to face, inches from each other. Terry looked into his son's eyes as the helmet fell into place, the visor still up.

"Alright?"

Danny nodded, his hair tucked out of his eyes.

"Ready?"

Danny nodded. As soon as the helmet was on, the son wasn't there, and the driver had arrived.

Terry gently held his sons' shoulders.

"I don't care if you win or lose," he said with a kind word but stern eyes.

Danny nodded.

"I just care that you're my son and I'm your old man."

Danny nodded again; the ritual words spoken by his dad before any race.

"But if it's not too much trouble," said Terry with a smile, "can you please just put this Goddamned bucket over the line before anyone else."

"Yes sir," said Danny and they rested their foreheads against each other's and silently counted to three.

———·———

The atmosphere in their little camp lifted itself out of the doldrums when they knew for certain that their car was on the track. They had sat in silence for ten minutes, which under normal circumstances was plenty of time for Uncle Tone to finish his can; in this instance he had not even drunk a third. They sat in cold silence and watched and waited. Then it started, as it always did – a murmur from the grandstands that filtered across the front of the paddock, gently wafting over everyone and to the little hill that they ritually occupied. The murmur became chatter, excited and dripping with apprehension. The family sat in their line and their hearts sped up, the breath caught in their mouths. Then they would see a few people in the grandstand begin to stand up, a few more in the smaller stands, and a few more, until a roar erupted and a wave of people leaving their seats swept the circuit; the roar and the applause a tsunami over the paddock.

For a few seconds the family didn't stand. Chris was the first to relent, he got to his feet, then everyone followed. They did not clap or cheer for their boy because they knew him, and they knew what was at stake. They knew the seriousness of it all and the focus required. They also could not but bask in the mania and adulation that engulfed the whole circuit. The boy-wonder, the unsigned, unsponsored lad from a one-car team was on the track. The car came first, pushed out on to the grid by the lad's old man. And then, after some agonising moments, he appeared like a rockstar, walking out on his own and down the centre of the empty starting grid towards his ride. The audience lapped it up. What a star, milking every ounce of drama. The potential team directors and sponsors felt their bank balances skyrocket with every step the unsigned lad took. Chris and his family knew the truth: Danny was not milking anything. He did what he always did, always had done. He waited and just took a few moments on his own to calm himself down. Perhaps he was confident, perhaps he was terrified, perhaps he was praying – the visor was down, so who knew? But they knew him, and they knew that whatever it was that made Danny delay his entrance was for his own personal reasons. The crowd's delight at his perceived showmanship was just a wonderful by-product. There he was.

Danny Redding walked the empty grid. His father had parked the car and already stepped out of the way – nothing more to say or do for his son. Danny felt each step to be like concrete. He wanted to get in the car, he wanted the open track. As was his way, he walked around the car before finally stepping into it. The crowd loved it, but he did not hear anything. He strapped himself in and took a few seconds to close his eyes and flex his hands on the wheel. Nobody knew it, but in those few seconds on the grid, he did not revise his strategy, he did not recall his meditations on the carpet in his bedroom, his feet miming the pedal actions like James Hunt. He discarded all that and concentrated on the feeling of Julie's fingers running through his hair. He smiled wryly and snapped his eyes open just as the lights changed.

Contact.

Pedal down.

Engine roar.

Away.

Chapter 12
A Friendly Interrogation

anny stepped on to the winner's podium to rapturous applause from the crowd and respectful claps from the rest of the drivers. The wreaths were placed around each driver's neck and a bottle of sparkling wine handed to the winner. Though he dreamed of spraying it liberally over everyone like real Formula One drivers did, he knew better of it and kept hold of the bottle until the ceremony was over, whereupon he handed it over to Uncle Tone who grabbed it from him and clutched it to his chest. Danny shook hands with his father, hugged his mother, kissed Julie and gave Chris a dead arm. The rest of the teams continued to celebrate, some having come from all over the city, delaying their long journey home as much as possible in order to enjoy the atmosphere for as long as possible. The Redding family were together and so they left the reverie and headed to the pit garage where the stewards had wheeled their car back.

They walked along the pit lane in quiet contemplation. Danny mulled over the race, knowing that he had missed out on the lap record by a few tenths of a second because he took the Benz chicane imperfectly. He knew it the moment he had done it, but fought hard to regain the time. He had not and that mistake scratched at the roof of his mouth. Next to Danny, Julie walked quietly thinking of bands and gangs – the other girls in school who were getting ready for their nights out, drinking and fooling at the reservoir underneath the Stivyakino TV tower. She could not deny that a part of her wanted to be there, with her friends but the thought of the drink and the requisite headaches, let alone the ugly, lecherous boys that would try their luck, it was more than enough to make her feel happy where she was. Julie hoped her love for Danny in some ways helped him or, at the very least, was no hindrance in his preparation and his racing – most of all, she hoped that she wasn't some sort of passive accessory or vague character in his story. She hoped he saw her as she saw herself and what she did for him. Danny never told her the last thing that went through his mind before every race. He never thought to. It just never crossed his mind.

Terry and Janine walked hand in hand, both thinking the same thing – 'I love my boy, but we can't afford this forever. What happens when the money runs out, or the car breaks? What then? What then?'

Behind them, Uncle Tone held his bottle of sparkling wine and focused his gaze on the back of Julie. She reminded him of a girl once, years ago. Mary something. Man, he loved her, and then she was gone. Couldn't stand his ways, couldn't stand the state he got into after every rejection letter from publishers and literary agents fell through the letterbox. She loved him; he kind of remembered that, but everyone has to say "enough is enough" at some point, even he knew that. They were both young then… perhaps too young and too clever to make it. Who knew? That was years ago and he had blotted her out well enough, almost completely but some things of hers remained and some things were put in front of him to remind Tone of what he had done and what he should be doing. He looked at the back of Julie and thought: 'I need to do some writing soon or I am going to end up dead in a pub toilet and good riddance'.

Chris noticed the glazed look in his uncle's eyes and the direction they were pointing. A chance glance up from Julie's back had revealed to Chris that his uncle was sharing the view. Chris gave his uncle a shove.

"Perv," he said quietly.

"What's that, Kit?" said Uncle Tone, falling back to the world. Chris nodded to the back of Julie.

"Perv," he repeated.

"And what would you know of it?" said Uncle Tone wryly. Chris went red in an instant.

"Ah, so you fancy the old boiler, do you?" chided his uncle, shoving Chris a little too hard; his half-drunk senses forgetting their true strength. Chris was forced to recalibrate by taking a side-step.

"Shut up, idiot," he said.

Uncle Tone broke into a wide smile, and bent down a little but kept on walking. He looked like one of those vultures from The Jungle Book that Chris used to love nearly as much as his mother did.

"Go on," he whispered, "what do you know about it, have you got a woman? Have you kissed anyone?"

Chris scowled and looked down at the asphalt and tried to train his thoughts back to those he had conjured on the tyre bridge to the paddock.

"You have, I bet you have," continued Uncle Tone, "I bet you used tongues." And at that he stuck his tongue out and started sloshing it around.

"Shut up!" snapped Chris, a little too loudly, causing his mother to look around and survey the scene. Uncle Tone righted himself and gave her a reassuring look that said: 'It's fine, I'll handle this.'

Janine tutted and turned away from them.

"Almost got me done in there, Kit" whispered Uncle Tone.

"My name's Christopher," he whispered back, glowering at the floor ahead.

"It's Christopher when you're in the doghouse, Chris normally," replied Uncle Tone.

"Eh?"

"It's why you have a name that can be shortened. So you know when you are in the shit. Same with your brother. When he's got the cheek on, five gets you ten that your mum bellows up the stairs 'Daniel'!"

"I hadn't thought of it like that," replied Chris.

"Not so bright are you, Kit?"

"Chris."

"I said 'kid'."

"What?"

"I'm just teasing you. Christ you can be touchy."

"Only with timewasting idiots. And you said 'Kit', I bet my MegaSystem on it."

"You haven't got a MegaSystem, boy – don't be making bets you can't cash. And what's wrong with Kit?"

"It's gimp. If I called myself 'Kit' at school, I'd get a shooing. Rightly so."

"Really? Jesus, your school is full of idiots. If I was called 'Christopher'."

"Chris."

"Or Chris, you can bet your bum I would be referred to as 'Kit'. It's way cooler."

"It's gimp."

"You're just saying that because you fancy Julie."

"So annoying. I do not, for the last time, fancy J-u-l-i-e," whispered Chris angrily, and having the prescience to spell out her name silently.

"I would, if I were you," smiled Uncle Tone, smiling.

Chris couldn't go on. His uncle was infuriating, but he loved him. Chris spurted out a laugh and Uncle Tone put his arm around him, pulling him into his side. Janine turned around to make sure everything was alright. She smiled, genuinely, at her brother-in-law. An idiot, yes, but their idiot.

———•———

Uncle Tone poured out the sparkling wine into mugs on the counter in the pit garage. Everyone took one and, after an approving nod from Terry, Uncle Tone was allowed to hand one to Chris, but not before he had topped it up significantly with lemonade. They all toasted Danny and with three cheers, took a big sip. Chris could not understand it, they all seemed so happy with their drinks. To him it tasted utterly vile. They finished their sips with overtly satisfied gasps, while he finished his with a gag. 'They're crazy,' he thought as he placed his mug on the side. 'The Midnight Boy won't ever drink. It makes women cackle like witches and men act like idiots and neither drive well. The Midnight Boy will be pure and for the road and for justice.'

Though the only drunken adults he had every really had any close contact with were his mum, dad and uncle, Chris was certain that his observation was a hard and fast rule. Indeed, of late he had noticed a particular influx of adverts on the TV advocating the dangers of combining drinking and driving. He had never noticed them before and wasn't sure if they were a new thing, or perhaps another sign of his burgeoning maturity. Adult signs, messages and ways of doing and seeing things were creeping into his life and displacing some of his older and more favourite things. Some of his toys that were his best two years ago were happily taken to charity shops – replaced by newer, more grown-up looking toys. Was he now starting on a journey that would displace even these? Indeed, a few times in the last few weeks, Uncle Tone had asked on numerous occasions when Chris would be fourteen. Whenever Chris answered, Uncle Tone would ask a follow-up question about whether he still played with toys. Chris answered in the affirmative. Then, Uncle Tone would state that "it won't be long before your toy soldiers aren't your favourite toy any more" with a big, mysterious grin. Then, even more cryptically, he would turn to his mother and warn her to install a lock on the bathroom and to not disturb if Chris was inside "with both taps on".

Chris had no idea what he was referring to – why would he want to play in the bathroom with the taps on? Was it some strange initiation into adulthood that a child could never know, nor ever ask? Whatever the reason, when Uncle Tone had gone down this little line of questioning, his statement had always been the same and it had always received a slap on the arm from his mum and a flustered, almost disgusted expression on her face that Chris hadn't seen before. During all this, his brother remained strangely silent, looking at the floor and almost blushing. It was a mystery, but maybe the awareness of the drink and drug adverts that had cropped up and his approaching birthday might all be tied together. Maybe the revolting taste of the sparkling wine would be replaced with the gasps of joy. Maybe the mystery of the bathroom taps would be explained. 'Whatever it all means,' he thought, 'the Midnight Boy won't ever drink.'

They all sat in the van. Chris was in the front passenger seat waiting. He knew it wasn't his proper place; his proper place was in the back of the van, sat on the MDF benches with his uncle and Julie. But they weren't going anywhere just yet. The SuperKart was on the trailer attached to the back of the van, Uncle Tone and Julie were in the back. Uncle Tone was 'somewhere else' in one of his strange faraway moods that seemed to come and go with no warning, head tilted back against the panelling and leaned to the side, eyes glazed over. There, but somewhere else. In the rear mirror, Chris could see that look and recognised it as what he must look like when he was The Midnight Boy, sitting on his carpet in his little bedroom staring blankly at the TV because, really, he was burning through the city in the Midnight Special. Chris hoped that it was so, but couldn't be sure – Uncle Tone was a strange one, but Chris hoped it was so.

Julie, on the bench opposite, looked at the space between herself and her boyfriend's drunk uncle wondering if the endless drinking was hereditary. Chris noted her awkward position and smiled to himself, deciphering her look and language in an instant. He was sitting on the front bench next to his mother who was reading her Detective Giallo novel. Chris knew which one it was as she had read the ten-book series over and over again – in fact he could barely remember seeing her holding a different book in her hand. He shook his head maturely, he felt, and cast his eyes out of the passenger window. Ahead he saw his father and brother standing outside the Drive Team's entrance. They were in deep conversation with two men in posh suits. They all looked serious. His father and his brother had their arms folded in what, to Chris, seemed quite defensive and impolite. There was some nodding and shaking of heads. His father rubbed his chin like he did when considering something, like when Chris asked for a new bike out of the blue, but instead of the chin stroke and thoughtful nod which always led to a roar of laughter, this chin stroke and head nod ended with a furrowed brow and a look to Danny who shrugged, which in turn caused the two men to break out into smiles. The whole gesture from his father seemed to say to Chris 'sounds reasonable enough' which was something he never said, which meant that Chris had no doubt grossly misunderstood the situation.

He squinted at the four men and concentrated, knowing that the Midnight Boy needed to be skilled in situational awareness and also fluent in lip-reading in all languages. How else to fight crime, and prevent crime all over the city? How else to anticipate traffic and pedestrians around a blind corner when approaching at 275mph in the Special? This was a test, and so he leaned forward a little as if the extra few inches closer to his targets somehow granted extra powers. He clenched his jaw and squinted even more.

His father was making a point, counting on his fingers, his brother was nodding in compliance, the two men were staring at the finger counting, a look of slight fear increasing across their faces with each new finger counted. Finally, Chris's dad stopped counting and folded his arms. Danny copied. The two men in the suits conversed with each other, annoyingly shielding their mouths so that Chris could not see, nor practise lip-reading. Finally they stopped their confab and smiled at Danny and Terry. The two men held out their hands to shake. Chris crinkled his lip in disbelief as Danny and his father nodded to each other and shook the two suited men's hands. Nobody said goodbye. Danny and his father peeled away and started to walk towards the van, calm faces, matching strides. Chris knew that they were about to leave and so had to climb into the back to sit on the bench. He was about to do so when he noticed the two men in the posh suits were watching Danny and his dad walk to the van. Why hadn't they turned around? Then, they both reached into their breast pockets. The Midnight Boy thought 'gun!' but the two men drew out long cigars and lit them in unison. Chris snarled at them and their evil cigar-smoking ways, in those posh suits. 'Villains,' the Midnight Boy said to himself.

Chris heaved himself over the front seat and clambered down next to Julie. It was a split-second decision. Sit across and look at her, or sit next to her and be closer. He sat next to her. The driver and passenger doors opened, and Danny and his dad climbed into the cabin, Janine shuffling into the middle of the front bench to accommodate them. Chris saw his dad put the keys in the ignition and hold them there. His brother did not turn to look ast the passengers in the back. Then Chris's dad leaned over and gave his mum a huge, loud kiss on her cheek. He then turned to address the passengers.

"How about a curry, on me?!" he said with a broad smile.

"Yes please," said Julie.

"He ain't heavy," said Uncle Tone, which confused Chris somewhat.

Terry hit the front bench to signify that the discussion was happily over and the decision made. He turned the ignition and began to back the car up. Chris mimicked his gag reflex when drinking the sparkling wine and made a mental note to strike curry from the Midnight Boy's future diet. That stuff was awful.

Chapter 13
'We Race as a Family'

hris could not deny that he was hungry. He tried to resist as best he could – the silver dishes of gloopy food slathered in strange gravy and garnished in bits of green really did not seem appealing. The bread didn't look like bread and the giant crisps that everyone took great pleasure in breaking and devouring looked plain and uninviting. Everyone wolfed down their curries and took great pleasure in sweating and proclaiming how hot everything was. Chris sat for a bit, pushing some light brown mush around his plate.

"Hey bro," said Danny who was sitting next to him, "try this," dumping a wing of what, possibly, could be chicken on to Chris' plate. It had the shape of a chicken leg, but it was a lurid red. Chris peered over his plate and looked at the radioactive food staring back at him. "Have a bit," said his brother, dumping a bone on his own plate and licking his bright red fingertips. "It's not spicy, I promise."

Chris looked up at the rest of the diners. Everyone at the table was staring at him, half smiling. Uncle Tone had his glass of beer resting against his lips, just waiting to be poured down his gullet. Chris wasn't stupid, he knew it was a trap. It was as plain as those strange twins in his class – as soon as he took a bite, his mouth would erupt as the red lava hit his tongue. Everyone would laugh and point, and he would never be able to taste anything for days. But he was super hungry. Chris looked up at his mum, sitting opposite. She gave him a reassuring nod. Surely his own mother wouldn't betray him, surely not even she would be evil enough to be in on the joke?

Chris took a resigned breath and picked up the chicken leg daintily in his fingers. He sniffed it. Nobody ate, they all waited. Finally, Chris sunk his teeth into the red chicken leg and tore off a chunk. He held it in his mouth and didn't chew – he knew he couldn't spit it out in a restaurant, he had to swallow, therefore he had to chew…thus he had to taste. He began.

It was merely three seconds after chewing that Chris Redding's gastronomical universe changed. His eyes lit up a bit, his shoulders raised and he looked across at his family, smiling through red, greasy lips. Tandoori chicken was utterly divine.

Chris nodded to all and took another, huge bite. The table cheered and toasted, before tucking into their own delicacies. Chris could barely believe it. What the hell had he been so afraid of? It was the best thing he had ever tasted. He sucked the bone clean and looked around at the other plates. His mother knew what he wanted; he used to do the same with cabbage on people's plates when he was a little boy. Never the roast beef or potatoes – always the cabbage. Janine surreptitiously forked one of her tandoori legs on to his plate. Like a hungry stray, Chris grabbed it and sank his teeth in.

"See," said his mother, "what was all the fuss about?"

Chris shrugged and nodded in agreement.

"Good man," said Uncle Tone, butting in. He was on to his third pint of the meal and his plate was pretty empty. He barely ate. He leaned over the table a little and went "psst" at Chris, who looked up, bone clamped in his jaws. "Remember, Kit: you only have one life and you will never know what you like and what you don't until you try it."

Chris nodded.

"Gentlemen!" announced Uncle Tone to the table, thrusting his glass down on the table and sending a splosh of beer on to his plate. "…and ladies."

Everybody was too happy to tut or ignore the impromptu toast and instead picked up their glasses and awaited the speech.

"Remember this day, young Kit my lad, today you learned to try anything once. So please, try everything once so that come the end when you're facing Old Tick Tock, you can travel light across the Styx because you're left it all behind!" He thrust his glass into the middle of the table, and everyone acquiesced, a little cheer went up as the glasses chinked. Uncle Tone then blurted out happily, "except folk dancing!" He broke into a broad, satisfied smile. Terry laughed; Janine rolled her eyes. Julie stifled a laugh and Danny nodded in agreement. Sound advice indeed.

"Aaaanyway," said Janine, butting in and diverting the conversation, "how about after this we go back to ours for a drink and a dance?"

The cheer at the table was a little louder than before. Terry ordered another round.

"Danny," said Terry in his unmistakable tipsy drawl, always adding a 'DZ' to the start of Danny's name. "You've had your one, son," and he tossed the van keys over to him. "You be Des."

Danny gratefully grabbed the keys and pocketed them, understanding 'Des' to mean 'designated driver'.

The yawns had become more frequent and the music a little quieter. Chris was wide awake though, of course having not taken anything more than half a glass of shandy. Danny and Julie sat slumped arm in arm in the sofa, Terry on his special armchair with Janine sat on his lap, her legs draped over the arm. The TV was on, but the sound off. Uncle Tone was at the record player, flicking through his brother's rubbish collection of bland vinyl.

"This is the worst collection I have ever seen," he said. "Kit, pour a final round, would you?"

Chris got up from his beanbag (previously fetched from his bedroom and dumped down beside Uncle Tone's chair).

"What does everyone want?" said Chris. "Cup of tea, Dad?"

"I will have a beer, my boy. Get your old man a beer."

"Uncle Tone?"

"Beer," he replied into the box of records as his fingers flicked through them.

Chris's mum yawned and shook her head. Danny and Julie shook their heads too.

"Two beers," said Chris, leaving the sitting room and walking into the kitchen. As soon as he had left the room, Terry clicked his fingers at Danny and nodded to the ceiling. Danny smiled and quietly left the room. Julie got up too, and went to the kitchen.

Chris stood by the kitchen sink and looked out at the black garden, the cloudy night shielding the stars. The two cans of beer were by the counter, both opened and awaiting to be poured. He could see, in the murk, the red blinking light from the top of the TV tower. Chris nodded at it and turned from the window, leaning against the counter and looking down at the floor, arms folded, eyes glazed over.

Julie walked into the kitchen and stopped when she saw Chris in a serene pensive state. She leaned against the wall, careful that her head didn't knock the cork pinboard riddled with takeaway menus. She crocked a leg against the wall and looked at Chris for a few moments. He was totally unaware of his surroundings, he was someplace else. She recognised the look about him, same as his brother…but somehow different. He was at no racetrack, monotonously rehearsing every bend and every swerve in some circuit or other. The little flutters on his eyelids and the slight side smiles and smirks told Julie that the boy was somewhere of his own creation. Some place nobody knew about. Julie looked at him, framed by the dark window behind him she had a strange, irrevocable feeling that sometime in the future, everybody in the city would know where he went to when he closed his eyes. He was sure to do something. 'You're gonna be so cool,' she thought.

Chris remembered where he was and opened his eyes, taking in a deep breath as if waking from his dream. He looked at the two cans and recalled why he was in the kitchen. He grabbed two clean glasses and jumped a little to see Julie by the wall, smiling at him.

"Penny for them," she said.

"Eh?"

"What's on your mind, kiddo?"

"Oh nothing, you know. School, bullies, girls, the usual."

"Bullies?" she said, a half-smile curling on her lips and a tone of voice that suggested that Chris wasn't telling the truth.

He shrugged. "Whatever, the usual," he said, reaching up and opening a cabinet and taking down two empty glasses. He poured one can straight into it, and the head rocketed up the glass.

"Rats!" he said, putting the glass and can down.

"Tilt the glass and the can at equal angles and pour slowly," said Julie, from the wall.

"Cheers," said Chris, attempting to pour again, this time getting it just right.

"How's that?" he said.

"Perfect," said Julie, craning her neck and looking down the hallway and into the living room to see Janine shaking her head and giving the international sign for 'more time, more time.'

Julie left the wall and hopped up on the counter behind Chris.

"So, how is school?" she said, obviously stalling for time. Chris did not sense it.

"Alright, starts soon. New year, same old."

"Moving up to Middle School though, yeah?

"Yeah."

"Miss Gardner is head of that year. English teacher?"

"That's right," said Chris, half-looking over his shoulder.

"She's cool. I remember her, very cool. Strict as anything, but if you get on her good side then she's the best. They say that everyone has one teacher in their life."

"What do you mean?"

"Just that everyone has a teacher that is more than just someone who tells you a bunch of facts and figures. Like a friend, or a mentor. A teacher that directs you a little in life, and is always with you. Gardner is that for me. She's cool."

Chris didn't reply. Julie's faraway tone suggested that she wasn't really talking to him which was fortunate because Chris had no idea what she was talking about. He could not relate to a single word.

"So," continued Julie, reverting to her normal tone of voice, "what you looking forward to most?"

"Art, probably," said Chris, pouring the second beer painfully slowly so that he did not spill a drop. "Haven't really thought about it."

"Not just before?" she said. Chris stopped pouring for a second. Julie hopped off the counter and leaned against the cupboard next to Chris.

"What were you thinking about?"

Chris smiled to himself and shrugged, "Nothing really, just thinking on things, places, the future."

"Good to be alone sometimes, ain't it?" said Julie, quietly. Chris looked up at her and saw that, once again, she wasn't really talking to him.

"You okay?" he asked.

Julie winked at him.

"Tell you a secret?" she said.

Chris nodded.

"Your brother is soon to be a legend, a famous driver. Racing all over, he'll have everything at his feet. Everybody will want a piece of him, everybody will want to be close."

"And you're worried that you're going to get pushed aside?" said Chris. Julie furrowed her brow and smirked a little incredulously. "Are you worried that he doesn't see how much you love him? Are you worried that when he's rich and famous you'll be out the door?"

Julie looked at Chris, unsure just how he suddenly had become so perceptive. Finally, she simply nodded. Chris sighed and turned to lean against the counter beside her. He rested his head against her shoulder.

"Well, if he does," said Chris, "I'll kick the crap out of him."

Julie let out a laugh as Chris picked up the two glasses of beer.

"You are so cool – cooler than Danny, for sure."

"No, I'm not."

"Yeah, you are," said Julie, suddenly a little more seriously. She bent down to Chris so they were eye to eye. "Whatever is in there," she said, tapping his head, "wherever you go to when you're alone, it's yours. That's what's really cool," and she leaned forward and gave him a kiss on the forehead. "Remember that," she said.

"This kiss or…"

"That's what I am talking about," she said with a laugh, "that's the coolness that will make you stand out."

"Thanks," said Chris.

"You're welcome," said Julie, "now, let's give them their beers."

Chris took the glasses and stepped in front of Julie, who walked behind him, her soft hands on his shoulders, guiding him around the corner, down the landing and into the sitting room where everyone was standing up.

Chris looked a little confused and handed the beer to his dad and his uncle, neither of whom said "thank you".

Julie stepped over to Danny and wrapped her arm around him.

"Now," said Terry addressing the whole room, "couple of announcements. Firstly, after today's race…" A cheer came from all for Danny who accepted the applause gracefully. "…and a first-rate mechanical job from yours truly, anyway there may be an opportunity for Danny to progress up a division. Perhaps to the Formulas…"

Janine gasped and put her hands up to her mouth. Uncle Tone swayed a little and smiled a smile that said 'saw that one coming'. Danny looked down to the floor, the focus on him a little bit more than he would have liked. Chris looked at Julie and saw a happy smile, but worried eyes. She darted a glance at Chris that said to him 'told you so'. Chris simply winked at her and the unease behind her eyes fell away.

"It's early days yet," continued Terry, "lots of ins and outs, lots of this's and that's…but there is a chance that Danny can progress up into real racing and not only that but, on his orders let us not forget, the race team will go with him."

Everyone looked at each other with a slight note of confusion. Terry hung his head.

"Me, you fools, me. Danny and I thrashed out some riders and demands and the money men seemed to be up for it. Meeting tomorrow about it, but there is a good chance that Danny can fulfil his potential and can do so with all of us at his side."

"We race as a family," added Danny, putting his arm around Julie and pulling her in tightly. Janine blubbed a little, the tears falling over her hands. Uncle Tone also sniffed.

"So," finished Terry, "the future looks like it could be a bit brighter for us. Maybe a few new comforts around here, no more cheap booze, no more tick."

"A MegaSystem for me," said Chris, with glee, knowing that it was a joke but hoping that the reminder might not go missed,

"That'll be the day, son" laughed his dad.

"Don't I know it," replied Chris, happily, much to the delight of the room. Possibly the first time he had made an entire room of adults laugh with him, rather than at him. He felt taller, slightly more adult.

"So, let's have it for Danny boy and our family!" said Terry, clapping his hands, the sound muting as he was holding his glass of beer. Everybody cheered and clapped. Chris finished clapping first and slumped happily down in his beanbag ready to continue the night and feeling like a real grown-up among peers. As if they were not a 'family' as such, but a little 'group' – a big, yet subtle difference, strange as that sounds.

Terry made that groan he always made before sitting down. Janine cleared her throat. Terry halted, mid seat.

"Oh yes, one more thing," he said in his best/worst Colombo voice. Terry stood back up. "As it seems that Danny is moving up, and that things change and you know, time marches on and everything. I'm a sentimental so-and-so, as well you all know." They didn't. "And I want to keep hold of the good times, I want to relive a few memories but at the same time create some brand-new ones."

"Oh, skip to it," heckled Uncle Tone.

Terry smiled at Chris. "Up you get, boy," he said.

Chris stood up. Suddenly, everyone was looking at him.

"It's your birthday soon, but before that I have something for you...well, something to ask you."

"It's £249.99 from Barrett Games," said Chris, "you can get three games with it and a spare controller for an extra £25" he said, with a smile.

Another burst of laughter from the room.

"He ain't letting it go, Tel," said Uncle Tone. "Stubborn is that Kit. Good luck getting him to listen to team orders" and he reached over and ruffled Chris's hair.

"Eh?" said Chris, the penny not dropping.

Terry smiled at his son. It was a warm smile that Chris couldn't recall seeing before. Terry nodded at Danny who reached behind the sofa and handed over a wrapped-up present. Chris couldn't help but beam – wrapping paper! A present! Brilliant. The parcel was soft, as it bent when held and was the size of one of their large sofa cushions. Terry took the parcel and handed it over to his youngest son. Chris looked tentatively at the room of expectant adults before taking the gift.

"It's not one of the sofa cushions is it?"

"Well, you won't know until you open it," said his mother, wisely.

Chris looked at the parcel, the wrapping little more than yesterday's newspaper. He paused for a few seconds, milking the moment before tearing it open. He and the room gasped as he pulled out a set of old racing overalls. No sponsors, just jet black with blue piping. Chris held them up, eyes wide in awe.

"Now," said his father, "they're your brother's old ones but they should fit good enough. We'll get you on the boxkarts to start off with. Just to start, but we'll get you into a real car faster than you know it."

Chris looked into the chest of the overalls, the size of them blotting out the rest of the room. He bit his lip and swallowed, fighting back the hard impulse to cry. He took a breath and lowered the overalls and saw the faces in the room, each looking at him, his brother proud, Julie smiling wide, his mother crying and Uncle Tone nodding slowly with conviction.

"What do you reckon," said his father, bending down so that he was eye-level with his youngest. "You want to go racing with your old man? You wanna go faster than your slug of a brother? You and me, eh?"

Janine blubbed even more. Chris could even swear that Danny wiped away a tear. Chris looked at his father for a few seconds, finding a new person before him. Not so much a giant any more. Not so much a silent mountain.

Chris stepped across the room. His old man opened his arms to hug his boy. Chris held out his hand instead and the two men shook on it.

CHAPTER 14
4 A.M.

Chris sat on the sofa, dressed in his black overalls.

"You look the mutt's nuts, my man," said Uncle Tone, slumped in his brother's arm chair. Everyone else had taken themselves off to bed. After the surprise gift had been given, they had all talked excitedly for another forty minutes before Janine and Terry went to bed. Danny stayed around another twenty minutes and then was taken upstairs by a sleepy Julie, who yawned a goodnight to Uncle Tone and blew a kiss to Chris. It was getting on for half-two in the morning, the music had finished, and the supply of cans was running low. Chris brushed down his overalls, not caring that the crisp remnants fell on the floor.

"You think so?"

"Yeah mate, you'll be grand," confirmed Uncle Tone, his eyes wavering, his head falling to the side.

"Just boxkarts though," sighed Chris.

"That doesn't matter, Kit. Just because they're not Formula One doesn't mean they're not cool in their own right."

"I guess."

"And you get to build them yourself. That's cool – you can paint them up, design them. If you're not fast enough, at least you can look good. Create a bit of spectacle. The mob love that. That's entertainment."

"Nah, I'll be like Danny, I'll just stick to being fast."

"What's the point?" slurred Uncle Tone, his eyes opening and flashing with anger for a split second. "Why do you want to be someone else?"

"I don't Uncle Tone, just want to be fast like him, beat his records."

Uncle Tone pulled an expression that was supposed to be ambivalence but looked more like gurning to Chris.

"Don't compare yourself to no one, just be yourself, Kit, that's what's really cool. Him up there," – Uncle Tone waved a finger haphazardly at the ceiling – "he is a great man, already a legend. Everybody loves him. But you…" – the finger came down sharply and pointed at Chris – "you're on the outside. The brother of a champion. In the inner circle and yet not. You're a mystery, you'll be something else as long as you come out good, honest and strong. Will you do that? Will you be good?"

"I will, I will."

Uncle Tone smiled and his eyes drew heavy. "You'll go far, my boy. Records are broken, champions come and go, people move on. Give them something they've never seen, something they will never forget, something they can measure themselves against. A legend. They'll sings songs about you, they'll write books about you… hell on wheels, I'll write a book about you!" His eyes closed and his head slumped to the side.

"I will be a legend," said Chris quietly to himself, "me and the Midnight Special."

Uncle Tone began murmuring a song that Chris had never heard. However, amid the snores and the garbled words, he heard 'Midnight Special' and assumed Uncle Tone was singing a song about him. Chris smiled and stood up, he reached over and grabbed a throw from the back of the sofa and draped it over his snoring uncle, patting his shoulder and left him asleep. Chris retired upstairs to bed, turning the light off in the lounge as he did so.

———

It was nearing 4am when it happened. The idea had formed a day earlier, but the courage to execute the plan had not arrived until that moment. Chris knelt on his bed, still in his racing overalls, chin on hands, elbows on the sill and staring out across the suburbs and at the blinking red light atop the Stivyakino TV Tower.

The overalls were a snug fit, padded and warm. He did not mind that they were hand-me-downs. Most of his clothes were, and there was something poetic, he thought, something right about wearing his brother's old racing gear. Chris smiled at the recollection of his dad, asking him to race together. To join the team. It was going to be a great partnership. As the red light blinked at Chris, he thought out the path of his future that led all the way across the city.. He imagined racing a black boxkart and becoming a champion, perhaps the youngest ever. Then, with his father moving on to karts, then SuperKarts and before his fifteenth birthday becoming Formula One champion. No sponsors, just the black car and the team. No one would believe it.

Then some sort of disaster. Chris casually imagined his father being gunned down in the street by some thug, perhaps Chris injured too. A national scandal, a bankrupt team. Chris in recuperation, to emerge some years later as the Boxkart Rebel whose first mission was to roam the streets searching for the thug that killed his father. The trail taking him all the way to City Hall. He takes down the administration, the mayor falling to his death from the top of his skyscraper like all the bad guys in the movies. Then he would realise that crime would never be over, the streets never safe and so the former child racing prodigy would bocame the masked driver, the dark saviour of the city: the Midnight Boy.

Chris smiled when he joined the dots from his bedroom, through his imagined life all the way across time and space to the beacon atop the Stivyakino TV Tower. 'Who knows,' he thought, suddenly developing the world further, 'maybe I could be on a case of a masked vigilante who is seemingly terrorising the city. I track him down, and we fight almost to the death. I spare him and he tells me his story. It seems he is the good guy after all, and the powers-that-be are pinning crimes on him. He became a masked hero after his father was shot, like mine. He is The Batman, and we team up!' Chris smiled at the thought. 'Or, a case could lead me out to Gotham City, I could get mixed up in the Batman's turf. His case and my case are the same. After a brutal fight, we team up.' Chris smiled and nodded to himself – a helluva future. He turned his gaze from the Stivyakino TV Tower and was about to get into bed when his eyes fell on the lock-up beside the garden. He looked at the small garage, last in the row of eleven, the moonlight glinting off the padlock. He knew where the key to that padlock lay.

Chris looked at the bedside clock: 4:05a.m

"Eff it," he said quietly, zipping up his racing overall and creeping out of his room and across the landing.

——•——

Chris stood in the dark living room and looked across at Uncle Tone, who was still snoring loudly on the armchair, curled into a little ball, the blanket pulled over him. Chris stood motionless, a black silhouette, waiting for a few moments. The carriage clock on the fake mantelpiece ticked. The drunken uncle breathed heavily. Slowly, purposefully, the black shadow turned from the scene and walked silently into the kitchen.

Next to the cork chalkboard on the kitchen hung a row of keys. Chris stood, assuming the silent, stern face of the Midnight Boy. He knew exactly which keys to go for, but still he ran his finger along the wall, slowly down the line until he came to the set he wanted. He clasped the dangling keys so that they did not chink and carefully lifted them from the hook. He turned from wall and bent down to the lock at the backdoor. He envisioned it to be a lock to a vault, or to some official building that he needed to get in to. He held out the long key for the lock and with one hand steadying the other, he inserted it into the lock without scraping the edges – the skill and accuracy of a surgeon. He gave a cursory look back around, down the hall to the living room. The coast was clear, yet he could feel the imaginary sweat across his brow. He held his breath as he turned the key, certain that the activating lock would creak and crack, loudly echoing around the house. He turned the key just enough to pull the door too, knowing that a full revolution of the key would set the lock loudly in place. He reached up and slid his fingers around the door handle, slowly pulling it down and opening the door slightly. The cold night breeze flittered through the door. The Midnight Boy slid up the wall and stepped through the narrow crack in the door, closing it silently behind him.

He walked slowly, almost menacingly down the cold concrete alleyway, the lock-ups to the left of him closed, a few clattering in the bracing wind. His eyes glinted in the moonlight as he stared ahead at the door he wanted.

The lock-up door slid upwards to reveal the outline of the Midnight Boy, framed by the blue night sky behind. A shaft of moonlight fell into the garage and caressed the fairing of the Special. Sitting there, facing the door and waiting to be driven.

Upon seeing the car, Chris stepped forward in his mind and put the Midnight Boy away for a few seconds. The adventure of busting out of his house was one thing, doing what he was about to was another. His stomach pulled tight, a sudden urge to go to the toilet gripping him. He held on to the top of the door above his head, gripping it tightly. He was not wearing any gloves and already his knuckles were freezing. He looked down at the clear line on the ground, knowing that if he took a step into the garage, he was committed. It was not too late to turn back. Not too late at all. He took a breath and stepped in.

Chris knew where everything was in the garage without need for the main light. He sidestepped around the car and grabbed the torch that was on the side. He covered the bulb and turned the torch on, wise enough to let only a fraction of the beam escape, lest it shoot out of the door like a spotlight, directly into his parent's bedroom. He knelt down to the car and shone some light on the engine first, then the wheels and finally into the cockpit. It was all present and correct. Chris turned the light off and gripped the front wheel with one hand, while holding on to the back of the rear wing with the other.

"Okay kid," he whispered, "let's go be badass." And with that he slowly began to push the car out of the lock-up.

Chris steered the SuperKart to the alleyway and aimed it down towards the road, alongside the house. He quickly crept back to the garage and closed the door, placing the padlock back through the loop but leaving it unlocked. If his father should wake and look out the window, he wouldn't suspect a thing. Chris looked back up at the house and gripped the car once more. On the count of three, he began to push it along the alleyway. The grind of the tyres on the loose stones scattering on the alleyway seemed like canon-fire in the still night. He winced as he kept pushing the kart along. The grind getting louder. His nerve faltered as the car passed alongside the house. As the entrance to the road approached, he sped up to a near run. He always assumed the car to be light as a feather, considering how Danny flung it around the track, but to push it at speed was draining and as they hit the dip from the pavement on to the road, the inertia of the car almost got away from him. Chris leaned back and swung the wheel around, turning the car safely on to the road and alongside his dad's parked van. In an ideal world, he would have been able to get into the car there and then, but it was too dangerous. Firing that beast up would alert the cops for sure. Chris flexed his cold knuckles and gripped the wheel, knowing that it would be a long walk to get the kart to a safe distance. He put his head down, looked at the asphalt, gritted his teeth and began to push the SuperKart away from the house.

———

He had come far enough – it was time. Chris stood up from the car, his back aching a little. He had pushed the beast for half an hour, far from the house and out of the suburb. He had taken himself to Solly Lane, by his school. The lane was wide, pedestrianized and flanked with trees and bushes. It was also long, perhaps a kilometre in length. The lane led from the school car park, out towards

Solly Park, which was where the stoners gathered – those kids in the sixth form who let their hair grow long and smelt strange. The cool kids in the years above Chris hung out at the filled-in reservoir, under the TV Tower where they drank and smashed bottles. The kids in Solly Park just seemed to lie about smoking and giggling. His mother always warned him about those kids and their ways. Chris couldn't see why. They seemed harmless enough.

Anyway, at this time of night the location was perfect. Solly Park was not a 'park' as such but more of a concrete plain – a twisted climbing frame at one end, a disused bunker covered in tags at the other. The entrance of the park was wide enough for a bus to drive through and had a four-foot concrete wall around its perimeter. It was completely deserted. Chris positioned the car at the top of the lane and looked ahead – a long straight and then through the wide entrance and out into the park where he would have free rein to 'turn and burn' as his brother would say – to really get a feel for the Midnight Special. 'If this goes well, tomorrow night, take her to Palmerston Road and do some serious downhill racing.'

Chris pulled the chord on the engine, firing her into life. The roar echoed around the school grounds and the kart began to jiggle on the spot, begging to go. He held on to the car and slipped into the seat. It was unexpectedly low as his feet disappeared under the cowling and rested on the pedals. He felt the vibrations of the engine against the back of the seat, the car seeming to shake all around him. The noise hurt his ears and the kart felt tight around him, almost constricted. He gripped the wheel in an effort to stop the fierce vibrations, which tightened the knot in his stomach awfully.

Chris tried to calm his heart and overcome the volcano in his guts. It was a long way and the entrance to the park was wide, flanked by the concrete walls. But that wasn't the real problem. He was a good kid; he never really got into trouble at school, but now here he was, committing grand theft auto against his own family and about to go joyriding.

'What the hell are you thinking?' he thought, clamping his eyes shut and gritting his teeth. The noise and the vibration were almost too much. He was so far away from home and really, really scared. He snapped his eyes open.

"Let's ride," said the Midnight Boy and the pedal went down.

Chapter 15
Burying the Body

He could barely breathe, he could barely see. The car was too fast, the thick hedges lining the wide alley were a blur, the noise and the stink of the engine overwhelming. Chris held on to the wheel for his life, the rattle and anger of the wheel wrestling with him. He squinted and tried to focus on the end of the black tunnel, to the wide opening of the park where he would be able to break out of the confines of the lane and feel freer, perhaps even breathe. He could not ease off the accelerator, the speed and his fear held the foot down, coupled with the shake and bite of the engine – it was all too much for Chris to take in, how was he supposed to think and react to all these stimuli? He tried to lean forward, to turn his head and look around, at least get some bearings but the force of his acceleration pinned his head to the back of the chair, the pounding of the engine hitting the seat against his head. Teeth chattering, eyes streaming, entrance approaching. He had walked that alleyway countless times, even been into the park, he knew the entrance was wide enough to drive a bus though, but now, careening towards it, the dark alleyway contra-zooming in and his vision narrowing he knew that the entrance was too narrow. He'd never make it. He managed to close his eyes for a second before reopening them. Big mistake. In that second, he must have covered half the distance, the opening already upon him. The Midnight Boy said nothing; Chris simply thought *'I'm going to die.'*

Suddenly, his body took over. Before he could chain the thoughts together, he had taken his foot off the gas and slammed his left foot on to the break and spun the wheel around. The car screeched to its side, pitching on to two wheels. The twist of metal piercing the air, the engine wailing, Chris looked to his side in horror to see the concrete wall bearing down upon him. Impact. The car broadsided the wall full on. The inertia caused Chris to whip his head to the side, taking a glancing blow against the wall. Before he could react, the car fell down, landing painfully on all four wheels. He sat there for a few moments, in a daze, the side of his face wet and warm. He blinked slowly. The engine was still on, but the noise seemed somehow distant – a faraway thunderstorm. Chris looked ahead, the concrete wall to his immediate right stretching off into the distance as it ran the perimeter of the park.

The engine slowed to a purr before running empty. Chris's eyes were heavy, the edge of his world blurring, a strange vignette filled his view. The distant thunderstorm seemed to have dissipated. His eyes were so heavy. He managed to look up, before darkness came. The last thing he saw before his eyes closed was the distant glow of the red beacon atop the Stivyakino TV Tower. Chris Redding slumped forward, his head resting on the wheel.

He awoke with gasp, as if finding the surface of a dark lake after being pulled under and taken down to the depths and to the very edge. His eyes burst open, his inhalation fierce and loud. Chris sat back and looked around. Where was he? He was not in his bedroom. The sky was a shade of purple and the air was crisp. He pinched the bridge of his nose and looked at his lap. He was still in the car. Chris winced and touched the side of his head; the wound had stopped bleeding and the blood had dried. He looked down the adjacent alleyway that led to his school, still a little unsure about what he was doing there. Slowly, it came back to him. At first it was disbelief, then slowly he assured himself that it was the truth. When he believed the truth, fear came. Panic first, a cold sweat breaking and then that grip in his belly. Sharper than a knife, the urgency greater than anything he had ever experienced. He had no words, it seemed his tongue still didn't quite believe it. Eyes wide, he gripped the wheel and pulled himself out of the wreckage.

Chris stood aghast as he looked at the broken car, slammed against the wall, its right side buckled and twisted. The rear wheel pointing to the sky, the front twisted under the chassis. He had seen crashes on the TV – they tumbled and spun like his toy cars when he launched them from the top step, debris spinning off in all directions. The driver always managed to climb out. With all his heart, Chris Redding wished that he had been that unfortunate statistic, that dark figure that blighted a perfect safety record. But he was alive, and no pit crew or safety cars were coming to get him. He was alive, alone and leaden with guilt.

"Oh hell, oh hell, oh hell," was all he could whisper as he looked at the sad car. There was no way he could push it home, and even if he did, what then? He was done for.

He turned from the car to collect his thoughts, the sight of the victim clouding all his judgement.

"Come on, think, think, think," he said, before his frantic gaze fell on the thick hedges that lined the alleyway to his school. It was a rubbish idea, but the only one available.

Chris turned back to the car, grabbed the wheel and the rear fender. The crippled side of the car seemed to exaggerate the weight. His head throbbed and he gritted his teeth as he pushed with all his might. The car did not budge an inch. The front wheel was tucked under itself and jammed any progress. Chris swore loudly, knowing that dawn was fast approaching. He could not be caught.

"I'm not going down," he spat, as he rushed around to the front wing and pulled the buckled wheel out. The twisted axle snapped easily and the wheel came free in his hands. He unceremoniously dumped it in the driver's seat and grabbed the steering wheel again. This time, the car moved. It was heavy and awkward work, but it was moving, the front axle scraping against the tarmac and leaving a tell-tale mark as he pushed and dragged the car towards the thick hedges. 'Nothing you can do about the scrape marks, just get the car hidden.'

Finally, with a mighty push against the rear spoiler, he was able to pitch the car into the hedge and down a ditch on the other side. He grabbed some low branches, twisting and snapping them so that they hung low and covered the vehicle. After ten minutes' work he stepped back and viewed the crime scene. He looked at his watch: 5:45am.

"Good enough," he said, a strange sense of excitement coming over him as the adrenaline swelled. He might get away with it, either way the hard part was done with. Chris gently touched the wound on his head. His hair was sticky and matted. Worry about that later. He left the crime scene and jogged home, mentally preparing for phase two of his getaway plan.

———

Chris made it back to his house in 15 minutes flat, running on pure adrenaline. He stopped for a few seconds beside his father's van, leaning against it and coughing into his hands. Nearly there. Chris peered through the front window of the van towards his house. From the outside all appeared fine. No unexpected lights on, no activity within. A final, cursory glance down the street told him that the coast was clear.

Chris crept down the side alley to their lock-up, hugging the garden fence so that he could remain unseen from the back windows of his house. He grabbed the door to the lock-up and opened it slightly, rolling underneath and into the garage. As quickly and as quietly as he could, he took various tools from their hooks and placed them 'randomly' on the counter, he scattered some oily rags on the floor and carefully laid the car's old stanchions on their sides. A final look at the mess and he knew, to the untrained eye, that it appeared to be a pretty convincing crime scene. A clear burglary. One final action needed to be done. He grabbed a crowbar from the counter and bent down to the padlock bar on the ground. On the count of three, he prised the metal plate from the ground. After replacing the bar on the counter and wiping his prints from it, Chris rolled out under the garage. Finally, he grabbed the padlock that was hanging from the door, wiped it and tossed it to the small grass verge by the garden fence. Phase two complete. Chris left the second crime scene of the night and crept towards the house. The backdoor was still open, and so he slipped inside and replaced his father's keys on their hook. That was it, he had done it. A calmness overcame him. It was done. It was over. Chris allowed himself a little smile before pouring a glass of water and leaving the kitchen and going up to bed.

Upon the chair, curled up and under the warm blanket, Uncle Tone regarded Chris' movements with one eye. He saw the boy, dressed in his racing overalls, sneak through the room when the dawn light was breaking. Uncle Tone was sleepy, but not stupid. He filed the information away and went back to sleep.

Chris got out of his overalls, folded them neatly and slid under the covers. The moment he pulled the blanket up to his chin and felt the warmth and safety of home, the magnitude of his crimes hit him. The room grew smaller, like a prison, his stomach turned, and a million different eventualities exploded like supernovas in his mind. His eyes filled up, he wanted to die like he had done in the car a few hours prior. He wanted to die, to flee, to get away from that house. He was a murderer, living in secret with the family of his victim. He was Judas at the dinner table, the assassin in the council. Chris pulled the covers over his head, trying to block out the endless analogies that filtered through him. His own family, everything they had done together. Suddenly he began recalling all the little incidents and moments that had been labelled as 'normal' before but now seemed like a montage of loving remembrance played out to soft music at the end of love films. A hug from his mother; that time his father brought home surprise fried chicken from the store across town; the time his mother made him cry and his brother hugged him. The red push-car, his brother holding it up so that he could race. His childhood, golden and warm and now gone. Chris' stomach turned and threatened to explode.

He whipped off the covers and dashed to the bathroom. He slammed the door shut and knelt, vomiting water and bile into the bowl. As soon as it was expelled, he felt better, though his head throbbed slightly. Chris flushed the toilet and cupped some water into his mouth from the sink.

He looked at his tired face in the shaving mirror. Eyes heavy, bags under them. To himself, he looked like guilt incarnate. He turned to inspect the wound on the side of his head, pulling apart the matted hair. It wasn't so bad, but it needed cleaning. Chris turned on the hot tap and dabbed his wound clean, before breaking apart the matted hairs. He stood up to inspect the cleanliness. The vapour from the hot tap had condensed over the mirror. He could not see his face, save for the streaks that were visible through clear words he had drawn earlier with his finger. The vapour revealed it all: "The Midnight Boy Drives".

Chapter 16
Taking Confession

He lay awake in his bed, staring at the ceiling and the luminous plastic galaxy of stars and planets stuck on it. The sun was up, the Milky Way dull and Chris lay with his arms across his chest like a corpse. He had slept maybe two hours – a dreamless, light sleep, waiting for the moment to arrive. At 8:30 in the morning, it came. First with the slam of the back door, then some frantic rushing up and down the stairs. And then the commotion hit. Chris lay awake, wishing he was dead as he began to hear his father's voice rise and rise until it was a torrent of foul language, each word blending into one like the ramblings of a madman. Chris held his blanket up to his chin and clamped his eyes shut. Whenever he had a nightmare, his brother would always tell him to imagine doing press-ups in the dream. Say to yourself: "It isn't real, it isn't real" and press yourself up – the trick would pull you out of your nightmare and back to the safety of reality.

"When it gets dark, and you're terrified, chances are that you are dreaming," he told Chris once, when aliens had invaded the city and the mayor had elected to detonate a nuclear device to wipe everything out. In that nightmare, Chris remembered the family gathering outside in the street, along with the other neighbours. They all looked at the horizon and awaited the detonation. The aliens were also running down the street towards them all – death by nuclear blast or Xenomorph. The family hugged, and Chris closed his eyes. A blinding flash and everything became hot. And then he awoke in tears, covered in sweat. It was so real, that he checked his body for burn marks in the bathroom mirror. His brother calmed him and taught Chris the trick to outrun your terror and rebel against your nightmares.

As the commotion raged downstairs, Chris whispered: "It's just a dream, it's just a dream, it's just a dream."

There was a smash of glass from downstairs and Chris's eyes snapped open. It was no nightmare, it was real. Chris climbed out of bed and left his bedroom, throwing his dressing gown on and heading into the warzone.

———

Uncle Tone was awake and staring out of the living room window, nursing a steaming cup of coffee. Janine sat pale-faced on the sofa, staring at the fireplace blankly. Chris stood at the foot of the stairs. He peered down the hallway to see his dad hugging his older brother. For a second, confusion filled Chris. Maybe something even more terrible had happened to warrant the strange reaction from everyone. His mother turned to see Chris, she smiled a teary smile and leapt up from the sofa, hugging him tightly.

"What's going on?" said Chris with a genuine tone of confusion. "Did someone die?"

"Kind of," said Uncle Tone, still staring out of the window.

Chris looked down the hallway and saw his brother. His dad had broken off the hug and was putting on his paint and plaster-spattered denim work-coat. Chris hugged his mother tightly and looked at Danny. Danny looked at his younger brother with bloodshot eyes, cheeks wet with tears. Chris hardly recognised him. A fallen giant. A broken boy.

"What happened?" whispered Chris, hoping beyond hope that someone had died, even Julie, so that his own crime could be absolved from what he was now witnessing. His brother defeated.

"Someone stole the car," whispered his mother. Chris clamped his eyes shut and buried his face into his mother's chest. It was true, of course it was.

"Right, enough of that," snapped his father, striding into the living room. "Janine, get your coat. Tone, take Christopher and… I don't know, just look after him."

"Sure bro," said Uncle Tone. "You and me today, Kit," smiled Uncle Tone, "boy's day out while your old man sorts out this mess. What say you?"

"Sure," whispered Chris, in a daze.

Janine put on her coat and threaded her arm through her husband's. They walked to the front door.

"Where's Julie?" asked Chris.

Danny stopped at the door and turned back. "She's at work. See you later, bro. I love you, mate."

"It'll be alright," said Chris, flatly.

Danny smiled, sniffed and nodded. He took a breath and seemed to grow a few inches. He looked over at Uncle Tone, who gave Danny a stern nod, the type Chris had seen in war movies when soldiers were about to go 'over the top'. Danny nodded back like a soldier and zipped up his windbreaker before leaving the house. The door closed. Chris and Uncle Tone stood in the living room for a few moments, the air heavy with dread – the only sound coming from the carriage clock on the mantelpiece.

"Right then," said Uncle Tone, "get washed and dressed and we'll go out."

"Where are we going?"

"We'll go to the tracks, have a bit of fun."

"Sure," said Chris, turning to ascend the stairs.

"Buy you a shake and then you can tell me how you got that knock on your noggin, in the early hours of the morning."

Chris halted halfway up the stairs for a few moments. His stomach went over the peak of Palmerston Road. He gripped the banister and walked on to get ready. Uncle Tone watched him with sharp eyes, as he blew the vapour from his mug of coffee.

———

Uncle Tone had shouted for a taxi to take them across town towards the indoor go-kart tracks and chatted to the taxi driver all the way, as if they were old friends while Chris sat in the back, his eyes fixed on the magazine pocket on the back of the front passenger seat. Every once in a while, Tone would flick a glance in the rear view at his nephew and with each look, his suspicions were confirmed. The boy was drowning in fear and guilt.

They arrived at the circuit by 11am. The racetrack was housed inside a large warehouse in an industrial park. The taxi had to drive past block after block of depressing buildings that housed offices, storage units and electronic manufacturers. Buried at the back, lay Hot Wheelz Trax. The go-karts weren't professional by any standards, but they were fast enough and a good day out for kids and families. Chris had been a few times and enjoyed it, but never as much as he would have liked – mainly because he felt that it was a kiddy's version of sport. Sometimes he had to race alongside children 2 or even 3 years younger than he was. They were fast, sure, but it was because they were light, he reasoned. They entered the foyer and Uncle Tone paid for two sessions for Chris. The lady behind the counter smiled politely when Uncle Tone asked if the bar was open yet. She nodded that it was, but her look carried a disapproving tinge to it. Uncle Tone paid no mind.

"Alright, Chris," he said, handing him a plastic token, "go get your suit." And he pointed off to the race-shop where young drivers hired their gear. Chris smiled and tried to appear calm, but really, he was feeling nauseous. Utter fear inside him – fear of the look in his uncle's eyes, fear of what would happen later that day, and the day after that, and after that. He felt how criminals must feel when the gavel comes down and the sentence is delivered. Any hopes, dreams or plans smashed away with one swoop of the little wooden hammer. But he had done the crime, there was no escaping. Chris took the token and walked to the shop.

Uncle Tone watched Chris disappear into the store, before walking to the viewing gallery to get a beer and a hot dog.

——————

Chris zipped up his red racing overalls. They were a general fit, so they were loose around his waist, but tight around his shoulders and his gloves stank of other people. The other kids in the changing rooms were chatting excitedly about the sessions ahead. Chris recognised a few from other times he had been there, but nobody spoke to him. He was thankful for that. The kids zipped up their overalls, picked up their helmets and dashed out of the changing rooms. Chris sat back down on the wooden bench and rested his helmet on his knees. He held out his hands. They were trembling, a coldness breaking out over his head. Beads of sweat formed across the back of his neck and ran down his back, a sensation that he could not recall ever happening before. He knew he could not stay in the changing room forever and so, on the count of three, he walked out to get into his car.

Uncle Tone sat above the circuit, dangling his arms over the railing of the viewing gallery. The small course twisted over itself in a classic figure-of-eight configuration with some tight chicanes thrown in, here and there. The diner was cheap and cheerful – soggy burgers and limp hot dogs served in paper trays, and some various soft drinks. But there was beer too. Tone poured a plastic cup of foamy, overly cold beer and bought a hotdog. He took position and waited. The drivers walked out to the line of cars on the start grid, engines already running, jiggling in the spot, eager to go. The kids all climbed inside. Chris was last out, just like his older brother, but with a slovenly gait. Though Uncle Tone suspected that the reasons for the younger brother's delay were different, he could not help but be struck by the similarities between them. He sighed as he watched the sad boy slump towards his kart, and he thought he understood the pain and angst inside. An hour ago, he had had no idea how to handle the situation, his own anger clouding things but now he could not help but feel sorry for the boy. He took a sip of his beer. "You're just going your own way, ain't you, Kit?" he said to himself.

Chris got into his car and Uncle Tone looked to the front of the grid, waiting for the lights. Red. Second Red. Green. The roar of the engines erupted and the karts lurched forward, each one jostling for position as they burned towards the first bend. All except one car. At the back of the grid, Chris remained motionless. Uncle Tone stood up and looked down at his nephew. A few stewards were waving the car forward. It did not budge.

"Oh hell," whispered Tone.

A steward rushed towards Chris's car and began to push it, shouting and pointing at the car to go. Chris began to wave his hands and shake his head. Suddenly he pushed the steward aside and climbed out of the car, running back along the lane and climbing over the crash board. Uncle Tone dropped his beer and left the viewing gallery to get to his pal.

———

Tone checked the foyer, the gift shop and the changing rooms until, eventually, he found Chris. The kid was sitting outside, hugging his knees by the wall. Uncle Tone saw him and sighed in relief, half expecting the boy to have run off into the city, perhaps home, perhaps who knows? He could see that Chis was crying, the tell-tale signs all there – the jiggling shoulders, head buried in his folded arms, the barely concealed sniffs. Uncle Tone took a few cautious steps. Chris sensed him coming, and shuffled away from him, trying to conceal his distress. Uncle Tone put his hands on his hips and hung his head, thinking over his best course of action. After a few moments, he continued up to his nephew and sat down next to him, hugging his knees also.

"What's up, Kit?" he asked softly.

"Nothing, leave me alone," said Chris, his teary voice muffled by his sleeve.

"Doesn't look like nothing," pushed Tone. "Is it about this morning?"

"It's nothing, I said! I'm fine!"

"Not about this morning, I get you… perhaps about last night then?"

Chris's shoulders began to jiggle more and he turned a little further away from his Uncle.

"Want to talk about it?"

Chris shook his head.

"Wanna tell me what happened in there?"

"Just didn't feel like racing. Is that a crime? Piss off!"

"Hey, Kit," said Uncle Tone firmly, "I get that you're upset for whatever reason but watch the language, understand?"

"Sorry," mumbled Chris.

"Pardon?"

Chris sat up, taking his head from his arms and leering at Uncle Tone.

"I said 'sorry', okay?" he blurted out in angry frustration, his eyes red and fierce, his top lip thin.

"What happened to your head, knock it in your sleep?"

Chris's anger faded and his lip wobbled. He was undone. Uncle Tone nodded.

"You have to tell them."

"How?"

Uncle Tone shrugged, "I don't know, mate," he said, putting his arm around Chris. "You gotta come clean."

"They are gonna kill me. I have ruined everything."

"Well, they ain't gonna be pleased for sure. But they'll forgive you, they'll understand. It'll be fine."

"Why? How do you know that?"

"Family mate, that's what families do. Look, can I talk to you man-to-man?"

Chris shrugged.

"Can I?"

Chris sniffed up his tears and nodded.

"Wipe your nose then, for God's sake" said Uncle Tone with a smile. Chris spluttered a laugh and drew his hand across his sleeve.

"Look," began Uncle Tone, "we all mess up – everyone does. Lord knows I have for most of my life. I've pissed away whatever talent I had as a kid, drank it or gambled it away – always been carried by your dad. Well, you see him as your dad, but he's my brother. He forgives me, and I forgive him too."

"For what?"

"Well, your old man isn't exactly a saint – he can be a right old idiot when he wants to be."

Chris laughed a little more.

"Point is, we do things, we screw up – for whatever reasons. I don't know the reasons for you doing what you did; don't ask me to tell you if it was right or wrong. That's your own thing, that's your own guilt to come to terms with, I guess. But I do know that you never set out to hurt anyone. You never meant to cause trouble, did you, Kit?"

Chris shook his head, "No, I never meant for anything."

"Well, if you can admit that, if you can admit that you never meant to hurt anyone, then they will see that. They'll forgive you…but you have to come clean."

"Can't we just forget it, pretend it never happened?"

"Sure, sure you can. Look I ain't going to tell them. I won't say anything. I'm on your side, you believe that, don't you?"

Chris nodded meekly.

"Say it then."

"You're on my side."

"Always have been, always will be. I'm on your side, I'm in your corner. If you want me there when you come clean, I will be. If you want me to chip off, I can do that. But that's if you choose to come clean. You gotta choice here, Kit. You can come clean, or you can ignore it – pretend it never happened and let time heal the wounds and it'll pass."

Uncle Tone looked at Chris who was staring off over the concrete car park, deep in thought.

"But, if you do trust time to bury this, it will eat you alive. The guilt will consume you, it will live in your gut and take over your whole being. It will dominate your will and your thoughts. The pain and guilt will infect everything, and it will define you."

Chris sighed and looked at the kerb.

"Just wanted to be like Danny. Just wanted to prove that I could do something on my own."

"Well, messed up as life is, I would say that you got the best opportunity to do that."

"How do you mean?"

"Well, you got a chance now to look your old man in the eye and confess. He'll be angry but, by Christ, he will see the courage it took to come clean. He'll see the strength and will that it took. He won't be angry at his son-the-boy, but at his son-the-man. Here's your chance to make a stand, grow up, confess your crimes and be defined by your actions. For good. What do you reckon?"

Chris sniffed and nodded.

"Good man," said Uncle Tone and held out his hand to shake. Chris took it.

"Thanks Uncle Tone,"

"Hey don't thank me Kit, I'm just speaking from lack of experience. I ain't never taken responsibility for nothing, I've run at every turn because the other path is too damn hard. Every time. You're nearly fourteen and you're about to become more a man than I will ever be. Just do it right."

"I will."

"I know you will."

Uncle Tone took his arm from around Chris and sat back against the wall. Chris leaned back also. Uncle Tone fished in his pocket for his smokes. He took out his last and lit it.

"So, you wanna tell me what happened in there, now?"

"I got scared. The engine. The noise. Too fast for me."

"I shouldn't have brought you, I guess. That was my fault."

"You weren't to know."

"Saw you come home last night. Then this morning and everything... should've taken you to the park. Easier ways to get the confession I guess."

"I pissed myself," said Chris.

"You looked scared."

"No, I mean, I really did."

Uncle Tone looked at Chris and furrowed his brow.

"I couldn't help it. The engine. Guilt, I guess. Couldn't hold it in. Don't tell anyone."

"Not a chance mate, that's nothing to be ashamed off anyway – Christ, I do it all the time."

"Really?"

"Yeah – when you reach my age, cheap cider goes through you like water down a drain."

Chris chuckled to himself.

"But don't worry, I won't tell nobody. Trust me."

"Thanks Uncle."

———

They had sat and chatted for two hours. Chris' stomach had eased, and Uncle Tone had gone in to pay for the cleaning of the overalls and to buy some new clothes, some hot dogs and shakes. Together they sat out in the sun and laughed and joked. Chris told his uncle about middle school, and they even talked about girls. Though they never spoke about the incident the night before, Tone understood exactly why Chris had wanted to take the kart out, what he was trying to do and what he was trying to become. They spoke about everything and nothing and

Chris almost forgot his pain and guilt until a quarter past two in the afternoon when his father's van pulled into the car park. Their laughter died down and they both stood up. The van pulled up alongside them. Danny and his father looked tired and pale, neither regarding Chris nor Uncle Tone. Janine, in the passenger seat, rolled down the window.

"Hi, boys, alright?"

"Not bad Janine," said Uncle Tone. "Didn't do much racing – too nice a day for that so we sat outside and yapped a bit. Bright kid, this one," he said ruffling Chris's hair. "Get everything sorted?"

"Made a start," said Janine sternly.

Uncle Tone nodded and reached for the van's side door and slid it open. He turned to Chris.

"Want me to come?" said Tone quietly. Chris looked at his parents and brother on the front bench of their van. His stomach began to turn again at the thought of what he had to do. He shook his head.

"No, you go. I got this," replied Chris, and he slapped his uncle on the shoulder before climbing into the back of the van. He sat down and looked at the open door. His uncle stood for a moment, before thumping his heart and nodding. Chris took a deep breath, buckled himself up and nodded back. He was ready. Uncle Tone smiled and slid the van door shut.

"I'm going to have a word with a few locals in some of the pubs around," he said to Janine, "see if anyone knows anything."

Janine smiled and nodded, "Thanks, Tone. Afterwards, come over for dinner, maybe? Not in the mood for cooking so perhaps a takeaway?"

"Sure."

Uncle Tone patted the side of the van and smiled at his sister-in-law. His brother did not look at him. Janine smiled kindly and the van started up and they drove away.

Uncle Tone watched the van drive out of the parking lot and sent Chris all his best wishes and courage. Something inside Tone told him that it was going to be alright.

———

They had driven in silence for twenty minutes. In the back of the van, Chris fixated on the rusting panelling opposite. Every pitch and roll of the van as it made its way through the city caused him to slide a little on the wooden bench. He went through every variation of his confession. Straight out with the truth; a gentle build up; perhaps the excuses first; perhaps some tears; perhaps some curse words to prove that he was a man; perhaps quietly and matter-of-fact. Before he knew it, the van reached the top of Palmerston Avenue. There were no windows in the back of the van, but the moment of sharp descent told Chris all he needed to know. They were driving down the steepest road in the city. His favourite part of the city. He felt it apt, the sharp descent acting as a natural countdown. He had planned to wait until he was home, to sit them down and hand out some calming beers before spilling the beans but no, at the bottom of the road would be best. He counted down from five.

"Dad," he said, firmly, "I have something to say."

"What's that, son?" said his dad over the din of the traffic and the engine.

"I have something to say," repeated Chris, a little louder.

"What?" shouted Terry in frustration, taking his eye off the road and trying to look over his shoulder. "What you on about?"

"It was me!" shouted Chris, his delivery unlike any he had rehearsed.

"What was?"

"It was m—"

Nobody but Janine saw the old lady step out from behind the parked car. She screamed. Terry snapped his attention from his son and yanked the wheel to the side to avoid the lady.

Chris was lurched forward, his belt bracing the impact and dragging the air from him. The van pitched awfully, Terry fighting for control. Things seemed to slow for Chris. He heard his mother scream and he looked to the side, past his family on the front bench and through the windscreen. There seemed to be no air to breath, no sounds came from him. He saw a truck come screaming towards the van. He clamped his eyes shut and heard the loudest, most awful sound he had ever heard. Like being inside that nuclear explosion from his nightmare. Whiteness filled his vision. He saw strange silhouettes cast over the panelling in front, then something heavy and wet hit him in the side of the head. Another awful twist of metal, like being inside a crushed can of Coke… then blackness came.

———

Chris opened his eyes slowly. The first shape to appear, a flashing red dot. He squinted slightly, thinking it to be the red beacon atop the Stivyakino TV Tower. The slight ringing in his ears changed to a more metronomic beep. He opened his eyes fully and the blurry shape in front of him pulled focus and became a life support machine. His head throbbed. He tried to sit up, but a firm hand against his chest prevented him from doing so.

"Don't try to sit up. Stay as you are," came a soft, yet firm voice that did not belong to his mother.

"Hey, Kit," same the familiar voice of Uncle Tone.

Chris winced and smiled.

"Where's Mum?" he croaked.

"Just get some rest," Uncle Tone replied, a worrying waiver in his voice.

"Danny? Does my bro know I'm here?"

"He does."

"Dad coming to get me?"

"Just get some rest, Kit," replied Uncle Tone, his voice drifting off into a croak at the end of his sentence. Chris had no willpower to fight the desire to sleep. He wanted to sit up and see his uncle or ask more questions and analyse that strange tone that seemed to fill him with dread. Instead, the beep of the machine he was plugged into became a lullaby. He let his eyes close and the red blinking light of the Stivyakino TV Tower took him far away.

Uncle Tone stood up when he saw Chris fall asleep. He looked over to the nurse by the bedside. She gave him a warm, bedside smile. Her eyes were red too. Both she and Uncle Tone knew that the road ahead for Chris was dark and painful. Uncle Tone knew that they were in hell.

Uncle Tone left his sleeping nephew to make his way to the waiting room where he found Julie, in the corner, inconsolable. He sat next to her and she fell into his arms, sobbing her life away. Tone Redding wanted to cry too, he wanted to howl and wail but no tears came. He cradled Julie and stared blankly at the wall, trying to figure out just how to tell Chris Redding that his entire family was dead and was never coming back.

TWO
WARRIORS

Chapter 17
Now What?

Chris flexed his red knuckles and winced as the cold water ran over the cuts and scrapes; the red blood flowing pink as it diluted down to the small drain outside Sibley Hall. He grimaced as the blood finally stopped swirling.

"Shit," he mumbled, the right side of his jaw aching more than the left – the result of a vicious final blow. He turned off the tap and looked up to the roof of the tall building; the student halls of residence that stood in the middle of a field where Chris's peers gathered to play football and fight. The phrase 'Sibley Hall, 4 o'clock' was a challenge thrown down countless times by some kid or other who felt disgruntled or affronted by another at school. As soon as that phrase was uttered, the news spread around the school like wildfire: 'X is fighting Y at Sibley Hall, spread it.' The challenger was generally serious, or else they wouldn't have thrown the challenge down. If someone was challenged, they had to go. They had to fight. If they didn't: ridicule, or perhaps something worse. Perhaps they would be ambushed after school or at the weekend when they were least expecting it and by more than just one. A proper shoeing.

At Sibley Hall it was one-on-one and all the better for it. Also, often, the fight consisted of lots of pushing and shoving and insults before it petered out and both parties lost interest in actual brawling. If a punch was thrown, it had better land and knock the guy out or else you'd be dead. Most of the kids just wanted the rep, they didn't actually want to fight and get hit in the face. There were some kids though, some kids wanted it, needed it. They would fight anyone – weak kids, older kids, kids from other schools. They were crazy and to be avoided. Chris Redding was not one of those kids, but when one of them insulted his dead mother, the challenge had to be thrown down. Chris Redding was to fight the perfectly named Lee Hardman. Chris knew he was going to lose; he knew it was suicide but as soon as the challenge was thrown down, he felt better about it. Maybe Lee would kill him. Wouldn't be so bad.

Chris waited by himself at Sibley Hall. A crowd came and they bayed and jeered at him. Then Lee Hardman came on his bike. He was short and angry, hair cropped tightly and a permanent look of rage about him. A pitbull. He dumped his bike and walked through the crowd. Chris made two fists and readied for death. Lee didn't break stride, and clocked Chris right in the jaw, sending him down to the ground in an instant. The crowd laughed. Lee spat on Chris and made an obscene accusation about his mother's sexual proclivities before walking back to his bike and cycling off without acknowledging the crowd. The audience laughed and dispersed, leaving Chris lying on the grass in a daze. When everybody had gone, he got to his feet and limped over to the little tap by the wall of the building.

His limp not caused by the fall, but by the crash one year before – the collision that had claimed the lives of his mother, father and brother, but had denied Chris the chance to remain with them in everlasting peace. Instead, he was left behind on earth with a busted jaw that caused him pain when he spoke, a bald patch on the side of his head from countless operations. His limp was caused by the pins and plates that enabled him to walk again. There was a time when the doctors had thought he never would, instead being confined to a wheelchair. The thought of being stuck in a vehicle for the rest of his life terrified Chris more than the reality of his parents' death. A lifetime in prison. It galvanised him and he fought to walk again. Uncle Tone said he'd never been so proud to see Chris fight on and he really did until he left hospital and could walk at pace. Chris should've been vaguely happy that at least he had that part of his life. But instead of hope from the victory over his injuries, Chris found out that there was nothing left inside. No fight left, just anger and confusion.

Chris walked over to the wall and turned on the tap and splashed some water over his face. It was bracingly cold, like the late February air. He had 'died' in the later summer and been reborn in late winter, a whole portion of his life gone. Chris went back to school and found it an alien landscape. His friends not seeming to be as close any more. Not that they had abandoned him, it was just that they felt like ghosts.

Chris rested his head against the wall and felt the tears welling up, the sickness in his stomach returning as it always did. Then the anger came back and Chris bit his lip and punched the brick wall, two jabs and a right, with such ferocity that the skin split instantly and the blood gushed forth. He looked down at the water washing the blood away, the stream turning pink as it flowed down the drain, and he felt better. Something inside retreated into its cave to sleep.

He turned the tap off and flexed his knuckles. The bleeding had stopped. Chris zipped up his duffel coat and walked out of Sibley Hall, to make his way across town to what was supposed to be his home.

———

Uncle Tone heard the key in the lock turn and the front door open, the draught of wintery wind bothering his feet and ankles. The door slammed shut and then came the stomp of feet, down the small hallway and into the living room. He didn't turn to look at the visitor. Instead, he continued to stare blankly at the TV that had not been switched on in months.

Chris stood in the doorway of the living room and surveyed the scene. The room was tiny, barely bigger than his old bedroom. A narrow staircase ran up the side wall, leading to two bedrooms and an awful bathroom. The wallpaper was cream and peeling. It had probably been white at some point, but now it was tobacco-stained. The TV stood in the corner, under a little alcove beneath the staircase. In front of that, and next to the window was a threadbare, busted armchair. Next to that, a sofa that had no covers over the foam cushions. A glass coffee table in the middle of the room and that was that for furniture. The room was decorated with maybe a thousand empty beer cans and various bottles of spirits dotted around. Huge, mountainous ashtrays and tinfoil takeaway containers with remnants of food inside, cigarette butts jabbed into leftovers like gravestones. In the armchair, under a little blanket sat a zombie.

Chris looked at Uncle Tone and felt no anger or sadness. He felt nothing. The zombie was unshaven, unruly hair, sallow skin and grey eyes. He could truly be dead because Uncle Tone never moved. Although he must do at some point because Chris sometimes heard him shuffling around, perhaps heaving into the toilet, perhaps the 'tzissch' of a freshly opened can at any hour. Tone barely spoke. He had seemed strong and courageous during those months when Chris was in the hospital, learning to walk properly and undergoing numerous operations. He was vivacious and determined as if the death of the family had lit a fire under him. Indeed, when he told Chris that they would be living together, Chris was almost glad and excited for the future. He even dared to think of the phrase: 'a new start'. That all went to hell when they first arrived back at the squalid flat. They closed the front door and sat down on the sofa and that was that. The fighting had been done, the battles over and they were home. What now for the two warriors? Life.

"Hey Unc," said Chris.

Uncle Tone lolled his head to the side and for a few moments seemed to not recognise Chris. It was a painful expression, as if he had dementia and was rifling through his mind for a name to latch to the strange face. His eyes drifted into the middle distance, zoning out for a few moments before they snapped back to reality.

"What happened to your hands?" said Uncle Tone finally, his lips barely parting as the voice croaked out.

Chris shrugged. Uncle Tone turned his attention back to the TV. Chris looked to the floor and began to ascend the stairs.

"Where are you going?" murmured Uncle Tone.

"Do my homework for tomorrow," Chris lied. Uncle Tone furrowed his brow, the change in his dead face coming on like a drastic morph.

"Homework, what day is it?"

"Wednesday," said Chris, continuing up to his bedroom and leaving Uncle Tone in his armchair with nothing to do but drink and worry the armrests.

"Wednesday," he whispered to himself, as if the word itself held some lost and mystical meaning. He tried to crack a smile, but it wasn't worth the effort. He blinked slowly and fell into a drunken, dreamless sleep.

———

Chris closed his bedroom door and slumped on his narrow bed. The room was tiny and filled with stuff. He had most of his old possessions and many of his brother's too. The white CRT TV stood in the corner of the room, balanced precariously on a pile of comics that Chris was now too old to read. His brother's posters were stuck up on the walls, with Chris's haphazardly pinned over them – every image jostling for position and attention. Videos stacked up next to the little dresser, a box of old toys in the middle of the room. Chris looked up at the ceiling, no plastic glow-in-the-dark stars and comets. Nothing. Just the cracking plaster.

Chris lay there for a few moments, before he heard Uncle Tone opening another can. Chris rolled on to his side and looked at the blank TV. He reached over and picked up a video from the top of the pile. He had no intention of really watching it, but nevertheless, he leaned over and stuck the video in the machine. The TV wobbled on the uneasy stack of comics, and he noticed a few scraps of white paper poking out from the middle of the pile. He knew what they were but couldn't bring himself to regard them properly. He knew what happened when he did. The TV flickered on, and the trailers began to play. Chris ignored them and continued to stare at the edges of the paper.

"To hell with it," he said finally, before lifting the TV and sliding the stack of papers out. He rested the TV down and sat back on his bed. He paid no attention to the video; he'd seen the film a thousand times and now it was just white noise. He looked at the papers – twelve drawings of the Midnight Boy and the Special, drawn at a time when that future was as gleaming as the Stivyakino TV Tower depicted in them, and which now taunted Chris in his daily life. He ran his fingers over the drawings, trying to remember the adventures of the Midnight Boy and how it made him feel way back when he was alive. He recalled nothing. The tears began to force their way out again, the drawbridge raised, and his anger marched out to meet them. Chris snarled and slowly tore each picture into shreds, feeling no relief in the action, nor satisfaction in the sound of the rip. He lay back on the bed and let the shreds fall to the ground. They drifted on to the carpet, and some fell under the bed where they landed next to a boxed-up MegaSystem – a welcome home present from Uncle Tone that remained unopened and stashed away. What the hell use was that to him now?

CHAPTER 18
ROAD SAFETY

C hris awoke, dressed, washed in the small, filthy sink, grabbed a juice box from the kitchen counter, ripped the date off the paper calendar pad and left for school without breakfast. He was getting painfully thin, but nobody seemed to notice, at least nobody in his immediate circle, which included his uncle and the kids at school who didn't notice anything other than themselves. Of course, the teachers noticed. Most of them cast sad looks Chris's way when he limped by and they shook their heads and wrung their hands in private, unsure just what exactly to do about it. Let time take its course and heal his wounds? Let him forge his own path, or intercede and perhaps make a few serious calls to the local social services? Chris didn't know any of this, he just had a continuous knot in his stomach that he used to attribute to hunger in his other life but was now simply labelled 'guilt'. It twisted inside like his mother wringing out a wet towel, or the towrope on his father's old van and trailer. He hunched over, pulling his anorak tightly around him as he walked on. It was a couple of miles to the school, and he didn't want to take the bus. No moving transport for Chris. And it wasn't because he was scared, alright? He just liked to walk.

He crossed through the 'concrete meadow' – a car park next to a closed-down petrol station that some kids used to race remote-controlled cars in the summer. Chris looked down at the cold grey concrete and noticed the remnants of tyre tracks as the little cars once skidded and careened around the course. A winding trail of imperfection. He could not see the perfect racing line within the tracks and their miniscule width made them seem as if he were a giant, staring down at the racetrack of old – or perhaps floating above it, a great distance between himself and that perfect line that his dead brother never failed to find and that was now out of reach for the kid.

Chris hocked the contents of his nose to the back of his throat and rocketed them out, dashing the sludge across the concrete as he pulled the collar of his coat up tighter and looked ahead to the cityscape, grey and veiled in the early morning mist. His uncle lived up in Denmark Heights, which was a high part of the city – not nearly as high as Palmerston Road, which was, blessedly, behind Chris on the other side of the town, but still high enough to see the expanse laid out before him and the TV tower glinting away. It was a prison. Nobody left the city, they were born, they grew up, a few maybe set some records that stood for a season or a year or two and then they, like their records, were beaten by time. Chris sighed, bored already of his depressing thoughts and panorama. He trudged on towards school.

—·—

Tony awoke in his chair with a start, his eyes snapping open like awaking from a nightmare, despite his dreamless sleep. For a second or two, he felt cold dread on the back of his neck as if a telephone carrying the worst news had started to ring. He looked around, in a panic, his hands gripping the arms of his chair. Nothing. Still the same cans everywhere and the ashtray mountain range. He sighed in relief and slumped back in his armchair. It was a clearly a nightmare, but one of feeling over vision. He could not remember a single image, just utter dread. He wiped his eyes and pinched his nose, hoping to dispel the last of the phantom nightmare back into the void. His heart calmed down and some feeling returned to him. His toes were cold, his knuckles too, having slept exposed from the meagre blanket. Tone looked at the TV and saw the bottles on it, and on the little dresser beside – at least seven bottles of hard liquor and three bottles of wine. Not one of them was entirely empty. Some had a third left, some a dreg, some barely touched. Tone rubbed his head as he stared at the bottles, his eyes welling up. He had a problem, that's what she used to say long ago when she was still around, before she left him. He would write, he would drink and pretty much ignore her… just as he would ignore what he was drinking. He would leave half-drunk bottles in each room, he thought it was a whimsy – never far out of reach of a drink, but she said it was him forgetting and blindly reaching out for more, more, more. He couldn't see it then, but in that cold morning after the nightmare he couldn't even remember an image of, he knew she was right. What else could it be, what else did anyone expect?

Tone heaved himself up from the chair and slumped against the banister, leaning over and looking up at Chris's bedroom door.

"Let's go, Kit. Monday morning, new school week, new sixth-formers to crack on to, hot Art Teacher TAs to shine on, let's go!" He clapped his hands and turned to survey the scene. He shook his head.

"Looks like a flipping soap opera in here," he said to himself as he walked into the galley kitchen and grabbed a roll of black bags from under the sink. As he stood up, he noticed that it was one in the afternoon.

"Holy hell," he said with mild disbelief. He almost smiled at the extent of his blackout and considered smashing out the cleaning and taking himself for a well-earned pint, just one, when he noticed the calendar pad next to the bread bin. It was Wednesday. Tone leaned back against the fridge, smearing the vulgar poetry of magnetic letters he had composed some time, some when. For five seconds the sadness stormed his castle and the black bag fell to the floor. He drifted his gaze to an unopened bottle of wine lying inside the breadbin. Unopened! A divine gift from Dionysus himself. Tone took a step forward, his foot sliding on the black bag. He almost lost his balance but righted himself by grabbing the counter. He bent down and picked up the black bag. The battle was over. Tone completely forgot about the bottle of wine that almost felled him and walked into the living room. He felt alive and full of vim, of course he knew that he was still drunk, but he was going to put it good use… until about 15:30 when, if he wasn't in the pub taking one then he would crash hard.

"Do this, sink a few pints… but take your notepad," he said aloud as he began to throw the empty cans and the takeaway graveyards into the bin bag. "Take your pad and write something down, do a bit of work, sounds good."

Uncle Tone began to sing an obscure folk song as he worked, determined to outrace his dying drunken state and get a top-up before the see-saw tipped too far into sobriety and it all went to hell.

———

It was the last period of school and the day, thankfully, had been alright. Chris hadn't seen Lee and his gang all day (different half of the year). People hadn't taken the mick out of him for getting smashed in the face – a few people gave him that encouraging nod that said, "You're alright, you". In fact, in Geography he even received a smile from a table of girls as he limped into the room. He played it down by ignoring them as it was a very real possibility that they were smiling at someone behind him, but as the day wore on and his collection of nods and acknowledgments amassed, he thought back to the table of girls and dared to think 'Maybe that was for me?' Get smashed in the face and get a smile. Must be easier ways.

Chris sat on his own outside the classroom, waiting for the lesson to finish so that his class could occupy the space. His classmates filled the hallway. Chris had to sit down because his leg ached and so he did so, on a little bench that ran along the wall. The bodies all around him became a sea of white blouses and blazers. The chatter was intense, a strange symphony of discordant voices. Boy and girl and, curiously, man and woman. As the days and weeks wore on, the timbre and baritone of the hubbub had changed, almost a rumble sometimes and then if things were really heated, there would be a piercing squeal that cut through the air like a PE whistle, causing the group all to stop at once and, as one, burst out laughing – except one boy who would turn red, his voice having chosen the worst time to break, his full vocal range as yet unfinished. Chris looked at the floor and listened to the curious sound and felt even more excluded. He rubbed his jaw and throat, feeling the scars of his operations and knowing that his voice would never amount to anything other than a barely audible whisper. 'It's not so bad,' he thought, thinking of movies and enigmatic, silent types. 'What you got to say anyway?'

The door opened, one class rushed out of the room and one class stampeded inside. Chris was about to get to his feet when some unwieldy, large girl trod on his ankle and fell into a group of people. They laughed, quickly called her a collection of mean names and pushed her on. The girl fell on her knees and huffed, the regular insults chipping away at her. She was tough and had sustained the abuse for as long as she could remember but even she had limits, and she knew soon that they would be reached. She swore at the kids as they gaggled through the doorway, and she grabbed the strap for her bag. She looked around to see Chris Redding standing over her.

"Sorry, did I hurt your leg?" she said, swinging acutely from anger to horror as she realised that she had kicked 'Chris Cripple' (what her mates called him).

Chris winked and shook his head, curling his lip to suggest "Me? Not at all, never."

He reached down to her, extending his hand. The girl took it, and Chris heaved her up, trying his best not to let her weight show on his strain.

"I'm Kate," she said, smiling.

"Kit Redding," he said. "Sorry about the twats, they're…"

"Twats."

"You got it kiddo,"

Kate blushed a little.

"Do you know what this class is about?" asked Chris. "Saw a special notice up."

Kate shrugged. "Probably some exam prep rubbish."

"Sit next to me?" asked Chris.

"Really?"

Chris offered the way to Kate who smiled in disbelief (when her face was turned from Chris', lest he see). He walked behind her into the classroom.

The teacher, a tall, balding man, was at the front of the class and wheeling a huge TV in front of the blackboard. The lights were already dim.

Kate and Chris sat down next to each other. Nobody paid any attention to them. Those that mocked Kate seconds before had already forgotten about it; why should they remember? A few kids talked in hushed circles about Chris, some mentioned the 'fight', others talked about the accident. They whispered so quickly and quietly that it was barely audible even to each other. They all did agree on one thing though: Chris's brother Danny was an absolute legend.

"Settle down," said the teacher as he wrote his name on the blackboard, unaware that it was completely obscured by the huge TV.

"That's me. Mr Baker has the flu, so I'm the sub."

The kids weren't stupid – Scott had started a rumour in CDT that Baker was caught by his wife, English teacher Mrs Baker, getting a hand job from the PE Teacher Ms Germaine in the ball cupboard – the delicious irony not lost on them. The rumour spread and that was gospel. In truth, Mrs Baker had recently been diagnosed with cancer and Mr Baker, on her return, would be in for a serious grilling from them other kids about what happened in that cupboard. With his wife in hospital, he would just have to take the jibes and jokes on the chin. That's just the way it was with kids, rumours and teachers. Big deal, nobody gets hurt.

The substitute teacher closed the door and noted the class was still whispering.

"I said settle down!"

A helpful young girl in the front row, pointed to the TV. The teacher realised that his name was obscured and wheeled the TV to the side, to the sarcastic applause of some students. He ignored them. His name was Mr Baron.

"Alright, alright. Today for this lesson you just need to watch a video for 30 minutes, and then after that we'll have an open discussion about what we've seen. Understand?"

There was the requested collective "Yes, Sir" that had been marinating in boredom for 14 years.

"Excellent. Remember, questions at the end."

Mr Baron turned the lights off fully and switched on the TV, bathing the room in an eerie blue glow.

Chris rested his head on the palm of his hand, already bored. Kate, next to him, could hardly suppress her smile and rifled through every permutation of instigating some light petting in the dark with the gallant kid next to her. His walk was funny, sure, his voice was messed up but as her friend Stacie said, it was 'kinda hot' and of course his brother was a legend. Imagine a dalliance with that?

The static on the TV cleared and the video started. The atmosphere in the room remained exactly the same. Exactly the same except for Chris Redding, the only one in the room to move. He sat upright, his eyes a little wide, the wet rope in his belly tightening as if it were attached to a galleon's unmanned helm in a maelstrom. He grew instantly cold across the brow. Next to him, Kate didn't notice at all.

On the screen, a slow-motion sequence of a car smashing into a wall, the crash-test-dummies flying through the windscreen and crunching awfully into the bricks. The title card appeared: "Road Safety Part One: Careless Crossing Costs Lives!"

CHAPTER 19
A FLASH OF ANGER

Three crashes into the video and Chris snapped. The images were coming thick and fast in that dark room as if just for him and his own private torment nearly caused his stomach near rupture. The cold sweat over his brow, the trickling sweat down his back and the slideshow of memories returning from a deeply sealed vault inside that had now been cracked. Up until that moment, he had barely any recollection of the crash – he remembered his father turning to him, asking Chris to speak up. He remembered the full beam headlights flooding the interior of the van, bright, searing and altogether out of place, the shadows from the beam unlike any he had seen before. Upon reflection, when asked by the doctors what he could remember and he thought on those beams of light, the only thing he could liken it to was being abducted by aliens. Now, things were coming back. A look on his mother's face, a manipulation of the shadows as a hand was raised to protect a face, a strange and slow shadow-puppet theatre playing out against the metal panelling of the van, opposite Chris's bench. The thud and twist of the impact, the roar of an engine. The feeling of warm liquid spattering his face. Something heavy and wet colliding with the back of his head. These images came back to him now, in that class in front of the video. But there was more to recall. The accident over, the deathly silence that followed as if the whole of existence had held its breath in shock. The van having fallen on to its side, Chris saw the contents of his dad's glove box broken free and scattered across the floor, pulling the blood into smears and patterns that looked like tyre streaks – some oily gloves, a cassette tape with its innards blasted out, a grubby A-to-Z and a half-eaten sausage roll. As Chris lay there in silence, he looked at the items, unblinking. His father, his family. The details of them all.

The fourth crash played out and Chris, before he knew what was happening, had leapt out of his seat in class and staggered backwards. Everybody gasped and looked around. His eyes wild, Chris had no control over his actions, his thoughts racing to conclusions faster than he could control, making decisions faster than he could rationalise. Immediately Mr Baron stood up and flicked the light switch to see Chris Redding ashen white. The substitute teacher looked at the other students to see a similar look of shock.

"What's the matter?" he blurted out.

Chris felt his bowels issue the warning sign. Expulsion imminent. He had to get out of there. He pushed his way through the desks.

"Where do you think you are you going?" snapped Mr Baron.

Chris didn't even consider the truth, it was too horrific, to visceral to admit and so he deflected.

"Got to go, Sir," he said, a bewildered smile breaking across his face. He turned and smiled to the class, "It's Kate… she's got a fishy fanny and I can't stand it!"

It made no sense, but that didn't matter. The class erupted into laughter, immediately forgetting the shock and understanding it to be a great stunt. Kate's jaw dropped and she found what seemed like a million fingers pointed, a million eyes gleaming with laughter – her instant humiliation equal only to the noise. All her life she had put up with the jibes over her weight and her looks which did not sit well with the dominant ideology of the times and especially not in her school. Kate screamed, not in fear as Chris had, but in utter anger. Whereas something snapped in Chris, for Kate in that moment it was released. The laughter didn't stop, but the scream still came. She stood up and with remarkable strength upturned her desk to more jeers. But when she picked up the wooden chair and swung it like a hammer throw over the kids' heads and against the wall, shattering it into kindling did the jeers turn to fearful screams. Mr Baron darted from the door over to the violent beast to suppress it and save the class. Chris could not linger, and he chose his moment to slip out and hobble as fast as he could to the nearest toilet. He slammed the cubicle door shut and only just managed to sit down on the seat before the volcano erupted. No relief as the exodus came, just grief and guilt. The cubicle was mercifully small and so, without moving from the seat, he was able to jab the door with both hands repeatedly until he had reopened the wounds on his knuckles.

———•—

The flat had been cleaned to an appropriate standard and Tone had gathered up all the loose change from the various trousers and jackets littered around the place. A few coins here, even a note there. Enough for at least three pints. Three pints in the Arms, or eight cans in the park. Simple maths.

Tone sat on the park bench with the blue plastic bag next to him, a heavy coat pulled tightly around himself to preserve the cold. Winter was breaking and soon it would be warm spring but until then, staying outside was an activity reserved for postmen, dog-walkers and the drunks in beer-jackets. Tone observed the walkers in the early afternoon, strolling through the park throwing balls and sticks for their dogs. They seemed happy in their lives, almost blissful and he wondered what they would think of him if they deemed to cast a look his way.

"Poor drunk idiot," Tone answered aloud, smirking to himself that they didn't have a clue what he had been through in his life, let alone the last year. He pulled a raggedy notebook from his pocket and opened it. He took a sip of beer from one of the cans and tapped the pen against his jaw, looking at the dog walkers and then down at the blank page. Would their lives not inspire him? There could be anyone over there, imagine a circumstance for them. Nothing came to him, so he drank on, but remained staring at the blank page hoping to pull some inspiration from the mire of memory. Something divine. Something good. Something to fire up his engines and get him writing again. Anything. Nothing.

———

They had caught up with Chris. After he had calmed down in the toilets, he crept out. He couldn't sneak home as his school bag containing his house keys was still in the classroom. He decided to wait around until class was over and then, in the salmon stream of children coming and going from classroom to classroom, he could dart in and grab the bag.

Chris skulked around the empty corridors and open-plan areas of the middle school – the tiny microcosm of the larger school in general. There was a general sense of segregation in the school system – a lower school and then middle school and finally the upper school which contained the cool sixth formers who wore suits instead of uniforms. Some of them had cars and were allowed to park among the teachers. Chris sat on a bench in an empty corridor, resting his aching leg and looking down at his bloodied knuckles. He flexed them and thought about Kate. He was angry, and full of pain, that much was obvious but nothing like what Kate was going through. Nothing near it and he wondered then about all the other children in his school – even the bullies, even Lee Hardman. He was surely the only orphan in school, but everyone else must be going through their own hell. Chris stood up, knowing that he should make his way to Ms Gardner's office, the head of middle school, and own up. As he approached her door, he was distracted by a hubbub from a classroom, an unusual sound in the sense that it was clearly not due to any lesson, or any kind or trouble. There was laughter and jokery in the noise, unfettered and unfiltered. The kind of laughter that was loaded with relief that parents or teachers weren't around: an after-school club.

Chris looked at the half-opened door for a few moments, trying to guess the ages and even the identities of the kids inside, assessing whether it was safe to enter. If they were tough kids and he just strolled inside, what then? The laughter was light, and the language seemed tame enough, but what convinced him to open the door was another sound – unmistakable. An engine. A high-pitched rev and whir that peaked and descended in a pleasant two second burst. Chris reached out and pushed the door open. Inside the room, six young kids were leaning over a table inspecting a radio-controlled car. One kid, chubby and with greasy hair was holding a radio controller. Another slight kid in glasses leaned over to the upturned car and jammed a precision screwdriver into the engine, tweaking the car slightly. He nodded to the chubby kid who gave the controller a twist. This time the engine sounded less whiny, more real and angrier.

"It's got some bite," said Chris from the doorway. The kids stopped and looked at him. Chris leaned against the frame to take the weight off his leg. The kids just thought he was being cool, leaning like a rock star with bloody knuckles.

"You're Danny Redding's brother," whispered the slight kid. The other kids stood up to look at the brother of a legend.

"I'm really sorry for what happened," said the chubby kid, looking down at the floor.

"Thanks," said Chris, "is this a club?"

"Yeah, it's a racing...I mean, a radio-controlled car club."

"You race?" asked Chris.

The kids looked at each other. Though he was the brother of a legend, he had interrupted their club and had blood on his knuckles. He was an unknown quantity.

"On the weekends," piped up a gangly kid from the back of the group. "They turn the gym into an RC raceway at the weekends."

"Private?"

"Public."

Chris stepped into the room. The boys stepped backwards, just slightly. Each of them sure that any one of them was about to get decked. Chris looked down at the car.

"My brother used to have an RC."

"I bet," the gangly kid dared to say. "He was the greatest ever."

"Yeah, well, he's dead now," said Chris, looking at the underside of the car and inspecting the innards.

The other boys looked at each other once again. Chris stood from his stoop. The kids leaned back.

"On the weekends?" he said, "I might pop along. Would that be okay?"

The gangly kid looked at the chubby kid with a confused expression.

"Sure," he said finally, "if you want to race, there are club fees. It's 50p to –"

"Free for you, of course" interrupted the slight kid.

"Why free?"

"Because you're Danny Redding's brother. You're a legend."

Chris smirked. "He's the legend, I'm just the brother."

Chris held out his hand to each and they tentatively shook it one at a time.

"Kit Redding," he said.

They all replied at once – Chris thought he heard a Martin, a Paul and perhaps another Chris. He was about to ask them to repeat it when the fateful and feared sound of Ms Gardner clearing her throat came from the doorway. Chris sighed and turned around. Ms Gardner, a petite woman with jet-black hair who always seemed to be half-running/half-walking everywhere extended her arm and showed the way to her office. Chris was normally a good kid – well, he used to be – and so any reason for him to be in her office was usually based in his fantasies. There were no two ways about it, Gardner was fit, and most of the kids in middle school, rushing into adolescence, held her up as an ideal. She looked sternly at Chris with her brown eyes.

Chris winked at the RC club and walked out of the room, trying his best to hide his limp and appear strong and cool. When the door closed, the attention from the lads was no longer on the car, but on the cool kid who was now their friend.

———•———

Ms Gardner looked over her desk at Chris, her arms folded. She had his file on her desk, closed – more of an affectation of dread than a reminder of who the boy was. She knew, of course she did. Everyone knew and the teachers had held quiet and sad meetings soon after the accident about what would happen should Chris ever return to school and how to track his behaviour and flag up any problems. Nobody wanted him to fail; they wanted him to be strong and they were happy to hear that he had learned to walk again, that he had no obvious brain damage and though his jaw was broken in several places, he would be able to talk. But the emotional scars? The teachers took it upon themselves to keep a distanced, private eye on him and head off any more disasters at the pass.

Chris sat opposite Ms Gardner and looked at the desk, rather than at her.

"We let you down," she said finally in a flat tone. Chris looked at his lap.

"Mr Baron is from another school and though he had heard about what happened, the whole city knows, he didn't realise you were in his class. He was following the curriculum. I will have a word with him."

"It's okay," said Chris, massaging his aching knee a little, "it wasn't his fault."

"It must've been awful, utterly distressing,"

Chris shrugged.

"No?"

Chris sniffed and looked up at Ms Gardner, meeting her gaze with fierce, watery eyes. His jaw clamped shut as best he could to help maintain his composure.

"What happened?" he muttered.

Ms Gardner too felt the sad tide rising inside for the kid.

Chris looked suddenly to the wall and wiped a tear away. He took a breath and sniffed again.

"It's okay, Chris"

"What I did," he said, meeting her gaze once more, "to Kate. That wasn't me. That's not…"

"I know," said Ms Gardner. "It's perfectly normal to feel what you're feeling."

"Have you spoken to her?" interrupted Chris. "What will happen?"

"She has been suspended for a week."

"But…"

"She damaged school property and that cannot be tolerated, but that's a minor matter considering. The psychological damage, it will be better for her if she took some time off. Hopefully, in a week she might feel confident enough to come back to school. Hopefully the memories of her peers are short"

"I should apologise to her. Now, rather than in a week I should think. Shouldn't I?"

Ms Gardner unfolded her arms and sighed. She nodded.

"But how?" she asked.

Chris looked at his lap and thought for a few seconds.

"I will write her a letter," he said finally. "I am not good at writing, that's my uncle and maybe he can help me say what I want to say"

"As long as it is what you want to say."

"Yes Miss, would be little point in getting him to do it for me, wouldn't it?"

Ms Gardner smiled and sat back, "Yes, yes it would."

"Miss, if I bring the letter in tomorrow to you, will you send it on?"

"I will."

"You can read it if you want."

"It's not for me to do."

"Okay, well, can you do me a favour?"

Ms Gardner raised an eyebrow that forced a little grin from Chris and the faintest of blushes.

"If the letter works, can she be allowed to have her suspension cut short if she is ready to come back?

Otherwise, she will miss the school trip on Friday and that's not fair. Not for something I did."

Ms Gardner smiled and nodded. "I will think about it."

Chris broke out into a relieved smile.

"Go along home," she said finally. "We'll write this up as a detention. There's no need for you to stay back any longer."

Chris took his cue and stood up, wincing a little as he did so. He walked to the door.

"You know," said Ms Gardner as Chris reached the door, "I taught your brother when he was your age. English."

"What was he like?" asked Chris.

"Different from you," she said, with a sincere, hopeful smile.

Chris rested his head against the edge of the door, looking down at his shoes. He smirked and nodded. "Yeah," he said, tilting his head and looking back at the Head of Year, "that's what everybody says."

Chris left the office and shut the door quietly behind him.

"Bo good, Kit," Ms Gardner said to herself.

Until the day she died, she could not recall what had caused her to take the risk then and there; to put upon the broken boy such weight and invoke the shared memory of his dead brother. But she did so and until the day she died, Marisa Gardner never once regretted doing so.

Tone was running out of cans, and his beer jacket was wearing thin. The cold air was penetrating and causing his left leg to jig. God knows how long he had been in the park; the sun was setting, and the dog walkers were starting to come back for the second walk of the day. Still, he sat, looking down at the blank page on his notebook. He opened the last can, the 'tssch' of the ring-pull at once both warming him and reminding him that it was the last one in the bag. He took a sip and looked across the park, hoping for last gasp of sudden inspiration. He froze mid-pour when across the way he saw a young woman and man, walking arm in arm, pulling each other close to share their body heat against the breeze. Uncle Tone squinted at the couple, wiping his mouth with his sleeve. It was her. He smiled broadly upon seeing Julie across the park, arm interlinked with a new boy. She was moving on, getting on with her life, breaking away.

"Good for you, girl," said Tone to himself and he looked down at the blank page and scrawled.

> 'There was a boy who had a brother and the boy lived fast in drink in words. But the brother was taken away and with him the words. What was left was the drink and on that ocean floated buoys of pain, guilt and fear.'

"Well, it's a start. A ropey one, but you can only go up from there," he said with a satisfied grin. Tone nodded his thanks to Julie and her new man, pocketed his notebook and decided to head home, finishing the can along the way. Just a short paragraph written, and certainly not the greatest ever put down, not even the greatest he had ever written but he felt that a corner had been turned and that was worth so much. So much.

Chapter 20
Kalimotxo

The downstairs was relatively clean, the upstairs still a disaster zone. Tone returned from the park, swaying slightly and feeling woozy from the impetus the little paragraph had given him. He stood in the entrance of the cramped living room and leaned against the wall. He pulled out his notebook and reread the paragraph hoping that a second idea might spring to life. Then maybe a trail or a string to follow, a single idea, maybe an event or an ending that would birth a universe in him – that Big Bang of a story and a chain reaction of ideas and feelings to burst into life and rejuvenate his dull mind. Nothing came to him at that moment. He sighed and stowed the book away, looking up the staircase to the rooms upstairs. May as well finish at least one thing he had started. Under the vigour of drink, he grabbed the roll of black binbags lying handily on the chest of drawers nearby and marched up stairs to clear the cans from his room and, in another bag, grab the laundry from both rooms.

Tone blitzed through his own room in minutes. The room was bare – just a rickety old bed, a bookcase with a few well-read books upon it and a dusty typewriter on a desk by the window. Next to the typewriter, a little plate of mouldy bread ringed by crushed cans. The cans, the food and even the plate went into the bag. It was too far gone, too encased in festering mould to be used again in any healthy manner. Into the bag it went. It was the only way to be sure. Laundry into the other bag. He smiled at the discarded clothes, a few socks, then trousers, then shirt dropped in a manner that made it appear as if the owner had slowly disappeared, leaving only a breadcrumb trail of vestments leading up to the bed. Into the bag and the job was done. Still encouraged by the booze, Tone turned and went into Chris' room. He flung the door open and couldn't remember the last time he had been in there. The room was the opposite to his own: full of clutter. Old toys kept from his previous house and life, boxes of salvaged family possessions stacked up in the corner, the TV on a stack of comics. A living shrine. Uncle Tone took a deep breath and surveyed the scene. He was drunk, but not stupid. Chris was not home but would be any second and, as an angry young man, probably wouldn't think too kindly at discovering an adult rifling around in his room. Plus, the sheer scale of the operation felt too daunting to undertake. Where to start, what to do? Uncle Tone suddenly felt the need to go to the bathroom, the cans of beer catching up with him.

"To hell with it," he said, motioning to close the door. He stopped when his attention fell to the floor and to the pile of torn up papers by the bed. He could see crayons and pen marks, clearly drawings ripped up. Art broken. Uncle Tone had, in moments of anger, torn up countless pages of scribbles, even whole manuscripts that used to be brilliant but suddenly appeared awful in moments of dark despair. He had torn, discarded, flushed and burnt so much and always, always bitterly regretted it later, for he knew when the dark clouds part, the horrible realisation that a brilliant idea, a beautiful darling had been destroyed and cast into the ether to be forever forgotten. Tone rarely thought as passionately about anything save the self-destruction of his work. He knelt and scooped up the fragments of paper and stuffed them into his pockets. Now it really was time to relieve himself, and so he dumped the bags, turned ninety degrees and stood facing the bathroom door.

—·—

When Chris walked into the living room, he almost double-took and backtracked outside to check the address. The place had changed, the cans gone, the ashtrays cleaned and the cushions on the sofa turned over. The only thing that confirmed that this was his address was his uncle, sitting on his chair as usual, no longer staring blankly at the TV, but hunched over the cleared coffee table, poring over little scraps of paper, moving them about, considering, and then moving then back again.

"What you up to?" asked Chris.

"How was school?"

Chris clapped his hands, the sudden snap bringing Tone up from his task.

"What are you doing?" asked Chris, this time a little louder and with a little more labour. Uncle Tone looked around, his eyeballs rolling about the room like pinballs. Then they glinted.

"I'm doing a jigsaw," he said, looking back down at his game, "I was tidying up…"

"I can see," said Chris dumping his school bag down and slumping into his chair.

"Went into your room, don't worry, didn't touch anything, didn't find your mucky mags…found these on your floor. Fascinating."

Chris rolled his head to the side, his interest in his uncle's game suddenly piqued. He instantly recognised one of the fragments – a car wheel and a slice of black cowling.

"That's private," he said sitting up.

"It's now public," said Uncle Tone, reaching down beside his chair and lifting three complete puzzles, haphazardly re-assembled and bound with sticky tape. Chris reached over and snatched the remade drawings from his uncle.

"They're for the bin," he said, motioning to rip them up. Uncle Tone lurched from the table, both hands out like a springing zombie.

"No, don't!" he yelled.

Chris sat back, a little startled at the sudden outburst.

"Sorry about that," said Uncle Tone, "took me ages to rebuild those. They're great."

"It's just pictures, just shit pictures. That's why I ripped them up. Meaningless."

"Meaningless pieces of paper are scrunched up and tossed into the bin. Pieces of import are torn to shreds. It's a statement," said Uncle Tone. "They are great, what are they about? What do they mean?"

"Nothing, just some stupid character."

"Wait!" said Uncle Tone, halting Chris with one finger and leaping from his chair and darting into the kitchen where followed the requisite clattering and crashing of an inspired drunk going about his business.

Chris sighed and smiled, happy to have his uncle back from the dead. Tone returned and slammed down an unopened bottle of wine on the coffee table.

"Found this beast in the bread bin!" He said, before putting down two glasses.

"I'm not really a wine kind of guy," said Chris having tasted only shandy and some vile sparkling stuff once, a long time ago when it was summer, and the smell of grease and petrol was in the air.

"Fear not," said Uncle Tone, producing a bottle of Coke from under his arm and slamming it down on the coffee table, causing the glasses to chink. He opened and poured the wine, sensibly giving Chris only a little and himself way too much, pouring it as if it were a pint. He opened the Coke and topped up Chris' glass.

"It's called Kalimotxo, the Spanish kids drink it. Let's go!" and he clapped his hands, grabbed his drink and sat back in his chair, both eyes on his nephew.

Chris hesitated.

"If you don't like it, I'll have it but at least try a sip and tell me about this character of yours."

Chris took a deep breath and picked up the glass.

"Good man," said his uncle. "Don't gulp it down, just sip it and if you don't like it, leave it to one side."

Chris took a sip. It was sweet, but with a pleasant sting. He smiled and sat back, keeping hold of the glass.

"So then," said Uncle Tone, his notebook out and resting on the arm of the chair.

Chris looked at the reassembled picture by his side.

"It's nothing, a stupid thing. Just something I came up with back…before…"

"If you don't want to talk, it's fine," said Uncle Tone, suddenly hit with the realisation that of course it was a painful topic, of course it was from before, why else would he have torn it to shreds? Most of the time, drunks really don't think a lot about going too far.

Chris took a sip of his drink, a slow, nostalgic smile breaking out, as if recalling an old friend long forgotten.

"He's called The Midnight Boy and he drives."

It was approaching ten at night before Chris came to the end of his tales of the Midnight Boy. At first, his outlining was slight, but his uncle kept asking questions, kept probing and kept offering up suggestions and ideas which Chris either took on board or batted back. To his amazement, Chris found that he could field any and every question thrown at him – as if he knew every facet and detail of the entire world he had once created. Not only that, but a sense of right and wrong when it came to story and structure. He intrinsically knew what 'felt' right so when Uncle Tone suggested that the Midnight Special could be upgraded after one adventure so that it could fly, or if one time he fought off vampires, Chris found himself arguing back vigorously and convincingly that it didn't fit the tone of the world. By nine o'clock he had the complete makings of a huge ongoing series of stories, all linked, all leading to the next, all building up – twenty central characters and their hopes and fears, their wants and desires. Uncle Tone was relentless in his questions, but never once took a single note down in his book.

When ten o'clock rolled around and the carriage clock chimed on the mantelpiece, the Midnight Boy had driven his last adventure, defeating the Big Bad and driving off, out of the city and towards another; a definite end to the story, but a tasty hint that the story could continue one day. Chris, on realising this ending, tailed off into a slight daze and then he sat back in the chair.

"Yeah, so that's about it."

Uncle Tone sat back in his chair and looked at his nephew. "Quite a story. Quite a story indeed."

Chris poured the last of the wine and mixed himself a kalimotxo. He nodded in agreement.

"So why did you tear it all up?"

Chris couldn't answer. He couldn't believe that he had done it. He shook his head.

"Incredible, isn't it?" said Tone, "what we destroy when we are on our knees, what we give up on. And look what you have created from all those shreds. Not just your pictures and a few fantasies any more, are they?"

Chris shook his head, amazed at his creative achievement and realising then what his uncle went through from time to time and how, in the days, months and years in between inspiration, how futile and cold the real world must be.

"But then," said Chris, still looking at the pictures, "if I hadn't ripped 'em up, we could never have rebuilt them."

"Indeed. Out of the ashes and all that." Uncle Tone leaned forward. "Kit, Kit, my boy…,"

Chris looked at him. Uncle Tone tapped the pictures and fixed him with a fierce and committed stare.

"These aren't just pictures, it's not just a world that exists in your head. This can be your ticket out of here. This can give you whatever you want, in reality, in this life. This is the life that really matters because this is all you've got. If you want warmth, if you want hope… if you want your red beacon on the TV Tower, whatever it represents to you in your future. In this world, this is your way to get it. Understand?"

Chris nodded. "I think so."

Uncle Tone smiled. "You're gonna be something. Something that nobody will ever forget. This is how you're going to do it."

"You think so?"

Uncle Tone nodded. "I do. Now it's late, go to bed."

Chris smiled and stood up, grabbing his school bag. "Got a piece of homework to complete first, then bed." He walked to the staircase, halting at the third step.

"All things considered," he said, "it's been a good day. Thanks, Unc."

Uncle Tone raised his glass and smiled. Chris ascended. Uncle Tone waited to hear the bedroom door close before looking at the pictures and opening his notebook. He drew a line under the paragraph he had written in the park and wrote a second statement.

> 'The boy was a rebel and he railed against The Man. All in the city felt the pressure of The Man's jackboot. The Man was everywhere and in everyone, but he seemed to manifest himself inside the boy more than anywhere else in the city. But The Man was not a crooked politician, or an evil corporation, it wasn't the military industrial complex or any other form of authority. The Man was their weapon. The Man in this instance was fear itself and the boy would rebel against it. None of us knew if he would ever win, but we all knew deep down that he would never give in, never kneel. The boy would always rebel.'

Uncle Tone smiled and closed his eyes as he closed his book, falling into a dream-filled sleep. Above him, Chris sat on his bedroom floor, resting against his bedframe and writing a long, flowing and illuminating letter to Kate.

Chapter 21
Benson and Weatherly

The kalimotxo wasn't the best idea either of them had ever struck upon. While Uncle Tone slept, as he always did, in his armchair, Chris arose twenty minutes later than he usually would. His wake-up call was a bastard of a headache. On any normal day in the past, he would have played it up to his mum and got her to let him stay at home. It would be all too easy to get Uncle Tone to ring the school, if anyone would understand the severity of the situation, it would be a fellow soak. Chris looked at the clock beside his bed and almost convinced himself to pull the covers back over his head, but he remembered his duty for the day. He had a letter to deliver to Gardner, who would pass it on to Kate and if it worked out as he hoped, she would get the courage to return to school early and go on the school trip. Chris pinched his nose and heaved himself out of bed. Twenty minutes late. It was a near impossible task, but he had to get to school on time. He gave himself a cursory wash and covered up the unwashed parts with deodorant, threw on his uniform and rushed out of the house before even doing up his tie. In the armchair, Uncle Tone slept peacefully and contentedly, drifting through a world filled with dreams and promise. The first time in months.

Chris limped across town as fast as his tired legs could muster. The faster he went, the more incapacitated he looked, his movements enhancing his disability. As he hobbled passed a parade of shops, some old dears in the café tutted and sighed at the kid. One of them concluded that the boy must have suffered a bout of polio when he was a young boy. The letter in Chris's pocket spurred him on. It was his job to deliver and though the pain was great, he pushed on. The shopping bags his mother used to load him with now seeming like feathers on his shoulders. His goddamned leg. The wind was biting and did not help his mobility whatsoever. In fact, everything seemed to exacerbate the thumping headache. 'This is what Tone must feel like every day,' he thought as he rounded the corner to school and entered through the wide gates. The general population had already made their way to registration. Chris slowed down and his burning lungs caught up with him, but he had made it. There were a few late stragglers, the usual suspects, ambling up late as if it were no big thing. Chris walked over the grounds to middle school, trying to regain his breath and feeling the awful battle between hot sweat under his clothes and cold wind on his face. If his mother had been alive, she would no doubt have chastised him for playing out too long in the cold and foretold a bout of flu to hit him hard. Chris wiped his brow and pushed the double doors open and walked into the school and to his classroom.

Mr Sharma, Chris' tutor, was already taking registration when Chris opened the door.

"Mr Redding," he said as sternly as possible. Sharma was never strict or angry, but that by no means meant he was a pushover. Indeed, when the class first met him, they were dumbstruck by his demeanour. They had been assigned their tutor when they had first joined middle school and he or she would guide them through the next three years. Most tutors were fair enough, but Sharma was different – he treated them like adults, like friends. The first teacher to have ever done that and so there was never any backchat, just banter because he was a good man.

"Sorry, Sir," said Chris as he walked to his desk. Mr Sharma smiled and continued with the register. He had only reached the Bs and Chris smiled and tutted to himself knowing that he could have eased off in his frantic dash to school for at least 45 seconds and still arrived before his name was called.

Sharma finished the register and put the folder to the side and leaned against his desk.

"So then," he said, rubbing his hands together, "special treat for you all today. A lovely, special assembly."

Groans around the class.

"I know, I know," he said. "But think how I feel? I have to sit through the whole thing keeping an eye on you lot. None of what is said means anything to me, and still I've got to go. So, spare a thought for Sharma, will you?"

"Tough life!" called out Stuart from the back of the class.

"Has been since you lot landed on my doorstep," smiled Sharma. "By the way, Stuart, Mr Baker came by earlier and told me that you requested a transfer from rugby to the girl's netball team."

The class laughed.

"That's right, Sir. Better etiquette in the shower!"

The class laughed and so did Mr Sharma. 'You'll go far,' he thought. He looked to the side and saw the top of Ms Gardner's head through the circular window in the door, as she was too petite to stare through it fully.

"Alright, alright settle down, ladies and gentlemen, settle down."

The laughter petered out.

Gardner, as if on cue, opened the door. The class shut up and sat bolt upright, all eyes on the blackboard. Only Chris looked across at her as she scanned the room with her stern, brown eyes. He felt that they shared a connection. Something private and unknown, except to each other. The class remained deathly still. Why the hell was Gardner in their tutor room?

"Right then, ladies and gentlemen, off you go."

The class looked at each other and slowly got out of their seats. Gardner extended her arm and gestured for the children to file out, the class now suddenly all hoping that they were going to an assembly, rather than what seemed like an execution. Chris waited at the back of the class, wanting to tag on to the line and be the last out. Sharma smiled at his tutor group filing out, while

Gardner remained stoic until Chris came to the doorway. She reached out and halted him with a hand on his chest. Chris stopped and looked at her, that private connection seemed to be broken. She had that same stern look in her eyes. Had yesterday meant nothing to her? He looked at Mr Sharma who gave him a warm, kind smile with a subtext that said to Chris "Sorry, mate. Nothing I can do about it… good luck."

"This way please, Christopher," said Gardner quietly as she redirected her arm to the opposite direction from the class who were now merging with the rest of the tutor groups as they were vomited out of their respective classrooms. She was pointing towards her office. Chris assumed that it was to do with the letter, at least he hoped it was. He walked out of the room.

"Mr Sharma," she said professionally.

"Ms Gardner," he replied.

Gardner closed the door and scuttled up to walk beside Chris.

Before Chris could say anything, they had reached her office. He entered and sat in his seat, she in hers.

"Good morning," she said, folding her arms.

"Morning, Miss," he replied.

A heavily pregnant pause, and then she raised that eyebrow.

"Oh yes," said Chris, reaching into his inside blazer pocket and producing his letter. He handed it over to Gardner who took it.

"You wrote it. Good."

"Always do my homework, ma'am." He chanced a smile. It was countered with a stern 'hmmm'.

Chris motioned to stand, but before he could brace the armrests, he was halted by her outstretched hand.

"Please, not just yet, Christopher," she said, her expression changing in an instant from one of stern authority to one that, to Chris anyway, almost broached genuine concern. He sat down slowly. Gardner sat forward and sighed.

"You won't be going to assembly today, Chris," she said. For a moment, Chris had that feeling that something was up – chiefly because she had shortened his name from Christopher to Chris. The opposite to when he was in trouble with his mum, but no less serious.

"There are a couple of gentlemen in school today," she began, her words stretched out a little as she searched for the right tact.

"Police?"

"No, no not police," she said, furrowing her brow and wondering why he would immediately go to 'police'. "These gentlemen own one of the racetracks in the city."

"Oh."

"Indeed. They knew your family; I don't know if you ever met them, but they had big plans for your brother."

Chris looked down at his lap.

"And they are here today to make an announcement. I deemed it appropriate to talk to you privately first, rather than you hear it from the rest of the school because… well, it might be a little too sensitive for you."

"What's the announcement?"

A perfectly timed knock on the door.

"Seems like they have already made it," she said, standing up from her desk and walking to the door. As she passed Chris, she rested her hand on his shoulder and gave it a tender, encouraging squeeze. She opened the door.

"Gentlemen, please."

Gardner led two men into the room. Chris looked up and recognised them immediately – the two men who had been talking to his father and brother after Danny had won his last race. Chris motioned to stand up. The two men halted him, and sat on a bench against the wall, their caps in their hands.

"Mr Redding, it's a great pleasure to meet you" said the first and fattest of the two. My name is Mr Benson, and this gentleman is Mr Weatherly."

"Hello, Mr Redding."

"Hello," replied Chris darting a look towards Gardner who was sat forward, her chin on her hands. He could not read the look in her eyes.

"We had the great, great honour of meeting your father and your brother."

Both men crossed themselves, a gesture that Chris immediately filed under 'false' for reasons he couldn't quite fathom.

"Your brother was a true legend," picked up Benson, "and we had such high hopes for him. It really, really was a terrible accident. One minute they are here and then all our plans are…"

Gardner cleared her throat, her teacher's voice snapping Benson out of his inappropriate ramble.

"Thank you, Sir," said Chris, graciously.

"Well, we've just come from assembly where we made an announcement and we'd just like to run something by you,"

"After you've already made the announcement?" said Chris.

Gardner gave him a wry smile, but he didn't see it. He was looking at Benson and Weatherly with sharp eyes. The two men cleared their throats with embarrassment.

"Good point," said Benson, nudging Weatherly who reached into his briefcase and pulled out a green flyer.

"Well, we've announced that in six weeks we will be holding, in honour of your father and your brother, a charity street race."

"Not a street race, as such, more of a derby," said Weatherly. "A fun, family day of boxkart and soapbox racing." He handed the flyer to Chris who regarded it.

"We've got permission from the council, the route is set, food stalls, drink stands, face painting. Fun boxkarts – open to all, the wackier the better."

Chris was staring at the paper, seeing his family name plastered over a crude poster detailing the events of the day. Gardner looked keenly at his profile, unsure what the young man would do next.

He was sitting like a coiled spring, his grip on the paper tight.

"The proceeds from the race, sponsors and all that will go to setting up a foundation at the circuit to help bring up young racing blood. Who knows, there might be another Danny Redding out there just waiting to be discovered?"

Chris darted his eyes from the flyer and locked them on Weatherly. Both men stared back with wide, embarrassed eyes.

"Of course," corrected Benson, "there will only ever be one Danny Redding. What we mean by that is discovering a hidden talent, a gem out there who might not have the necessary means to drive like your brother did – bravely, fearlessly and with beautiful panache."

Chris smirked and looked back at the flyers. You could almost hear the two men exhale.

"We were hoping," said Benson, "that you would come along, maybe start the race, or wave the chequered flag?"

Chris gently put the flyer down on Gardner's desk.

"What if I wanted to race?" he said.

The two men looked at each other.

"Sure… I mean… sure, in theory, if you wanted to," said Benson.

"It's just that it's a circuit, many laps."

"So?"

"So, these aren't motor cars, these are boxkarts and soapbox cars…. pedal cars you see."

"And what with your…"

Both men gestured identically to Chris's busted leg with their flat caps.

"If it were downhill slalom then sure, but a circuit… well, it would last longer, more revenue from sponsors and trade stands. I mean, by all means enter… it's just…"

"The pedals," picked up Weatherly.

"I understand," said Chris, rubbing his leg. He picked up the flyer and rubbed his chin.

"80/20" he said finally.

The two men looked at each other and then to Gardner who shrugged.

"I'm sorry?" said Benson.

"80% of proceeds go to the special unit that helped me walk again, 20% to your pockets."

"I'm not sure I…"

"It's simple, gentlemen," said Chris, folding his arms and affecting as best approximation of his father's voice as he could. "You need my family name on your posters to get people there and get karts on the grid. And you've come here to ask if I could wave the flag, but what you're really asking is: 'Can we use your name?'"

"It's a great programme, a great academy we have in…"

"No doubt, but 80/20 in favour of the charity or you don't get the Redding name."

Chris looked at the two men.

"50/50?"

"60/40?"

Chris motioned to stand up, "Gentleman, I have to get to class."

The two men sighed and stood up. "80/20" they said, quietly.

Chris extended his hand. Benson and Weatherly reluctantly shook it.

"Ma'am," they said, putting their hats on and tipping them to her. She remained in her seat and smiled, politely.

They went to the door, stopping and turning back before leaving.

"80/20?" said Benson with a smile. "You are your father's son."

"My mother's too," replied Chris.

The two men left.

Chris turned and picked the flyer from the desk and folded it into his pocket.

"Are you okay?" asked Gardner standing from her desk and dusting down her jacket and pencil skirt.

"Yes miss," he said, flatly.

"You handled that very well, very mature."

"Thank you, ma'am," he said, "please do not forget to pass the letter to Kate."

"I will not. You may go to class."

Chris turned to the door.

"I'm sorry," she suddenly blurted out.

Chris turned back to her.

"Sorry you won't be driving," she said, a little sheepishly. "I'm sure you would've been great."

"Driving is not for me, Miss. My brother was the racer."

"I understand," she said with a smile and a shrug. "Still, flag-waving will be cool."

Chris opened the door, "I ain't no cheerleader either ma'am," he said with a mysterious smile and a glint in his eye. He closed the door and left Gardner alone. Privately, she had no qualms in thinking: 'You're really gonna be something.'

Chapter 22
Day Drinking

The day had started relatively well for Tone. He awoke with a meagre hangover, after a long, deep and dream-filled sleep. The place was still clean and fairly tidy but most remarkable of all was that he could remember everything from the night before. He didn't sit in his chair for a good hour after awakening as he usually did. That old ritual of warming up his bones like they used to have to do with Terry's van in the winter; keep her ticking over, and all that. Instead, on this day, his eyes pinged open and he remembered everything and so, with rejuvenated knees he sprang up, walked into the kitchen and made himself a cuppa. Slightly less remarkable than his total recall, but a near miracle nevertheless was that he found milk in the fridge that was not green paste and was entirely drinkable. The day was bright and crisp with puffy white clouds in the air. He poured the milk into his tea and smiled as he thought about the Midnight Boy and the ideas it had inspired in him. A book was forming in his mind – and as creativity germinates, the wider picture began to be revealed. The book would be his masterpiece and would be seen on every bookshelf throughout the city; they'd move out of the cubby-hole house and into something with a garden, a dog maybe, and a woman in a white cotton dress to bake bread and look after them both. Chris would go off to a good school, get his leg seen to and become whatever he wanted to become, maybe even a graphic novelist. Tone drank his tea and wallowed in the fantasy that was sure to come true, all because of the Midnight Boy and his Midnight Special.

"It's going to be a glorious day," he said to himself as he blew across the brim of his mug and looked out at the city though the grimy kitchen window.

—————

Glorious days, searing, bright and crisp, inspire great things in men and no idea on days like those are greater than that glorious one-word plan that can be an edict or a question, whatever suits you. The great declaration. And so, after washing and generally spending some time enjoying relative sobriety, Tone stood in the centre of the living room, stretched and then drummed his hands on his chest and to no one and everyone he said: "Pub?"

Tone grabbed his coat and scarf, flung them on, took his wallet and marched out of the house and towards whatever pub he deemed appropriate for his mood. This was his first mistake. Tone felt invincible, he walked head held high with a broad, satisfied grin on his face. Notebook in hand and money in his pocket, to the College Arms he went. It was a stupidly bold manoeuvre. To drink in the flat-roof pub that stood on the very edge of Palmerston Road? Lunacy. Before Tone knew it, his feet had taken him there and before he could turn back and flee the scene of his brother's death, he had pushed open the rickety pub door and stepped inside. His armour was noticeably chinked from the sight of the road and its precipice hill, like a concrete waterfall with the pub on the very edge, but the smell of the fetid carpet, mixing with the waft of those blue disc things in the urinals that turned his stomach every time someone went to the gents went some way to assuage the tickling dread in the roof of his mouth.

That road, that waterfall, that crash. What the hell was he doing there? He stood for a second in the doorway, looking around. The huge square bar in the middle of the room, some tables and chairs to the left, some booths to the right of it, pool tables and more seats at the back and a barmaid in the middle. He hadn't gone too far in. His back was still against the door. 'How about leaving and getting across town to the Swan?' he thought. 'Couple in there, a bite in the Greyhound, a few in the Denmark Tavern, to the offie, kebabs for dinner and back home for movies and food. How about that?' Tone reached behind his back and grabbed the door handle. 'But that goddamned road. Safer inside.'

"Alright, Tony?" came a hoarse, yet feminine voice from the bar. Angela, the barmaid had spotted him. She was short, pretty, pale and had her hair scrapped back across her scalp so tightly that she looked as if she had tied her ponytail to Concorde. "Haven't seen you in…" she cleared her throat realising when it was that she last saw him. "What can I get you?"She reached above her head, fingers ready to grab a pint glass.

'In for a penny,' thought Tone and he let go of the door handle and stepped forward.

"Pint of lager," he said with a smile. "Got any peanuts?"

"You bet."

"And some peanuts then," he said as he pulled a barstool from the bar and plonked himself down.

"Mind if I sit at the bar?" he said, after already committing to it.

"Not at all, quiet today. Usuals aren't in yet. Happy for the company."

Tony looked around the bar, it was indeed deserted, a fact that he hadn't taken into consideration when he was standing at the door. He looked up at the clock next to the dreaded bell that would throw them into the street. It was eleven in the morning.

"Jesus, I assumed it was lunchtime."

"Near enough for a liquid lunch," said Angela as she put Tone's pint down in front of him. The tasty beverage now caused him to think twice. Even a soak like him knew he probably shouldn't be smashing pints at eleven in the morning. If he did that, he would be hammered by three o'clock. Nothing worse than walking home smashed when the kids are coming out of school. That's a real wake-up call that you've gone wrong somewhere. Weekends are different, of course – schools are closed. He sighed and took up his pint.

"So, how have you been keeping?" said Angela as she bent down to bottle up the fridges underneath the bar.

"Same old," said Tone, "getting by day-by-day."

"I hear that. How's your nephew, what's his name? Cal?"

"Kit."

"Kit, that's the one."

"Ah he's just grand, he's a real beaut."

"How old is he know?"

"Nearly 15."

"Jesus, I'll probably be ID-ing him in here in not so long."

"Probably, probably," said Tony, taking another sip and not realising that he had drunk a third of his pint in two gulps.

"School going okay?" she asked as she threw the empty box over the bar and pulled a full box along the floor towards her. Angela ripped it open and started stocking up the second fridge.

"Yeah, well, I guess. Gets into a few scrapes. I think he had a dust up the other day."

"Really? That sucks."

"Nah, he's alright," said Tone casually.

"Well, you keep an eye on that."

"Nought wrong with a little fisticuffs," said Tony into his glass, the last of his early morning pint already making him say stuff that he would not normally.

Angela smiled and threw the empty box over the bar to join its brother.

He had made it past 3pm, just. The glory of his early morning wake-up and level head had inspired him to do little more than drink like a maniac. Pint after pint, and only three packets of peanuts in between. Tone tried to pace himself and had not done a bad job. He wasn't so hammered. A few of the locals had come and gone, a few had chatted to him, a few had ignored him. But they all knew who he was on account of his brother and what had happened to him.

"One more, darling," said Tone.

Angela surveyed his presence, he was good for a few more. 'Unless he vomits all over the bar or a patron, he's good to at least seven. Of course, if he starts on the back bar then that will probably be about four-thirty. But for now, pints are going down well.'

"Can I put a few creds on?" said Tone, leaning over the bar and trying to paw at a little black box on the wall, his fingers searching for the tiny red button on the box's side. Angela slapped his hand away.

"Bad boy, back in your box."

Tony smiled goofily and sat back on his chair, steadying himself on the bar rail lest he fall back off his stool.

"Go on, just a few then. Put it on random!"

Angela sighed and hit the button five times.

"You got five credits, knock yourself out."

Tony double fist pumped as if he had scored a winning goal and stepped over to the wall mounted jukebox.

"Any requests?"

"Nah, mate," said Angela as the pub door opened and a group of sixth-formers walked in, loud voices, strange teenage language, huge laughs. They immediately walked around the bar and plonked themselves down in the booths. Angela leaned over to Tony.

"What do you reckon?"

Tony leaned around the jukebox and looked at the young kids, surveying their youthful faces and noting their barely disguised apprehension of being in some place they shouldn't. Tone squinted one eye and knew that he could get Angela to ID them all and have them booted out into the streets. He smiled broadly.

"Yeah, go on, let 'em be. They're alright. A few weeks shy of eighteen, but it's a sunny day so who's counting?"

Angela nodded in agreement and turned from the jukebox to face the young adults in the booth.

One of the kids plucked up the courage to come to the bar. He ordered pints all round and put straws into the pints for the girls, a gesture which made Angela wince.

The songs started playing and Tone sat back in his chair. He began to drink his pint. This was his second mistake. Like his feet had taken him to the College Arms and the very edge of Palmerston Road, his fingers had chosen songs that they really should not have. Tony made it through the first two minutes of the first song before his demeanour went over the precipice. His eyes glazed over, his thoughts drifting from the pub and into memory. He brought forth the face of his brother as a young man, and then as a boy. Playing together, holidays at the seaside, arguments and fights.

Angela was a great barmaid and she saw it in an instant. Tone's shoulders had slumped a few inches, his head tilting to the side, his pint held at half-mast. Then he looked around the pub. An old man was sitting alone in a corner table, reading the racing news. Tone stood up, wobbled a little bit and walked over to him. He plonked himself down on a little stool by the table. The old man sighed and looked up from his paper.

"You ever meet Terry Redding?" slurred Tony, "he was the best, the real best. We used to go for runs in the… scouts too. And he was always first in races. Always… always that was Terry and he cooked. Remember the cherries and the apples? Remember that time we beat up Daz in the because of the… remember? Ah that was him. What a guy eh? My brother!"

Tony picked up his pint and smiled, but his eyes told the old man that he was lost. The old man tapped his glass and returned to his paper.

"I can see you want to be left alone, sir… good day!"

"Good day."

Tony's head wavered slightly as he looked around the pub, the potency of the drink exacerbated by the sad songs and the searing memories. Full inebriation was approaching like a bullet train. Tony spotted two men playing pool. He picked up his pint and weaved his way over to them.

"You ever meet Terry Redding lads?" he said, bumping into the table and disturbing the balls.

"Piss off, mate" snapped one of the men.

"Terry Redding, my brother. He was…he'll have you! He'll fuggin… box your ears!"

Both men stood up from their game and looked at the drunk. They didn't want to hit him; he was just drunk but there are only some many times you can be irritated in one minute by the same stranger.

"Tone!" shouted Angela, from the bar having kept her beady eye on him. Tony turned around to her.

"Come have a sit down, have a pint with me."

Tone smiled and flicked the V at the pool players. They swore back and returned to their game.

Tone left the pool area but instead of walking around to his seat, decided to walk the long way around. Angela moved around the bar too, so that she could keep an eye on him. Tone walked, running his hand along the bar until he spotted the group of sixth-formers. He locked eyes with a young, pretty girl whose demeanour immediately screamed out 'oh no' when she saw the drunk smile and walk over to the group. Tone did not sit down but stood at the opening of their booth and swayed for a few moments, staring at the girl with a stupid grin on his face.

"Can I help you, mate?" said one lad, a tall handsome man with his whole life ahead of him. Probably some gap year in a foreign land, loads of photos of beaches and sea fishing. The kind of kid hated by drunks. Tone didn't say anything. The group laughed and huddled in together.

"You know Kit?" asked Tone.

They ignored the drunk, instead giggling into to a huddle over their barely sipped pints. Tony did not like it. A sneer broke out on his face.

"I said, you know Kit?"

"No, mate," snapped one of the girls.

"Kit."

"Yeah, we heard you mate," said the boy with the future. "We don't know Kit."

"Kit Redding, about this big. Great boy, you must know him."

"We don't know him."

"Danny Redding?"

The group looked at each other.

"Yeah mate, course we have. That kid that died."

"That's right," said Tony swaying, "you know him?"

"No...why, was he your boyfriend?"

Some of the group laughed, the others saw the look in the drunk's squinted eye and thought that their mate might have just kicked a pitbull in the balls.

"What?" slurred Tone.

The boy with the future stood up. He was tall – taller than Tony, strong and sober.

"Alright lads," said Angela from the bar. "How about that drink, Tony?"

The lad with the future leaned into Tony. "Why don't you get lost, Granddad?"

Tony smiled and looked over his shoulder at the pretty girl he had originally zeroed in on. She looked uncomfortable.

"You look like someone I knew," he said, with that sense of conviction drunks possess. As if they were outing a spy or revealing a dangerous piece of information hitherto kept secret by the other party.

"Err... okay."

"What did you say?" said the lad.

Tony smiled and shrugged.

"Look Grandad, wh–"

Tony pushed the young man, sending him crashing on his back on to the table, knocking over the glasses like bowling pins. The other kids screamed and tried to climb out of the booth. Angela rushed around the bar and the pool players dropped their cues.

Tone grabbed the boy by the lapels and tried to punch him in the jaw. The boy was fast and whipped his head out of the way as Tone's fist slammed into the table. The pool players reached Tone. They were bouncers at a local boozer and so knew how to subdue drunks. In seconds, Tony was on the floor with a knee in his back. He began to scream and lash out, the music, memory and booze now taking over completely.

"Get the hell out," said Angela to the group of kids.

"But…" began one of them. Then they saw the look in Angela's eyes, and they rushed out of the pub.

"What about this idiot?" said the bouncer who was now currently using Tone as a beanbag. Angela looked down at Tony whose screams had changed to whimpers.

"Him too."

"Door, or window?"

"Door," smiled Angela, turning to Tony. She held his face in her hands. "Tony, love, sober up and get back to your old self. Till then, piss off mate."

The two men grabbed Tony by the arms and pushed him out of the door. Tony staggered around in the street for a few moments, the inertia of his exit threatening to barrel him on to the floor and down the precipice of Palmerston Road. He halted at the last second and stood on the edge. He looked down to the very end, to the crash site and the crosstown traffic that bisected the very nadir of that huge stretch. He wiped the tears away, but it didn't work. More came, then more and soon he was like a child. He turned away and trudged home.

———

Chris had been prostrate on his bed for hours after coming home from school. He had been staring at the green flyer, at the list of stalls and stands and of the outline of the proposed circuit, imagining all the brightly painted boxkarts and pedal cars racing around in the name of his dead family. He did not know if it was a good thing to do so, but he could not help but succumb to the fantasy. Chris heard the door open, and the clatter of Uncle Tone come through the hallway and into the living room as it always did. Chris got off his bed and went to see his uncle and inform him about the charity event. He halted at the door when he heard not giggles nor singing nor the 'tssch' of opening cans. He just heard sobs. Chris listened on, trying to find the right words to say. Trying to find the courage to go downstairs and witness a broken adult and still have the courage to remain strong and talk them down. He felt his own tears threatening to break free. He knew he was not strong enough and so he returned to bed, got under the covers and pulled his pillow over his ears to drown out the cries from the broken adult downstairs.

CHAPTER 23
PALMERSTON ROAD

O ne half of the middle school congregated around the three huge coaches parked outside the school, all dressed in their home clothes and talking excitedly and loudly about the trip ahead. A simple excursion to the observatory where they would sit in the dark and watch a long, boring video about the solar system, its creation and all other inconsequential matters. Still, they would not be in school, and they were dressed how they wanted to be dressed – in school, the groups and gangs were merged in their uniforms and their guard was usually down. They could not choose who they sat with, most of the time having that privilege taken from them. For that, they were forced to mix with the other kids and unlikely friendships had been formed over millennia-long maths classes, or over bunsen burners or apple pies in Home Ec that tasted awful. Most of these friendships were forgotten when the uniforms were switched to civvies. And as such, the groups outside the coaches were smaller, more tightly packed, more intimate, more intense – bands of brothers and sisters, little groups that always were and always would be. Until university.

The tutors tried to corral their pupils and pull them from their groups, but it was fruitless. The sun was up, the air hinting at a warm spring and the day ahead promised everything: kisses on the back seats, gropes in the dark.

The teachers had no chance of getting the students into their tutor groups so that registration could be taken. That is until Ms Gardner exited the school double-doors and scuttled over to the coaches. She was dressed as she always was: pencil skirt, white blouse and black blazer, a few books and a binder clasped to her chest as she hurried along. Even the other teachers had dressed down for the day. Gardner had not. She reached the hubbub and only had to raise her voice in one high noted 'um' and silence befell them all. The coach drivers stopped yapping and were suddenly overcome with an urge to hide their smokes.

"Tutor groups, please," she commanded.

There was a general harrumph from the pupils before they began to rearrange themselves, a great sea of heads moving about, a strange hive-mind activity that automatically took each pupil from wherever they were to wherever they had to be in moments.

Gardner nodded to the tutors who took out their registers and began to take the notice. Gardner, not content with controlling the classes, took the time to walk a lap of the coaches. She even kicked the tyres, just to be sure. Of what, she did not know but it made the coach drivers straighten their clip-on ties and remove the half-eaten sausage rolls from the dashboard. By the time she had finished her lap, the registers had been taken.

"All here," said each tutor as she passed them.

"Missing Redding," said Sharma, at the front coach. Gardner looked towards the school gates, then to her watch. They were fast approaching the minute that they should be on the road, and the pupils hadn't even boarded. She sighed.

"Let's go," she said, and stepped to the side of the coach door, offering a way for the teacher and pupils. Each class filed on to their coache. They passed their teachers on the steps of the coach in a dignified manner, but as soon as they were aboard there was a mad dash for the prime seats. Bags were thrown down as reservation markers, coats hung over other seats, pushing and shoving and general calamity until all were aboard and seated. The majority found themselves in undesirable seats – perhaps away from their friends, perhaps too far forward and within earshot of their tutor thus discouraging any illicit talk.

Sharma's group, along with another class, had boarded and he sat behind the driver. Gardner remained outside the coach. She looked towards the gates once more. No Chris. She climbed aboard and stood in the centre aisle.

"Ladies and gentlemen."

The pupils shut up and faced front.

"We'll be off shortly. It should be a good day. We have lots of exciting and educational activities for you."

Gardner looked down at the nearest pupil, a young boy with glasses who seemed to be years behind his classmates in terms of adolescence. He looked more like eight than fourteen. Gardner handed him a stack of green leaflets.

The boy took them and began to walk down the aisle handing them out to the pupils.

"Here are your activity packs. While we are travelling to the observatory, I would like you to read them carefully and discuss them with the person sitting next to you."

The pupils began to chatter, assuming that they were allowed to.

"*Only*," stressed Gardner, causing the chatter to cease and regaining control again expertly, "with the person sitting next to you. I want no noise, no leaving your seat, no messing about and disturbing the driver. Understand?"

"Yes, Miss," answered the hive mind.

Gardner surveyed the pupils for a moment. There was a general maudlin air in the coach. She smiled.

"There will be a gift shop."

Smiles and chatter once more. Gardner sat down in one of the front two seats, parallel to the driver, a full view of the road ahead.

"Off we go, Ma'am?" asked the driver.

Gardner ignored him and began leafing through her travel bag, and then through her clipboard and notes. The driver sat back and huffed, folding his arms and waiting to move out. The engine was rumbling over. Gardner read through the registers, she scanned the activity leaflet and she read her own notes on the plan for the day, all the while darting glances up ahead at the school gates, hoping to see him. Eventually, she could stall no longer. She put her clipboard on the empty seat next to her and nodded to the driver who tutted and pushed the coach off. There was a loud cheer from the pupils, instigated by the lads on the back row, which was countered with an even louder 'sssssh' from the girls on the seats in front. They moved towards the gate.

Chris Redding wiped the sweat from his brow and took a moment to catch his breath. He had overslept again, not because of drinking kalimotxo but through anxiety. His uncle, who had seemed to have turned a corner just two days ago, had now appeared to have turned back on himself. When Chris woke up, he found Tone slumped on the floor, kneeling penitently at his armchair, his head resting on the seat, a puddle of drool soaking through the cushion. Too drunk to even sit down properly, half-drunk bottles of the hard stuff all around. Next to those, shreds of paper. Chris picked up paper remains and inspected them. They were not the drawings of the Midnight Boy, those had been gathered and placed on top of the television, underneath a framed picture of their dead family. A shrine to the past and a declaration for the future. The shred of paper came from Tone's notebook. Chris knelt and found the cover and spine of the book on the floor. Eviscerated. Even the blank pages, the hopeful canvasses of future masterworks destroyed and dashed on the floor. Chris sighed and wiped the matted hair from his uncle's face.

"Hey," he whispered, "you should get up."

Uncle Tone opened a dead eye and looked blankly up at Chris.

"Sad song," he said, cryptically.

"Up you get, Uncle."

Tone's eye fell from Chris and focused on the inside of the arm rest and the frayed threads and weave, the foam inside exposed.

"Sad song," he said again.

Chris tutted and stood up. He clapped his hands. Uncle Tone didn't move. Instead, he waved a shaking finger at the door.

"Go to school" he said flatly.

"Sod ya, then," replied Chris, picking up his bag and leaving the house to make his way to school. The slamming of the door snapped Uncle Tone fully awake, and he sat bolt upright from his armchair prayer. His head was throbbing in a way that it hadn't done for years. A real bastard back there. He pawed at his hair, scraping at his eyes and cheeks.

"I'm not supposed to be here," he said as his other hand reached down for the nearest bottle of hard stuff.

———

Chris walked as fast as he could and had gone twenty minutes forward when he stopped outside the parade of shops and cursed into the air. The old women inside the café heard and looked out of the window and tutted. They saw the boy look one way down the street, before turning to look the other way, before looking at his watch, thumping his leg, and then hobbling off.

"Poor lamb must've had polio," said one, before returning to her tea.

Chris swore and swore and swore as he made his way to school. He had gone too far to turn back and knew that he would just have to suffer the laughs and jokes when he got there. He had overslept and had to deal with Uncle Tone before leaving and as such, had totally forgotten that it was a school trip day. He could have worn his own clothes and fitted in, but in his haste, he had put on his uniform. He reached the corner of the school grounds and halted. He wiped his brow and regained his breath. He stepped out and was almost flattened by a coach the size of an ocean liner. The brakes applied sharply, and the coach pitched forward. Chris stood for a second, frozen with an expression of stupid shock on his face. The coach pitched back and Chris stepped out of its path. He saw Gardner in the front seat, looking out at him. The door to the coach opened and he sheepishly climbed aboard.

Chris stood in the centre aisle and looked down at the eyes staring up at him. The further down the coach he went, the more kids had to angle out of their seat to look at him.

"You're late," snapped Gardner, looking at her notes. "Find a seat, and hurry."

"Yes, Miss," replied Chris and secured his bag on his shoulder. He walked down the aisle. Every seat was taken, he knew it would be and yet he went to the very back, passing the eyes and hearing the whispers, before turning back and walking to the front where he heard the sniggers behind his back and caught a few "twat" and "crippled bell-boy" remarks from the kids. He reached the front of the coach. Gardner looked up at him, both eyebrows raised.

"No seats, Miss," he said.

Gardner huffed and stood up, gathering her notes and her bag. She stepped out into the aisle and offered the window seat next to her.

"You'll have to sit next to me," she said.

"Yes, Miss," said Chris, unhooking his bag and sitting down. He placed his bag on his lap and looked ahead. Gardner sat back down next to him and re-organised her notes. She handed Chris an activity leaflet.

"Study this," she said.

"Yes, Miss."

Gardner turned to the driver and nodded. Again, the driver tutted and put the coach back into gear, checking his mirrors and driving out of the school slowly.

———

They had driven for twenty minutes and in that time, Chris had not said a word, he hadn't even looked at the leaflet, let alone looked ahead, through the great glass windscreen. Instead, he had held on to the plastic grab-rail in front of him and looked down at his backpack, his eyes fixed on the threadbare weave and the broken zip help together by a paperclip. His heart was beating fast, and heavily – the type of heartbeat that makes you convinced it's audible to the outside world. He tried to collect and order his thoughts. Go over the Midnight Boy, run through and galvanise the grand story and explore the world. It was tricky to do so for with each passing moment a dark voice in the back of his mind cackled at him 'you're in a vehicle, in a vehicle, in a vehicle' and it was true. It could possibly have been the first time he had been in a bus, car, coach or train since the accident. He walked everywhere and Uncle Tone was normally too drunk to drive. Maybe he had actively avoided transport, he could not be sure. What he was sure of was that he was now aboard a mighty vehicle, at the front and facing forward and cold sweat was beginning to break out across his brow. He could make it, he wanted to get to the observatory, forget about the journey for a few hours, then spend the next few hours preparing for the journey home. Maybe get a better seat on the way back and talk to someone, get his mind taken off this. Taken off the images flashing through his mind, strange shadow plays in the back of the van, cassette tapes smeared in blood, heavy, wet and unnamed objects striking the side of his head, that terrible sound of twisting metal, of being inside a Coke can that is being crushed by a giant. 'Think, Midnight Boy. Think, Midnight Boy'.

The coach pulled to a halt and Chris smiled to himself, relaxing his grip in the grab-rail. He had made it. He dared to look up and ahead. His smile dropped. The road had been cordoned off, a few police cars blocking the way, beyond them a fire engine and an ambulance. A policeman began walking towards the coach. Chris sucked in a lungful of dead air. Gardner looked up from her book and saw the scene ahead. Without thinking, her hand shot across and grabbed Chris'. She held it tight, her thumb over his knuckle. The policeman tapped on the coach door; the driver opened it. The policeman stepped aboard. The pupils all craned out of their seats to see what was going on.

The young officer leaned forward and spoke to the driver quietly. The driver nodded and the policeman smiled politely at Gardner before stepping off the coach. The door closed and the driver began to shift the coach right, being directed by the policeman.

"Been a pile-up," said the driver, frankly, "going to have to follow the diversion."

Chris sunk in his seat and turned from the window. As the coach flanked the scene, the pupils on the left-hand side pressed themselves against the window to see if they could see anything disgusting. The pupils on the right of the coach also leaned out of their seats to see if they could grab any details.

Gardner knew it was happening but could not stop it. Instead, she held Chris, pressing his head into her shoulder and looked out of the window. She could feel his heart beating and the sweat on his brow. His breathing heavy, his hand on the rail, knuckles white. The coach passed the scene fully and Gardner saw a fireman holding an awful piece of machinery that looked like a mechanical pair of dinosaur jaws cutting open a crushed vehicle. She pulled Chris in tighter until they had driven from the scene. The diversion took them around some side streets and for five minutes, Gardner did not let go of Chris. Sharma looked over to see and his heart nearly broke for the poor lad, his friend. The excitement of the incident was already a fading memory for the rest of the class, and they had settled back into the general natter and banter of school coach travel.

The bus swung a hard left and Gardner looked out ahead of the window. When she saw what was approaching, she forgot herself and her profession.

"Oh Jesus," she said, quietly.

The diversion had taken the coaches well off course and they had come to the precipice of Palmerston Road. The driver thought nothing of it. In fact, he was quite pleased – a nice bit of driving for once. The coach teetered on the edge and then tipped down. The class all laughed as their stomachs rose. Chris's heart froze. Without looking, he knew where they were. He had felt that tip more than anyone else in the city. Gardner felt Chris grow stiff as a board for an awful moment, and then she felt her left leg grow warm as Chris Redding lost control of himself.

Chapter 24
That Redding Boy

Gardner took a sharp inhalation of breath as she realised what was happening. The young man had regressed to terrified boy.

"Stop the coach," she snapped just as it was about to get interesting for the driver and the rest of the pupils.

"Eh?" replied the driver

"Stop the coach, now!" Gardner commanded. The brakes were applied so hard that they almost felt the back of the coach pitch so far forward as to topple over and upend itself.

"Open the door. Mr Sharma, see to the others."

Sharma stood up instantly and chanced a look at Gardner's seat. He saw Chris, hunched over and mortified, skin ashen, eyes in terror. He had seen that look many times before and knew what had happened. He looked at Ms Gardner and recognised sadness and concern in her eyes, indeed they were almost moist. The door to the coach opened agonisingly slowly.

"Right," said Mr Sharma to the rest of the class. "Settle down, settle down. Just a quick stop and we're on our way."

Gardner stood up and blocked the aisle so that nobody could see. Chris picked up his bag and left the coach. The children nearest, craned their necks to see and chatter immediately began to spread back along the coach, the dissemination of fact and rumour mixing as it went.

"Settle down, settle down," said Sharma, a little more loudly and a little more forcefully.

Gardner leaned into his ear.

"You take over. I'll take him back to school and sort it out. Okay?"

"Okay, good luck," whispered Sharma.

Gardner collected her things and exited the vehicle.

Chris was standing away from the coach, facing a brick wall, trying desperately to hide himself from the world. The door to the coach closed. Gardner approached Chris.

"Are you okay?"

Chris sniffed and wiped his eyes. He shrugged, his back still to her. The coach pulled away, the faces of his peers pressed against the windows. In a few minutes they would all understand what had happened and the reason behind it, but for now it was a spectacle beyond compare and had to be witnessed. Chris watched the coaches disappear down the hill and as the last coach passed him, he chanced a look up to the rear window. He saw Kate peering out at him. All the other kids were talking – and laughing. She looked so concerned. She waved at him. Chris waved back and finally turned to face Gardner who had her hand over her mouth.

"I'm sorry, Miss," said Chris.

Gardner's bottom lip almost went and she stepped forward and hugged the young boy, pulling him tight and rocking him a little, as her mother used to do to her when she had fallen or suffered some form of humiliation – and when Marisa Gardner was young, that happened a lot.

"No, no, I'm sorry. How terrible. It's not your fault, it's not your fault."

They broke off the embrace and Gardner looked at him.

"Just the road and…"

"I know, you don't have to explain, it's… come on, let's get you back to school."

Gardner looked around and spotted a pub just up the hill. The College Arms.

"We'll go to the public house, you can clean yourself up a bit in the gents and I'll phone a taxi to take us back to school. From there, I can get my car and take you home. That okay for you?"

Chris nodded, too tired to think of any alternative, let alone think about the two car journeys.

Gardner held out her hand and Chris took it. Together, they walked into the College Arms.

———

Chris waited by the door on the inside of the pub. It was exactly as he imagined it would be. There was a strange, unwelcoming smell that seemed to not affect the old men who sat at various spots around the pub. A dull carpet, a smoky atmosphere and a lethargic sense of general apathy. Gardner scuttled over to the bar and chatted with a barmaid with scraped back hair. After a few moments and a couple of glances in Chris' direction that made him feel uncomfortable, Gardner came back.

"You can use the gents to clean up. It's round the back and to the left."

"Okay," said Chris, quietly.

"Want me to hold your bag for you?"

Chris handed over his school bag and walked cautiously round the bar. As he passed, he caught eyes with the barmaid who gave him a cheery smile and a wink. Chris half smiled back. He walked past a row of empty booths, the backing taped up where it had been ripped, the tables chipped and stained with glass rings. He came to a black door with no handle that had a hanging sign on it: Gents. He pushed it open and was immediately hit by the smell of disinfectant battling away with bad guts. The light was flickering, and it was unearthly cold inside. How the hell could people spend time in a place like this, knowing that they would have to venture into here every once in a while? It was disgusting. Chris stepped inside and removed his school trousers. At home, the washing machine had an on/off relationship with the working world and so he had often washed his clothes in the sink. There was, miraculously, a full bottle of liquid soap next to the sink that, if one were feeling cynical, could glean a lot about the hygiene habits of the locals. Chris set about washing his trousers, before drying them on the hand dryer.

Chris emerged from the gents ten minutes later, clean and vaguely dry. He walked over to the bar where Gardner was having an orange juice and talking to the barmaid.

"Taxi will be here in a few moments," she said. "Do you want a Coke?"

"Okay," said Chris, hopping up on the barstool next to her. Angela smiled and grabbed the pre-mix dispenser and jetted some Coke into a glass.

"Ice, and a slice, doll?" she said.

Chris shook his head.

"How's Tony?" asked Angela as she put the glass down in front of Chris.

"How do you know him?"

"Bit of a local that one. He's always in here, havering on about you. Showed me your picture, so I clocked you when you came in."

Gardner smiled and sipped her orange, remembering her few meetings with the sweet drunk man when Chris was convalescing, and she had had to deal with him. Meetings about the future of Chris' education, about his recovery. Tone, always with bloodshot eyes from grief and booze, had conducted the affairs with grit and integrity. A faint waver here and there, and a fog of booze around him, but the few meetings they had held together reinforced in Gardner that the Redding family were of good stock.

"He alright?" said Angela.

Chris sniffed and shook his head.

"Hungover? He had a skinful last night."

There was the toot of a taxi horn outside.

"He's sad," said Chris.

"You mean sad as in 'rubbish', like kids say, or sad as in…"

Chris stood up and downed his Coke.

"Properly sad."

He began to walk to the door.

"Thank you for letting us use the facilities," said Gardner as she gathered her things.

"No worries," said Angela. "You look after that one."

Gardner smiled politely.

"And you, squirt," called out Angela to Chris who turned at the door. "You look after that soak of an Uncle. Tell him 'Angela says no more sad songs'."

Chris nodded and left the pub.

———

Gardner sat in the front of the taxi, Chris in the back. The doors where closed and the driver started backing up the vehicle.

"School is it?" he said.

"That's right," replied Gardner.

"Alright, well do you mind if we take a little bit of a scenic route?" he asked, swinging the car around. "won't take longer than five extra and I won't charge. Just don't like that Palmerston Road," he said.

"That's fine, perfectly fine," said Gardner and she fumbled in her bag to get her book to read for the journey.

"Yeah, used to," continued the driver, oblivious to the fact that nobody was really listening. In the back Chris rested his head against the window and felt his eyes grow heavy. It was mid-afternoon and he should have been wide awake, but he felt tired and hollow inside.

"Used to bomb down that one whenever I got the chance," continued the burly driver with piggy eyes, "but you heard what happened? To that family?"

Chris closed his eyes. The driver's words sounded as if they were spoken from one end of a tunnel and he was at the other.

"Can we just drive?" asked Gardner, hoping to curtail the driver's friendly banter.

"Sure," he replied. "Yeah, that family. I loved them, really did."

The tunnel between Chris and the driver suddenly disappeared and he opened his eyes.

"I mean, I didn't know them or ought, but they were great. Still are. Do you follow racing?"

"I really thi –"

"It's okay," said Chris, seeing Gardner looking at him via the wing mirror. The driver didn't pay any attention.

"Well, I follow racing. You should too. Effing great sport, pardon my language. Real drama and passion, energy – ah! Great days out at the circuits. Take the family down, me and my wife. I love my wife. The kids, great day out. Always sit in the stands, sneak some sangers and fizzy pop in, and some cans for me and the missus. Seeing the karts, the formulas… what a day! Not much brings us all together these days. The city I mean, not just the family. Good times. Well, the Redding family they were the real deal, family outfit you see. Family is so important. They were real outsiders, no sponsors, practically hand-built car…"

Chris sank a little in his seat and closed his eyes. Gardner did not take her gaze off him.

"But when they raced, eff me – mind the language – did they go. Their driver, eldest boy, best damned racer I have ever seen. My youngest, seven he is, lovely kid, wanted posters of him on his wall. 'Course you can't get posters of that driver, unsigned you see' – so I got my kid some poster paper – great roll of it, you know that lining paper you use for wallpapering? Got him a roll of that and some pens and told him to make his own poster. He was moody at first, he wanted a real one. But I said to him that if he did it himself, nobody in the city would have that poster. It would be the only one, just like his hero was the only one. My kid made twenty different posters from that one role of paper. You should see his room, it's an effing – mind the language – gallery to that legend. I don't mind. I love it. When I go to kiss my boy good night, I can see the pictures and I know my boy is beautiful, and I can also remember that racer and his family, his team – the outsiders. Well, don't need to tell you what happened to them, it was in the papers. Effing tragedy that was. Effing tragedy. That's why I don't go down Palmerston Road if

I can help it. Reminds me of it all, and then I think about my boys and my wife and the posters on his wall. Nope, not going down there.

"But it's all right, its life for the rest of us I guess, hard as that is. Youngest survived though, brave lad. Learned to walk again they said, papers didn't report it. Why bother, he weren't a racer. That's how they think, wouldn't sell any papers, that story. That's what it's all about, ain't it?"

The driver rubbed his thumb and forefinger together in the universal gesture for 'lots of money' – "...but you hear things driving a taxi, from passengers you pick up, here and there. They say he learned to walk again. Can you imagine that? Waking up, finding out what happened, then finding out you might not be able to walk again and then buckling up and getting on with it? Effing – mind the language – brave boy that one. My boy wouldn't admit it, but you ask me as a parent and if you could ask them Redding parents up there looking down, they'd say the same. It's a parent thing. That Redding boy, the one who learned to walk again, he's the real legend. Here we are."

The car pulled into the school car park and came to a stop. The cheery driver turned to the woman in the passenger seat and awaited payment. He was a little taken aback to see her wiping away what looked like a tear before rummaging around in her purse for some change. She handed it over.

"You alright, love?" he said.

"Yes, I am fine, thank you."

"No problem."

She looked over at the back seat of the car to see Chris asleep.

"Time to go Chris."

Chris woke up and groggily stepped out of the car. Gardner tipped the driver an extra fiver.

"Thanks, ma'am."

Gardner smiled and got out of the car. The driver watched them walk to school and noted the boy's pronounced limp and reconciled it with the name the woman had called him. He smiled. It couldn't be. It really couldn't be. He hoped it was. He believed it was. The driver shied off the rest of his shift, electing to drive straight home at speed so he could see his family and tell them all about the day he had that Redding boy in the back of his cab.

Chapter 25
Chris Makes a Fist

Gardener led Chris towards the double doors to middle school. "I'll get my things, then drive you home," she said.

"Okay," said Chris as they entered the building. It was just after lunchtime and so most of the classes were on break. Some dashed from classroom to classroom to relay messages about who fancied whom, while others organised trips to Sibley Hall for 4 o'clock when so-and-so was about to fight so-and-so. The teachers on patrol kept things in relative order. It was a gentle form of controlled chaos.

As Gardner walked through the corridors, most of the activity was temporarily halted until she was out of sight and earshot. Chris walked a little behind her, head down, looking at the floor. Most of the kids who saw him assumed he had done something bad and was being hauled to her office to get done. In truth, Chris was staring at the floor and hoping that nobody would spot any remnants of the stain on his trousers. Of course, they would have to be eagle-eyed and really looking for it, but Chris knew that when it came to his peers, you never could tell. Luckily, he passed through the corridors and open areas to Gardner's office without incident.

"Just wait here," she said quietly as she unlocked her office.

Chris sat down on the row of chairs outside, usually reserved for those waiting to get a beasting. He put his bag on his lap and looked over the notice board directly opposite. Drawings from the lower years, class timetables, school team results, notices of items for sale from other kids – as sanctioned and regulated through one of the teachers after they had discovered and broken up an underground football sticker trading ring that had scammed a year seven out of a shiny and caused three other kids to get 'mugged' in the PE changing rooms for their stash. Now, all trading was above board.

Most of the ads were for used computer games – strangely, the ones that had seen the most use were the most valuable as they were the ones that the previous owner had spent the time in unlocked secret levels and power-ups. Chris thought about his MegaSystem, hidden under his bed, unopened. A pang of shame hit him at the recollection – it cost a fair whack and Tony didn't have much and so it must have cost even more. Tony would have sacrificed more than the other kid's parents who had two cars, colour TVs and holidays in strange sounding places. Chris felt the rope in his stomach begin to twist. He took his gaze from the ad and found the green flyer for the Charity Boxkart Derby held by Benson and Weatherly. The knot tightened. Chris stood up and paced a little, his breath catching him. The cackling voice in his head returned. This time it didn't mention vehicles – it first started by saying: 'You just think about yourself, you just think about yourself'.

He walked back and forth outside the office, his eyes darting to the noticeboard and his mind thinking over Tony counting out his pennies for that MegaSystem that had gone unused. He started to conjure different scenarios: perhaps Tony robbing an off-licence for the money, maybe selling a kidney or, worse still, selling off all his notebooks and ideas to some shady businessman who happily took them for the price of a games console when they were actually worth a fortune of happiness. He thought of his own convalescence and, for perhaps the first time since he left the hospital, he began to imagine what Uncle Tone had gone through: the loss of his brother whom he had known far longer than Chris had known his own. The selling of the house and possessions, the responsibility of taking care of all the adult stuff just so Chris could come home and feel safe, come home into a warm place and sit with his games console and play. All that and what did Tony get? Chris was a kid and kids need adults, Tony was an adult and adults need someone. The knot reached critical, and Chris stopped pacing. He stared at the board.

"It's all your fault," he said with quiet venom. Chris didn't think, he just reacted to the truth. He punched the noticeboard so hard that his fist punctured the cork. He punched it again and again before tearing off all the notices and papers and throwing them on the floor. A pupil from a lower year, happy on his breaktime rushed around the corner, only to be confronted with the mad beast in an upper-year uniform. Before the boy could hit the brakes, he had crashed into Chris, who then fell and whacked his knee against the wall, the pain causing him to curse loudly. The kid gasped as Chris got to his feet and grabbed the boy by the lapels, his strength far too great for the young lad. Chris snarled and made a fist. The young boy closed his eyes and grimaced, awaiting the punch. Chris's fist wavered behind his head.

"What the hell is this?" shouted Gardner.

Chris snapped out of his rage and dropped the poor kid, who darted away like a mouse. He turned to see Gardner standing in the door of her office.

"Get the hell in here," she snarled, pointing to the office.

Chris knew that he had gone too far, and so he could only go a little further.

"Piss off," he snapped, before pushing past her and rushing out of the school.

Gardner stood rooted on the spot for a few moments, shocked at the scene she had witnessed, the threat of violence and the destruction of her noticeboard, not to mention the language. Rage welled in her – the boy was troubled, sure, the boy had been humiliated, but there was a line. She turned on her heels and marched out of the school towards him.

Chris hadn't got far before he felt a hand clasp his arm, spinning him around.

"Let go of me," he snapped as he reeled around to see Gardner's face of thunder.

"You need to calm down, young man" she said. "You need to calm down and get back into school and into my office right now. Do you hear me?"

Chris still had further to go.

"Why should I? Why? So you can pretend to look out for me? That it? Pretend you care. You're a teacher, you're not my mum."

"Lis –"

Chris yanked his arm out of Gardner's grip with such force that she was pulled forward.

"You're not my mum," snarled Chris, his face close to Gardner's, his eyes aflame and causing her to lean back a little. The boy was strong, and his rage tempered and focused. Chris was stronger than Gardner, and his size intimidated her, bringing her back to her youth and that damned father of hers. Suddenly she felt herself shrinking, recoiling under the feudal grip of masculine aggression.

"You're not my goddamned mum, understand?" Chris felt the righteous rage taking over him, "because my mum is bloody dead, alright? She's dead and it's my fault, so stay out of my way. Understand?"

Gardner could only nod meekly. The troubled young boy now appeared before her as a monster, a corporeal nightmare from her past. Chris saw the genuine fear in Gardner's eyes, a fear that went beyond the present moment, a deep fear that seemed to have been buried and had now taken over the woman, reducing her to the equivalent of the boy he almost decked. Chris's rage was beaten back, and a calm inner voice said to him: 'You did that.'

Chris turned from his teacher and rushed away as fast as he could, down the leafy driveway at the rear of the school – that long narrow bush-lined driveway that he had avoided ever since that night he had driven down it at breakneck speed. Gardner stood for a few moments, alone in the school grounds. She was visibly trembling. She felt sick. She put a hand to her mouth and her panicked eyes darted around the scene. The bell rang to signify the end of break-time. Suddenly she was surrounded by a few hundred children all laughing and screaming, heading off to their respective classes. Gardner marshalled all her resources and managed to regain her composure. For the rest of her life, she would never feel so alone as she did in that moment; a terrified child in an adult shell, surrounded by happy children, giddy with hope for their world.

———

Chris rushed down the drive, anger and fear ruling everything. He felt like a child being chased up the stairs by a monster, he felt like he had in that nightmare with the aliens and the nuclear warhead, but now there was no safety net, no wake up and no way out. He knew that he had destroyed it all, and there was no chance of recovery. In one, stupid, childish moment he had broken all ties with Ms Gardner and ruined his chances of just getting by at school and gradually rebuilding his life. His uncle was a drunk and now he was going to be suspended, maybe expelled – who knew? Who cared? It was over. He rushed on, each dark thought of the past coalescing with the bleak future. He forgot the pain in his leg and the instinct to run like before overwhelmed him. His disability won out over his instinct, and he toppled over, crashing to the ground in a painful heap, tearing his trousers and cutting up his knee. He whacked his head on the concrete and grazed the side of his cheek. But he could not linger, he tried to scramble forward, but the pain prevented him. He fell on to his hands and knees and watched as the blood dripped from his head and spattered on to the concrete. His anger remained, but the fear was replaced by guilt. Chris sat up and held his head, wincing as the blood trickled down his wrist and under his sleeve.

"Dammit," he spat as he clamoured on to his right knee. He was about to get to his feet when he looked down into the ditch beside the road. It was still there, still buried by branches and bracken – totally obscured unless one were searching for it. The wreckage of his brother's SuperKart. The rage boiled back up and Chris grabbed the nearest broken branch to hand, scrambled down the ditch and started beating the hell out of the car wreck, gurning and grunting with every strike, hoping that it would bring some kind of catharsis. It did not. All it did was make his anger and guilt compound and his arms burn with exertion.

Eventually he was spent. A few stamps and kicks on the car and that was that, nothing left. He felt raw, compact, like an animal or a madman from a comic. Breathing loudly from his mouth, he clamoured up from the ditch, dirty and wild. He staggered out of the driveway, across the road and into the concrete wasteland of Solly Park.

He was exhausted, battered, broken and bloodied, his limp more pronounced than ever. He just wanted to get home, maybe even set fire to the house, maybe stick his head in the oven or take a razor to his wrists. Maybe even pack a bag and get the hell out of the district and take his particular brand of pain and destruction with him. Tony would be free and could move on. Gardner would never again have to bear witness to that look of fear. Chris could take their pain and just go. Just get gone. That was what he was going to do.

As soon as that thought came to him, a few things clicked into place. The rage transformed from a wild beast into a more controlled animal. He stood upright and began to walk a little more purposefully through the concrete park. He was halfway across and nearing the exit when he saw them: two lovers on a bench, kissing, their arms around each other, their world as one. Julie and some new guy.

That focused beast snarled and said: 'One more swipe before we get gone. One more lash for the bastard world.' Chris bent down and picked up a conker-sized stone and hurled it in their general direction before walking on, not bothering to check where it had landed. He hoped for the wall near them, just to shock them out of their kiss. The new guy would be bemused, and Julie would look up and see the damaged boy, broken and alone, limping off into his bleak future and she would feel the greatest shame of all for betraying her love for his dead brother.

The stone arched high in the air. Chris was almost at the exit when he heard a little thud, followed by a scream and a shout. He turned to see Julie clutching the side of her head, while the giant of a boy was tearing towards him. No more anger, just fear now. Flight. Chris turned and made for the exit as fast as he could. He was within ten feet of it when the new boy slammed into his waist, rugby tackling him to the ground. Chris hit the deck and the wind was immediately blown from him. The other lad began belting Chris in the body and legs, each flailing fist trying to make contact with the boy's jaw, but Chris was wriggling and jerking on the ground as if he were having a fit, trying to deflect the blows and make himself small. He could vaguely hear Julie screaming out: "Darren, leave him! Leave him!", her voice getting louder and louder as she approached.

Darren got one in, right in the side of Chris's head. Bang. Stars. Julie reached her new boyfriend and hauled him off Chris.

"I said leave it!" she screamed, a thin trickle of blood running down her temple from where the stone had struck.

Chris crawled away, getting to his feet, his head feeling groggy, his breathing laboured. Julie pushed her boyfriend away and ran over to Chris.

"Are you okay?" she asked, her eyes streaming with tears, blood running down her face.

Chris was despondent. 'You did that too,' the cackling voice said.

"Please leave me," he whimpered before turning and walking out of the park as best he could. Home and packing were the only things now on his mind.

Julie turned away and her new boyfriend stepped up to her, holding her face and inspecting the wound.

"It's nothing," she said, bravely, "a glancing blow."

"You were lucky, who was that little shitbag?"

"Danny's brother."

CHAPTER 26
'THIS IS NOT MY HOME'

Chris opened the front door to the house and walked straight upstairs to the bathroom. He dampened a dirty towel and dabbed it on his eye and lip, already ballooned from one of the punches. He winced before splashing some water on the welt on his head. Everything hurt, inside and out.

He left the bathroom and entered his bedroom, slumping down on the mattress and closing his eyes. The trouble and pain would be there in the morning, so he could still pack then. For now, dream.

Downstairs, Uncle Tone did not hear Chris enter the flat, having passed out some hours before, after a furious drinking spree aimed at outrunning the hangover and the realities that came with it. The hangover was coming soon, perhaps at any moment, but until then he would fight side-by-side with the bottle to keep it from his door. He lay on the sofa, a line of drool dangling out of his mouth and pooling into the ashtray on the floor, the carriage clock on the mantelpiece ticking louder than bombs.

———

The night had arrived, and they occupied a twilight land between the waking world and their dark dreamless selves. The doorbell rang three times before Tone awoke. At first with a sniff, then a splutter, then a jolt. He said something unintelligible, even to himself, before he rolled off the sofa and landed on the floor, faceplanting in the ashtray. He coughed and spluttered out the butts, dusted himself off and groggily stood up. The doorbell rang a fourth time, and he said something else equally unintelligible. He staggered to the door, managed to unlatch it before staggering back to the sofa and collapsed upon it, instantly falling back into his slumber. Outside the house, as Julie tapped the door ajar, it creaked open a little.

"Hello?" she whispered.

The house within appeared dark and smelt rank. The door swung back and tapped upon its latch. Julie held it to before it had the chance to lock itself. She pushed open the door and cautiously stepped inside. She walked slowly down the little hallway and into the tiny living room. There she saw Tone collapsed on the sofa. He could have been a corpse and, figuratively, he was. Nothing had changed for the better since she had last been there, all those months before. They had sat together on the sofa and talked things through. They had shared a few drinks and she had wept before falling asleep only to find that Tone had gently laid a blanket over her. She had felt safe and reassured that morning and had left rejuvenated and with the strength to move on. Now she had returned to find the place a tomb and the kind, tipsy protector a broken-down drunk not fit for park benches or underpasses. Julie sighed and walked to his armchair, pulling the threadbare blanket from the backrest and draping it over the snoring man. She backed away from the sofa, kissed her hand and held it over Tony before turning and ascending the staircase.

The fourth ring of the doorbell had awoken Chris from his slumber, but he made no motion to answer it. The noise could have been anything. The only use of it was to wake him. He lay on his bed and looked up at the chip-paper ceiling, counting the little pieces of rice painted into it and hoped that by the time he reached one hundred, he would be asleep once more. His head throbbed, his side ached, and his heart was heavy. He just wanted to sleep. Just to regain enough energy so that he could pack and leave in the morning.

There then came a knock at his bedroom door. Chris furrowed his brow. Uncle Tony rarely knocked, and if he did, he only hit the door once. A triple rap came again. Chris sat up and watched as the handle turned and the door opened a crack.

"What do you want, Unc? It's late. Have another bloody drink or something," he said sleepily holding his head.

"It's Julie."

Chris sat up properly as the door opened a little further and a set of slender fingers curled around the edge.

"May I come in?"

"Sure," said Chris, darting a cursory look around his bedroom. Nothing he could do about it now anyway. Julie slid into the room, closed the door behind her and leaned against it, her hands clasping the handle.

"You okay?" she asked.

Chris hugged his knees. The darkness in his room masked the wound on her head but did not conceal his shame. He shrugged.

Julie sighed and looked at the floor. They both remained like that for a few moments before she spoke.

"I'm sorry for what you saw."

Chris knew that he should have been the one to apologise, but Julie had beaten him to it. She was the better person and that stung even more than the cut on his eye. He turned from her.

"That looks pretty bad," she said, gesturing to his bruised cheek. A shiner already formed, reflecting the moonlight.

"May I sit?"

"Sure," said Chris and he slumped off his bed and on to the floor, resting against the side of the duvet. Julie took off her leather jacket and draped it over the foot of the bed, before joining Chris on the floor.

"Guess I should apologise," she began. "Fill you in, tell you a few things."

"You don't have to. I understand," said Chris. "You've forgotten about my brother. It's fine."

"I didn't forget about him, Chris, that's not fair. That's mean."

Chris held his knees a little tighter. Julie took a deep breath.

"It's just…" – she stopped and rubbed her chin. "God, this is hard."

"Then don't say nothing," he said. "Why are you even here? I don't understand why you're here."

Chris' anger rose and he looked at Julie, eyes more wet than wild.

"I don't bloody understand," he spat.

Julie saw through Chris. She clenched her jaw to remain strong and carefully reached out, like a vet trying to calmly touch a mad dog. Chris did not recoil. Julie threaded her fingers through his hair.

"I know you don't. I don't either," she said, "on the way here I thought of a million different ways to tell you a million different things. I just…I love your brother. I love your brother so damn much that when he went, I tried to go myself. I wanted to die."

Chris was disarmed instantly. For the second time that day he saw a childlike, innocent fear in the eyes of someone else and he couldn't help but realise that he had driven them there. 'You did this.'

Julie's eyes were stern, but her bottom lip was wavering. "I tried to. You were in hospital, I tried to end it all. But I didn't. Tony saved me. He found me in a park and took me home. He laid me on the sofa and put a blanket over me. We didn't talk about it, we just sat in silence. Then we talked about other things. It got me through. He gave me the courage to take the first step and then inside I found the strength to go on. To get stronger and to take that love

I have for your brother and keep it in a box inside, keep it safe or else it would kill me. I moved on, but I never forgot. I never forgot. You can throw a rock at me or call me slut or bitch. I don't care, but when you say that I forgot Danny, that I forgot about your brother, that really fucking hurts, okay?"

The tears had come, and her eyes were searing. Chris knew then that he had so, so far to go before he even approximated the strength that Julie had inside. His tears came also, and he held out his arms.

"I'm so sorry," he said, "I'm sorry for everything."

Julie fell into his arms and held on to him tight.

"I miss them so much and it's my fault," he said, "It's my fault for everything."

"Shhh, baby," she said, into his chest. "It's not your fault, it's not your fault."

"I feel so angry," he said, pulling away from the embrace and standing up. It was time to let a few things out. Chris began to pace around his small room, while Julie wiped away her tears and pulled her hands through her hair.

"I just don't understand anything. I don't understand this stuff inside. I can't control myself, one second I feel okay and I am good to people and then something inside… and I just…. I just."

"Just what, Chris, just what?"

Julie got up from the floor and sat on the bed. Chris looked at her, lips pursed, hands clenched in fists.

"You can say it, it's not a bad thing."

"I just want to die, alright?" he shouted, thumping his chest with a fist. "I just want to go. I want it to be over. There. Happy now?"

Julie smiled a little and reached over to her jacket, grabbing her smokes.

"Do you think it's a bad thing?" she said.

Chris anger evaporated in an instant by her questions. He looked up and to the left, to his rational brain.

"I… er…."

Julie lit her cigarette.

"After everything you've been though, you think anyone would want to live? You think anyone would want to continue?"

"I don't give a damn about anyone."

"Apart from me," she said with a smile. Chris found himself smiling a little.

"Apart from you," he agreed.

"And Uncle Tony. And your mates at school. And maybe a teacher or two."

It hurt to admit that she had a point.

"But I don't understand. How do you…?"

"Doesn't matter about me," she said matter-of-factly, her raging tears of a moment ago now seeming like a distant memory. "I figured it out for myself. I went my own way. It got bad, sure, but it got good too." She patted the bed next to her. Chris slumped down next to her. She offered him a smoke. He declined. She smiled and put her arm around him.

"There is no right answer, no right path except the one you find for yourself, the pathway you create for yourself. You're good Chris, you're good inside and you always were."

Chris shrugged to agree unconvincingly.

"Can I be frank?" she asked.

"Only if I can still be Chris," he said with a little laugh, as he wiped his nose across his sleeve.

"Look at me."

He turned to her. Julie held his face gently in her hands.

"They are gone, my love. They are. But you're not, you're still here and though you're in hell right now, you will come out of it. You will. Your mum never had half your kindness, you're already tougher than your dad and you're stronger than your brother ever was. He was a racer, the fastest in the city, but you have a deep soul, a way of seeing and feeling things. I know it, I can sense it in you. You taste everything just a little more, feel things a little more acutely so your struggle will always seem harder. The way will always seem longer, the path darker. But only you will be the one to walk it, only you Chris. Only you. Understand?"

Julie sat back and looked at the boy.

"Everyone says stuff like this to you, right?"

Chris nodded.

"Just words right?"

Chris shrugged.

"Lie on the bed."

Chris furrowed his brow.

"Trust me, lie on the bed."

Chris lay down and Julie stood up.

"I can save your life in five minutes and seven seconds," she said, with a quiet, yet overwhelming grandeur.

"I... er..."

Julie smiled and turned to her bag, fishing out a cassette that she promptly put into Chris's stereo. She rewound it to the end of the second side before pressing play. She turned back to the bed and lay down next to Chris, managing to thread her arm under his.

"Anyone with half a heart knows that the right song at that right time in your life will change you forever. And then, when you get lost, or you need help you can find that song and it will be your beacon."

Chris lay back, staring at the ceiling, feeling uncomfortable with the proximity of the woman. She sparked up another cigarette.

"Let's listen," she said, "and let the music save your life."

The song started.

———

They lay there, listening to the same song eight times in a row before finally Julie, whose arm had gone dead from having Chris's weight upon it, finally stood up.

"Don't go," said Chris sitting up on his bed.

"I have to. I don't live here."

"You could, if you wanted."

Julie smiled and looked around the room, looking at the old posters and pictures of Danny in the room. She lit up again.

"No," she said, exhaling a plume expertly. "No, I couldn't."

She fished in her bag and pulled out her Walkman and headphones. She rested them on the bed.

"Take this, keep the tape. Listen to the whole album, but remember the song and remember me."

"I will," said Chris "I will al–"

Julie held out her finger and rested against the door, looking at Chris.

"Take a picture in your mind," she said.

They remained like that, looking at each other for a few moments.

"Remember this photograph, where you were, what colour the moonlight was, remember every detail about the moment a song saved your life."

"I love you," said Chris.

"No, you don't," smiled Julie, "but you will say it one day and mean it. And you will always remember that day too."

Julie left the room and Chris lay back down. He reached over to his tape player, rewound the song and started to listen once more. Out of hell, he had found just one flicker of hope. The song started and he found that he was holding on to the green flyer. He regarded it, and the glimmer of hope formed the start of a pathway.

Julie descended the stairs feeling weightless. The hour she had spent in Chris Redding's bedroom was worth a thousand in her new boyfriend's, maybe even a thousand in Danny's. They had shared so much, in an unspoken exchange while listening to that song on repeat that she knew she would never forget – and she hoped she would never be quite the same again. As if she were a ship that had been heading straight for a storm and at the last second caught sight of a beacon. She had been given a new heading. Julie hopped off the last two steps and walked over to Tone who was still lying on the sofa. She bent down to him and ran her hands through his hair. He murmured slightly and opened his eyes to see a pair of brown eyes staring back at him. His own eyes widened in awe, and he chanced a smile at the angel.

"Am I dreaming?" he whispered.

Julie shook her head.

"You're really real?" he murmured.

She nodded. "It's Julie."

Tony furrowed his brow as the voice and the name pulled the angel face into sharp focus and recognition, like an oven in the winter was ignited. He smiled, contentedly. What a face to wake up to. Then the music filtered into his awakening moment.

"What's that song?"

"It's called Mayonnaise," she whispered back, running her fingers through his hair and fondling his scalp.

"Mayon–" He furrowed his brow. "Where am I?"

"Home," she said.

"Kit?"

Julie smiled, leaned in and kissed Tony on the lips, softly, gently.

"You look after each other," she said quietly, standing and zipping up her coat.

"Don't go," said Tone, unable to get up properly.

"I can't stay here," she replied, "this is not my home."

She turned to leave, stopping at the doorway and looking back at him.

"You look after each other, Tony. You're the only two left. You don't need to be alone. You don't need to be lost."

Julie blew Tony a kiss and left the house. Tony rolled on to his back and looked up at the chip-paper on the ceiling. He listened to the song with the strange name and saw a spark light up in his mind's eye.

Chapter 27
In Hell

Marisa Gardner had drunk three quarters of a bottle of fine wine but hadn't really tasted any of it. She had watched two movies after eating her lonely dinner, but she hadn't really taken in anything on screen or tasted anything from the plate. The dishes had been washed, the kitchen squared away, and throughout the autonomy she simple was not present. Ordinarily, after school she looked forward to getting back to her small one-bed flat. It was her little island: family pictures on the wall, comfy cushions on the large sofa that was big enough to sleep on if she became too comfy under her quilt. The flat wasn't posh, but it wasn't squalid, it was just right – every little detail that she had added, the trinkets on the shelves, the books she had amassed, all of it a perfect representation of who she was, and what she was about. She took pride in the place, and it was what she loved most in the world. No children and no lover any more… but those things were transient anyway. The flat, or at least her feeling of safety and warmth within it, was and always would be. But this evening it did not offer her much sanctuary.

Since Chris Redding had loomed over and poured his vitriol into her, she had felt rattled and out of sorts for the rest of the day. Her two classes that afternoon were taken off the curriculum, and instead she instructed her classes to spend the hour in quiet reading and study while she sat in her chair at the head of the class and looked out of the window. Indeed, she couldn't even remember driving home, and it was fortunate that she hadn't come across any reckless drivers on the road. The car seemed to have driven her home. So, she sat on the sofa, looking at the TV, wearing thick socks and wrapped in a quilt, drinking wine and the only real feeling that she had was fear. She feared the boy. He had violence inside him, bubbling away. Marisa Gardner was not afraid of the other troubled kids who fought at Sibley Hall, even Lee Hardman who once spat at her and threatened to set his dad's dog on her – he was just a brat who could be dealt with. Chris Redding was another matter. A boy in turmoil, a man on the edge and she was afraid of him.

The film finished and Marisa finished her glass of wine. She leaned forward and topped it up. The credits rolled and a decision was made. She turned the TV off and reached beside the sofa for her red, fake vintage telephone, took a deep breath and dialled.

"Hello," came a sleepy female voice at the other end.

"Hello. It's Marisa, is Peter there?"

"You know what time it is?"

"Yes, is he there?"

"Why do you want to speak to him?"

"Look, it's of a professional nature that, of course, you wouldn't understand so I won't waste your time and bore you with the details. If you could just put him on the line then you can get back to your soap opera."

Marisa heard the phone being dumped down on the sideboard at the other end. She cursed under her breath.

"Peter!" bellowed the woman at the other end, "It's your bloody ex-wife again. Give her ten minutes and then come back to bed... Hello?" the woman's voice now appeared back at the receiver. "He's just towelling off," she demurred, the last remark spoken with relish into the mouthpiece.

"Jolly good," replied Marisa, expertly deflecting the strike with an insouciant tone. There came no reply, just heavy footsteps stomping away from the phone. Marisa smiled and took a sip of wine.

"Hello Mari?" came Peter's soft voice. "What's up?"

"Hi Peter, how are you?"

"Oh not bad, not bad."

"How's the baby?"

"Like a baby – cries and screams all the time."

"And the newborn?" she said with a wry smile.

"Touché" chuckled Peter down the line.

"Anyway, enough of the pleasantries," said Marisa sitting up in her seat and pulling the quilt over her knees, "I'm looking for a bit of advice."

"Life or work?"

"Work."

"As always. What's going on?"

"Well, I have a kid at school, one of my middle schoolers. Coming up to fifteen."

"Trouble?"

"Troubled. He used to be a blank boy."

"A what?"

"Blank boy. It's what we call the kids in school that are neither good nor bad. Average test results, homework done. Unremarkable in that sense. The kind you have to look in the register before addressing them, so you're reminded of their names."

"That is remarkably depressing, but I get you."

"Well, used to be one of those and then something happened. Something terrible and then now... I don't know, we've all tried to look out for him. He's got farther and farther away."

"Drugs?"

"Don't think so, I mean he doesn't really have any friends at school. Doesn't have a crowd."

"A loner?"

"Yes, and he's got so much anger. And today he nearly hit a lower-year child and... and..."

"He didn't hit you?"

"No, no, Christ no we're not there yet... just he's so angry and I think I can't reach him and if I tell you the truth, I am afraid of him. Afraid of what he might do in a class, or to a teacher... he's very volatile."

"Have you suspended him for striking the young kid?"

"Well, not officially. After the incident he took off and I am not sure he will come back."

"Home life?"

"Lives with his uncle who has a dri– …he's a sweet man, good hearted. He worked out the boy's programme while he was in convalescence. We almost went on a da– …I digress, point is, the guardian is honest, but he hits the bottle something fierce."

"I see."

"I can tell by your tone what you're thinking" said Marisa, looking into the dark red of her wine.

"That's why you called me, right? To find out your options? As a counsellor, I would need to meet the young man before I can make an assessment, but it sounds like something that social services should be informed about immediately."

"You really think so?"

"Look, love, he's threatening kids, you're scared for your own safety and that of your students and faculty. He's volatile and you say he lives with an alcoholic. It's not something anyone should go through, let alone a young man at such a pivotal age. I can't see him, because of you and me – I would be compromised – but my feeling, professionally, is that you should contact social services and get them on the scene. They will take your statements, maybe poke around the school a bit and visit the uncle. If the man is unfit, then things can be done. We don't know what is happening at home, it could be an abusive relationship, we don't know so you should at once get more professionals involved. On a personal note, if you are really afraid of the boy, you must steer clear of him. I want you to do that for me, understand?"

"I understand."

"I mean it, I know how you get around cases that you care about, you need to be ultra-clinical on this one. It's vital. Anything you do beyond the remit of your profession could not only harm him, but also any cases that might be brought up. Above all, distance must be applied. Understand?"

"Yes."

"Promise?"

"I promise, Peter."

"Because I love you, I always will and your welfare is important to me."

"So that's it," sighed Marisa, electing to ignore Peter's last statement. "We cut the kid lose from school, take him from his uncle and let the system look after him until he's eighteen and then he's on his own?"

"Worst case scenario."

"These things always are," said Marisa.

"You'll do the right thing, Mari, I know you will. Look, I've got to go but, in the morning, I will dig out some contact details of colleagues and recommended professionals and I will call you at work. Let's get some more opinions on this, before we start getting Services involved."

"Would you do that?"

"Sure hun. Listen, you'll be alright, it's never easy, nothing ever is but you're a tough old boot."

"Okay."

"I gotta go. Night night, love you."

"Goodnight."

Marisa sighed deeply and sat back in the sofa, lolling her head on the rest and staring up at the plaster patterns on her ceiling.

———

It was almost dawn when Chris sat up in bed. The tape had been played over and over and he knew nearly every beat and lyric to every song. The first rays of sun crept through the curtains and he hadn't slept a wink. Chris had tried to fight time and preserve the perfect moment but it was, of course, fruitless. But it was no great shakes, he had the memory. He could still smell Julie's perfume on the pillow beside him. He could still almost feel her arm on the back of his neck. He smiled to himself as he sat up and stretched. He looked down at the flyer on his bed, a sunbeam falling upon it. Chris smiled to himself. There was only one thing left to do, but it would require everything he had left to give. He stood up and left the bedroom.

Tone had slept lightly, lying on his back, his arms arranged corpse-like across his chest. The music from Chris' room had been a lullaby that had sent him off and caressed his dreamscape. He awoke to the sound of vigorous clapping. At first, he thought it was the dream, but as the clapping got louder and his dreamscape began to get duller, he began to wake up. The room was a little cold, as he hadn't slept under his usual blanket and his feet were freezing. He didn't remember taking off his boots – he rarely did when he slept for the very reason of not wanting to wake up with ten ice cubes at the end of his feet. Someone must have taken the shoes off. More clapping. Tone pinched his nose and looked to the stairs to see Chris standing there, clapping loudly.

"What the fu–" he was too tired to finish.

"Up you get. Jesus, you're a wreck" said Chris.

Uncle Tone, not the greatest of rousers, sneered at the boy and furrowed his brow when he noted that the young man didn't look too great either. He reached for the nearest smoke, lit it and used it to point at his nephew.

"What happened to you?"

Chris had forgotten about his wounds. He reached up and gently touched the scrape on his cheek and the bruise around his eye.

"Long story."

"Wanna talk about it?" said Uncle Tone sitting back in the chair.

"Not really," said Chris.

"You know we only have each other," said Tony, the words coming to him in a strange prophetic manner, as if he had heard them long ago, perhaps lifetimes passed and only now the relevance being revealed to him.

"I know, Uncle, I know."

"So then…"

"It's not important. But we do need to talk about something."

"Okay, can I have a dump first?"

"Sure," said Chris, stepping away from the table and walking into the kitchen.

"If you find anything, pour me one," said Tony, standing up and making the groaning noises that adults make when they get in and out of chairs.

"You get coffee," said Chris from the kitchen as he flicked the kettle on.

"You're the worst," said Tone to himself as he stomped up the stairs to the toilet.

Chris prepared two coffees and sat down in his uncle's favourite chair and waited for the toilet to flush. Ten minutes passed and eventually, his uncle returned downstairs.

"Ten stone lighter," he said proudly as he patted his belly. "May I?" and he gestured to his chair.

"Please," replied Chris, offering the sofa and handing a mug of coffee to his uncle.

"As you wish," he said, sitting down on the sofa and sipping his warm drink.

"You make a great coffee; can you make it Irish? Never mind. What do you want to talk about?"

"You and me," began Chris, "we get by."

"We do alright?" agreed Tone.

"Alight… alright," said Chris quietly, weighing up his uncle's assessment with barely concealed incredulity. Finally, he sighed and looked deadset at the pair of bloodshot eyes staring back at him.

"No, we don't, Tony. Look at us, we're an effing disgrace."

"Hey, just watch the mouth, Kit"

"I'm serious, Uncle," said Chris standing up. "Look at this place, look at the state of it, look how we live. We are on our knees, and you know what? I think we want to be here, beaten up and on our knees. I think we want this and why? Because we're too scared. Too damn scared to grow up and move on."

Uncle Tone looked into his drink and said nothing.

"Julie made it, Julie got through this, but us? We're a mess Uncle. We've destroyed everything because we're scared little kids."

"Look, I know it's been rough, but it'll get better, I'll get a job. Things won't stay so bad."

"We're in hell, Tony, it's been hell since the crash and it's hell right now and we're gonna stay in hell forever unless we do something about it now."

"You got some great plan up in that noggin of yours then?"

Chris smiled and handed the flyer to his uncle who took it and looked it over.

"You want to go to this circus? Cashing in on our names?"

"Nope," said Chris snatching it back from Tony.

"We're gonna race," he said, kneeling so that he could be eye-to-eye with his uncle. Tony looked up from his coffee. A spark lit inside him.

"Race?"

Chris nodded.

Another few sparks igniting others.

"You're gonna race?"

"We're going to build a car, and we're going to race it. A black car with electric blue trim."

"The Midnight Special?" gasped Tony with childlike wonder.

"You bet your arse the Midnight Special," replied Chris with a broad grin. He held out his hand.

"Shall we pull each other out of hell, Uncle T?"

Tony thought for a moment, before breaking out into a laugh. "You are nothing like your old man, you know. You're a real badass!" And he thrust his hand into Chris'.

They shook hands and stood up, pact created, decision made, and to work they went.

Chapter 28
Cleaning House

They slumped themselves down on the sofa, allowing just two minutes' respite. The house was transformed. It was remarkable. As soon as Chris had made his offer and Tone had accepted, they set to work. Chris assumed they would rush out of the house immediately like avenging superheroes, racing into action. Instead, Tony said: "We can't change the world out there, only to come back to this. If we're gonna do it, we're really gonna go for it. All in…so let's clean this bastard up!"

They started collecting cans, bottles and ashtrays, then when the general waste was done, they moved on to the more detailed cleaning of the living room and the kitchen. When the original colour of the tiles had been revealed, they scrubbed harder; when the pattern on the counter service was revealed, they really put their backs into it. They were almost demented in their cleaning – nothing cursory, nothing hidden away or swept into a corner. They finished the downstairs, but it wasn't enough. Not nearly enough. They surveyed the spotless room, utterly liveable and almost quaint before craning their necks in unison to the upstairs – the bedrooms and the plague pit that was the bathroom.

"Hell with it," said Uncle Tone, downing his break-time tea, "I'm not scared. You?"

"Bring it," answered Chris.

Tone slapped him across the chest with a pair of marigolds. They two men put on their rubber gauntlets and ascended.

The cleaning of the bathroom was first and the hardest in terms of elbow grease required. The bath had a tidemark around it that they first thought would have to be either blown off or burnt off with hazardous chemicals. They chipped away at it with a paint scraper and when they were halfway round, they began to feel better about it all – that they were winning, that no bathroom could beat them. The sink, the toilet, the cupboard, even the inside of the toothbrush jar was seen to. They cleaned until Tone stopped suddenly, standing back to inspect the room, rubbing his chin and surveying it like an artist at his canvas and judging whether his work upon it was done. Finally, he said: "Yes, a human could wash themselves in here without fear of infection. Our work is done." And so, they turned to their bedrooms.

Their private chambers were more of an emotional task than a laborious one and so they tackled them separately. They both knew that a scrub and a polish would not be enough. Chris had hoarded too much stuff, clung on to too many things from the past and it was time for a clear out and so he marched up and down the stairs until his leg burned and his knee ached, taking down piles of old comics and annuals, old pictures and clothes that didn't fit any more, toys that he once loved more than his own brother were now dumped into boxes and taped up. The things he kept: the TV and some videos, his stereo and some cassettes and, of course, Julie's Walkman. The posters were taken down and after a moment of uncertainty, were all rolled up. The walls now clear for lining paper to be pasted up and designs for the Midnight Special to be pinned. His clothes were organised, folded and placed away. Then, as he was just about to finish, he moved aside the last pile of clothes to reveal his racing suit, formally his brother's. Chris halted for a few moments, staring down at it. He dropped the pile of clothes in his hand and picked up the suit, holding it by the epaulettes and inspecting it. At the doorway, Uncle Tone was scrubbing down his own bedroom door. The cessation of activity from within Chris' room caused him to stop his own work and peer around the door. He saw his nephew standing in the middle of the room, holding up the suit. Chris turned to him, eyes stinging with moisture.

"You alright Kit?" he said, quietly, hoping that this discovery wasn't going to be the straw that broke his back. Chris broke into a smile and nodded.

"Found my brother's first suit. Remember when my dad gave it to me?"

"Sure, sure I do."

Chris folded the suit carefully and placed it on his bed.

"You know, I think that was the last time we were all together and happy," he said.

Uncle Tone sighed and leaned against the door frame. Chris stood back and regarded the suit.

"If you think I'm big enough, I'll race in it. What do you think, Uncle?"

Chris turned to his uncle, hoping to find reassurance.

"I think it was meant to be," he said with a wink before turning back to his work. Chris smiled and returned to clearing out his room.

Tony's room didn't take too long to clean up as he barely owned anything. He cleaned and scrubbed after collecting up the cans. The major change he committed was to heave the bed across the room to the far wall and then move his small desk to the window and place his dusty typewriter on it (which received a careful dusting). He placed the chair in front of the desk and sat down, satisfied with the new arrangement in his room. The bed was in a shadowy corner, which would better aid sleep now that he wouldn't be passing out so much. The typewriter was in front of the clean window. When he sat down to write, in the future, he would be looking out over the city instead of staring at the wall as it had been before. He would be able to sit and write and every so often, stare out at life going before him. It felt right and he was blessed with the giddy feeling that he was going to be prolific. For the first time in years, he thought about writing under sober sails, and it felt new, dynamic and exciting. It's good to be out of the comfort zone.

And so, as their work came to an end, they staggered downstairs and slumped on to the sofa to enjoy a hard-earned cup of tea. Even when brand new, the house didn't look as good as it did in that moment.

Chris sipped his tea before heaving on to the coffee table a large blank sketchbook and some pencils.

"We better start designing this thing soon," he said. "It ain't just four wheels and a steering column."

"Too right, youth," agreed Tone, looking at the blank page and feeling no fear, "it needs to be fast, obviously, you need to be able to drive it."

"Easy gears," added Chris, tapping his knee, "my gammy leg won't take too long."

"Which means we're gonna have to train you up. Get you on a push bike. It will be gruelling."

"Bit of pain won't hurt anyone," smiled Chris, "besides there are a lot of other things I gotta set right beforehand and I will also need to get to places quick smart. A bike is a smart choice."

"Right, that's that sorted. But I do have to raise a voice of concern. Three actually."

"Three voices?"

"Three concerns, one voice," said Tone placing his tea down on a coaster, the novelty of the very action causing him to chortle to himself.

"Hit me," said Chris.

"Well, firstly registration. We need to get you down to wherever and sign you up."

"Don't worry about that, I have that covered."

"Oh, alright then…secondly building this thing won't be cheap. I have some put aside for a rainy happy hour but we're gonna need some proper foldin' money."

"I got that covered too," said Chris.

"What you got going on?" asked Tone, suspiciously.

Chris reached behind the sofa and heaved the MegaSystem box on to the coffee table.

"I've never used it," he said. "Never once played. Too guilty perhaps, I don't know. Doesn't matter now anyway. This baby will fetch enough to get started. If that runs out, we'll figure it out."

"You sure? I mean it was a present."

"I know mate," said Chris, patting his uncle's knee. "It was a lovely gesture, and it was what I wanted before… but not what I need now, I think. Doing it this way is fitting. Put it to good use. You okay with that?"

Tone sighed and nodded.

"And the third concern?"

"The third thing," replied Tony, "is a practical question. This place is a too small for us two living in it, how the hell are we going to build a boxkart in here?"

"I've got that covered too."

"Really?"

"Yeah," said Chris, finishing his tea and standing up. "Put your coat on."

Uncle Tone unlocked the padlock and threw the metal door up on the old lock-up. He and Chris stood in the dark opening for a few moments before he reached inside and flicked the light switch. Not much had changed in the year since Chris had last been in the lockup, making tea for his old man and watching Danny tune up the SuperKart. The stanchions were still there, the work benches on the sides and the tools hanging up. A shrine. Opposite the benches, piled high against the wall stood a collage of cardboard boxes – the last of the Redding possessions put into storage.

"Christ, lad, I'm not sure about this," said Uncle Tone as he stepped into the lockup and stepped back in time. He walked around the workbenches and ran his finger through the dust, leaving a racing line over the white veneered surface. He jangled the hanging wrenches and spanners like a sad chime. He took a deep breath and turned to Chris.

"You sure?"

Chris stepped inside and looked around, the old smell almost sending him instantly into a nostalgic arrest.

"My dad built the best race car this city had ever seen, and he did it in here." He knelt down and observed the oil stains on the floor from the engine run-off. "My brother raced it like no other. They were legends and they did it in this lockup. That's why we have to build our Special here, it's perfect."

Chris stood up and looked over at Tony, who was leaning against the wall, hands in pockets.

"You think we can build a faster car?" he said, hopefully.

Chris shook his head.

"No," he said, with a smile, "not without my dad's brain and my brother's skill. But that's not why we're here. We don't need to beat them. "

"Just the others in the race," said Tony stepping from the wall, "and we can do that?"

Chris shook his head again, his smile even bigger.

"Not a hope in hell," he said, "but we can do something else."

"Come on, what?"

"If everything goes according to my plan, we'll give this city something they've never seen before and never will again."

"Yes!" said Uncle Tony. "By God, yes!" He strode past Chris out into the wide alleyway beside all the lock up.

"We'll show them something they have never seen!" he bellowed at the top of his voice, his arms over his head and fists clenched. "We'll show them a glorious thing and those that were not there shall hold their manhoods cheap while any other speaks aloud that they ate and drank and watched Chris Redding race on that day!"

Chris laughed and shook his head, "Come on, fool, help me shift these boxes."

Uncle Tony cleared his throat and stepped back into the lock-up.

"What was that manhood gubbins?" said Chris as he lifted the top box from the pile and placed it outside the lock-up.

"It's from a play," replied Tony. "Kinda." He picked up a box and placed it outside next to Chris. They both looked over the way to the house that overlooked the lock-up. Chris's old house.

"I wonder who lives there now? I wonder what their lives are like, and if they knew of ours?" pondered Chris.

Tony looked at the house and recalled the good times and bad that were had within its walls.

"They seemed like a good family, a nice set of people."

"Funny," he said, "never wanted to see her again."

"And now?"

"Just a house," he said. "The important stuff is in *here*," – he tapped his heart – "and in *here*." He tapped his head.

"Bravo" said his uncle, as he turned to get another box. Chris turned too, his attention caught by what he thought was a young boy sitting at his old bedroom window and looking down on him and his uncle. As the sun set, a dying sunbeam stung his eye. Chris shielded himself and looked at the window. The spectre was gone. Chris gave a smile and a nod to the heavens, before returning to work.

Chapter 29
Back in the Lock-up

The weekend sun was glorious. Tone had got up extra early having slept on his bed for the first time in weeks, perhaps months. At first, he could not drift off, his body telling him that it was the bed's fault. Too flat, too normal, not right…but his heart said otherwise. The whiff of adventure, the excitement of life to come kept him awake like a kid on Christmas Eve. Eventually he did drift into a contented, dream-filled sleep in which he saw the face of his love who had left him all those moons ago when he was twisted by the drink's black dog.

But this time he felt no sadness or malice when he recalled her face. The skies in his dreamscape didn't turn dark with storm clouds and no monsters came to chase him. It was a pleasant dream, meadows and sunshine like a shampoo advert on the TV. He awoke renewed and was doubly so when he stretched and found no aches or pains in his limbs. He felt young and alive, and he dared to think 'Pub'? He instantly stowed the idea and went about washing and dressing himself. He found that Chris was already up and out, getting stage two of their great plan underway. Tone found a note explaining what he was doing that day, as well as sweet little instructions on how to make coffee the way Chris made it. Tone followed the instructions to the letter and the drink tasted good, better than usual… but not quite like how Chris made it.

"Nobody makes coffee like my nephew," said Tony as he sipped it, standing in the living room and looking out of the window by the armchair.

It was then that a strange, sudden pang threw him. A vicious thought, a seditious thing that reared its head and spoke in a silky whisper. It said: 'This is how you'll remember him, when he's gone. Every time you smell coffee for the rest of your days.' For some reason, Tony could not quite fathom, this suggestion made him sigh with heavy melancholia, one of the more dangerous strikes upon a drinker in recovery – a feeling that takes control of limbs and makes them reach for bottles, an idea that spreads through the heart and mind like a virus that says only 'drink, for what else is there'?

Tone turned from the window and looked down at the little note and read it again. It was in the quiet times when he was alone that he felt most vulnerable, most susceptible to the elements in the room – the chancing voices and tempting ideas to go down one easy path. 'This is how you will remember him,' came the voice again. 'Pub?'

No, it was not his time to fall and instead of letting his feet carry him to some watering hole, they instead took Tone to where he needed to be that afternoon. He walked through the city, jacket open, feeling the late-morning sun on his skin. Every step forward, every step taken, helped him beat back the dark thoughts until finally he reached his destination. He opened the padlock and heaved up the great metal door to the lockup. He took the little stool from the workstation and placed it on the threshold of the garage so that he could capture as much of the warm rays as possible.

He then took the first box of possessions he could find, placed it beside the chair and sat down. He knew it was potential suicide, what with having some money in his pocket and an off-licence a two-minute walk away but he felt strong and confident. He put his feet up, picked up the box and sifted through the old possessions of the family, looking for anything that might be of use to the current project. Something from the past that could help kick-start their future. After one hour and three boxes, he came across a neutron bomb – an old photo album with gold embossed lettering that said: "Mrs & Mrs Redding". His heart froze and he gasped a lungful of air that felt suspiciously cold. He ran his finger over the faux leather binding and opened the book. The first page was obscured by a protective layer of tissue paper. Through its fog he could see the blurry outlines of the polaroid photos. He wavered on the edge of memory, his fingers curled underneath it. For better or worse he turned the page and saw the wedding photo of his brother and his beautiful sister-in-law. What a day that was, how young they were.

Tony smiled to himself as he pored slowly over the pictures, setting aside his rummaging duty to spend a few sunlit hours time-travelling.

———

It was as plain as day; the push-bike was a piece of crap. More rust than machine. Paint chipped and flaking, cushioning on the saddle exposed, rubbish brakes and a chain that looked as delicate as raw spaghetti. Still, it had two things that Chris was on the lookout for. It was the only one at Woody's Cycles that had pegs on the back wheel – those just by themselves were out of his budget. The young chap who worked at the bike shop couldn't believe his luck that some kid actually wanted it. He didn't care if it was no doubt purchased solely to be thrown off an over-pass or into a canal, as that was pretty much all it was good for. He was just glad to be shot of the thing. He saw the kid who wanted it, noting his slightly ragged hand-me-down clothes and his almost painfully thin frame and felt sorry for him.

"Tell you what," he said, "promise you won't throw it into a canal, and I'll bung you a new chain."

"Really?"

The lad looked around the shop, the coast was clear, "Yeah dude, least I can do for taking this thing off our hands. Kinda feel bad even charging for it!"

"Thanks mate, that's really kind of you."

"Wait one second," and he dashed off back into the shop.

Chris bent down, holding his knee as he did so. He looked over the machine.

"You're an ugly little bitch, but you'll do."

"Say what," said the lad returning with a shining new chain for the bike.

"Nothing, just bonding," said Chris, standing up with a wince.

"You alright?"

"Yeah, just getting old."

"Right then," said the lad and he upturned the bike, resting it on its bars and saddle, "let's sort this out."

The new chain was fixed in no time and the bike right ended.

"All yours, kiddo," he said.

Chris smiled and swung his good leg over the saddle and sat upon it.

"Good luck with her."

"Thank mate," said Chris, extending his hand, "really appreciate it."

The chap shook his hand and watched as Chris started to cycle away. Wobbly at first and putting extra emphasis on his left leg with every revolution. The bike looked awkward to ride and the rider looked equally awkward. The lad shook his head and returned to work, suddenly feeling a little sad that the knackered bike would no longer be at the shop, degrading his stock. "Shame that," he said to himself.

Chris pushed the bike onwards and rounded a corner from the shop. Confident that he was out of view, he stopped for a second, exhausted.

"Jesus," he said under his breath while he rubbed his leg. Fifty yards and he was aching, his leg screaming 'no more, no more.'

"This was a really bad idea," he said as he lifted his leg back on to the pedal and started cycling again, slowly, steadily and surely.

———

Tone was almost lost in his nostalgia when a strange, painful grinding noise filled his ears, pulling him back to the present. An awful scrape and crunch of metal on metal. He looked up and around. There behind him at the end of the alleyway, he saw a kid awkwardly trying to cycle a push-bike. He was weaving about the place, standing out of the saddle and leaning forward.

Uncle Tone stood up and scratched his head in amazement as Chris 'cycled' up to him and applied the brakes, the squeaking sending nearby birds from the trees.

"Got… the… bike," wheezed Chris, leaning over the handlebars and panting hard. Sweat poured from him.

"Please tell me you fished that out of a canal," said Tone as he grabbed the handlebar and steadied the bike. Chris dismounted and staggered back a little, the strength in his legs gone.

"You alright?"

Chris nodded and put his hands on his knees, coughing and spitting on the ground.

"Look, this might not be…"

"It'll be fine," said Chris, regaining his composure, "I have a week or two to get used to it. Besides, I'll be sitting down which will be easier on the pins."

"If you say so," said Tone, wheeling the bike into the garage.

Chris staggered past the little chair and noticed the photo album. He stopped and picked it up.

"Jesus, they were young," said Chris, running his fingers over a picture of his mother and father in an embrace.

"Long time ago, long time ago," said Tony, quietly.

Chris turned the page and laughed out loud.

"Look at you! Amazing haircut, look at your sideburns!"

Tone stepped over to the book and snatched it from Chris.

"Those burners were all the rage back then. I was scoring more than Joe Friday with those bad boys."

"Who?"

"Jesus, the things you don't know."

Tone turned the page to reveal a group shot of everyone together.

"Bet you don't recognise half these people, do you?"

Chris shook his head.

"A lot of them are extended family, on your mum's side. Don't hear much from them these days. Look at her!" Tony pointed to a brunette with a skirt wholly inappropriate in length to be worn in a house of God. "She was your mum's best mate from school. I had it bad

for her, the things I would do to try and get a date with her
to the sock hop."

"The what?"

"It's a dance. A school dance. Can't wear shoes in the
gymnasium, hence 'sock hop'. Anyway, I wrote her poems,
can you believe that?! Songs too."

"And did it work?"

"Did it heck. She got with your old man… before he
met your mum, that is."

"Ha! I don't believe you."

"True story, he was a hound, your old man, back in the
day. You heard of Mods and Rockers, right?"

"Yeah."

"Well, he was a Greaser. You know what that is?"

Chris shook his head. Tone smiled.

"Me and your old man were into motorbikes when we
were kids. Used to hang out at the cafes and bike shops
around town. Now the Mods and the Rockers would head
down to the city limits every weekend to ruck with each
other."

"Yeah, I heard about huge gangs piling in."

"That's right… well the Greasers were different in that
respect."

"How so?"

"We beat the crap out of Mods and Rockers alike! We
were very democratic in our punch ups!"

"It's mad," sighed Chris. "Don't really think about parents in that way. You know, what they did before I was born."

"It's not natural to," said Tone, snapping the book shut. "So then, back to the plot. What we have here is a bike with a good chain. We chop it up and weld our chassis out of it, no?"

Chris shook his head, "No, I need to train on Little Bitch. Get my strength up. We design first and when I flog the MegaSystem we'll get new materials for the chassis – can't scrimp on that. Prime chassis and wheels, we'll clean up the cogs on the bike and salvage what we can once I'm done with it. Until then…"

Chris walked over to the corner of the garage and picked up the stanchion for the SuperKart. He pulled out the metal plugs at the sides and manoeuvred the bike in between them, slotting the rear pegs into the stanchion holdings. He climbed back on, the bike now converted into a stationary exercise machine.

"Tell me more about those days," he said as he began to peddle, the pain returning almost instantly.

"Kit, you're crazy," said Uncle Tone with a smile as he sat down on his chair.

"I know."

"You also know James Dean's Porsche was called Little Bastard, right?"

Chris nodded.

"And that he died in it, yeah?"

"You gotta do something, right?" replied Chris.

Tone shook his head and opened the photo album at the first page once again. As the evening wore on, Chris trained while his uncle regaled him with stories from a bygone time.

Chapter 30

The Underground Grapevine

Sunday brought a morning of rest for the two men. Chris had near worn himself out on the exercise bike the evening before and had barely made it home before wolfing down a Pot Noodle, staggering upstairs and slumping down in his bed, falling asleep instantly.

They both awoke around noon, not a bad time by their standards and spent the day on the sofa watching movies, Tone making notes in his notebook and Chris designing like mad. Everything from the chassis construction to the paint scheme and livery was considered. There was a silent agreement and division of sign-off for the design. Chris had the final say on the artistic side of things, but for the more technical aspects of the boxkart's construction, he defaulted to Tone, who looked them over and supplied critical opinion, which was well handled by Chris. The first design was too radical and unrealistic for their budget, time and expertise. When Tony saw it, he simply handed the paper back to Chris after considering it for three seconds. "May as well have an ejector seat in it, an' all" he said. And so, the editing process went on through the day as videos were put in the machine and taken out, coffees and teas drunk. Come seven in the evening, the telephone was picked up and a takeaway was ordered. They ate it from plates and Tone allowed himself a few glasses of wine which led to nothing stronger than the ideas the booze gave him. By ten o'clock Chris handed his uncle a set of drawings which he pored over. The design was simple and elegant: the skeleton of the car seemed light, yet strong and well within their grasp. He had even provided a cost breakdown of materials, offset against a modest projection of what he thought the MegaSystem would fetch. They would even have some cash left over if all went to plan. Of course, Little Bitch would have to be gutted before the gears and chain could be added, brakes too which meant his training regime would have to be cut a little short so that they could get the Midnight Special finished on time. When Tony pointed this out, Chris shrugged and simply said "Guess I will have to train harder then."

And that was that. The car was designed, and the next stage was about to begin.

"Best get an early night," said Tone. "Got a lot of ducks to line up tomorrow, plus school too."

"Yep, school," said Chris, packing up his pens, papers and pencils. "Night, Uncle," he said as he walked cheerily up the stairs to his room.

"Night, lad," replied Tone, watching his movie and studying the plans. The wine tasted good, and for the first time perhaps ever he thought that it tasted 'good enough'. A satisfaction filling him that was as rare as 2-for-1 in a pub. He finished the bottle and also retired.

———

Chris was up before Tone as usual and he washed, dressed and prepared himself a hearty breakfast of scrambled eggs on brown bread. His brother used to eat something similar and had said it gave him lots of energy and protein. Chris hated it back then – who the hell could eat eggs in the morning without bacon, sausages and beans? Who? Only an idiot health freak. Still, his brother knew more than Chris about these things and he deferred to his brother's expertise and scoffed down the food, seasoning it with pepper and ketchup. After downing half a pint of orange juice, he was out the door, wheeling Little Bitch along the narrow corridor and out on to the road. His leg still ached from Saturday, but it was a good pain, the pain that seemed to say: 'It's nothing, I can take more.' Chris looked at his watch. Loads of time. He smiled to himself and pulled the bike away.

———

Nobody was going to nick Little Bitch, not unless they wanted to throw her into a canal and there wasn't one for miles around, so Chris didn't bother padlocking her up. He cycled to the school grounds and stashed the bike around the corner of one of the shops on the parade outside the front and waited. He got there early as some of the teachers were still arriving and parking, so he kept well hidden. After five minutes, the children started to arrive. He kept a keen eye out for his target. After a further ten minutes, he spotted him – the tall, gangly lad who belonged to the radio-controlled car after-school club.

Chris looked around, no teachers to collar him. Gardner no doubt already inside her office, thinking of ways to rule the school. Chris dashed across the school gates, through the crowd, pushing into the oncoming traffic until he reached Martin and his little gang.

"Hey Chr…"

"Dude, I need a word, can we?" said Chris, darting his eyes to see if any teachers were around and feeling like one of those spies in the movies who were being chased by numerous unseen enemies.

"Sure."

Chris grabbed Martin's arm and pulled him out of the crowd and into the doorway of an unopened shop. Martin's gang hovered around.

"Keep an eye out, lads," whispered Chris.

The gang turned and looked out, bunching together and feeling like rebels or freedom fighters. They knew what they were looking for.

"What's going on?" asked Martin.

"Got kicked out of school," replied Chris, adding a layer of false bravado to his tone.

"You haven't!" exclaimed Martin, his eyes lighting up with excitement.

"You can't tell anyone, understand, this is between you and me, right?"

"Right," nodded Martin, "you can rely on me sure."

"You're my lieutenant, right?"

"You got it buddy."

"I knew I could count on you. Listen, I got a favour to ask."

"You name it," whispered Martin, hunkering down in the doorway. Chris winced as he knelt to meet Martin's eye.

"I need you to fence something for me. Can't be on the noticeboard, just put the word out on the underground."

"You want to fence some footie stickers? Easy, I know a few people who'll put the word out. Who you got? Any shinys?"

"No, not stickers. I got a MegaSystem, unused, unopened, still boxed. Need a fast sale, cash."

"A MegaSystem…I don't know, that's pretty big to sell underground."

"Not for a guy like you, right? You know people, I'm sure you do."

Martin swelled with pride. "Yeah, I know a few people."

"Well, you see what you can do?" said Chris, handing Martin a piece of paper. "This is the deal: if you can get a sale ASAP for cash, we can do the exchange here. Make a deal and phone this number, it's my home."

"Wow!"

"It's just a number, make a deal and phone this number. I will be by the phone at 15:30 every day for ten minutes. Make the call at the phone-box over there. Got it?"

"You bet."

"Say it."

"Make a deal, phone you, that phone-box over there…"

"And…"

"Tell nobody about you. Silent seller." Martin tapped his nose.

Chris smiled and held out his hand. Martin happily shook it.

"You're the man," said Chris, standing up and looking around, popping his collar and pulling his blazer up around his neck in a gesture designed to emphasise the clandestine nature of their deal. It worked a treat and Martin followed suit. Chris nodded to the rest of the gang and disappeared into the crowd, smiling as he walked away. The gang turned to Martin, one of them asked what was going on.

"Get on the underground grapevine, put the word out that some footie stickers are going under the counter. Get a few deals done."

"What for?"

"When the operation is up and running again, then we hit them with the motherload."

"What is it?"

"Gentlemen, we gotta fence a MegaSystem."

They all gasped. It was a monumental mission. They performed their gang handshake and walked through the school gates, dissidents in the making.

———

Gardner sat in her office and flicked a silver ball in the Newton's Cradle on her desk, setting off the little distraction. She looked at the clock. It was just past 1pm and she could hear the entire middle school finish their lunches and begin to move from room to room to get to their next lessons. She stood from her desk and opened her door, standing in the doorway, leaning against the frame, watching the multitude of faces rushing past. Some she recognised from their outstanding achievement; others she knew from her dealings with them. The rest a sea of anonymity. She watched and was struck with the notion that any one of them could be anyone or anything, their blank faces masking their insides. What were they going through? At home, in the changing rooms, after school? In the parks and out of reach of adults? Who were the anonymous ones? The blank faces. Gardner was filled with shame at how desensitised she had become to the majority of young adults that passed through her corridors, year in, year out. It seemed that unless they were great or terrible and stood out, then they could live forever or die that day and it seemed as if she were indifferent. How many were maintaining an emotional lie? Laughing and joking at school, crying and confused at home? They were all entirely out of reach of her and he she felt ashamed and helpless. Gardner was about to turn into her office when she caught sight of Sharma pushing his way through the masses, a few smiles and hellos from his pupils; they really seemed to like him. Gardner caught the eye of her colleague who smiled at her. She nodded to him to enter her office. He deviated from his course and stepped inside.

"Have a seat, Ousman," she said.

Ousman Sharma obliged, sitting down and crossing his legs, taking the time to fold away his glasses. Gardner sat at her desk, the Newton's cradle still click-clacking.

"This is about Mr Redding, isn't it?" he said.

Gardner nodded.

"Did he come in this morning?"

Sharma shook his head.

"Any phone call from his uncle?"

Gardner sighed, leaned forward and halted the Newton's cradle.

"I spoke to Peter on Friday. You know he's a professional in these matters?"

"Are you thinking of Social Services?" said Sharma, sitting forward in his chair.

"Chris is volatile."

"He's in a lot of pain. I mean, in the coach on the trip…"

"I know, I know. I felt so humiliated for him. Also…"

"Protective."

"That's right, we had a moment. I thought I connected with him, I really thought I had reached him. You know he destroyed the notice board."

"I heard that was Lee Hardman."

Gardner shook her head, "No, it was obvious some pupils… some teachers even, would have pinned it on Lee. It was Chris and he threatened a year nine boy."

"Physically? I can't believe that."

"It's true, I saw it. Had him by the lapels, made a fist."

"Did he hit him?

"No, I was there just in time."

"Do you think he would have?"

"I don't know, I really don't. He rushed off and I caught up with him and he swore at me. Now I've been sworn at before, but there was so much anger in him. I was genuinely afraid. That kind of anger could go either way."

"So we cut him loose?"

"What would you do, in my position?"

Sharma billowed an exhalation and sat forward.

"Normally, I would say give him time. If he was disruptive in class, I'd say give him time. But violence? Even if episodic, I mean we can diagnose the source, that's quite obvious... but we can't have that. Can't have students afraid. Staff either. "

"I'd like to really be sure before I do anything."

"Of course."

"Do you think he will come back this week?"

"After what you've told me? I doubt it – shame, anger or belief that he's unwanted will probably keep him away," said Sharma.

"Out in the cold is probably even worse for him. If he isn't here by the end of the week, do you think we should visit his home?"

"I don't know, Marisa, that's... you can't just turn up at a student's house like that. Not without a letter first. Authorities would have a field day and any legitimate concerns you had would be swept aside by the illegality. You'd probably do more harm than good, to be honest. You can't get too close, too emotionally attached. Professionally, if you want to help him then you have to remember that. Don't cloud the issue with your feelings. Sounds harsh, I know. I love the lad too, my heart was broken for him, really… but if you want to help him you have to be his teacher, a professional adult in his life. Hard to hear, hard to say even but that's my opinion on it."

"No, you're right. Okay, well then if he hasn't turned up by the end of the week I will call some of Peter's contacts and get some advice on the next stage. Would you be so kind as to pop your head around the door and let me know after registration? I would come to your class and observe first-hand but I don't want to upset the other pupils or draw attention to concerns. If anyone asks, we'll say that he is in hospital for a few check-ups. Jesus, it sounds like we are about to disappear someone."

Sharma smiled to himself and stood up, buttoning his blazer and putting his glasses back on.

"You'll do the right thing," he said. "Always have, always will."

"Until the day that I don't" she replied with a sigh. Gardner stood up and shook Sharma's hand.

"Thank you for your time and your counsel, Ousman."

"Very welcome, Marisa."

Sharma reactivated the Newton's cradle and left, leaving Gardner alone in her office with the click-clacking of the desk toy. She slumped back in her chair. The toy clacked one too many times and she grabbed the thing and dumped it aggressively in her desk drawer. It provided no satisfaction.

Chris lay on the pavement, staring up at the sky, his heart beating fast and sweat pouring off him. He looked at his watch, ten to three. "Five more minutes," he said. A woman pushing a pram walked past him, struggling to manoeuvre the pram around Little Bitch, which was dumped on the pavement next to Chris. He saw the woman and grabbed the frame of the bike, dragging it out of her way.

"You alright dear?" she asked, looking down at the boy. "Did you fall off?"

Chris shook his head, "No, just taking a breather ma'am."

The woman looked confused at the strange, sweat-soaked boy and pushed the pram off, leaving him be.

Chris sat up and looked down the road ahead, taking in the slight gradient and gentle left turn. He pulled the green flyer out of his pocket and unfolded it. He turned the paper over and took a pen from his pocket. The back of the flyer was covered in timings. He scrawled his latest, and fastest, after spending the entire morning practicing the circuit over and over until he couldn't pedal any more.

"Come on kiddo," he said to himself, "let's be having you." He got to his feet, picking the bike up as he did so.

He looked at his watch. There was half an hour until the end of school. Time for one more lap. He mounted the bike and pushed off.

He broke down the road and took the sweeping left turn at a gentle pace. He had a few minutes to kill and decided to take the course at a gentler pace. He had belted around as best he could before and thought it prudent to drive slowly around it, take in the sights and sounds, maybe pick up a few idiosyncrasies in the racing line that he might have missed before, maybe find a quicker line through it all. He came almost full circle and stopped twenty yards from the finishing line. Up ahead, he imagined the huge banner and chequered flag and the crowds lining the streets, hanging over the barriers, waving and cheering. He was at the top of a T-junction, the proposed racing circuit taking over the long straight horizontal line. He turned and looked to his right. In the far distance, he saw the Stivyakino TV Tower, its red light blinking away. In between him and there, a few streets down the T-junction lay Palmerston Road. Chris had not even noticed it before, having concentrated on the road ahead as he cycled around. Maybe a subconscious defence system had been built. Moving forward and not seeing it, not thinking about it... but it was there, and it always would be. The knot in his stomach appeared once more and began to tighten. His heart on the rack once more, his guts burning. He thought that the decision to race would have been enough to dispel that ghost of the past but now, standing there so close to it, he understood that he had been quite, quite wrong.

"Goddamn," he said despondently as he gripped the handlebars of the bike. 'You haven't registered yet, you've done enough, made some positives. People will understand. You don't have to race, you don't have to race, you don't have to race…'

Chris swung his leg over the bike and began to push it away from the track, his memory of the lap times fading as the burning in his stomach and his leg owned him.

CHAPTER 31
SIBLEY HALL, 4 O'CLOCK

I t took Martin two full days and first period on the third to sell the console. He and the rest of the RC club had kept it under wraps as their operation was highly illegal. They started with some football stickers sold to the lower years, and word got around that the racket was open again. And then, with a judicious application of shiny stickers here and there, harvested from their own collections, they soon had the entire lower and middle school trading. Then it was time to break out the big guns. A word in the changing rooms here, a note in class there. Conspiratorial nods across halls. Soon the desire to get hands on the console was like wildfire. A few offers came in, some from jokers, a few serious and then after school on the Wednesday in the RC club classroom, a quiet auction was held. The bidding was frenzied up to the value of £50 and once that barrier was shattered only two kids remained in contest. Paul and another guy called Chris. Both lived in the nicer part of the district, with wall-like coniferous trees lining the front of their gardens, shielding their detached houses from view. Sand coloured gravel driveways, white walled houses with Tudor-effect wooden beams all over the place. Huge gardens. Probably had swimming pools in the back, but most of the other kids in school wouldn't know. The kids who lived in those sorts of houses socialised among themselves. Martin was pleased when the bidding came down to these two boys because he knew they could get the money for the console. Probably didn't even have to explain to their parents what the pocket money advance was for. Probably just scoop it out from under the sofa, or inside the cookie jar. The hammer came down at an incredible £135, which was only £50 cheaper than a brand-new system. Martin assumed that the excitement of the bid and the illicit nature of the sale had got the better of them. Paul won and the other Chris sloped away, sworn to secrecy about what had happened in the room, lest some adult found out.

Paul shook hands with Martin and asked about the details of the trade. He almost turned white when Martin simply said: "Sibley Hall, 4 o'clock."

———

The moment the bell rang, Martin dashed out of school to the nearest phone-box to call Chris Redding and relay the good news. He garbled in an excited voice and in detail the operation and hard work he had gone through, embellishing the details here and there – adding in a few narrow scrapes with teachers, having almost been caught out, having been threatened by Hardman to hand over the console in exchange for a month without slapsies in the changing rooms. He got through all that and then finally said how much he had got for it.

"Outstanding," said Chris, calmly on the other end, "see you at Sibley," and he hung up. Martin put the phone down and looked around at the kids walking past the booth. He wanted to tell the nearest person, share the information and brag about how he was the right-hand man of Danny Redding's brother. Perhaps set himself up as the year's 'fixer' – the guy who could get things done, get anything for anyone. He giggled to himself and left the booth to make his way to Sibley Hall without even going home to dump his heavy school bag.

Chris put the phone down calmly, but the minute the receiver hit the holding, he punched the air and did a little dance. He grabbed the console box beside the sofa and stuffed it into his backpack.

"Just popping out, Unc," he shouted up the stairs.

"Don't be late," came the answer, underscored by the tapping of typewriter keys.

Chris wheeled Little Bitch out of the house and made his way to Sibley hall. After two and a half days pedalling around the circuit, his legs were already feeling stronger and he was more confident on the machine. The race was approaching and while it kind of felt like an approaching exam and something he could no longer get out of, he did feel as though he was putting in enough preparation so that on the day, hopefully, he might get through it. Anything after that, who knew? Just get through the race, show the city what you can do then get down to the business of living.

Chris arrived at Sibley Hall at ten to four in the afternoon. He crossed the bumpy field, beside the huge tower block to the far end, into the copse that encircled the park. He dumped Little Bitch in the tall grass and hunched down out of view. The deal was on, but he wasn't stupid. Of course, word could have spread around school that the exchange was happening and there would be a MegaSystem and some ready cash out in the open. Anyone could turn up and nab the lot.

"Good call on the location," he spat, cursing himself for his stupidity. Even if the hand-off didn't get hijacked, there was still the chance that the park would be hosting some fight or other. Hardly the most isolated of locations.

"Too late now," he said, as he scanned the park.

It passed the hour by one minute and he saw two bicycles emerge from the tree line at opposite ends of the park, cycling towards each other, riders standing up on their pedals to get their bikes over the uneven ground. Chris recognised Martin instantly and guessed the other to be Paul. The two met in the middle of the park. Chris stood up and whistled. They turned to him, and he waved them over. The boys cycled across the way to meet Chris in the bushes.

Martin and Paul hopped off their bikes and let them fall on to the grass. They made the final few yards on foot with Martin stepping in between Paul and Chris. He thought it prudent that he should take on the role of mediator.

"Chris, this is Paul."

"Alright."

"Alright."

This was serious business.

"You got the cash?" said Chris. Paul patted his thigh.

"You got the console?"

Chris looked around before unzipping his school bag a fraction and opening it so that Paul could look inside.

"I see the box," he replied.

"I see the outline of your wallet" countered Chris.

"Gentlemen, please," said Martin, raising his hands to supplicate the two and ease the tension.

Chris smiled and unzipped the bag a little further so that he could reach in and open the flap of the box. He held the opening for Paul to see.

"Console, pads, cables, couple of games. Bagged, boxed, never played."

Paul took his wallet out and showed the edges of the notes.

"How did you get the money so quick?"

"Pocket money lying around from the last month."

Martin whistled in amazement, Chris smirked.

"So then…"

"So then…"

"Gentlemen, on three," said Martin, officially.

"One…two…three."

Chris put the bag on the floor between them, at the same time Paul dropped the wallet. They both snatched up their payment. Chris scanned through the notes. Everything was there. He held out his hand. Paul looked in the bag and was satisfied. He took Chris's hand and shook it.

"See you around," he said, backing away to his bicycle, wary of turning his back and suffering an ambush.

"Never can tell," replied Chris, keeping near the edge of the copse. Martin waited with him and watched as Paul shouldered the bag and cycled away at speed.

"Easy as pie," said Martin.

Chris took out a fiver and handed it to Martin who was gobsmacked to receive it. He genuinely hadn't even considered a commission.

"You sure?"

"You earned it… got one more favour to ask," said Chris

"Name it."

Chris reached into his pocket and pulled out an envelope. He handed it over.

"Instructions inside, just a simple action, no harm no foul, but super-important that you carry it out tomorrow. Can you do that?"

"You betcha."

Chris winked at Martin and picked up his bike.

"Stay out of trouble, kiddo," he said as he started to cycle away.

Martin waited till Chris had disappeared from view before he dared to open the envelope. He pulled out the letter and read the few bullet-point instructions. He understood the words, of course he did, but the meaning of them – why he had been asked to carry out the task was a mystery. He shrugged and pocketed the note before picking up his bike and heading off home for dinner.

———

Chris got home in record time, even chancing a few dangerous crossings and taking a few of the busier streets, rather than sticking to the quieter, safer back roads. He got home and rushed upstairs to Tone's room. He knocked and didn't wait for an answer before throwing open the door. His uncle was at his desk, all around him scrunched up pieces of paper, a mountain of an ashtray beside the typewriter. He turned to Chris, a tired expression on his face.

"You alright?" said Chris, the wind taken out of his sails a little.

"Yeah, yeah… just this. Tricky business this writing malarkey."

"No ideas?"

"Loads, mostly rubbish, some good… none great. I'll get there though," he said with a sigh, turning his chair around so that he could face Chris properly.

"So what brings you belting up the stairs at this hour, haven't you got homework or something?"

"Yeah, loads," he lied. "I'll get to that in a moment. First, check this out."

Chris fished in his pocket and tossed the wallet to Tone whose eyes nearly bulged out of their sockets when he saw the wedge inside.

"Mary Mother be, you sold it?"

"Yep!"

Tony stood up and they high-fived, their hands clasping and gripping in a manly and satisfying way.

"After school tomorrow, let's get what we need then. Might be enough left over for a pizza and a pint?"

"Balls to school, let's go in the morning."

"No chance, school first. Above everything, school – shopping and boxkart shenanigans after, capisce?"

Chris released his uncle's hand.

"Sure," he said.

"Good man, now get some homework under your belt and I'll see what's in the freezer for dinner."

Chris left Tone alone with the cash. He whistled to himself as he thumbed through the notes, counting not the monetary value, but the number of pints he could acquire. Chris entered his room and turned his cassette player on to listen to Julie's album. He lay on his bed and looked at the ceiling. How the hell could he go back to school now? After all this? He was determined to see it all through to the end. It was all that mattered.

"Balls to school," he said to himself as the music started and though he believed the sentiment deeply, a quiet voice came to him and said 'You have wronged Ms Gardner, you have wronged Ms Gardner…'

Chris sighed and put his hands behind his head and thought of the future while the music guided him.

Chapter 32
Dealing with Adults

A painful compromise was made. Chris wanted to get the materials straight away and hang school. Tone wanted to wait until after class. Both wanted to go together. When Chris explained that if they waited until after school, most of the day would be wasted and time was catching up. The race was around the corner, and they hadn't even begun the actual construction. This valid point led to one startlingly obvious answer. They were loath to admit it, but they would have to go before school so that Tone could spend the day welding the frame and doing all the grown-up stuff. Going before school meant getting up before six in the morning to get to the depot when it opened.

They agreed to do it and retired to bed almost instantly. The fear of oversleeping forcing them awake around four in the morning and cursing them thereafter with only batches of light sleep for ten minutes every twenty. They awoke each time and grabbed their alarm clocks, sure that it was way past due, only to find that they had time enough to doze.

But they did not sleep in, the living-dead awakening and washing haphazardly. Chris got into his uniform and took his bike to the bus stop to catch the early morning ride across town to the home store. The bus driver was none too keen on having Chris's bike on board but when

Chris over emphasised his limp, the driver huffed and relented. The two partners in crime crossed town as the sun came up. They had limited time and were excited for the mission ahead. On the bus, Chris never once thought about the incident in the school coach a few weeks before, or the fact that he was even inside a moving vehicle. His mind was on the mission and as they talked over what they needed to buy, Chris mentally ran over the steps in his own internal masterplan. There was no time to look out of the window and daydream, or to relent to fear. Mission first. The focus worked and they reached the depot in time. Chris locked up Little Bitch while Tony grabbed a trolley. They went over their shopping list in rapid fire back and forth, high-fived and then rushed into the store.

———

They caught many bargains in the store and easily bought all they needed and had money to spare. They bought good parts too, no expense spared. The trouble was that Chris had to get to school and so he took Little Bitch from the depot and cycled off, leaving Tone with all the raw materials. He could, if he broke his back, get it to the workshop in one go. He could leave some behind the counter and make a second journey but that was hassle. He fished in his pockets for coins and notes and adding to the change left over from the shop he pleasingly had enough for a taxi.

Tony arrived at the lock-ups before nine. He had made excellent time. He chatted with the driver all the way there, informing him of what the materials were for. The driver was so impressed and excited for the project that he even helped unload the boot and carry the goods from the roadside, down to the lock-up at the end of the alley. He was paid and he tooted the horn before driving off.

Tony looked down at the boxes. Inside all the pipes, wheels, chains and plastics there was a boxkart waiting to bust out.

He stepped inside the lock up and flicked the kettle on. While it boiled, he took all the bits out of the boxes and laid them out on the floor, neatly in regiment. He recalled a time long ago when he received a model Spitfire for his eighth birthday. He wanted to build it straight away, but his older brother insisted on setting out all the sprue trees and regarding them in detail. Finding what bit went where, what order to assemble and paint certain parts. At the time, Tony slumped on the table in boredom as Terry inspected the unmade kit. The older brother was right though. The kettle whistled and Tony made his tea, taking twenty more minutes to study the instructions he and Chris had made up. Tea finished, order of play established, no more messing around.

"Right then," he said, putting his mug down on the sideboard, "let's be having you."

———

Of course, Chris hadn't gone to school but instead used the early morning to cycle the circuit repeatedly until 11am. There was no doubting that he was getting faster, his legs stronger and he was beginning to shave half-seconds off his time here and there, recalling tricks and tips his brother used to impart as well as adding his own that he had discovered while playing racing games on his crappy old games system. The only niggling doubt in the back of his mind was that final straight and bend, leading to the line. That final stretch that passed by a T-junction that broke off and led straight to the top of Palmerston Road. Every time he had reached it in practice, he had shut his eyes and powered past it. He knew that he would not be able to do so in the race, unless he was in the lead. If he was boxed in, with cars all around him and he closed his eyes and flinched, then that would be it. He tried, he really tried to keep his eyes open when he passed but he could not. His stomach turned unpleasantly each time, like being in a car going over a humpback bridge.

Chris looked at his watch. He had no time to do another lap and try to beat that involuntary spasm.

"Balls to it" he spat, before wheeling Little Bitch around and making off across town to his meeting.

———•———

A pretty receptionist sat behind the counter in the entrance hall of the race circuit. Chris was nearly late as he cycled through the gates and towards the reception. He hit his breaks, the squeal causing the receptionist to look up from her desk as he swung his leg over the bike and let it fall unceremoniously into the concrete. He rushed through the glass sliding doors as fast as he could, the sweat beading across his brow.

The receptionist was young, perhaps just sixteen and already out of school. She tilted her head, flashing a fake smile, which was the only way to maintain it for nine hours a day, six days a week.

"Hello, Sir, how can I help you?" she chirped.

"Here to see Benson and Weatherly," spluttered Chris, his words staccato as he regained his breath.

"Your name, Sir?"

"Chris Redding," he said.

The receptionist's demeanour changed immediately upon hearing the surname. Her smile dropped a little and she sat up straight.

"You're his brother," she said quietly, a voice carrying a note of disbelief to it.

"That's me," said Chris, his breath still erratic.

The receptionist could've picked up the phone, but instead and for a reason unknown even to her, she stood up from the desk and scuttled off towards a fake mahogany veneered door at the end of the large atrium, that was lined with classic race cars of all divisions. Chris craned his neck and watched her leave. He smiled as he recognised the same scuttle in her as with Ms Gardner. People with jobs really need to get to places quickly it seemed. He walked around the desk and over to the cars. Eight, gleaming as new, parked in a row by the glass-fronted building. Huge engines, huge wheels, tiny cockpits. Up close to these machines it was barely possible to imagine a human being wanting to climb inside and fire then up – you could only conclude that race car drivers were crazy.

Chris smirked as he knelt. No pain in his knee. He held on to the open cockpit of one car that resembled a silver bullet strapped to the front of what could only be described as a church organ mating with an atomic bomb. He peered into the cockpit and whistled to himself as he saw the leather seat, the analogue dials and the tiny pedals half hidden in the shadows at the front of the car.

"Magnificent, isn't she?" came a throaty voice behind him. Chris stood up from the cockpit. Benson and Weatherly were stood by the wooden door.

"Beautiful," agreed Chris.

"If you wouldn't mind though," said Weatherly, gesturing to Chris' hand on the rim of the cockpit.

"Oh, sorry," he said, retrieving his hand and wiping it on his jacket. He walked forward. The cessation in exercise had locked his leg and his limp suddenly came back with vengeance. He didn't notice at all, but the two men did. The receptionist saw too. She sighed and looked at him with pity, much like nurses and teachers did when they saw him walking about.

"Thank you, Beverly," said Benson as the two men stepped up to Chris. The receptionist nodded. Chris looked at her and winked, something inside making him do it before he even thought to. Similarly, the receptionist found herself offering the faintest giggle and a blush before scuttling back to her desk. She sat down and concluded that it was because of the Redding name, and his older brother whom to her had all the makings of a ragged version of James Hunt.

"I must admit," said Benson, shaking Chris' hand, "that we didn't expect to see you here. A phone call would have done, no need to trouble you at all."

"I hope I am not inconveniencing you, gentlemen?"

"No, no," added Weatherly, "not at all. We were just going over the finer details of the event. Would you like to come through to the office and see it all?"

"No, that's fine. You gentlemen are very busy indeed. I just came to ask about what I was expected to do on the day."

"Shall we, then?" said Benson, offering a way towards an arrangement of comfy sofas in the foyer. The three men sat down, Chris wincing slightly as he held his left leg with both hands and extended it out. The two men thought it best to ignore it.

"So, we were thinking of the start flag. Maybe a little announcement and then you come up to the podium, if you want, acknowledge the crowd, then take the flag and wave it. Then, come the finish line, same again but with the old chequered. That's it, really. Hospitality will be provided for you and your uncle of course. Fine food, salmon, crudités, no expense spared."

"Pot Noodles?"

"Excuse me?"

"Kidding!" smiled Chris. "It seems agreeable, but I was wondering if it would be possible, could I just do the chequered flag? I am sure you can get some genuine local celebrity to start the race, but I would so like to finish it. For my brother you see, he loved to win as you know, and I think it would be a fitting tribute to him if I were to be the one to welcome home the derby champion."

The two men looked at each other before nodding.

"I think that is an excellent idea," said Benson.

"So, arrive whenever you like, make you way to the VIP section and make yourself known and we'll send someone to chaperone you around. Get some sarnies in that skinny frame of yours and then up to the finish line when the time is right."

"Perfect," said Chris, "and that, gentlemen, was all I came to ask of you. I trust that the charities have been notified and the changes made to the promotional items as I requested?"

"Oh yes, yes…all taken care off," they both said, overlapping each other as they stood up.

"Then I will see you on race day."

Chris shook their hands and walked towards the glass doors.

"Shouldn't he be at school?" said Benson, under his breath.

Weatherly shrugged. "Probably one of those teacher training days," he replied.

"Goodbye, Beverly," said Chris as he limped past her.

Beverly only waved at his back.

Chris heaved Little Bitch up on to her wheels and swung his leg over. He nodded a salute to the adults inside the building and made his way off.

"Jesus, he cycled here," said Benson, with mild whimsy.

"Got a bit of his brother's grit in him after all," added Weatherly.

The two men turned back to their office and went about their day.

Chris killed time on his way to the lock-up. He had hours to waste and so he did a few more laps of the circuit, but his times were getting slower and slower and his stomach getting tighter and tighter with each lap. And so, he meandered slowly back.

He arrived at 14:30, turned the corner beside his old house, now repainted and with nice cars in the driveway. It had changed so much that it didn't even seem like it was the house he was born in. He stopped at the mouth of the alleyway and sat back on his bike, a broad smile breaking out across his face. Right at the end of the alleyway, from the open lock-up at the end, a shower of gold and amber sparks spraying out intermittently, as if someone inside had their thumb over a hose spouting sparks like a roman candle. The grinding nose, the 'blueamph' sound of a welding torch being lit and the fierce sound of the flame focusing like an afterburner filled Chris with joy. He dismounted and pushed the bike the rest of the way.

Tony was covered in grime, grease and sweat. Chris leaned Little Bitch against the wall outside and peered into the garage. There it was, on the stanchions, gleaming bright and burnished – the frame of their Midnight Special. Tony saw Chris and smiled, turning the welding torch off as he did so.

"Hey, Kit! You're home early, how was school?"

"Last period was a free, so I skipped out," he said stepping into the garage and looking in amazement at the chassis.

"You've been busy," he said.

"Thirsty work this," said Tone, wiping the sweat from his brow. "What do you think?"

"It's brilliant, it's perfect!"

"Feel the heft of the bugger."

Chris walked around to the front of the chassis and gripped the warm front axle and lifted her up. It was like nothing. He looked at Tony in amazement.

"She is going to fly, my boy, she is going to fly."

"I can't believe it. I can't believe how light it is… and how badass she looks in this raw state."

"You know it kiddo, just don't clutter her up with loads of cowling and what not. Simple elegance. Brutal design."

Chris nodded, instantly revising the design in his mind to accommodate the recommendation.

"But now is the hard part," said Tony.

"What do you mean?"

Tony gestured towards Little Bitch in the corner. "Time to gut the bugger for her cogs and chain. Put the bite into our beast."

Chris sighed and walked over to his bike. When he bought her, he never imagined that she would come to mean so much to him. He reluctantly wheeled her over.

"She's had a good innings," said Uncle Tone, noting the melancholic look in Chris's eyes. He bent down to the bike and rubbed his hand tenderly along the crossbar as if the bike was an old dog or horse. "It's to the Knacker's Yard for you, old girl," he said softly.

The two then upended Little Bitch and set about their work, taking her to pieces. They worked together into the late afternoon, neither thinking about their bellies even though they growled for sustenance. They each took a cog from the gear and scrubbed them with wire wool until the rust was gone and they were gleaming like new. The chain was linked with another that they had bought so it was long enough, the pedals and crank-arms salvaged and cleaned up – everything they could take from Little Bitch they did until the Midnight Special was sitting on the ground, wheels on, gears in place, handbrake by the small bucket seat, steering wheel attached. Naked as a newborn, but ready to go.

"She needs some cowling and a lick of paint," said Tony.

"Tomorrow," said Chris, "I need a night to think it over. I don't want to rush into it and balls it up."

"Smart thinking," said Tony. "Let's get out of here and get to the chippie."

He put his arm around his nephew, and they spent a moment looking at the skeleton of the Midnight Special, already looking eager to get out on to the open road and cut loose.

They both nodded and rubbed their chins in appreciation of their creation at the same time, before leaving the garage, turning the light off and locking up.

CHAPTER 33
DATE NIGHT

It was nearly done. Just a few finishing touches and she'd be ready. Chris left the flat early in the morning. He knew that he needed the whole uninterrupted day in the lock-up to construct the cowling and paint up the Midnight Special. But it was a school day and Uncle Tone would not allow him to pull a sickie, and so Chris played with fire. They were at home, eating their fish and chips, watching a movie and feeling good about their day and their direction when Chris suggested he fix his uncle a drink. It was a tactical move, for sure, but a dangerous one. Uncle Tone was concentrating on the movie, relaxed in his armchair so the question caught him with his guard down. Before he could think of the consequences, he agreed to a few well-earned drinks. Chris fixed the wine and the whiskey and kept it gently flowing until Tone fell asleep in his chair. While preparing drinks, Chris had ensured that they would run the supply out before Tone fell over the edge and so, for every drink he poured in the kitchen, he tipped some more wine down the sink. There could be none left over so that Tone could suddenly get his thirst back and go off on one. It was a dangerous game, but Chris needed Tone out of the picture on the following day so that he could spend it in the lock-up alone.

It worked. In the morning, Chris, dressed in his uniform just in case, crept downstairs to find Tone asleep on his chair, snoring loudly. He probably wouldn't wake up till midday, and would need an hour to have a coffee and generally come fully awake. Then half an hour at least to decide what to do, then an hour to get over to the lock-up where he would find Chris working away around about the time school chucked out. The time was bought, and Chris did not feel bad for taking his uncle out of the equation in such a fashion.

He got to the garage as the morning sun was warming everything up. He opened the door and was filled with love when he saw her parked there, naked and gleaming. He dumped down his bag and got straight to work. The redesign was in his head, and he knew every facet, every contour and every detail of the paint job. He pulled the thin sheets of plastic from the bench and laid them down, before pinning over an equal sized sheet of tracing paper. He began to draw out the parts. The cowling, spoiler and wings needed to be light, and so the plastic was easily cut into shape with a Stanley knife.

By four in the afternoon, the test was complete. She looked even better with the thin curved cover over the steering column, two swept and flared wings and a fin shaped spoiler at the back. Time for priming and painting. Chris unhooked the parts and laid them out on newspaper in the alleyway under the warm spring air.

———

The time had come. The week was out, the kids had gone home, and the teachers had started to pull out of the car park. Gardner sat in her office, looking out of the window and watching the last of them all leave. In her hand she held a piece of paper with a list of names and corresponding telephone numbers. Peter had been true to his word and supplied his list of professional contacts and Marisa had kept her promise also. She had given Chris to the end of the week to come back in from the cold, but he had not done so. She turned from the window and placed the paper next to the telephone, picking up the receiver and clamping it between her shoulder and ear, her finger wavering over the buttons. She took a deep breath and dialled the first tone. The line connected and it rang once, before a panic overcame her and she hung the phone up.

"Dammit," she spat.

Marisa drummed her fingers on the table and glared at the piece of paper.

"Oh, to hell with it," she whispered, and she picked up the receiver and dialled a number from memory.

———

The shell parts were painted. Just like the Midnight Special, Chris had sprayed the bulk of the parts matte black and masked off the edges and sprayed them electric blue. A satin application of varnish and that was nearly that. He attached all the parts and applied a large reflective oblong across the back of the spoiler. He grabbed a little paintbrush and a pot of white paint. Kneeling down in front of the cowling covering the steering column, he painted on a large zero and underneath that, he wrote

'The Midnight Special – "Little Bitch II" and underlined it with a little flourish. He flipped the cap back on the paint and stood back. She was done. She was finished. A beautiful, sleek machine – dark covering with dashes of the gleaming, burnished skeleton underneath. A sparkling shadow. Chris folded his arms and rested against the workbench, taking in every detail of her. He smiled and nodded to himself. He picked up his bag and walked to the door.

"See you soon," he said, before locking her up and leaving.

Chris returned home expecting to be greeted by the sound of the TV and the fug of cigarette smoke as Uncle Tone eased out his hangover. He opened the door and halted in his tracks. The TV was off and a record was playing, but that wasn't wholly unusual. What was strange, was the smell. Aftershave. Chris walked into the living room to see Uncle Tone standing by the little mirror on the wall, tutting and cursing to himself as he battled with a tie. Tone was dressed in a clean white shirt that was ironed, against all odds, smartish trousers and shoes that looked like they had been introduced to some polish. His hair was washed and slicked back, his face shaved. An entirely suspicious miracle.

"What's going on?" said Chris, cautiously from the hallway. Tone craned his neck and smiled.

"Ah my boy, how was school?"

"Good. It was good."

"Did you get to the lock-up?"

"Yeah…finished her up."

"You what? You finished her! Without me?"

"Yeah, sorry…I was on a roll and got carried away. You'll see her tomorrow at the race."

"I guess… balls to this!" he said in frustration, pulling the tie loose again. Chris stepped up to him and took hold of the garment. He attempted to tie it.

"So, what's going on, what's all this?"

"I have a date," said Uncle Tone.

"Get out."

"True facts. Phone call this arvo. Woke me up. How many did I have last night?"

"Just a few," said Chris, undoing the tie and attempting it again. "Sorry, it's tricky doing it on someone else. Backwards."

"So, out for dinner. I'll be back. I mean, I don't want to be if you know what I mean, but chances are I'll be back tonight so we can take the Special to the track together."

Chris undid the tie and pulled it from his uncle. "Hang on," he said, looping the tie around his own neck and tying it loosely.

"That'll do it," he said, flinging it back at Tone who looped it back on and pulled the knot up neatly around his neck. He brushed himself down. Chris picked up Tone's leather jacket and held it open for him.

"Sir," he said.

"Thank you, my good man," replied Tone, threading his arms into the jacket and pulling it on.

"How do I look?"

"It'll do," said Chris walking into the kitchen and opening the fridge. "We got anything in?"

Tone fished in his pocket and pulled out a fiver. "Get a takeout," he said, dropping the note on the coffee table.

"So anyway, who is this boiler then?" said Chris, head still buried in the fridge.

"You know her, actually," replied Tony, picking up his wallet and keys. "That teacher of yours. Marisa."

Chris turned from the fridge and looked at Tony.

"Oh yeah, they don't go by their first names to kids. Gardner, Marisa Gardner. Yeah, when you were inside, we met up a few times to talk over your educational career so to speak. We had a connection… didn't quite work out due to, well, never mind, anyway she called me up this arvo and asked me out for dinner and a drink. Lucky me, eh?"

"Yeah, lucky you," said Chris vacantly.

"Hey, you alright with this? Not embarrassed that, you know… if you're not comfortable or anything no harm. Plenty more fish in the sea."

Chris thought for a few seconds before regarding Tone's hopeful expression.

"No, you're good. Say 'hi' from me…if, you know, I get mentioned."

Tone broke out into a smile. "Thanks mate," he said, before turning and making for the door.

"The worm has turned for us, my man, the worm has turned for us!" and he exited the house with a new, never-before-seen spring in his step.

"Shit," spat Chris to himself, turning back into the kitchen. He knew what the deal was. The anger turned in an instant and he swung out and punched the fridge door closed. The pain flared up in his knuckles and he rubbed his fist, the concentration on the impact calming his rage slightly as he began to focus. He took a deep breath.

"Alright then, only one thing left to do." he said, walking into the living room, grabbing the phone and dialling a number.

"Hello, Mrs McIntyre? Would it be possible to speak to Martin? It's Chris Redding. Thank you."

Chris looked around the house, feeling a sense of impending departure coming over him. A strange nostalgia for things that were still there, but now seemed to have been long gone. For the few seconds hanging on the line, he felt as if he was inside a living memory.

"Hey, Chris!"

"Martin, how you doing? Listen, I have one more favour to ask of you. A big one, but it's super important."

"You got it man, what can I do? Need me to fence something?"

"No mate… I need you to steal something."

Tone walked up to the little lectern at the front of the restaurant and waited. The carpet and walls were red, the waiting staff in starched white shirts and black trousers. Tone all at once felt completely out of place. If it had been his idea, then a few beers and a burger at the College Arms would have been perfect. But, having seen the sort of place that Marisa liked to frequent, he knew that there was no way the Arms would be acceptable. Which probably meant that it could never work between them.

A young woman walked over.

"Good evening, Sir."

"Good evening, Ma'am. I believe I am here to meet a friend. Ms Gardner."

The young woman looked down the list of bookings on the lectern and smiled when she matched the name.

"Follow me, Sir" she said, handing a faux-leather-bound menu to Tone.

"Thank you," he said as they made their way through the restaurant. The place was swanky, areas sectioned off with tie-back curtains, round tables with white cloths, matching white cloths binding the cutlery. As they walked around, Tone looked at the clientele – pleasant looking people, happy and well groomed, enjoying the mysterious looking food. Strange colours and formations on plates that did not appear to be of anything earthly bound. He took particular note of the gentleman, hoping to see one with the napkin either on their lap or tucked into their ties so that when he sat down at the table he would know the correct etiquette. He saw men using their napkins both ways, which was no help.

They turned a little corner and he saw her, sitting at a little corner table against the wall. Marisa was dressed in a pleasant blue dress, hair up. Perhaps not the ravishing and tiny cocktail dress that Tone had fantasised about on the way there, and equally not the comfortable jeans and a jumper that friends wore when they meet each other. A lovely middle ground. He was shown to his seat. Marisa stood up and held out her hand.

"Hi, Tony."

"Hello, Mari," he replied, shaking her hand but not kissing her cheek. "You look lovely."

"Thank you," she replied, offering the seat to Tone.

The waitress disappeared.

"It's about Chris," said Marisa, instantly regretting diving straight to the point of their discussion.

"I see," said Tone, gracefully although inside he felt the hit straight to the gut.

"Wine?" said Marisa, hovering the bottle over his glass.

"No thank you, water is fine," said Tone, pouring himself.

"Oh… you sure?"

"I'm sure, thank you," he said, with a smile.

Marisa topped up her glass and sat down.

"So, how are you?" said Tone. "No harm in a little chit-chat before we get down to business."

Marisa smiled, feeling a little uncomfortable about the situation. When she was getting ready and when sitting alone and waiting for Tone to turn up, she did dare to wonder how he was and what he would be wearing. Then she thought about laughing and joking. She conjured up an actual date in her mind. But no, her opening gambit had dispelled that.

"Oh, you know, this and that," she replied with a non-committed tone.

———

Chris put the cap on his pen and folded the letter closed. He picked it up, along with a second letter beside it and walked into his uncle's room. He placed one letter on Tone's pillow and put the other in his inside pocket. He then walked over to Tone's desk and opened the thin drawer. Chris riffled through the papers inside until he found what he was looking for – a small Moleskine address book. He flicked through the pages, stowing away a twinge of sadness at noting the disparate entries. His uncle really did not have any friends, at least none that were contactable outside of the local pubs. Chris clenched his jaw as he flicked past his father's name in the book, simply noted down as 'Big Bro'. Tone had not erased the name or number. Chris sighed and flicked on. Finally, he found the address he was looking for. He smiled to himself, consigning the details to memory before returning the book to the drawer and closing it.

Chris looked around the room before regarding himself fully in his uncle's mirror. The night had come, the moon arisen; the silver light filled the room and illuminated Chris. He regarded both his form and the expression of conviction on his face It was time. He zipped up his brother's black racing overalls and left the house.

Chris walked in the shadows, down the side streets and back alleys, keeping himself covered by darkness until he came to the lock-up. The door was opened, and the Midnight Special was wheeled out. He walked around the kart, running his hand over the cowling, wing and wheel.

"Ready for a test drive, Little Bitch?" he said, before climbing inside. His feet hit the pedals and he adjusted himself in the seat, holding on to the wheel and flexing his leather driving gloves. The car was low to the ground, and she felt lean, sturdy and hungry. Chris threw a cursory look up at his old bedroom window and curled a smile, remembering living in that ancient building and looking out over the city and dreaming of becoming the Midnight Boy and he knew, for one night at least, it had become so.

He lifted the hand brake from beside the seat and set off. The silent shadow moving out of the alleyway and turning on to the road. He began to pick up speed as he felt more and more comfortable behind the wheel. She was strong and handled beautifully, his legs did not ache, and he found great power was at his fingertips. He smiled and really opened her up, only one destination on his

mind. A place over the way, signalling out to him. A red
light, flashing in the night sky. A beacon calling him home.

Chapter 34
Finding the Body

Marisa rested her chin in the palm of her hand and thought for a few moments, trying to find the right words to say.

"You have to understand," said Marisa, "I really have been as patient and as…"

"As what?" said Tone, as he rolled his large whiskey around in the palms of his hands. After five minutes of initially stilted conversation, they had circled the main issue tentatively. Their food tasted bland, so they both forwent any dessert. The 'date' had turned into a sort of business meeting. Out of his comfort zone, Tone had found himself reverting to type over the course of the evening. The water switched to wine, and he drank two glasses to every one Marisa drank. Come the end of the meal, he ordered whiskey while Marisa finished her wine. She had spoken at length about Chris and his time between the accident and a few weeks prior: how he progressed at school, how the other children saw him. All of which Tone knew, as he had been there, and as the evening progressed, he began to just wish she would come out with it. He could see that she was physically uncomfortable. Shifting in her seat, unable to maintain eye contact, talking quietly and contradicting herself as if she were holding an internal discussion out loud. Eventually, the side roads and back-alleys led on to the highway and with a sigh and a heavy heart, Marisa began to address her fears.

"As what?" repeated Tone, looking keenly at the woman, sensing some sort of attack or ambush. He sipped his whiskey.

"These last weeks – well… month, really – at school he has become disruptive."

"He's been through a lot," deflected Tone.

"Yes, of course. Nobody knows that more than him, you or I… but there is disruption and then there is disruption."

"So, he plays the fool in class, he's a young man, he's changing. You might not remember what that's like but…"

"You forget that I spend most of my life engaging with young men and women. I wager that I have more experience in this than yourself. Please do not patronise me or my profession in that manner. I am trying to be as straight with you as I can."

Tone downed his whiskey and saw a flash of frustration on Marisa's face at his truculence. He nodded at a nearby waiter and tapped his glass for a top up.

"You were saying," he said as his drink was replenished.

"It's not the disruption. It's more than that. I think he has deeper problems. Something that may need to be discussed with professionals."

"You talking about therapy? He doesn't need a shrink. He's fine, he's doing great. Trust me, I know."

"Did you know he's become violent?"

"What are you talking about?"

"He attacked a younger pupil."

"A bully?"

"No… and even if it were so, it's not something to be applauded or excused. He attacked a younger boy, without provocation after destroying my noticeboard."

Tone's truculence fell away slightly. Marisa wasn't lying, why would she? He had no reply and so sat back in his chair.

"He threatened me…"

"He threatened to hit you?"

"No… no, not as such. He was just angry, aggressive but you must believe me. I have dealt with troubled children before. But with Chris… his anger is very real and present and, difficult to explain, but he made me afraid for my own safety. And those of my staff and children."

"Jesus Christ…" said Tone softly, sitting forward again and resting his head on his hand.

"We can't have that, and I am duty bound to contact authorities…"

"How long ago was this?"

"Two weeks ago."

"Two weeks? And since then, no incident?"

Marisa sighed and sat forward.

"Well, as you know, he hasn't been at school for two weeks. Not since the incident."

"Excuse me?"

Marisa furrowed her brow. Her eyes widened slightly as the penny dropped.

"He left school and hasn't been back."

"He's been... I mean..."

"What?"

"He's been leaving for school every day."

"Do you know where he has been going?"

"I'm going to effing kill him."

"Look, Tone..." Marisa reached across the table and cupped Tone's hand, trying to ease his agitation.

"I should have called the authorities as soon as he left that day, but I couldn't. I wanted to believe that he would come back. I needed to believe that I could reach him... I've grown very fond of him, and I don't believe anyone is beyond saving. But I can't hold on any longer. I must call them and then –"

"Then what?"

"Then they will ask questions. Awkward questions. About his home life."

"What's that supposed to mean?"

"Look, you've been through hell, I know that. They know that because they will read it in a file. But they won't see that. They'll see how you are, how you two live and whether it is a stable environment. Whether his home life is... you know..."

"They are going to take him away from me?"

"Nobody is saying that Tone, please relax. Nobody is saying that it is a certainty. An absolute worst-case scenario. I just wanted to –"

"What, get me to shave and comb my hair, drag me out to a restaurant to blitzkrieg us like this? An official letter, perhaps, a meeting maybe?"

"I know, I should've… I just want to do the right thing by everyone. Especially for Chris."

Tone took his hand from Marisa's and stood up. He tossed some notes on the table and downed his drink.

"I have my problems, sure but I am good enough. I'll show you, or them or anyone who comes between me and the boy. So, make your calls, do what you must do and then you'll come see how we've been doing. You'll see and then it'll be too late for your apologies. Nobody is taking my Kit from me – understand, Marisa? Thanks for dinner."

Tone swung his coat on and marched away from the table, leaving Marisa alone and shocked. She watched him leave before sinking in her chair and cupping his mouth, her eyes spilling over. The nearby diners tried to ignore the scene and returned to their desserts.

———

The Midnight Boy pulled the special into the private car park outside an eight-storey apartment block. He drove slowly alongside the line of parked cars. Each one respectable, designed for people with good jobs and families. No vans, no sports cars. The private area was pleasantly landscaped: sloping lawn, a line of fir trees and potted plants. He rolled the car up to a wall and parked her up, hidden in the shadows. He climbed out and walked over to the entrance hall and entered. He walked through the entrance hallway, all the while reciting the address from Tone's notebook in his mind. He reached the lift and called it. Inside the box, he ran his finger over the buttons until he found the relevant floor.

The lift dinged and the doors opened. Out walked the Midnight Boy, who made his way along the apartment corridor. It was late at night and the block was silent. The building was relatively well-to-do. The internal corridors were carpeted in a light brown a few shades lighter than the walls. Orange lights above each door. He looked at the door numbers as he passed until he came to the one he was looking for: 817. The Midnight Boy stood in front of the door and craned his ear against it. Silence. He stood back and fished the second letter from inside his overalls and slid it under the door. Mission complete, he turned away from the door and back to the awaiting Special.

———

Tone's anger deserted him the moment he left the restaurant. No longer feeling righteous, he truly reverted to type and walked without thinking straight to the nearest off-licence and spent the rest of his money on beer and a small bottle of whiskey. Purchase made, he started drinking the beer before leaving the shop. He walked off into the night, headed next for the nearest park bench in which to sit himself down, drink into the night and try to reconcile the irrefutable truth that repeated like a stuck vinyl over and over in his mind: 'They are going to take him away, they are going to take him away, they are going to take him away.'

———•———

Marisa unlocked her front door and before taking off her coat she walked to the little sideboard and poured herself a large glass of rum. She had blown it and she knew that her chances of gaining a little bit of common ground with Tone and Chris had been destroyed. She took a long gulp of drink and sighed as the warm drink did little to assuage her anger at Tone. She walked back to the door to hang up her coat when she saw the envelope on the floor. She hung her coat up grabbed the letter and went to the sofa to read and finish her drink. She opened it and nearly dropped her drink when she saw who it was from. Marisa sat up, set her drink aside and read the letter from Chris.

———•———

The beers had been drunk, crunched up and thrown from the bench. Tone staggered home, sipping the whiskey and dribbling as he yammered and babbled to the night. After five failed attempts, the key went into the lock and the door was flung open. Tone staggered into the living room, standing tall and throwing his neck back while he finished the last of the cheap whiskey, losing his balance and falling back, landing hard and awkwardly on the coffee table. He barely felt the impact and lay on his side, staring at the skirting board for a few moments before hauling himself up into his armchair. He stared ahead, eyes growing heavy and before they closed, he saw the reflection of himself in the grey TV screen in front. 'They are going to take him from me….What the hell took them so long?'

Marisa Gardner pulled into the school car park and drove to the far end, stopping at the mouth of the long straight, tree-lined driveway that opened out on to Solly Park. She waited for a few moments, the headlights on full beam, throwing their light down the dark driveway. The engine ticked over. She reached into her handbag and pulled out the letter. Opening the glovebox, she retrieved a torch, turned the engine off and exited the vehicle. The night was warm, but a breeze had kicked up. Marisa wrapped her coat around her and cautiously began to walk down the dark driveway, her torch beam on the ground a few feet in front of her. The silence was almost overbearing and as she walked, every permutation of possible danger leapt out at her. It was an entirely stupid place to put oneself at that time of night, but she was compelled to walk down that dark driveway. She passed the point of no return and stopped for a second, turning back and shining the torch back along the way towards her car. The beam reflected off the bonnet and she felt a little better, a little less alone. The car was still there in case she needed to get the hell out of that driveway. Marisa took a breath and turned from the car, walked on, this time moving her torch-beam from the pathway and off to the left, scanning the hedges, trees and ditch. She walked slowly, farther and farther along the driveway until she was a few yards from its mouth. Marisa thought she had walked too far and was about to turn back when her torch beam caught the glimpse of something metal, down in the ditch. Her breath caught for a second and she held the torch with both hands to steady the beam. She couldn't believe it, there it was. Marisa bent down and lifted the loose lying branches to reveal the broken and rusting SuperKart, left undiscovered for over a year, a buried secret revealed. Marisa welled up and put her hand over her mouth as she finally understood. She stood up and smiled a little, knowing that she had been right to hold out as long as she had.

———

The Midnight Special had been driven across town, all the way to the filled-in reservoir where the sixth-formers hung out. It was nearly three in the morning and the reservoir was deserted. In the centre of the concrete expanse, upon a small hill stood the great Stivyakino TV Tower, a sad steel giant, the tallest structure in the city. The Midnight Boy pushed the Special up the hill and parked her underneath the tower, tucked away behind a small, concrete hut. He climbed slowly up the concentric steel steps, level above level until finally he stood on the small platform at the very top, underneath the thin aerial and the blinking red light. Chris walked to the very edge and sat down, his legs dangling over the side and there for the rest of the night he remained, looking out over the city, underneath the red beacon, living a few more hours as the Midnight Boy.

CHAPTER 35
THE MIDNIGHT BOY AWAKES

The knock on the door awoke Tone with a start. He lurched out of the chair, eyes blasting open and a sudden profanity joyriding on the back of a coarse gasp. Another knock. He had no idea what time it was. Only that it was daytime, and the sun was up. With any luck it was early morning, worst case scenario, they had overslept and missed the start of the race. Another knock. Tone scrambled from the chair, grabbed a glass of stale water that was on the coffee table and threw it down his throat as he rushed to the door. He hoped it was Chris, perhaps having sneaked out to get breakfast materials – which would mean enough time for substantial bacon and sausages giving them more than enough energy to take the race. He grabbed the lock and flung the door open, double taking in shocked surprise to see Marisa Gardner standing there. They faced each other in silence for a few moments. Tone was completely confused. Perhaps he had slept for days, what the hell had happened? He remembered building the kart, then something about a tie, then maybe red carpets… then a park bench and the taste of cheap whiskey and the pain in his back offered the likely outcome that he had fallen over somewhere.

"Morning" said Marisa, finally. Her was coat buttoned up, her hands clasped around her waist penitently.

"Morning," said Tone, scratching his head.

"I came to talk, can I come in? It's important."

"Sure, but you have to be quick, big day today. What time is it?"

Marisa looked at her watch. "Eight in the morning."

"Oh, thank Christ for that."

Tone turned from the door and sloped off down the corridor, shouting up the stairs at Chris to wake up.

Marisa cleared her throat, took a deep breath and stepped through the doorway.

Tone had already gone into the kitchen and flicked the kettle on. Marisa entered the living room and halted. She looked around in sheer disbelief. Apart from the ashtray, and the empty bottle of scotch lying by the skirting board, the place was remarkably clean. No empties, no takeaway trays. No dust. It was not quite to her standards of cleanliness – nothing ever was – but it was good enough. She undid her coat and laid it over the arm of the sofa.

"Coffee?"

"Please," she called out, opening her handbag and taking out the letter.

Tone returned holding two cups. He placed them down on the table and bellowed up the stairs for Chris to wake up.

"Little bugger sleeps like the dead," he said with a smile, turning from the steps and slumping back into the chair.

"So, what can I do for you? Lovely to see you."

Marisa squinted at him. "You feeling alright?"

Tone scratched his head, "I think so. I had a few last night… celebrating something, must've been."

Marisa sighed.

"You don't remember the restaurant."

Tone looked up and to the left, trying to access the memories through the fog of booze.

"We met to discuss Chris… and his…."

The fog parted; the memories returned. He traced his way back from the floor by the coffee table, to the park, the off licence, back into the restaurant and to the table and the argument. His vague smile faded, and he stood up.

"Please," said Marisa, standing up to meet him, "I don't want to argue. That's not why I came here. I wanted to apologise for the ambush and to see if I could talk to Chris."

Tone remembered the truancy, the threat of social services, the falling off the wagon.

"Chris, get down here now!" he shouted.

"Please, please don't be angry. It's me, it was me who was wrong."

"What do you mean?"

Marisa looked at the floor and handed the letter over to Tone who took it, pinched his nose so that he could focus on the handwriting. His expression soon changed from confusion to dismay. Marisa knew the letter by heart, having read and reread it. She could trace what line and what word Tone was on, just by the changes in micro-expressions on his face that seemed to her to be louder than bombs. Chris' letter was not to his teacher, but a confession to a friend. He had opened up to her and confessed everything – his anger, his pain, his fear but most of all, the secret that had been sitting upon his chest like a grotesque since it had happened. The theft of the car and the crash, the final look of despair on his brother's face, the destruction of the family dream – all on Chris.

Uncle Tone's knees grew weak, and he leaned against the stairs for support. He finished the letter and looked at Marisa.

"I found the car," she said quietly.

"I didn't really know the weight he was carrying. I just… I just drank."

Tone sloped past Marisa, resting his hand on her shoulder as he ascended the stairs to Chris' room. He knocked quietly.

"Chris, mate, I need to talk to you, can I come in?"

Silence.

"Chris, can I come in. Kit, mate…"

Nothing.

Tone opened the door to be greeted by an empty room.

"Shit!" he exclaimed before rushing down the stairs and throwing his coat on.

"You got a car?" he said frantically, taking up his keys and wallet.

"Sure, what's going on?"

"He's not in his room. I need you to drive me to the lock-up."

"The what?"

"I'll explain on the way,"

Tone was already out the door. Marisa grabbed her handbag and coat and gave chase.

———

The morning sun warmed Chris's face and his eyes fluttered open, straight into the sunlight. He had slept at the very top of the Stivyakino TV tower, resting against a great central spine, his legs on a latticed platform. He smiled and cricked his neck. The end was coming, and he felt strong and ready. He stood up, stretched and began to descend the helical steel steps down to the ground.

Chris reached the bottom of the tower and walked over to the Special, still there hidden behind the small concrete hut. He knelt down to her and ran his hand over the black cowling. He tried to think of the right words to say, but none came. Instead, he smiled, kissed his hand and touched the 'zero' number on the front. Leaning down around the boxkart, he retrieved a can of black spray-paint stashed under the seat and walked over to the hut. He stood back and regarded the wall – covered in tags and emblems from the gangs of the city. He took the lid off the can and shook it, the metal ball bearing rattling around inside. He stepped to the wall and in four-foot letters wrote: "The Midnight Boy Lives". It dominated the wall. He didn't stop to admire his work once finished, instead tossing the can on the floor, turning from the TV tower and its beacon. He walked away.

———

Tone flung the door to the lock-up open and was greeted by an empty garage.

"Shit!" he shouted, slamming the door down again and pacing around the alleyway. Marisa was standing beside him, confused and worried for the angry, hungover man.

"What does it mean?"

"Well, the kart's not there is it? He's taken it. How's he going to get it to the race? Ride it there? Push it there?"

"What's wrong with that?"

"Why do that, why go alone, why take it to the race without me? He's a smart kid, he's tricked me all this time, held dark secrets from you. He knew I was going to meet you. He knew it wasn't for a date, despite how hopeful I was…"

"What do you mean 'date'…"

"He knew that it would be an ambush and that I would find out…"

"So, he thought you would ground him and so he's taken the kart to the race?"

"I wouldn't ground him, he's not bloody twelve for Chrissakes… he's gone, I know it. He's the goddamned Midnight Boy. He's lost it… I… I…"

Marisa stepped up to Tone and steadied his pacing by grabbing his arms.

"Tone, you're not making any sense."

"He's gone. He's gone into the distance... off, he's gone."

"We don't know that."

"I know that."

"Well, beg my pardon but you're an idiot."

The panic wavered slightly.

"Well, that's true."

"Look, let's just calm down and take a moment. We've misjudged him all this time and he's gone his own way. Before we think the worst once again, let's just be hopeful and assume that he's gone to the race. Let's just go there and see. Okay?"

The voice of reason was strong and compelling. Tone calmed down and nodded.

"Okay, good idea, let's do that."

"Good man," said Marisa, turning back and scuttling off to the car.

———

Martin McIntyre and his RC Club mates arrived at the reservoir. Most were on bikes, the others taking a backie. They cycled up the incline to the base of the Stivyakino TV Tower. The six lads hopped off the bikes and stared at the great slogan sprayed over the concrete wall:

The Midnight Boy Lives

After a few moments, Martin walked around the side of the hut and soon remerged, pushing the hidden Special forward. The boys gasped in astonishment and gathered around the boxkart. It was a work of art, and they could barely comprehend what they were seeing.

"So then," said Martin, in an authoritative leadership tone that he felt appropriate, and which seemed to suit him, "let's steal this beauty."

The boys on the bikes mounted and made a little column, those that had taken a backie took a hold of the car and pushed her in between the row of bicycles. As one, they rolled out, the car flanked by bikes. Nobody dared sit inside the Special. It was sacred, that much was obvious.

———

Still dressed in his black racing overalls, Chris Redding walked into the cemetery. The huge, sprawling mass of crocked, jutting teeth, spreading out in all directions. Old, tangled trees lining the pathways. Chris paid no mind to the multitude of gravestones, crypts and shrines as he walked though – some with fresh flowers laid on them, some overgrown with ivy. The dead forgotten. He had been there only once, a painful day a year ago and though he had not dared return until now, his feet still knew the route. He had replayed the nightmare in his mind repeatedly, three maybe four times a day since then. He hoped he would never have to return, but then he had never predicted the situation he now faced. He arrived at his destination. A small family plot, sectioned off by a small, black-railed fence. He stood in front of his family and read their names and dates. A few flowers laid at his parents' headstones. He smiled when he saw his brother's stone. Flowers, notes, little toy racing cars. A shrine from the people of the city for their racer, their working-class boy who drove faster than they had ever seen.

"So, here I am," said Chris, "been a long time... you look well. Bit thin, but that can't be helped."

He tried to laugh at his nonchalant tone, trying to be flippant like his father had been whenever Chris was ill at home. "I'm sorry I haven't been around much... well, at all. I haven't been busy... I was just. It's been hard."

He knew it would go like this, he had tried to prepare for it, but it was useless. The tears came. "I miss you all so much and I want to talk to you and explain things and just fu–" He bit his lip. "Sorry for the language, Mum. School's been hard, tried to get along. Exams are coming up. I'll work hard at them, Dad. Danny, I saw Julie she's... she's great, still strong. She's happy. She came over the other day, we listened to music. She's alive, really is. Mum, I'm not so good, I've been in trouble at school. I guess I let my... what happened... become an excuse. I wasn't strong. I was a bully and a liar and it's not me. I let that happen. Dad, I'm trying to be good, I really am... Christ, I want to see you so much."

Chris reached over and touched each gravestone in turn. "I love you so much, bro. I don't care if you're up there calling me a bummer for saying it. I just love you, my brother. Nobody in this city has forgotten you, everywhere I turn people see me, but they wish they it were you. I'm so proud, so proud to have you as a big brother. You're the best, always were, always will be. I love you." Chris turned to his parent's headstones. "Mum, Dad, there's something I have to go do. You won't understand me and if you were alive, you would stop me. You would. But I must do it. I have made my own decisions, most of them the wrong ones, I have made myself the victim, I have been weak. But this thing, this one last thing, I have to do it. Shout and scream at me from up there if you have to, but it won't change my mind, it can't. You're in the ground and it's my fault. That's never going to change. But I am scared all the time, I have this rope in my stomach, I have this fear – like my chest is in a vice. I am just so, bloody tired of it all. And so, I'm doing this, they'll try and stop me, they won't understand. Uncle Tone will… but not for a long time. Right now, though… I just don't want to be afraid any more. I love you."

Chris kissed his hand and held it over the plot. "Be good, stay strong, enjoy the big race up in the sky. See you real soon."

Chris zipped up his overalls and walked away from his family.

CHAPTER 36
THE MIDNIGHT BOY WALKS

I t was difficult to maintain the sense of urgency. As soon as Marisa found a parking spot and they waded through the bustling crowds spilling out of every house and shop. The overall carnival atmosphere permeated. Houses on the side streets had clubbed together and set out trestle tables and were hosting street parties. Bunting from roof to roof, and the wide circuit was sectioned off with tyres, hay bales and, at junctions, A-frame barriers. People had got to the race early and the entire circuit was at least three deep. People lucky enough to have houses that lined the route had climbed up on to their extensions and their rooftops to afford a better view.

"Just like the Piazza Del Campo," said Marisa as she pushed through the crowds. Tone had no idea what she meant but concluded that it was some sort of party in some far-flung place. The precinct squares and car parks had opened out to trading stalls and food outlets. Children ran around drinking overpriced cola and stuffing huge, glistening hotdogs into their mouths. It was a glorious atmosphere and the sun had come to join in. Hot tarmac, the heat signature waving above it as if a real Grand Prix was underway. They pushed their way along, craning their necks to try and see where the starting grid was. They passed a VIP section, flanked by huge men in black bomber jackets and radio mics all set to fend off an invasion of sugar-high children or crazed parents eager to get out of the sun and into the VIP tents for Pimms. They were stern and fierce. Marisa saw the burly men and grabbed Tone's arm and pulled him over.

"There," she shouted, her natural teacher voice carrying louder than most.

"You see him?"

"No, but I have an idea."

They approached the bouncers and Marisa beckoned for one of them to bend down from his natural, twelve-foot height so that she could better communicate with him.

"Hello Sir, my name's Marisa Gardner, I need to see Mr Benson or Mr Weatherly, can you tell them that I am here?"

The bouncer looked up at his stoic mate before returning to his position, his eyes scanning the crowd.

Marisa turned red almost instantly. "Excuse me! I asked you a question."

The two bouncers began to chew imaginary gum in unison, their gaze far away.

Tone tapped Marisa on the shoulder.

"Forget it," he said. "You can't reason with them. I know their type."

Marisa was about to try again when, beside one of the statues she spotted Benson, unmistakable in his sheepskin coat with white fur collar.

"Mr Benson!" she yelled, not in her teacher voice, but in her 'Head of Middle School' voice. Tone cupped his ears and felt like a naughty eight-year-old once again. People nearby seemed to shut up a little. Even the bouncers cracked a flinch. Mr Benson heard his strict teacher calling his name from fifty years in the past. He stood bolt upright and instantly hid his cigar behind his back. He looked to the source of the foghorn and saw the petite Ms Gardner standing at the rope fence of the VIP area. She waved at him. He whistled to the bouncers and nodded to the teacher and her guest. The bouncers opened the rope barrier.

"Sorry, Miss," they both said sheepishly.

"I should think so too, and don't let me catch you being off-hand to people in the future, understand?"

"Yes, Miss. Sorry, Miss."

Marisa gave them her 'you have been warned' glare before marching haughtily past. Tone couldn't resist giving them each a patronising pat on the cheek as he passed.

"Bad luck, boys" he said gleefully.

Marisa and Tone reached Mr Benson who had resumed smoking his cigar the moment he realised that the voice wasn't Ms Sullivan from fifty years ago, but Ms Gardner from a few weeks back.

"Mr Benson, good morning."

"Ah good morning, Ms Gardner, and what a fine day this is to be sure. What a turnout and all in honour of the Redding name!"

Tone cleared his throat and Benson looked at him.

"Excuse me, Mr Benson," he said, sticking out his hand.

"Tone, Tone Redding."

The cigar nearly fell out of Benson's mouth.

"You're Terry's brother?"

"That I am."

"Well then you are a guest of honour. In my rare dealings with Terry, he spoke very highly of his family. Said his brother was a most gifted and talented writer."

Tone looked around to see if Benson was talking to someone else. Benson laughed.

"It's true, it's true," laughed Benson.

"Mr Benson," interrupted Marisa, "we need to know, have you seen Chris? Has he come?"

"No ma'am, not at all. You look worried, have you lost him or something?"

"You could say that."

"Well, that is a pickle. He's supposed to come to the VIP section when he arrives. We have a valet to look after him."

"He has a what?" said Tone, incredulously.

"Well, he is the guest of honour, he's waving the flag and everything."

"Waving the…"

"…Mr Benson, although we don't have VIP passes, do you think we could wait here until he does arrive? Would you be able to accommodate us?"

"Ms Gardner, Mr Redding, I can do better than that. Come with me."

And with that, Benson led Marisa and Tone through the concrete VIP 'paddock' past the champagne reception, where he handed out two flutes to his guests. They took the drinks. It was free and the weather warm, so why the hell not? Past the white tent and across the way to the starting grid. Of course, the VIPs and guests of honour had prime seats right on the grid and finish line. Marisa and Tone were taken to an A-frame barrier that sectioned off a junction to another road, right by the home straight. Ahead, they could see the finish line chalked into the pavement, and a large walkway straddling the road upon which stood a podium and five beautiful young women in leotards and sashes. Over the walkway, a banner that read: "First Annual Redding Boxkart Derby".

"You can wait here, I have to do some announcing," said Benson, shaking their hands and walking off.

Marisa and Tone leaned over the barrier and scanned the crowd on the other side of the track.

"It's impossible, he could be anywhere... even if he is coming," said Tone, forgetting about the champagne in his hand.

"Let's just stay here at least until the race starts. Better to stay in one place and let him come to us. Give it twenty minutes."

"Okay, bu–"

There was the typical whump-whump-whump of a finger on a microphone head, followed by the sharp tone of feedback.

"Ladies and gentlemen, is this thing on? Can you hear me?" came Benson's voice.

"We can hear you," answered various voices.

"Shout if you can hear me! Come on, this is race day!"

The crowd at the front of the grid immediately started cheering and soon more joined in. Tone and Marisa could soon feel the rumble in their ribcages as the crowd along the route began to cheer, the cacophony spreading along until it seemed as if the entire city was in glorious uproar.

"That's more like it!" said Benson, his voice relayed around the circuit via strategically placed soundstages so that one had the impression that his mighty voice was echoing all around.

"What a glorious day for racing! The city's most favourite and illustrious sport!"

More cheers.

"But let us not forget what price this great day has been bought with. Let us remember why we are here. A year ago, a tragedy that broke the heart of the city. Broke it in two."

Benson turned and looked up at the banner. He pointed to it.

"The name Redding was on the lips of all who loved sport, some of us were fortunate to watch Danny race in his father's car. Some of us privileged to know them personally…"

Benson's tone wavered, his voice cracking subtly but noticeably. It was a genuine rush of emotion. Marisa reached up and squeezed Tone's shoulder.

"They built their own car. They went their own way. As a family, always with dignity and courage. That is how they lived. Always…."

Reverential silence.

"…and by God did the boy drive fast!"

The loudest and proudest cheer erupted.

"So, to honour them and to raise funds for the physiotherapy wing of Sacred Heart Hospital at the request of our surprise special guest who will be appearing later, I declare the first annual Redding Boxkart Derby open!"

More cheers and applause.

"So, without further ado, let me hand over to my good man Mr Weatherly to introduce the parade of boxkarts that will race very shortly!"

Marisa and Tone could not help but suspend their anxiety for a moment as the parade started. From the distance, down the track, they saw two lines of boxkarts come trundling along, each being pushed by their teams. Beautiful, bizarre machines – a bathtub on wheels, a triple-winged propeller plane, a can of cola, a machine kitted out like an airboat from the Everglades. Stupid, whacky and wonderful, they paraded around, their teams and drivers waving and soaking up the adulation of everyone. But not all cars were of bizarre design, however. For every surreal machine, there came two or three karts built by serious competitors – gleaming, dangerous, vital machines full of anger and bite. Low to the ground and primed to race. The drivers waved like the others, but these guys had a look in their eyes, a point to prove and a desire to get over the line first in the inaugural race.

Tone held the rim of his plastic flute between his teeth as he clapped them all.

"Wonderful, aren't they?" said Marisa.

"What was that?" said Tone, turning to her.

"I said they are wonderful."

Tone said something that was stifled by the glass in his mouth. Marisa took it from his teeth.

"They are something. God, I wish he was here."

Tone turned back and clapped the competitors on, Marisa's small distraction causing them to miss the small, blacksteel car being pushed by schoolboys roll past. These guys were smaller than the other teams. These guys weren't waving at the crowds, but instead pushing their car through the parade, hidden by the other, grander machines.

The parade finished and the cars peeled off and took their pre-assigned positions on the grid. The crews stepped off the track, leaving the drivers alone by their vehicles. Weatherly handed the microphone back to Benson.

"And there we have it, what wonderful machines! What gallant drivers... what insane designers we also have! And so, what else is there left to do... but gen..."

Weatherly tapped Benson on the shoulder. Benson cupped the microphone and bent down to lend his ear. Weatherly whispered something frantic.

Benson stood up and looked out.

"Oh dear," he called out, "we seem to be missing a driver!" There was a little murmur from the crowd. The other drivers looked around.

Weatherly handed a piece of paper detailing the missing driver to his partner.

"We're still waiting for the driver of car, er... Zero."

More chatter and murmur. One car stood on the grid alone.

Tone and Marisa stood on tiptoes and craned their necks to see the car. Tone caught a glimpse of the rear spoiler and his heart dared to leap a little. He didn't recognise the spoiler with its blank white oblong stripe pasted on it, but he did recognise the exposed steel frame.

Then an excited tremor came from off down the way – back past the grid and around the bend, out of sight. The tremor was excited and at the same time hushed, a thousand whispers and gasps. Tone and Marisa, along with everyone at the very front of the grid turned to look down the track. A dot rounded the bend far away. The dot became a figure. A solitary figure on the track, walking towards the grid. A solitary figure in a black racing overall, walking with a limp.

Tone and Marisa were speechless. The man walked, all in black, his face covered in a black handkerchief. He walked down the centre of the drivers, each one turning as he passed.

Tone welled up as the Midnight Boy walked past him, not looking at the crowd, just looking on. Marisa could not take her eyes of the man in black. All she could do was reach across and thread her fingers through Tone's.

The Midnight Boy walked over to the solitary car, the Midnight Special sitting unmanned on the grid. The crowd was bursting with excitement and anticipation. They wanted to believe, all of them did, but they could not exclaim it without evidential proof lest it break the spell. He walked around to the back of the car, kneeling to the spoiler. Without any more ceremony, he ripped off the white oblong, the sticker peeling away instantly to reveal the name "REDDING" emblazoned across the spoiler. The crowd erupted into hysterical cheers. The noise was so loud that young children started crying. The Midnight Boy stood up by his car and took off the handkerchief around his face, revealing himself in full to the crowd. The crowd was at 99% but then Chris smiled and waved, and they all red-lined.

Benson tried to say something, bringing the microphone up to his lips, but he was speechless. He just looked down at the boy who held the city in his hand.

Chris looked at the drivers and though the crowd made him feel adored, the drivers made him feel proud. They all stood by their machines and applauded him. Chris saluted and as he did, he caught sight of Tone and Marisa in the crowd. He beckoned them over. Tone pointed to himself. Chris nodded.

Marisa nudged Tone forward. He bent under the A-frame and walked over, trying to wipe away his tears with his sleeve. Chris applauded his uncle as he walked. The crowd knew who he was. There was only one person it could have been. Somewhere around the track, on a TV screen, Angela saw Tone and cheered so loudly she fell off her deck chair, spilling her can all over her lunch. Tone walked up to Chris, and they stood in front of the Midnight Special.

"She looks great."

"Thanks," said Chris.

"Where did you go?"

"You didn't get the note? I left it on your bed."

Tone looked confused.

"We just assumed... what did it say?"

"Said 'See you at the race'," remarked Chris, oblivious to the anxiety he had caused through the miscommunication.

Tone laughed in relief.

"So, it's 'we' is it?" smiled Chris, nodding towards Gardner, still by the A-frame.

Tone turned and regarded the beaming woman.

Chris looked at Ms Gardner and nodded sincerely. She nodded back. Chris wasn't a blank face to Marisa Gardner, none of her pupils were any more.

"Yeah, what do you think?" said Tone, turning back to Chris.

Chris held out his hand. Tone laughed and shook it. A cheer. Chris turned the handshake into a tight embrace. Not a dry eye at the circuit. Chris grabbed his uncle's wrist and held up his arm as he had seen MCs do with champion boxers after they had gone the distance. In the crowd, fathers hugged sons, mothers cradled daughters. It was the Redding's city.

"Right then," said Tone, "only one thing left to do."

"Yeah?"

Tone stepped away from the Midnight Special.

"Put this lean bitch over the line before anyone else."

Chris smiled and nodded. Tone rushed back into Marisa's arms. The Midnight Boy looked down the grid at all the other drivers. He clapped his gloved hands and every driver replied likewise. They all climbed into their machines.

CHAPTER 37

SO GONE

He gripped the wheel. He flexed his gloves and tensed his legs, feeling the bite on the pedals. The heat in the suit was more than he had anticipated, the sweat already beading his brow. He looked to his left and right. Karts of all shapes and sizes, the rear view showing the same. He could instantly pick out the fast threats and the cumbersome ones. He had to readjust his game plan slightly. He had spent most of his time imagining similar cars to his own, much as he had witnessed when his brother raced. But now, even if he was on the perfect line coming into a bend and he came up against a boxkart built like a house, he was going to have to adapt. He smiled as he flexed his gloves.

"Got yourself a race here, Kit," he said to himself.

He looked at the lights and closed his eyes to gather his courage. He did not think of the race in that moment, almost taking himself by surprise when instead, he thought of Julie's scent and her fingers rifling through his hair. The song, their song; that defining moment. He knew that even if she wasn't watching the race, she was still there. He opened his eyes as the lights went green. Contact.

The start of the race was utter chaos. The crowd's cheers adding to the insanity. A boxkart built like a rubber duck lurched forward and made it two yards before it careened across the road, striking the windmill kart

,with both collapsing in an ill-constructed heap much to the delight of the audience and the drivers. Other karts behind stacked into the pile-up; some managed to weave slowly through. Chris was ahead and got off to a belter. He pushed the car on, the training on the course bringing him out in front. He pulled into the sharp first left and put the hammer down as he approached the first incline. A quick check in the mirrors, a steamship and a real race car just behind him, coasting in his wake. Chris tightened his line as a chicane approached, this was nothing like the million practice laps he had done on his own. The blur of colour from the people flanking the circuit, the sweat on his head and the sheer adrenaline of being chased caused him to slow slightly on approach to the chicane. Bang. A shunt from the steamship caused Chris to wobble, his grip loosening on his wheel slightly, the knot in his stomach tightening. That was it, the real racer behind burned past, the driver not even looking at Chris, then three others. Where the hell had they come from? Chris lost vital seconds and pedalled on, the stupid steamship causing him more bother than it was worth. He wiggled the steering wheel and threatened to shunt the steamship, which corrected. The driver swore at the boy and Chris acknowledged his sudden, fear-induced ungentlemanly manoeuvre. He waved at the steamship but he had chipped the guy off and suddenly he was looking at its stern, his view totally obscured. It was a disaster and Chris began to panic. He weaved all over the circuit trying to get a glimpse of the way past. Nothing.

Back at the start line, Benson was reading off the current positions as they were fed to him via spotters at the outer parts of the circuit. The crowd offered a muted cheer when Chris's position was said to be eighth... then corrected to ninth... then tenth.

Tone swore so loudly that a nearby mother tried to chastise him and had to be placated by Marisa. Tone lent on the A-frame, straining to look down the track and see the first lap conclude.

Chris was boxed in, but he was managing to keep pace with a swan and a bathtub. Sweat pouring and legs burning way before they normally did during practice runs. Not even a lap done, and he was almost spent and he knew it. Mistake after mistake. The proximity of the vehicles, the wheels right by his face, the occasional loose piece of gravel flicking up and striking him. Chris came into corners later and later and exited wider and wider. The swan and biplane soon passed him, and he was right at the back of the pack, among the cardboard boxes and the converted prams. He had known the race would be hard, but this was beyond the pale. He came out wide into the home straight. He heard the crowd cheering him on, he tried to speed up, but his legs had nothing, slower and slower until he passed Uncle Tone in dead last position. He chanced a look at his uncle and saw his expression –

the 'you gave it your best and I am proud of you' look that says to all kids: 'You're rubbish, but I still love you.'

His plan was still achievable but now it was looking desperate. He gritted his teeth, crossed the line in last place and did not hear his name called out like the others. Oversight? Doubtful. Shame, probably. Long straight now, up the chicane, nobody behind him now giving chase. Nothing creeping up except the soon-to-be-realised inevitability that he would be lapped. The straight afforded him fifteen seconds of solitude. It was dangerous, and stupid but he closed his eyes and pushed forward. The back of the van was black, and then the headlights filled everything with the twisting shadows of his parents, the wet lump that hit him in the side of the head. Chris opened his eyes as the chicane came up on him, but his mind's eye remained back inside that Coke can being crushed. The wet lump hit him again and Chris remembered it fully now, an arm spinning off from striking him – torn from his mother's shoulder and hitting the rear doors of the van. The knot inside pulled so tight his legs nearly coiled up to his chest. He was crawling to a stop by the chicane. The arm slopped down on to the bed of the van, the shadows twisting again. He saw the accident from outside the van, he saw it strike the traffic, he saw the van tumble through the air. He imagined the witnesses. Enough was enough.

"Fuck it," he shouted, and then he really put the hammer down.

A ripple of excited cheering spread from the chicane around the track. Chris Redding was making ground. Hitting the line well, his legs almost a blur. Fortune then played a great part as he rounded a tight left and saw the wreckage of the biplane and the steamship, another racing car spinning out of control. Chris gripped the wheel. The other car thumped into a tyre barrier and rolled back into the road, the brakes shot. Chris accelerated, weaved masterfully through the wreckage, regained his line and belted past the broken car ahead, holding his line and missing the wreckage by millimetres.

The incident was reported over the public address system. He was moving up the field. The longer the race went on, the more accidents and retirements. Chris moved up the field, maintaining his line, his eyes not on the road, his body taking over and shutting out the physical pain. All he could do was think of the accident, it was all coming back to him in slow motion, in real time, from the point of view of others. Everything. Total situational recall. He moved into eighth place. The noise from the crowd drowning out, the burning in his legs nothing. Seventh. He was in the hospital, he couldn't feel his legs, he tried to walk for the first time, he fell on his face, and thumped the tiled hospital floor. He crawled out of bed and into the toilet where he cried and cried. Gaining on sixth place now. He was hiding the broken and busted SuperKart, he was getting away with his dark crime. On the tail of fifth place. The look of despair on his brother's face that morning. Chris weaved wide, the car went to block him, Chris weaved back right and catapulted himself past. Fifth place. The noise of the track seemed to fall away, growing distant as something deep inside, a hidden voice took control of the young man. 'Fifth place, there is Uncle Tone and Gardner. Not the time to think about them just yet. Think only on what you got. Focus on that. Flush it out. Reconcile. Move on. Move on to fourth. First steps with the crutches, first visit to the cemetery.' Chris screamed in the car as he almost went up on two wheels as he aggressively took the chicane, shaving seconds off at every opportunity. 'Sitting next to Kate, the car crash video, her humiliation and rage. Jab, jab, jab against the toilet door.' There is fourth place dead ahead. Tone drinking. On the home straight, a few yards ahead. Tone's soldiering, Tone's pain. Pull up alongside fourth place. Neck and neck. This one is for Tone, pulling into third place as you pass both the car and Tone and Marisa, you got this, this one is for you. Point to Tone as you move on. I love you Tone, second place and then...well, that's for then. The letter to Kate, the school trip... no save that one, save that one. Second place, left turn, up ahead they are both there battling out, manoeuvre through wreckage, keep the line. The Midnight Boy, the Midnight Special, the world and the universe, that's your nitro. Hit it. Grip the wheel, grit your teeth, forget the pain, there is no outward pain, only inward. You almost punched a kid, you held him, and you saw the look in his eyes, you saw that, that was you. You are on them now, harrying second and first coming into the home straight. Top three, one more lap to go, you're in the place you never thought you could be, and you got yourself here but no time for self-aggrandisement, over the line, last lap, still in third. Gardner, chance after chance she gave you, you bore down on her and saw vulnerability in her eyes, her utter fear, you did that, you saw true terror. Pull out wide and bear in, cut in the middle of the battle. Second place bottled it, pulling back, giving umbrage, making way, you're in, get into first place's drift, stay on him, just half a lap and then on to the home straight and then… and then… you know what to do. Chicane, fighting Lee Hardman at Sibley Hall, the embarrassment of a one punch near knockout, chicane taken, two more corners and then… Stay on him, around the first, don't think of the crowd, don't think of the guy ahead, think of the past. Think of the entire crash, one last time, in detail, the death of your mother. The death of your father. The death of your brother. Home straight, up ahead is everything, up ahead is destiny… ease off, ease off. Leader is breaking away. He's going to win. Crowd on their feet, you have this, this is it, this is your time, show them something they have never seen. The leader crossed the line, but all eyes are you on Kit. Now! Hard right, straight into the crowd. This is it. They are diving out the way, get under the A-frame and off the circuit and you're clear! There it is, there it is up ahead. Palmerston Road. They are dead. Your mother, your father and your brother. They are dead. Wanna go join them?'

———

There were no cheers for the winner as he belted over the line. There was only mad panic. Chris Redding had steered into the crowd, headlong and reckless. Tone yanked Marisa out of the way as the crowd pushed aside. Chris charged through them all, straight under the barrier and off. Nobody announced anything, all people heard around the circuit was that strange and worrying whump and the tone of a microphone being dropped in shock.

Tone got to his feet, pulling Marisa up as he did so. Before anyone else realised, he knew what was happening. Chris was burning away, fast and straight. Tone made off after him, Marisa followed, and the rest of the crowd nearby charged after the boxkart racer who had gone off the circuit and was now belting headlong to the edge of Palmerston Road.

Marisa caught up with Tone, but it was too late. Chris didn't turn and didn't break but went so fast over the edge that he was airborne for three seconds. He hit the tarmac hard, weaving slightly, but the frame was strong. The Midnight Special could withstand anything.

Tone and Marisa stood at the top of the road and shouted down to the boy, but he didn't hear, he was so far gone. The crowd reached the precipice and they all looked on in horror.

In the car, Chris held his breath as the speed of his descent seemed faster than light. For a few seconds he remembered the coach journey and relieving himself in despair. It was time to let it all go. He pushed all his remaining angst and fear into his legs, and he aimed the car down the centre of the road, down to the intersection and the crosstown traffic where his family had died.

Everything now was behind him. All the adults screamed and hollered at the mad boy, some prayed to God to avert a tragedy, but Chris Redding was driving straight and faster than anyone had ever seen.

He was approaching the nadir of the road. This was it.

Marisa held Tone's hand and squeezed it in horror.

"Jesus, he's going to kill himself, he's going to die!"

Then, at that instant, in a divine moment of inspiration, Tone understood and felt calm and almost happy. Exalted, touched, an idea came to him. A fully formed story.

"No," he said, breaking out into a rapturous smile. "He's going to make it, he's going to live."

Chris was twenty metres from the bottom. The wind was so fierce, his hair flapping behind him, his chest pulled back into the seat. He closed his eyes and laughed, feeling the breath of his brother on the back of his neck, feeling his strong arms gripping the rear axle and lifting the car. Chris laughed like he had done when he was thirteen and hanging out with his brother.

Your mother, your father and your brother are dead, wanna go see them?

Chris kept his eyes closed and blotted out all sound. He didn't hear the wails of the cries and he didn't look into the rear-view mirror.

"Wanna go see them?"

Chris Redding stopped pedalling, his brother holding the rear of the car up and laughing, his mother in the kitchen, his father expecting a cup of tea. Chris leaned his head back in exaltation and lifted his hands from the wheel, holding them high above his head and feeling the wind rushing through his fingers. He approached the intersection, arms in the air and eyes closed. It was then, at the nadir of his descent, and travelling faster than any boy had ever done before that Chris snapped his eyes open. Focused and alive, he grabbed the wheel. The speed of the Special and the mania of the traffic – chaos and life all around and he was in the midst of it all. And within that hurricane, he found life. Painful, beautiful life. But, perhaps more than that, Chris Redding found the perfect line through it all. And then he drove. The Boxkart Rebel really drove.

...And the Boxkart Rebel Drives

Acknowledgements

With grateful and loving thanks to my family for
their encouragement and support. To my friends, in
particular Luke Searle, Craig Coole, Donatella Marena,
Chris Rolfe, Helena Caligari, the Tippler Crew,
Rebel Stationary and everyone in between.
To that one teacher, mentor and friend who set me
right – Mr John B Peacock – and, finally, with love and
thanks to the legends of TheNeverPress: Dave Hollander,
Leighton Johns, Felicity Bown, Francesca Clementi,
Ludo Lefevre, Dr Andy Parker and Claire Pagel.

I love all of you more than The Cure.

About the Author

As a wee lad, Graham Thomas wanted to be a pilot, a butler, a film-maker and an author. The only one that really stuck with him was 'author'.

So far it seems to have worked out well for him, creatively. As well as writing novels and poetry, Graham also runs a digital zine stuffed with curios and hosts a podcast about racehorses and movies. His eventual plan is to see out his days in a hacienda filled with animals and let the surrounding land do what she desires.

Alongside writing, Graham loves making models, cooking giant roasts, boxing, swimming, the Prince Charles Cinema and The Cure.

About TheNeverPress

TheNeverPress is an independent publishing house specialising in magical-realist fiction, poetry, and audio. We also have a digital zine and a podcast about movies and racehorses. All of it curiously off-beat.

We value our independence and plan to release a few publications each year in a unique fashion: paperbacks and zines, along with digital editions, online serialisations, podcasts, recitals and film screenings. Anything we can dream up, we'll try to make it happen. We might not be a publishing behemoth right now, but that's fine by us. We're just going our own way.

We're a collective of artists, writers, specialists and creatives who want to build a strange, punk label that is authentic, meaningful, ethical and always goes full tilt.

Find out all about us at: **www.theneverpress.com**
Get involved & subscribe to our zine: **www.theneverzine.com**

 @TheNeverPress

www.theneverpress.com